To Ella,
I hope you e
Els' journey.
    RL Seaton

A Silent Song

By

Rebecca Seaton

Published by New Generation Publishing in 2018

www.newgeneration-publishing.com

New Generation Publishing

This book has been produced with assistance from
The London Borough of Barking and Dagenham Library Service
Pen to Print Creative Writing Project 2017/8
with funding from
The Arts Council, England Grants for the Arts.

LOTTERY FUNDED | Supported using public funding by
**ARTS COUNCIL
ENGLAND**

London Borough of
Barking&Dagenham
lbbd.gov.uk

For Carolyn

'A friend loves at all times and a brother is born for adversity.'

Proverbs 17:17

Rima

GREAT SEA

ICE HILLS

Lila - Crith - Ile
RUCULIA
CASSAL
LANICE
Port-Nuar-Ile
Tonermead

North's Castle
Carbron

Burnt Land
Green Forest

Sea's End
Valley
ZARITT
12 K
SYRANMA
Krab
Islalan
Unit ana
AKRN
Annia
VEROSIA
Lutenna

CALAN
MYKRIA
Ocean's Eye
Suscta
RAZIKO
Red Cane
Vares / Gate

FROZEN MOUNTAINS

N
W E
S

A Silent Song: Characters

The North

Gods

Bronv Chief God of the North
Old Lok God of Wisdom
Cridf Messenger God
Fess Goddess of Finding

Garrtron

Els A young woman who is mute but has magical powers
Mavri Els' mother
Gron Els' father
Bronv Els' oldest brother, named for the chief northern god
Lissal Els' sister, one of the most popular girls in the village
Degra Els' middle brother, a talented singer
Cam Els' youngest brother, a drummer, not yet betrothed
Bronv-Grii the village elder
Shandum, Ardelyn Teachers
Sulys, Rehya Young women who are betrothed
Reesa, Gwen, Ceruth, Areev Girls not yet betrothed
Roga Lissal's betrothed, plays the message drum
Ben A young man who is betrothed
Hwym A boy not yet betrothed
Cressa, Liv Married women
Maimish Cressa's husband
Liv A notorious gossip
Sorab A mherl

Other

King Hurburt, King of the Northern continent
Lord Cranff, An advisor

Woh-Luhn the village elder of Burret Onri.
Cuhlm A warrior
Carlor, Ilsorn, Grint and Macie Soldiers

The South

Gods

L'ra Goddess of Adventure
Gax The Hunter God
Ellari Goddess of Mothers and Children
Arram God of Animals
Tadir God of the Land
Raz God of Fire
Myrrine Goddess of the Sea
Cala Goddess of the Air

Sytrannia

King Nahvib Ruler of Sytrannia
Princess Nubira His sister
Drayk First Minister
Lords Zachari and Lins Noblemen
Ladies Caree, Frani and Orlanda Noblewomen
Takka The king's coachwoman
Bataz Head groom
Brin A stable boy
Matzi A maid
Sousk A manservant
Skrella and Roro Chief Priestess and Priest of L'ra
Kyrria, Rayth and Plarina Priestesses of L'ra
Arrok A priest of L'ra
Timo A novice
Zritz, Pocack and Durrew Magi
Jayak A sorcerer
Vanya and Aashi Sorceresses
Alleri, Klara, Dayx, Cyru and Reynon Wizards
Sy A merchant

Lars A Publican
Karryn A resident of Jhrik-ansi
Nai-kin A ship's captain
Hrikki His second
Af The ship's cook
Dri-angk A young sailor
Vauram Townsman of L'ra's Town
Alkar Priest of L'ra's Town
Garihm An architect
Pinarv A builder

Zaritt

Queen Ashla The ruler of Zaritt
Prince Griorg Her husband
Lord Bik First Minister

Lykrosia

Queen Lidynne Joint ruler of Lykrosia
King Sedryk Joint ruler of Lykrosia
Lord Dekkomas First Minister

Akrin

King Vistar Ruler of Akrin
Queen Elaina His wife
Amsala First Minister
Tanvi Commander of the army

Izk

King Azabar Ruler of Izk
Queen Xyami His wife
Lady Taheya First Minister

East

Calan

Queen Wertle The ruler
Prince Alzin Her husband

West

Liance

King Eneb Ruler
Lady Rona First Minister

Cassal

King Ep Ruler
Lord Winnalio First minister

Rucilia

King Yacconi Ruler
Lord Amar First Minister

Other

Demon Lords

Quivviam and Xanesh Chiefs
High Lords
Demon Lords

Prologue

As Mavri walked through the forest, she quickened her pace against the driving rain. It was not much further now to the place where she usually paused to rest and eat something. She soon reached the heavily sheltered spot where the tree stumps seemed arranged as stools. Thankful, she settled down with her small pack, sighing deeply. The food lay in front of her for some minutes as she sat deep in thought, oblivious to the twittering birds and persistent pattering of the rain. As she decided she must eat something, Mavri heard a sudden crunch and noticed a movement on the other side of the clearing. She tensed and quickly picked up her stick. Most wild animals lived further into the forest but some wandered nearer to the village and bandits were also a possibility. It was with surprise, then, that Mavri saw a young woman of about her own age, though much darker of hair and skin. A Southerner?

'Please,' said the woman, 'Can I sit down? I have come a long way and was caught in the storm unprepared.' Indeed, Mavri could see how thin the woman's clothes were and how they stuck to her body. As the stranger walked over, her light shoes kept sinking into the sodden ground. She could not be used to the weather here, for sure, thought Mavri, remembering the tales she had heard of the blistering South. Gron, her husband, had a book of Southern songs and they had exclaimed together at the pictures of strange people and places in it.

'Of course, sit with me and eat.' said Mavri, beckoning the other woman towards the makeshift seat. Gratefully, the dark woman ate until, between them, all the food was gone.

'But I hadn't noticed your state!' she exclaimed, ' Here I am taking your food when you and your child have the greater need. I'm truly sorry.'

'No matter,' grinned Mavri, 'Truth told, it is worth it for

the company, I am nearly always alone here.'

'It's a lonely place. Why come here, especially on such an awful day?' she shivered and pulled her dress tighter about herself. 'Do your people not have a god to protect you and guide you on your way?'

There was a long pause and for a while it seemed Mavri would not answer. Then she spoke and it was with a sadness without hope, a fear that until now she had hidden from those closest to her.

'....We have a god, yes, a few. Not as many, or the same, as from the South, I hear, but ones we trust.' she raked her fingers through her hair and looked at the ground before continuing. 'But Bronv, our chief god, lord of music and celebration, has abandoned me for my sin and no longer guides me with happy songs.'

'Surely, you are kind and generous, what great fault could deserve such punishment?' Concern darkened the stranger's face.

'It was on Bronv's feast day. Music and singing are in every part of our life here, but on Bronv's day, no-one must sing until midday. Then all will celebrate, with feasting and music lasting into the night. This is in memory of Bronv's singing to the first travellers here to keep them going on to their new home. The first travellers did not sing until in sight of this land, that is why we are quiet and thoughtful the first half of his day and only sing later.'

'Well, I was collecting nuts for the feast and came through this forest. My mind was on the day, weather was good for it, but also on the new baby to be born soon and I was so happy at the thought of this new one and whether it may be a brother or sister for those I already have, I took to singing, forgetting it was before twelve. The earth shook and Bronv appeared before me. He swore my child would pay for my insolence and said she will never make a sound.' She brushed a tear from her cheek, remembering that terrible day.

'But there are worse punishments, surely?'

'In a land where singing is all? Birth, marriage, death, all are sung at. What other way can feeling be so well expressed? How else is there?'

'How else?' mused the Southern woman. 'There should be an else, there should be another way.'

'I do not know how.' sighed Mavri. 'I'm sorry, here I am whining and you a stranger. This is not your problem and I should not burden you with my troubles.'

'As you share your food, so I share your sorrow. But do not fear too much.'

'How can I not fear such a future? You cannot understand.' Mavri twisted her hands in frustration.

'Trust me, you need not fear so. I must be on my way now but my good wishes stay with you.' The woman looked intently at Mavri, who was surprised to find that the eyes beneath the dark lashes were bright green. 'Your child will be born mute, but she will not be without other talents. There will be an 'else', Mavri, I know it.'

She was walking off before Mavri could insist on the impossibility of any alternative to singing, and long gone before Mavri realised she had never told the woman her name.

Part One

Chapter 1

'Okay, lesson over! I can tell your minds are on other things.' Shandum sighed, 'Just don't forget the gods entirely, this is their celebration, too, you know.' But the teenagers whose attention he had struggled to hold were already gone. So Shandum, chins and belly wobbling in tandem, set off back to his own house.

The girls in the group headed for the riverbank to see if their festival clothes were dry yet. From a distance, they looked like fireflies, bright spots of colour twirling about excitedly.

'Does this green work?' Reesa asked.

'It matches your eyes. You'll draw in the one you want, surely,' Gwen said, soothing her anxious friend.

'Lissal, you look wonderful! You'll steal all the attention from the hopefuls though!' Areev said.

'Do you really think so?' Lissal sounded uncertain, but she made sure all saw the delicate edging on her skirt as she held its broad brim out for her friends' inspection.

'The orange suits you. It won't only be Roga looking, you know.' another said.

'Honestly, Ceruth!' Lissal giggled.

'Well, as long as someone turns my way, this is going to be my year,' Ceruth stated boldly.

'Why not?' Areev agreed. 'You're sixteen and I'm only the year younger. Besides, we are not unpleasant to look at,' she twirled her pale curls as she said this, 'And good singers too.'

'I shall play the bells too. I'm leaving nothing to chance.' added Gwen.

'I just hope my voice holds out. I'm sure I've chosen the wrong kind of piece for it.' Reesa frowned.

'You'll no doubt all find partners.' Lissal said, confidently, 'Then you'll be able to talk of wedding dress patterns and the such with Sulys and I.' Her blue eyes caught Sulys' green ones and both girls laughed knowingly.

'So, are you sure *everyone* will find someone this year?' Gwen asked.

Lissal made as if she was about to answer, but then she saw the only girl who did not speak and her heart sank. She had spent the last sixteen years doing her best to ignore her only sister - Bronv knew it wasn't usually difficult - but she was bound to mess this one up, even not coming would cause whispers. She was such a cause of shame. Why couldn't her parents have sent her away, sold her to merchants as a curiousity, just got rid of her for goodness' sake? She was nothing special to look at, that was embarrassing enough, but to not make a sound, well, it was unnatural.

Sitting at the edge of the water, Els was all too aware of their hostile glances. She had heard every word as she had been looking into the water, the river being the only way for her to know how she looked. Her dress was of the same pale blue as the sky, with soft brown ribbons on each shoulder. Her light brown hair, was tied in a neat plait which hung behind her. Her soft hazel eyes wore no make up, Els knew bright dyes, such as Lissal used, would only look ridiculous. She was well aware she was nothing amazing to look at, pointy little nose, freckles and that plain hair, but then, this was not something she had ever had to worry about. This would hardly be the first time she had been spoken of as if invisible, after all. No-one in the village of Garrtron had ever shown any desire to know someone who couldn't reply to them with speech or song. No, that was a lie, Cam bothered. The others would only speak to her to deliver a message, most likely some job to do, even her own family greeted her only briefly. Except for Cam. Youngest and most patient of all Gron and Mavri's children, Cam was not just a brother, but the only friend Els had. He alone would take sheets of paper to her so that she could 'talk' to him. If any other had heard of it, they would have reported it to Bronv-Grii immediately, she knew that. It was ungodly to communicate without sound. 'Voice first, instruments after, paper last.' Ardelyn, the music teacher, had said and that had been the view shared by all the important adults in the town, so there had been no opposition. Thank the gods for Cam! But then, he would not be with her forever. She had to face that.

For all the excitement the Festival of Fair Voice held for the other young girls, to Els it meant change and a future she faced with only uncertainty. Bronv, Degra and Lissal had all been paired before her and that was right enough, they were older. But would she be next, as she should, according to age? How was she to attract a young man when she lacked the words or music to do it? Desperately, she tried to think of ways in which she could somehow join in, if she could just do something to communicate with one of them. But even if she did, who would be brave enough to duet with her and risk the wrath of the village elders?

The fact remained; if she paired or he did, Cam would be taken from her and she would lose her link with other people then. Els knew she would be unaware of much news and companionship without her dear brother and a chill went through her as she thought of a lifetime spent with only her own thoughts. But here she was slipping off already, with Lissal looking daggers at her all the time.

'Maybe not everyone pairs, but all who count,' Lissal sneered, determined to distance herself from this reject in front of them, 'Those who are meant to pair and marry, those who join with music first over other ways.'

Els shrugged miserably. What do you want? she thought. Why do you even care? But she thought she knew. Lissal was unquestionably the prettiest girl in the village and she was not stupid. She had a voice and could play all the basic instruments, but she had little beyond that. The status she had built up in Garrtron rested on careful manipulation and Els was the single flaw in that.

Els walked away, leaving Lissal to turn conversation to her wedding plans instead. As she walked off, she found she could still hear her sister's voice with her mind long after it had stopped reaching her ears. Over the last few months, Els had done this more than once, usually when she was upset. Other things had begun happening, too. She had sometimes decided to grab a spoon or knife in the kitchen only to find it leap into her hand before she had actually moved towards it. There was no way she could tell anyone about these abilities, though, not even Cam. It was different, it was dangerous. Still, a tremor rippled through her that was not entirely fear. I can do things, she thought, just not the things you want.

She spent the afternoon trying to find a place to relax, away from the excitement of the festival. Its preparations, however, were all around her. Even at home, cramped into her room, Els could smell the desserts her mother was baking and hear Cam rehearsing with drums and voice in the room above. Her father and a neighbour were outside straining ale and discussing the feasting and drinking anticipated. Els sewed up her best dress, deciding she might as well look respectable - though no-one will look at one they can't hear, she thought - when a knock at the door revealed she hadn't managed to make herself invisible yet.

'Els! Els! There you are. Take this water over to the cooking area. It's no good you hiding away, we've all got to help in the festival preparations, okay?' Mavri sighed as Els nodded. She hated to be so abrupt but there really seemed no other way when Els was incapable of reply.

'Yeah, Els, you might as well help get ready, you can't exactly help celebrate,' laughed Degra cuttingly.

Drop dead, Degra. Els thought. If I could talk, I'd give you such an earful. Her mood darkened then. There was no easy revenge on him or Lissal. She had no voice to deliver the words in her head. Why me, she thought, trudging over to the cooking area with the heavy buckets. It couldn't be any of the others, oh no. Look at Lissal, the prettiest girl in the village and one of the best voices. No wonder Roga opened the last festival with a song to her, they were bound to duet. And Bronv and Degra found girls to sing with, Bronv's married now. Only me and Cam left now and Cam'll find a partner easily. He can sing.

'I'm amazed there's any water left, the way you're swinging those buckets about, Els,' boomed the baritone voice of Bronv-Grii, the village elder, 'Still, as you are here, you might as well help cook. Go and chop some shoots for Cressa and Liv, they could do with some help.'

The hut where the food was prepared was hot and crowded, old and young members of the village were preparing food in abundance for the annual Festival of Fair Voice, when the young people of the village would, if in luck, find their marriage partner. The air was buzzing with excitement and the chattering from the main hut was only drowned out by the tuning of instruments outside. Squeezing past men roasting the meat for the night's feast and old women mixing the traditional sauces for it, Els found Liv and Cressa, two women in their mid-twenties frantically chopping and steaming shoots.

'You're here to help us?' asked Liv, the older of the two, 'Very well, we need two bowls of greenwort and one of curly leaf. Let us know when you're finished.'

Els began chopping, trying to get on with her task and avoid those staring at her. She sometimes wished she could join the priesthood, that way she'd be away from all these daily duties, might even get sent to a small town to study, but most of the novices were male and all could sing. She doubted even the few priests dedicated to Old Lok would welcome her, gentle though they were. All the villagers mistrusted Els, nobody would talk to her except to tell her what to do. Liv and Cressa had gone outside to collect more shoots without so much as a 'goodbye' from either of them. Still thinking about them, Els found that though she could not hear them, she could catch their thoughts just as easily as she had those of her sister and her friends. However, she immediately wished she hadn't bothered, for the women's conversation was far from comforting.

'*She'll be ages yet. Half that water was spilt and it was late enough.*' Liv's voice was far away but the vicious

11

thoughts were all to easy to 'hear'. Cressa's feelings were more generous, Els was used to catching her musings.

'We don't know it was her fault, she was probably held up. Besides, the shoots will be done, Els is a good worker.'

'I suppose she has to be good at something.' Liv's thoughts were like rancid treacle, thickly unpleasant.

'That's not fair, it's only her voice that isn't...'

'Working? Normal? Cressa, you are kind but a fool. That girl is all wrong. Sixteen and no pairing yet for a start.'

'Lissal was seventeen last year.'

'Lissal was only waiting for the best. She only had problems in choosing. Good thing she did wait, Ben was the great singer a few years back but look at Roga now, that voice and the message drum. Ben and Rehya, that won't last.'

'Oh, Liv, you shouldn't say such things, it's cruel.'

'I'm only honest, Cressa. I tell you, that young girl of Mavri's is all wrong. She's not one of us with no voice. And born like it, that's no accident. You know what people say.'

'Well, people say all kinds of things. You can't trust such talk.'

'There's truth enough there, I reckon. Mavri knew something was wrong while she was still expecting her, her expression went from cheery to doomed in a single day and you know why?'

'No, go on,' Cressa said, resigned to Liv's tirade.

'Because she knew that baby was going to be born wrong. It's my guess Mavri did something wrong, reckon she was praying to false gods or something.'

'No! Mavri wouldn't do any such thing. Think what you're saying Liv!'

'You're soft, Cressa, you won't see bad in anyone. I say the proof's all there in that mad girl herself. Anyway, let's see what a mess she's made of our shoots.'

Els, waiting for them to reappear, fought to remain calm. Though she could not vent her anger verbally, she feared expressing her feelings physically. As they entered, she turned her face from them, scared they would read her mind as well as she could theirs. It was only in the last year that she had discovered new abilities and her fear had enabled her to keep them well hidden so far. Scared she would somehow reveal herself, she concentrated all her attention on the greenwort she was cooking.

'Els, you've done them all. Great work,' said Cressa.

Not like she's going to be stood chatting instead. Liv said nothing aloud but the spite inside her head filled Els'. It's not fair, thought Els, I can hear them but no-one hears me. How can you judge me when you don't know me? How can you be so nasty, yet so respected, just because you can sing well? It's wrong, it's wrong and I hate you! She felt a tingling then, similar to what happened when she was in a hurry and equipment seemed to jump into her hand. This was not impatience though, this was an anger borne out of years of rejection. She didn't mean to hurt Liv, but suddenly, all her fury was directed at the woman between her and her cooking. The pan quivered. Els tried to calm her feelings, but it was too late. As easily as she seemed to 'push' spoons when no-one was around, Els' mind became a wall of anger which lifted the pan with it like a great wave from the sea. The contents overflowed on Liv, who gasped and shrieked with pain. Horrified, Els ran to throw cold water on her, as did Cressa. Though Liv was barely hurt and soon calmed down, Els' head remained pounding, as the waves of fury abated into ripples of fear and shame.

'Thank goodness you were both here, I must have tipped it while we were talking.' Liv's apparent gratitude was little help to Els.

They know, they must know. Els shook, desperately trying to control the force that had consumed her.

This inexplicable power came upon her in the strangest ways. Sometimes she hardly felt it at all, just 'hearing' parts of distant conversations, catching private thoughts. Other times, she caught strong feelings of those nearby, often unfriendly towards her, several voices coming at once with confusing, mixed emotions. It scared Els that nobody except her did this. Another way I'm different, she silently wailed, another pain I have to hide. The 'pushing' particularly concerned her. At first, she hadn't realised it was her when things moved, but she had come to realise it was most noticeable when she was experiencing particularly strong emotions. Lately, she had tried to practice this strange ability and was pleased when she controlled this power, but the force that came out when someone like Liv threatened her was terrifying in its scope. She had felt the pan go, responding to her pain, the physical push coming with her mental frustration. This time, at least, it had done no harm and she gave thanks to Bronv that her powers had escaped notice.

* * *

By nightfall, the preparations had all been successfully completed. Fine smells pervaded the centre of the town, where benches and tables had been arranged in a circle. Most of the tables were empty except for glasses and piles of cutlery. The largest, however, groaned beneath the load of food upon it. Roasted meats still simmered in their juices, the light, herb-drenched aroma of the chickens mingling with the heavier, woody smell of the t'pors. Ale was there in plenty, along with a little wine, though this year's wine harvest was scarcely better than the previous one. The greenwort and curly leaf were in large bowls, as were the radishes, carrots and marsh beans. Mavri's desserts, like those made by some of the other women, were packed in ice, in hope that a cool end would be provided for an exciting night.

The area around where the benches were placed had been readied with an equal diligence. A small, low table stood with a stool either side. In less than thirty minutes now, the table would have instruments on it as those performing chose the means to show their true feelings to a loved one. Some would leave the stools to stand and sing, choosing their voice as the best of instruments. Others would open with a song, but sit down to play the instrument which worked in harmony with their personality. All the unpaired between thirteen and eighteen would be there, though it was normally those in the middle of this age range who would be paired during the night.

While small children peered curiously around the benches and adults busied themselves checking people were where they should be, those the Festival of Fair Voice was aimed at were anxiously anticipating events. From Cam's drums to Gwen's bells, instruments were checked and practised on. Voices were heard to gently rise and fall in every house containing a youngster and those already paired and married smiled softly, remembering their own festival times. Even the most modest of young men took extra care over lacing boots and tying tunic strings, some were hardly recognisable in suddenly washed hair. The young women were also in a state of nervous excitement. Clothes much admired that afternoon hardly looked right at all now. Areev thought she had never realised until now how stupid her nose looked, Gwen was convinced she had lost every melody she had ever known, whilst for some minutes Reesa couldn't brush her hair for her hand shaking.

At Gron and Mavri's home, Els was almost hopeful she would be ignored and not have to go to the festival when Cam moved into the doorway of her tiny room, blocking the light as he did so.

'Come on, Els.' he said gently. 'It's time to go now, everyone's ready.' She tried to look away, to pretend she had not heard, but Cam's blue eyes were fixed on hers and his left hand reached for her right. As she stood up, he shifted the large drum under his right arm away from her. Els knew Cam had been sent to get her on purpose, but she didn't really mind. Better than Lissal, all prettied up with juices on her eyelids and scarves all over. Or Degra, sniping at her. Bronv and her parents would not touch her, she felt there was nothing but contempt in their faces when they saw her.

If she had not been so preoccupied with the uncertainties of the festival, perhaps Els would have caught the thoughts of her mother. Mavri's face was grim. She hoped for a happy night but doubted it could be so.

Bronv was true to his word about my poor Els, she thought. For one foolish mistake of mine she will suffer the humiliation of rejection, more so here tonight than at any other time. What god of ours is this to offer no chance of atonement? As was often the case when she considered the unfairness of her chief god, Mavri's mind turned back, as a reflex, to that long ago encounter with the Southern woman. She wondered, what 'Els' was there ever for my poor speechless child? I was stupid to trust in the promises of a stranger.

'Come, Mavri, the players begin. Let's not let the young ones have all the fun.' Gron pulled at Mavri's sleeve and she smiled despite herself. True, she still had a husband and four other children to care for, she must celebrate with them all. Besides, all the wishing in the world would not help her youngest daughter, she knew that.

'Go on, Cam.'

'Degra, I can't, what if -'

'What if what? What if she won't duet? She'll hold your tune, Cam, all can see that. And besides, there'll be others to hear you if she won't. Play, brother, or you'll never know.'

Cam chuckled, Degra was not the kindest of brothers, Bronv knew! He was awful to Els, but he had a certain wily wit about him and maybe, well, maybe he did sometimes know what he was talking about.

The drum beat out, quiet yet insistant, Cam looking only at his instrument, desperate as he was to scan the crowd for Reesa. Everything was silent but the drum's steady beat, the tune played until it could be recognised, repeated, responded to. For there was Reesa, Cam didn't need to look up, he could tell the singer by the delicate tones of her voice, so often had he heard it in conversation. He did look up, though, he could not resist the warmth of her brown eyes and the smile on her face was worth every chance. Her smile widened then and he knew, knew what they had all known, what *he* had known, he and Reesa, a dual voice, this was what the festival meant.

It was towards the end of the night, when few were left, that Hwym sang, loud and strong. Hwym was a slim, blond lad of seventeen. It was probably only his shyness which had kept him from pairing before now. Quiet though he was in conversation, his love of music was strong even for one born in such a typical Northern village and he sang out a song which was eloquent in its hope. Those expecting a strong voice in answer turned in horror at the sound of a dull knocking. Els was banging on a piece of wood, responding in the only way left open to her. The sound was in time with Hwym's voice, but harsh and unmusical in comparison. Hwym had already stopped when Bronv-Grii strode forward and grabbed Els from the centre of the cleared area.

'What sacrilege is this?' he cried, paying no attention to the look of misery on her face. 'You have no voice, you were born without musical gift. This brazen display insults all our gods. Why, the swift Cridf himself is no doubt stopped in his tracks by such perversity.' Many of the villagers hissed their own disgust, not a voice was raised in protest at the elder's words.

'You are unable to duet and while I am Garrtron's village elder you will not.' he ranted. 'Get yourself home, you, you...abnormal child.'

Running, stumbling back to her parents house, Els thought she had never heard such cruel words. Oh, Liv was nasty, but she was only petty, but Bronv-Grii! It was him who had prevented her from learning an instrument, insisting that the laws of the gods must be obeyed. 'Voice is the gift that begins all others.' Els could hear him now, remember her mother's defeated look, her father's stern nod, forced to agree. If he had only let me, just one thing, one simple pipe! How different things might have been! There was no hope now, her hazel eyes began to fill with tears at the disaster the whole village had witnessed.

Never, even in her darkest moments, had Els foreseen that the village leader would so publically condemn her. The humiliation and general agreement that she was wrong for being so different was more than Els could bear. Oh, I'll go home all right, thought Els, but only to collect my belongings. Abnormal am I? Maybe I'll find somewhere I can be normal. Nothing to wait for here, where all hate me and Cam gets paired before me.

In the house, she snatched her few spare clothes, a water bottle and a doll her mother had made her, dark-haired and beautiful. It was special not just in its looks but in having been made for her alone. These scant items were in a knapsack and boots on her feet when she looked up to see Cam. He searched her face long and hard before he broke the silence.

'You are going away, then?' he sighed. 'Well, you might need these.' Cam offered her a package of bread and cheeses, along with a tattered book. 'It's a book of Southern songs. Dad gave it to me for the music but there's a map in the front. I don't know, maybe things are different in the South and it's a long way from those who are against you...' His voice trailed away then and he put an arm around the sobbing Els. 'Please don't hate me. I know I got Reesa and you got no-one, I'm sorry. I wish they'd let you play but, I can't make them. No-one's going to listen to a fifteen-year-old, most of them probably think Reesa could've done better.'

Els shook her head, she knew most people liked Cam and wished him and Reesa well. Assuming she was shaking her head in distress, Cam held out his hands helplessly. *No, I'm not angry with you.* Els thought, futilely willing him to hear her words, *Gods, why can't you hear this?* Smiling through her tears, she hugged Cam, wishing him well and praying to Cridf that he would convey this message. She pressed his hands in hers before walking off. Well, she thought, looks like the South it is.

Chapter 2

Els walked away quickly. She had no answer if she was halted, although she did not think this was likely. Moving out of the village, she looked at the darkening skies. Can I make it through the forest by nightfall? she wondered. What do I have to lose? she thought and quickened her pace with determination. Even in amongst the trees, she could hear the music and laughter of the festival behind her. Are they still laughing at me? Do all but Cam hate me? Tears fell but no sound was made even then. Els was oblivious to the animals in the forest, not knowing that they saw her but, feeling her sorrow, stayed away. So it was, then, that the exhausted Els fell to her feet and slept well on the mossy floor undisturbed by any creature.

Els woke to find the sounds of the festival over and the forest quiet, except for a small snuffling sound. She thought little of this noise until it became a cry of pain and her mind heard what her ears could not.

'Pain pain out pain out pain paw help.' The call was insistent and without end. Els clutched her head, the communication of torment nearly overwhelmed her. Searching for the source, Els found it in a tangle of branches behind a smallflower bush. Peering over the myriad blooms of the bush, her gaze was met by that of a frightened animal who tried to writhe away from her but remained trapped by the branches. *'It's okay, I'm a friend',* Els thought as hard as she could. At this, the creature lay still and waited for Els to pull off the deliberately twisted branches which entwined it.

Bandits! thought Els. The trap was clumsy and only bandits would catch a mherl. The creature was too small to be of use for food and its coat was too thin for human warmth. Its striped tail, however, was twice the length of its body and prized as an ornamental garment in other parts of Rima. If I leave it here, they will surely find it. The trap was laid for a purpose, she thought. Besides, it has alerted me that I cannot stay here, maybe saved me from capture by bandits. Els shuddered. Alone and without proper means of defence, she could easily be carried off by bandits, who would soon take her by ship to be sold as a servant or slave. That, or make off with her for their own ends. *'Come, friend,'* Els called, concentrating her mind to send her thoughts to the mherl. *'Come with me, little one. I shall call you Sorab. Let us go from this place quickly.'*

Breaking her bread and cheese to share with Sorab, Els hoisted the small creature gently into the top of her knapsack. His brown eyes looked at her without fear and Els wondered if he really could understand her. Well, if no human will understand me, why not a mherl? she thought. She smiled, then, suddenly feeling she was not alone. The day was bright and if she made good time, she could be away from all villages and nearly at the shore by evening. She had little idea what she would do when she came to the sea but decided that getting there must be her first step. Thinking this, she knelt on the ground and lowered her head in prayer to the only goddess of the North.

Noble Fess! she began, though I am called wrong by my people, know that I worship you just as they do. As we name you She Who Finds, help me to find a way to cross the Great Sea to the South. I give you praise that when I had to leave, Cam found that book. I know you have found me a chance. This is all I ask of you, once there I shall call upon you no more. I thank you for your help.

Midway through the day, however, Els found herself growing faint. Outside of the forest, the hills were forbidding and little grew there. Stumbling out onto steep slopes, Els scanned their surroundings for plant life. It's second season! Where is all that springs from the ground gone? Deciding to press on, Els realised that she could smell the sea, a cold alien tang which thrilled her with the promise of escape. A frantic chittering came from Sorab. *'I know, you're excited, too.'* Els grinned. *'But let's pass this next bank and see the water.'* The animal's squeaks gathered pitch but Els made for the hill bank ahead.

Stepping over, she saw the sea but her gasps of joy turned to horror as she saw the bandits waiting below.

'Gry! Lwry-ak.' the strange cries were meaningless to her ears but her mind understood only too well their intentions as those nearest grabbed her. She tried to hit them with the staff of her knapsack and was dimly aware of Sorab biting and scratching them. The creature was too small, though, and the pair were soon overpowered. *'Pretty enough little thing.'*

'And the mherl, too.' she picked up before finally collapsing.

* * *

Els awoke with a pounding headache. How much wine did I drink at the festival? she grimaced. Then she remembered how she had left the festival with no reason to celebrate. Looking up, she found herself in a small tent filled with numerous coloured fabrics, wooden gifts and bizarre weaponry. Aghast, she realised how she came to be in a bandit camp alone and her painful head seemed to worsen.

Alone was bad enough, but to be alone and unarmed - they had taken her staff - was an appalling situation to find herself in.

'Crrp!' muttered the mherl, reminding Els that she wasn't quite alone. What could they do now though? Els dearly wanted to cross Rima's Great Sea but she hadn't planned on doing it as bandits' booty.

The curtain in the tent moved then, and Els' thoughts were interrupted by a bandit carrying a bundle of outlandish clothes.

'Hryk-ya.' His meaning was clear but Els had no intention of wearing such flamboyant clothing, rich as some of the fabrics were. It'll only help fetch a price for me at a market and I don't want that, she thought.

As the heavy-set bandit approached, Els glowered and tried to back away, Sorab screeched oaths behind her. Els screamed in terror as the brazen thief advanced.

As she did so, however, he cried out and began slapping at his arms. Els looked closely, imagining some grass fly had bitten him, but saw nothing. Still the man waved his arms, flinging them about his body as if they were burning. He tried to grab Els then, but at that point collapsed on his knees in agony. 'Gryk! Nn-yran hi,' he wailed.

'Save me! The small ones torture now,' Els received.

I! I do this, she realised. A cruel look gleamed in her eyes then, as she saw her powers in all their frantic strength. Stepping outside the tent, she swept her gaze over the bandit group. *'Burn!'* she called, searching for their weaknesses with all her mind's force. *'Hurt as I have,'* she screamed inside. It was as if all the hate and frustration of her sixteen years had been released into a dangerous cloud of raw power. The bandit people clutched themselves in pain. There was not a single flame to be seen but still they rolled on the grass as if putting out a terrible fire.

'I could make it real,' Els said to herself, preparing her mind for this new task. She began to see real flames in her mind and the devastation they would cause her captors. Poor Sorab flattened himself against her, shaking in time with Els as the energy coursing through her made her seem to vibrate. Els, however, seemed barely to realise she *was* shaking, not stopping to see that her hands were unsteady, even as she raised them above her head to punctuate her screams.

Those screams were not alone, though. A thin, high voice called in sorrow over her wrathful cries. Turning, she at once noticed Sorab hunched into the ends of her dress. The mherl, however, was silent and staring. Whirling where she looked, she saw a small child lying on the floor, gasping in desperation with what voice it could summon. Children! The children! In all her rage and new-found power, Els had failed to see beyond the bandits as enemies. Looking, now, at the children of the group, she felt suddenly sick. But how to put it right? Searching deep within her mind, Els remembered Cam, saw how calm he was, how giving. Gradually, she felt the heat subsiding from her and her mind cooling. Rain began to fall then, great grey clouds emptying themselves, but no-one flinched from it. The rain was neither harsh nor pounding, rather a refreshing curtain that wrapped folds of relief slowly over the entire North.

'Come, Sorab,' called Els and hurried for the shore. While the bandits were struggling to recover, she knew she could snatch a boat. Finding a small one, she threw her belongings in, checked its oars were on board and unhooked it from its moorings with shaking hands. Sorab jumped in with an exuberant squeak and Els smiled despite herself.

Standing with the rope in her hands and her feet on the shoreline, Els looked out over the expanse of the Great Sea. Her heart skipped a beat when she faced it, fully aware now of the continuous water stretching in front of her. Nothing but a few ice flows would mark her way to the South now, it would be a landless horizon for a long while.

Doubt crept across her mind, that foe which had so often tortured her. All this water she must cross and for what? Could she really trust in an old map and the rumours of villagers? She had no covers against bad weather and her food supply was limited. Why risk peril at sea when she had never set foot in a boat in her life?

But she could hardly go back. Surviving in the forest alone and dealing with the bandits as she had, had been risky enough, but her village offered her no easier destiny. And hadn't Cam given her the map? Well, he knew about things like that, he must have believed she could make it. After all, Els realised, had not Bronv himself led her people miles to the North when the lands split? She knew people said her mother had offended Bronv, that she herself was cursed. But wasn't she a lot like Bronv, racing ahead to a dream? Well, if he could do it, why not her? Stepping in at last, Els would have giggled at the joke if she could, but as it was, that would only have rocked the boat.

Chapter 3

On her first day at sea, Els learnt how best to guide her boat, using her strength wisely in rowing and using her staff and knapsack as a makeshift sail. Her fear and excitement kept her on edge and she made good timing over the water as a result. When she grew tired enough to stop rowing she consulted her mapbook.

It looked as if her journey would take her to one of the three Northern-most countries of the South, sailing as she was in the straightest line she could manage. Els hoped for Zaritt, the largest of the three, as she guessed there would be more opportunities for some kind of work. Sytrannia or Akrin would be the only real alternatives, unless she made a serious error. Not unlikely, I'm no sailor, Els thought, although she was pleased with her maiden voyage so far. Sorab was busy enough at fetching fish from the sea, adept at diving quickly off the boat, returning with a silvery catch. Els closed her eyes briefly, giving thanks to Fess, for surely some power had been lent to Sorab. His ability to pluck fish out of the sea was uncanny. One minute, the sun was bouncing off gentle waves, the next there was a dash of brown fur breaking up the ripples, then leaving them as if never broken.

'Sorab, you are clever. And you are so good to help me in this way.'

'You're my friend. I help you now.' squeaked the mherl.

'Thanks! Let's hope we reach Zaritt soon and maybe I can provide some food there.'

On the third day, however, Els realised that she was not as near to her target as she thought. Instead of mountains, the objects which had made a craggy skyline from afar now became clear as icebergs. Smaller pieces lay directly in front of them but were overshadowed by the towering lumps above them. These fearsome things seemed to reach for the sun with their jagged tips.

Carefully, Els steered their little vessel through them.

Her line was straight until they met a lump so big it might have been a small island.

'We can always get back on course. Sorab, don't look so doubtful! Indeed, Sorab did look most unconvinced by this prospect. *'Big.'* was his primary thought and Els could hardly dispute that. As she sailed carefully round, she turned one way and then another, each corner revealing another bend streatching further than the last.

'Sorab, you were right. That was trickier than I thought.'

'Big cold bits. Little and big then big big.'

'Very big, yes. Well, I think if we turn South again, we shouldn't be too far out.'

At first, they could see nothing but sea in front of them and all they could do was hope for a safe return to their original course, such as that was. The sea was indeed great and Els was reminded that she was in a strange place and following an uncertain hope. Seeing not so much as a blade of grass, she felt as if the hills and forests of Garrtron had existed only in a dream. Gradually, however, the ice flows faded on the horizon behind them and the sea began to feel warmer. One particularly bright morning, the cloudless sky revealed a coastline not too far away.

'Zaritt! Wake up, Sorab, wake up. There is land in front of us. The South at last!'

'People? Mherl? Food?'

'Sorab, I have as many questions as you. Food I hope we will find soon and no doubt people. Mherl? I have no idea.'

Picking up her oars, Els rowed harder than she had found strength to in the last few days. The coast was long but the nearest port was straight, so Els aimed for this stretch. Gaining on her goal, she saw other, larger vessels, from fishing trawlers and family sailing boats to huge commercial ships. From the quiet of the sea, Els and Sorab now found themselves amid the bustle of a city port. The sounds were all foreign but Els guided her mind to understand, just as it could in the North.

'Silver, Silver for the king.'

'Papers?'

'Here, from Zaritt. Queen Ashla sends a message also. We are to bring her good wishes ourselves.'

'Fishing is getting hard work these days.'

'Grirgi, Shaz, Pinak. Let's unload.'

'Khan! How is your family? Come, you must be exhausted. Welcome to Sytrannia and Istalan.'

Istalan? Sytrannia? Els realised she had veered from her intended target. Sytrannia, though, seemed busy enough. If only she could attract some attention, get some help. Scanning the crowd, Els saw such a variety of people she had no idea where she could start or how even a visual greeting should be made in this unfamiliar land.

'Ahaz-ya! Hi mherl? Vra kin lan mherl ton sri garingha-ya?' an amused voice cried out.

Els turned to find a man only a few years older than her, pointing at her creature with obvious delight. If I could only reply, he seems friendly enough and Sorab is not anxious at his interest. Els smiled at the young man, then placed her hands over her mouth to indicate her problem. The Southern looked shocked momentarily, then continued chattering at a great rate, revealing himself to be Sy. Els understood not a word but mentally found the thoughts behind his words to be kind. He appeared to be a merchant. It seemed he could not entertain them long - he had some meeting - but would take them to a female friend of his, Kyrria. Els could easily see the thoughts in his head as powerful images, startling in their clarity. In one mental picture, Sy saw this Kyrria as unclothed, the next in gleaming robes addressing others with authority, again, humble, yet friendly. What manner of a woman do they raise on this continent? thought Els in wonder.

Sy's thoughts grew more anticipatory as they neared a golden building on the other side of Istalan's main gate. He easily passed through the gateway and seemed on good terms with the guards there, exchanging jokes as he explained that Els was with him.

The golden house was a different matter. Its two female guards were clearly dubious about Sy's presence. They will surely turn us away, thought Els, Why he wants to take me to a palace I don't know.

'Gqa! Kyrria ist es tikri-gran-ka? Ti lizx grit-ka tlank mi,' Sy gestured wildly in Els' direction, angry and pleading by turns. Els could suddenly see him in the market place, selling his goods. She couldn't help smiling, then, knowing that Sy also saw the situation this way. The guards suddenly tensed with the realisation that Els was following events, despite being mute and not learned of their language. One of them stepped forward and gently laid her hand on Els' forehead.

'I am Rayth. You hear this?' was all she communicated, yet her dark pupils betrayed her concentration and excitement.

'Yes, oh yes. I am Els, I hear you well,' Els exclaimed.

'Good, but calm down a little or you will give both of us a headache. I can see that this mind of yours is untrained but not to worry. It is no doubt for a purpose that you came here, so let us invite you properly.' She stood tall and proud then, joined by her companion. 'I, Rayth, and this, Plarina, welcome you to the temple of the goddess L'ra. We take you now to our sister priestess Kyrria.' Els and Sorab walked into the majestic building flanked by the two women, leaving a confused Sy on the steps below.

Rayth and Plarina opened the ornate doors at the top of the steps and Els gasped at the beauty of the temple's interior. A long hallway stretched in front of them, with incense burning in alcoves along it alternating with tablets proclaiming the virtues of L'ra. At the end of this corridor, they came to the statue of the goddess. Here, both guards knelt and bowed their heads to speak with she whom they worshipped. Els scarcely noticed.

'It's so...grand.' was all she could say, though the word barely covered the image. The woman in the statue was made from pure gold, but there was beauty in her even without this. Her smile was confident but gentle, almost as

if she was laughing at an inner joke which she could explain, should she want to. By her side was a large mherl, sheltered by L'ra's long hair. The mherl also had an expression of knowing a reason for humour, and with one forepaw raised, looked ready for action. Both were made of solid gold except that their eyes were cut from jade so that they seemed to shine. Several people knelt or stood near the statue, some talking quietly, though any sound was muffled by the gold thread carpet lapping the statue's base. Why should she be shown with a mherl? Els wondered, looking at Sorab, who had no more idea. And the way they all look at it, it's like Bronv is treated at home. Els was startled to find herself remembering Garrtron, but the parallel was obvious. Do I really want to meet this Kyrria? she thought. What if she thinks I am all wrong, like the others did?

'*Fear not, Els,*' Rayth gently pulled at Els' dress, reminding her that she was not alone. '*I do not know who it is you think of with such mixed thoughts, but no harm will come to you whilst among the followers of L'ra.*'

'*Kyrria will be most excited to meet a stranger. She will no doubt show you around and make you welcome,*' agreed Plarina.

'*I know. You are most kind. It's just... very different here,*' Els was hesitant in her sending at first but the others appeared to receive her thoughts with ease, so she continued, '*People have been very helpful already, Sy as well as both of you, but I don't know how to respond. What to wear, how to eat, how to greet people. Should I have knelt before the statue? I didn't think.*'

'*Stop panicking! Our heads whirl with yours. L'ra will take no offence. It's common for people to reaffirm their faith in her by bowing or kneeling -* ' Rayth put out.

' *- But not compulsory and you are a stranger -* ' interjected Plarina.

' *- So why would the goddess expect you to know our customs?*' Rayth said.

'*Well, thank you. If Kyrria is as friendly as you two, I*

will have little to fear,' gave Els.

'Come then, let us find her.'

Turning left beyond the statue, they went through a door onto another corridor. The many doors leading off on either side suggested living quarters. I will never find my way out alone, thought Els. Suddenly, the door at the far end of the corridor was flung open and a young woman came through, smiling to see her fellow priestesses.

'Rayth, Plarina. Do you go to the gardens this morning? The flowers seem all out now, the weather has been good. Bless L'ra and Tadir both.'

'Kyrria, greetings to you this fine morning. We were actually coming to see you,' said Plarina.

'Really? And is this a friend who comes with you? I would be honoured to meet any new friend of yours.'

'More a friend of Sy's actually,' Rayth grinned. 'She's mute and a Northener. Sy seems to have taken it upon himself to befriend her and thought you could help.'

'Sy taking a woman under his wing, eh? I am not surprised,' Kyrria laughed. 'But our friends have not introduced us,' she exchanged a glance with the priestesses. 'Do you know her name?'

'Surely - she told us herself,' Rayth said.

'Then - well, you can tell me yourself,' Kyrria looked at Els.

'I am Els. This is Sorab, a mherl I found in a trap. I am from Garrtron on the Northern continent. I come here because I, er, because I want to see what I can do somewhere different,' Els said.

'An adventurer? Then the goddess herself brings you here.'

'She does? I mean, I don't really understand. I left home reluctantly, I didn't even mean to come to Sytrannia,' Els apologised.

'L'ra, however, is the goddess of adventure. She favours well those who find their own fortune. Stop,' She put her hands up to block any argument, *'I know L'ra is as strange to you as some of your gods seem to us. But certainly there*

must be reason in your journey, for it cannot have been easy.'

'No,' agreed Rayth, *'I would not pry into your mind too far but feelings of fear and confusion are not long buried there.'*

'Your face alone tells of exhaustion that must have come from many trials,' Plarina sent.

'We are practised in our mental powers but you do not yet have that luxury,' Kyrria said. *'Stay with us and we can help you with it. It would also give you a chance to rest.'*

'Well, okay,' Els looked at the calm faces of her new friends, *'I'll stay.'* she said, and the mental voice that sent this message was surprisingly strong.

Chapter 4

That evening, Kyrria took Els to meet the chief priest and priestess of the temple, Roro and Skrella. The office they used was small but tidy, and brightened by the plants at the window. Although obviously interested in their visitor, the temple's leaders radiated the same sense of peace as the followers Els had already met.

'Kyrria? You bring us a friend?' enquired Skrella, in an alert voice.

'Yes, I believe so,' Kyrria said, 'This is Els. She has disobeyed her parents and fought others to travel the many miles over sea from the North.'

'A Northern adventurer?' Roro asked, exchanging looks with Skrella. 'Does she come as a novice?'

'Not exactly. Els is barely aware of our gods and goddeses, yet she is capable of great things - powers have surely been invested in her for a reason.'

Neither Skrella nor Roro spoke for a moment, yet they seemed to confer despite this. The silence was brief, but in that time they looked at Els and each other, as if to confirm an idea.

'We would like you to stay here a while,' Roro said, finally.

'You shall have a room next to Kyrria, there is one free there and it seems the two of you are already friends,' added Skrella.

'You are very kind. You don't even know me, yet you help me. Thank you,' Els said.

'Go, now, get some food and some sleep,' Skrella said gently.

Els ate with Kyrria, Rayth and Plarina in the dining hall, although this was now empty. The dining room spartan, as were the sleeping quarters, yet clean and tidy. The window in each also allowed plenty of air and sunlight. The door between Els' room and Kyrria's was lockable but the two girls used it often. Els found it strange

33

to be on her own after years sharing with her family and Kyrria's knock at the door was usually welcomed.

Although Rayth, Plarina and the other residents of the temple were kind to her, Els was close to Kyrria from that first day. As the weeks went on, she and Els soon got to know each other. Kyrria saw that Els wanted friendship, realising it was her shyness and pain that sometimes made her seem so wary, even rude, to others. She shared Els' love of animals and appreciated Els' affinity with Sorab. Els, for her part, grew to love Kyrria more than she ever had her sister, admiring her confidence, yet not feeling threatened by it as she had with Lissal.

Gentle as Kyrria was, there was a mischievous air to her which made her fun to be with. Her hair was, fortunately, short, for it always seemed to be swinging about. One afternoon, Els was practising pushing and sending with Kyrria and the pair decided to take turns receiving mental instructions and carrying them out with telekinesis.

'Move the cupboard a handspan to the right,' Els sent, only to throw her hands up in dismay as Kyrria turned the cupboard upside down. *Move to the right!* Els sent, with greater energy. This time, Kyrria herself stepped to the right. Before Els could send again, Kyrria burst out laughing, 'Oh, your face!' she cried, 'I really wondered what you would do next!'

Only in prayer did Kyrria stay motionless, the calm of her goddess was something Els could only marvel at. Normally, though, there was the sense of humour that she teased Els with, more than once feigning displeasure while Els performed her mental tasks.

Kyrria was not Els' only teacher, though. Arrok, a middle-aged priest, helped her with telekinesis, as Kyrria dwelt more on telepathy. Lessons with Arrok started off with breaking china, so quickly did Els send it across the temple, but her control improved and those on kitchen chores began to relax. Arrok was a quiet man yet his delight in a new pupil after many years enthused both of them. Els often tried to thank him to no avail.

'I need no thanks,' he would smile, 'How else would I get to play such games?'

Roro and Skrella encouraged Els to listen to the teachings of the temple, though nobody asked her to join in prayer. For this, Els was grateful. It fascinated her to hear of L'ra and the other Southern gods and goddesses but it meant little to her on a daily basis, so far removed was it from the teachings she was used to. Sometimes Skrella and Roro's words, or that of visiting temple leaders, would provoke a strange feeling of recognition, but this was usually fleeting and so alien she feared to invite it.

After a talk from a visiting priest, Els left the others in prayer and contemplation while she went to the garden. The sun was out and its light revealed the natural beauty of the garden. The flower beds were lovingly tended by the priest and priestesses and blooms of all colours flourished. Els wandered over to the pond, the ducks always seemed such funny creatures to her, there was nothing quite like them in the North.

'How are you?' she asked them, bending close to the water.

'Good. Much weed. Sun out,' the oldest duck answered.

'Help. The ringtail comes.' A young female bobbed under.

'Sorab! Must you scare them so?' Els scolded her pet.

'Stupid feathery things. They dive,' Sorab replied, all innocent, yet Els knew how he viewed the ducks. They were larger than the small rodents or insects he usually ate but they smelt good to him and Els feared the worst if he should ever encounter one on its own.

'Hello,' The mental call was weak but Els turned to see Timo approaching through the trees. A young novice, he was always keen to chat. 'I thought I'd give you a headshout before I got here,' he said, 'I know I'm pretty awful at it but I didn't want to disturb the others, some are still in prayer.'

'Not you?' Els asked.

'Hardly. I believe in Tadir, mind, you only have to look at this garden to see our earth is protected by him. It's just that all this stuff's a bit new. I'd rather do it on my own sometimes, so I escaped to my room for a bit, then I thought I'd have a wander out here.'

Els felt a huge sense of relief. It wasn't just she who felt strange, even this confident merchant's son could feel out of place at times. Really, she didn't feel that strange anymore. Those in the temple were familiar with Els' kind of communication, some could use it themselves. Arrok treated her like the pupil he had been waiting for, not an abnormality to be outcast. The acceptance of the temple community had washed over Els and she realised she had actually begun to relax with these people. She remembered one afternoon when she had been showing Kyrria her progress in telepathy, only to completely confuse the message she was trying to send. Looking up, she had been horrified by the rare sight of Kyrria frowning. When her friend collapsed into giggles, Els realised she had only been feigning disappointment. It was a welcome change both to be able to learn a skill and to be allowed to enjoy it.

Later that week, Els was performing another such task when Kyrria looked genuinely serious.

'What is it? Have I done wrong?' Els asked, anxiously.

'No, stop your worry. It is only that I realise how little I can teach you.'

'But you have helped so much. I hardly ever drop things now. And Arrok has done as much work in telekinesis, I am better.'

'Yes, a great deal better than us. You send and receive faster than we do, not to mention the speed you move items at. I know you can use your skills in other areas too,' Kyrria hesitated.

'Yes, what is it?' Els prompted.

'There are others whose job it is to practise such mind skills. Some can even travel using their souls, or bend the elements to their will, I hear.'

36

'Sorcerors?' said Els, faintly.

'Yes - now don't look so scared,' Kyrria said.

'But what do they do these things for? I don't want to hurt anyone,' Els suppressed thoughts of the bandit camp quickly.

'You wouldn't have to. In the South, you see how the gods are followed. Misuse of powers given by them would be strictly against the law of any part of this continent, as in the West.'

'Who can ensure such obedience, though, there must be those who try to gain by their strength?'

'Few who would be respected, or even tolerated, dare spite either the gods or a ruler such as ours. Tomorrow, I will take you to meet King Nahvib so you can see for yourself.'

Chapter 5

The palace was visible from a distance, a strong, stone building, embellished with various turrets and archways. From its size and strength, it was clear that the building, like the temple of L'ra, housed many and could look after them well.

'*Perhaps this is not such a harsh change?*' queried Els.

'*Indeed, just a progression,*' smiled Kyrria, '*King Nahvib will be most interested to meet you himself – I told him about your talents yesterday.*'

'*How? And why? Really? He's a king. I will just be a silly girl to him, one with daft ideas and no proper way of talking.*'

'*You certainly assume a great deal before meeting me,*' a third presence seemed to chuckle. '*Don't be so shocked, I too have strange ways.*'

'*King Nahvib, it's good to hear you again,*' Kyrria bowed low and transmitted the image mentally.

'*King Nahvib! I'm sorry, I was merely wondering. I mean, I didn't know what...*' Els' train of thought stuttered to a halt.

'*You didn't know what I was like? Why should you? But please, make your way to the palace gates and my servants will guide you to my rooms. I have not the mental talents to talk to you both like this for very long.*'

At the entrance, Els let Kyrria and the palace guards guide her to the king's chambers. Kyrria spoke almost continuously to the two guards and the valet within. Mostly, she smiled, but sometimes she frowned at what she heard. Els was too stunned to try to join in. The décor was luxurious and intriguing in style. Strange scenes on tapestries, instruments of celebration or ritual struck her. Metal dominated but jewels were also prevalent and Els wondered how they had been acquired. Staircases loomed above and people of all kinds – with many thoughts between them – appeared to fill the place. One only occupied Els – the king, and he can hear me, she thought.

The king awaited them in his drawing room. Smiling, he indicated a couch, which Els felt needed several more people to be full.

'So, you are Els. Kyrria's images are as accurate as ever, but it still surprises me to see one so young, so strong. Your people must be very proud of you.'

'Hardly, I am too different. But I came here and found friends, I am happy now.'

'Good. I hope you will continue to be so in your time here at the palace. You will stay and be taught here?'

'Yes, I would like to very much. You seem almost to understand.'

Maybe I do. A long while ago, I made a difficult journey of my own. I was a young prince and had been trusted with a message to the then king of Lykrozia. The message was safely delivered but on my return jurney a terrible illness fell upon my party.Two of my friends died and the others, fearing for themselves, left me for dead.'

Els leaned forward; even Sorab's eyes were wide, as if he were desperate to hear more, *'What did you do?'*

'I got up and walked on. The fever gripped me but I couldn't lie down and die, I had to show my father I could carry out affairs of state. When I reached sight of a town, I saw a beautiful woman beckoning me. I thought the lack of water and the sickness had caused me to hallucinate.'

'But you weren't,' said Kyrria.

'No. The woman who appeared was L'ra herself. She told me she would reward my courage and that I would have the strength to continue until I met help. L'ra also warned me that I would have this strength to call on in years to come, for it would be needed again.'

'Surely, she need not have made such a promise, this kingdom is strong,' Kyrria said.

'But for how long? Soon I fear I must use all the strength of myself and my friends to keep this country safe.'

'Why? What could you fear?' asked Els.

'War?' Kyrria suggested, disbelievingly, 'Our neighbours trade with us happily, it cannot be.'

'A war, yes, but not with a kingdom,' the king's broad brow wrinkled with concern, 'The Demon Lords are at war with us again.'

Kyrria shrank back on her chair, 'The Demon Lords?' she hissed.

'I only suspect but we must be prepared.'

'What makes you think they come now?'

'There have been a couple of strange deaths lately. A kitchen maid and one of my knights. Both appeared distant and distracted in the days before their deaths. When death came, it was sudden but the sorcerors and magi felt a tremendous surge of power at this time.'

'I'm sorry,' interrupted Els, *'But who are these Demon Lords?'*

'Once they were powerful sorcerers – magi – so legend has it. Hrai, some say, was the first to begin it.'

'Cursed be the dark one!' Kyrria cried with vehemence.

'Certainly,' agreed the king, 'All his magic was not enough, he craved immortality. He tried to summon the gods to perform this but found instead an old, dark magic.'

'This was always present,' continued Kyrria, 'But people had forgotten it. Hrai, however, used this power to become immortal and possessed of magic beyond that of his fellows. Soon, he found others to join him and so the dark ones above met the dark ones below and became what we call the Demon Lords.'

'For years, they appear to have gone. Then they meet a mind weak enough, corrupt such a person and take their power, draining their host. Or, worse still, they meet one like Hrai, with such a lust for power that he will willingly unite with them. And now they try us.' King Nahvib sighed, his moustaches drooping sadly.

'How can we combat such a dread force?' Els asked.

'Combining our strength is our only hope. I have briefed my people of magic and will soon speak to all in my kingdom.'

'The gods will also help us,' Kyrria said.

'Perhaps. Certainly we must look to them for guidance and not to other ways,' replied the king.

'Do you really want me here at this time?' asked Els, *'Isn't a stranger among you an extra burden?'*

'I hope not,' laughed the king, 'No, I look forward to helping you with your magic as you may be able to help us with this trouble in the kingdom. It is not as a stranger that you come but as a fellow adventurer – L'ra blesses us all in that.'

'Well, if you are happy with the arrangement, Els, I must return to the temple,' announced Kyrria. 'My home may also need protection if your majesty's fears are correct.'

'Kyrria…good luck. You'll visit? I do not wish to leave you forever.'

Els hugged Kyrria then, burying her face in Kyrria's shoulders in case the tears she shed began to show. Somehow, though, she doubted Kyrria would be much surprised, for she was gripping Els with an equal strength. Parting, Kyrria cupped her right hand over her left fist in the sign of protection through L'ra's blessing. Els nodded and waved until her friend was beyond sight of the palace grounds.

'Come, now, let me introduce you to your new home,' said King Nahvib, gently steering Els back inside.

'Our home!' Sorab chirped excitedly.

'I know!' Els laughed, *'I could never have dreamed of such a place when I was back in Garrtron. I think we will be happy here. Watch those stairs!'*

She shook her head as Sorab raced ahead, while the king led Els up three flights of stairs, richly carpeted in lush shades of green, until they reached a room at the top of the right-hand staircase. King Nahvib opened the door and led Els into the small room, not nearly as ornate as the king's quarters but not lacking in anything. A desk, chair and bed of some strange pale wood were all present, amid cushions and lengths of material in brightly coloured patterns.

'You like it?' asked the king.

'Of course. Who lives here, one of your sorcerers?' Els said.

'The room waits only for you, my dear, if you can accept it.'

'Accept it? But this is marvellous. I can't thank you enough, your majesty.'

'If it pleases you, I am happy. The room looks out onto the main courtyard and is sunny enough for you to write at the desk. A bathroom next door is shared with two apprentice magicians. I'll leave you to rest now, but the magi will send someone to bring you over to the teaching area in the morning. Goodnight, L'ra bless you.'

Els thought she would never sleep, she was so overwhelmed with everything that had happened that day. However, although very different to what she had grown up with, she soon found the fabrics very comfortable. Once Sorab had stopped sniffing every part of the room and had curled up with her, Els gave in to sleep before she knew it.

* * *

Tap, tap, tap. The gentle rapping finally broke through Els' dreaming state. Sitting up in bed, it took her a moment to realise where she was.

'Hello?' she tentatively put out.

'Els? I am Cyru,' replied a calm, male voice, *'If you can make yourself ready, I shall be pleased to take you to the magi.'*

'I will be with you shortly,' Els said.

Hastily, she threw on her tunic and leggings. She was so excited, she used her mental powers to open the door before she knew what she had done.

Els groaned inwardly. He probably thinks I'm a terrible showoff, she thought.

'Bye for now, Sorab,' she sent, *'I'll tell you all about it*

later!' Let's just hope I don't do anything else to embarrass myself, she thought.

Cyru, however, just grinned, *'Very impressive, but please, there is no need to tax yourself so early in the day.'*

Indeed, it had to be early, for it was dark even by the South's fourth season standards. Lights still shone gently inside the palace and the central courtyard, though the quiet revealed most people to be asleep. Cyru led Els in the opposite direction to where she had entered, bringing her to the East wing of the palace. Here, the wall hangings were more informative, with notices and letters displayed. Els saw that some of the rooms they passed contained workshops or meeting rooms and she caught sight of bright capes and strange symbols as she followed her guide.

Cyru knocked on a large, plain wooden door near the corner of the wing.

'Come in, Cyru, Els,' said a deep voice, so they entered, Cyru pulling the door shut behind them. Els turned to meet the gaze of a stocky Southerner whose dark hair was just beginning to turn grey.

'Welcome,' he said, 'You must be Els. Cyru, thank you very much for bringing our newest student down, you may go now,' he turned back to Els, 'Cyru is always so keen to help, we usually choose him to welcome newcomers. Anyway, I am Durrew and I shall be your main teacher here. Along with these two gentlemen,' he indicated two considerably older men behind him, 'Zritz and Pocack, I run the magical department of Sytrannia.'

'I am Els. It is good to meet you. What will I be doing here?'

'There will be some set classes, but also some time spent widening your abilities with magic in a class or a small group. This morning, I am taking a class for telepathy, what you call sending and receiving, shall we start there? I'll give you a cape – this short length indicates that you are an apprentice. I have no doubt it will grow in length very quickly.'

43

'Thank you. I look forward to learning from you, I hope I progress as well as you expect.'

'I'm sure you will, but we too, may learn from you, Els, do not forget that,' Durrew smiled.

He was still smiling in his class, where none of the sorcerers or students seemed surprised at his good humour. As Durrew greeted the class mentally, they all responded with an *'Alleri says good day,'* or *'Yarakob says good day,'* until they all turned to meet the new student, *'Els says good day,'* she sent, hoping they couldn't see her shaking.

'Els, where do you come from?' asked Alleri, a young woman with dark curls and a freckled nose.

'I come from Garrtron, on the Northern continent. More recently, I have been at the temple of L'ra,' Els answered.

'And you leave such exotic realms purely for an audience with Durrew? Surely, our teacher has been too modest!' laughed a tall, dark young man, the others joining in.

'Thank you very much, Jayak. Els, you have now met the South's youngest sorcerer. Fortunately, his magic is better than his wit.' Durrew said.

'Pleased to meet you, Els. Seriously, we will all help you if you need us,' said Jayak.

'I'm very grateful,' Els replied, trying not to blush. This young man was popular and powerful, yet he was paying her such attention.

The lecture was fascinating to Els, who listented intently to understand how to improve her magical skills. While listening to Durrew, she tried hard not to spend too much time gazing around the room at the others. She had become used to the dark skin and hair of the Southerners while at the temple, but the range of costume was much more varied here, the magic department attracting pupils from all over Sytrannia, as well as a few other outsiders. As she left the room, Els felt a gentle tug on her cape and turned to see Alleri behind her.

'We're going to get a snack from the kitchen, would you like to come?'

'That'd be great,' Els smiled.

'Okay, good. Dayx, Jayak, Klara, are you coming?'

The other young people were keen to join them and the little group made its way off. As they made their way down the corridor, Alleri and her friends chatted about themselves, their kingdom and their studies. So vibrant was their conversation that by the time they reached the kitchen, Els realised she had been talking almost as much herself.

As she sat with them, sipping a hot fruit drink and eating a nut cake, she knew she could enjoy being a person of magical talent, being herself. Surveying her new friends, Els grinned. Alleri was obviously leader of the group. She never stopped talking and the others listened to her. Her clothing was neat, from the ribbons tying her hair to the cloak which marked her as a magician. Dayx and Klara were clearly a couple. Klara's softly voiced arguments were always emphasied by Dayx' fervent agreements and the pair often seemed to think of things at the same time. Klara was a small woman with short hair who had been born in the South of Sytrannia. Dayx' hair was covered with the small, square hat typical of his farming background. Then there was Jayak. He was the tallest, yet it was his infectious laugh that alerted others to his presence. He was always happy and there was warmth in his smile. Els wondered if Jayak and Alleri were a couple: they appeared equally confident, but Els couldn't be sure. Whatever their situation, Els decided she was glad to be part of this group of friends.

'More juice, Els?' Jayak offered,breaking her thoughts.

'Give the girl a chance to rest,' Klara said, 'Honestly, Els, we are not all idle chatterboxes here.'

'Indeed, no, some of us mere mortals have to study,' laughed Dayx.

Jayak raised his left eyebrow in mock horror at this insult. Before he could comment, however, all chatter in the dining area stopped as Durrew sent an urgent message to them all,

'Trouble, important message. Main lecture room. All. Now.'

In the main lecture hall, every student of magic gathered, and Els was glad she had friends to help her find a seat. When all were seated, a hush fell as Zritz, Pocack and Durrew entered through a door in the rear of the auditorium. Their tread was heavy, not for effect but with the sincerest weight of the task that brought them here.

'Wow, even old Zritz woke up for this one,' said Jayak.

'Ssh,' hissed Dayx, 'I think this is about more than broken lab equipment.'

Pocack stepped forward, then, and spoke both verbally and mentally so all could hear.

'This is a serious occasion and I appreciate you all coming straight here. As the chief magus in Sytrannia, King Nahvib approached me this morning with grave news.'

'The king!' was the primary thought of the audience.

'The king himself is well,' Pocack hastily added, *'It is our country that has a sickness upon it. The Demon Lords are back.'*

'Calm!' called Zritz, as the students began to gasp and exclaim, *''This is an unexpected problem, and yes, a very severe one. We will deal with it, however. The king will tell all tomorrow, but we are trusted with early news, for we will be the ones to fight this menace.'*

'Yes,' added Durrew, joining his fellows at the front, *'This is now no longer a meeting but a council of war. We are the best weapon to stop this but it will be hard. Any who wish not to join us, say now and we will understand. Leave now, so that we may know who is left.'*

There was a ripple amongst the crowd and three left it. A young, pale girl with thin red hair drawn down her back severely, a wizard who could only just have been declared one, so awkwardly did he hold his cloak and an older man, who undid his cape and left it on the floor behind him.

'They must be really scared,' said Klara, 'And I'm scared enough.'

'Disloyal,' sniffed Alleri.

'Don't worry,' said Dayx, 'Plenty stay, what are three gone?'

A thunderclap brought them back to attention and Zritz grinned, though it was a weary attempt. Seeing this, however, many, apprentices and qualified alike, smiled too.

'If a man of ninety-one can fight, why do we fear?' Jayak demanded of his friends, his eyes flashing.

'Yes, my friend,' laughed Zritz, 'Forgive me eavesdropping but I celebrate your courage. Old or young and of whatever talent, we fight this together or it consumes us.'

'Yes,' agreed Pocack, 'We must be vigilant, any of you with telepathic talents, especially so. Those of you with telekinetic or elemental talents will be able to help defend us when the Demon Lords use physical force against us.'

'We will meet in groups to discuss exactly what we can do,' said Durrew, 'For now, you can have the afternoon free. We all have enough to think on for the moment. You are dismissed,'

'Enough to think on!' exclaimed Jayak later, sitting in Alleri's room.

'Can you believe it?' asked Dayx, 'I had no idea this was up.'

'I knew,' Els said hesitantly. She was still standing, having just come back from collecting Sorab, but knew she couldn't hide her knowledge any longer without feeling dishonest. 'When I came yesterday with Kyrria, the king told us.'

'He knew already!' shouted Alleri, 'When was he going to tell us?'

'It's not like that!' Els blasted back, 'He wanted to be sure, I think he was scared.'

'Scared? You do not know our ruler to question his power like this,' argued Alleri.

'Stop, Alleri. You are frightening a new friend who means us no harm.' Klara said.

'Plus,' mused Dayx, 'The room is beginning to shake and I fear Els is affecting our surroundings with her anxiety.'

Certainly, the room seemed to shimmer in the corners and their notebooks were rattling against each other. Sorab quivered violently, his eyes darting from Alleri to his mistress. Els held him tightly, looking back and forward between Dayx and Alleri. Then Jayak made a movement with his hands and a subtle noise and the room returned to order.

'Alleri, Els,' he said, each of his hands holding one of theirs, 'This is no time to fight, you heard what Pocack said.

'I'm sorry, Els, I just wasn't prepared for you knowing something I didn't. I suppose the king must think you're pretty important,' Alleri held out her other hand to Els.

'I know. I'm sorry too. I didn't mean to shout or mess your room up,' she grasped Alleri's hand firmly, *'It's just, it was like being at home again, falling out with everyone. I don't want that. I want to be your friend, not on my own.'*

'Els,' Klara said, 'Don't worry. We are all friends here. I don't know what happened amongst your own people, but here, an argument does not end our liking.'

'Well said, Klara,' Jayak grinned, 'Now can we teach Els to play Arram's game or are you scared she'll beat you?'

Chapter 6

The next time the friends met was at the auditorium again, where the three magi were busily distributing tasks.

'Alleri, Dayx, Cyru, Estella, go to laboratory three. We practise a chemical defence. You may be able to use your ability to 'throw' there,' Pocack waved them on.

'Jayak, Arak, Lufrie – see me in room fourteen for 'reading,' said Durrew.

'All new wizards or above not yet sent, either healing which Klara will direct– don't complain Klara – or with me here for sending and controlling,' Zritz leaned heavily on his stick, but his eyes were clear and bright.

Els looked around her. All her friends, indeed, everyone who had come to the Council, had found where they had to go. She had neither heard her name, nor recognised a suitable category. Typical, yet again, I don't fit in, she thought.

'Why do you still wait, child?' asked Zritz.

'Where do I go? My name is unknown, as is my magic.'

'I would not say that,' Zritz replied in a strong mental tone, *'We are excited enough by the little we do know of you. Let us say you train here with me awhile, but try the other groups too. Is this fair?'*

'Fair? Of course, thank you Zritz.'

Els smiled. Well, she thought, it seems I am welcome here. Looking about her, she saw that Zritz' group was mainly made up of new wizards, although a few more experienced ones were present, along with a woman who must be a sorceress, judging by her long, hooded robes.

Zritz started off by giving the group simple exercises in sending information. Els found that she could send as fast as the new wizards and some of the more experienced ones. Vanys, the sorceress, was both accurate and speedy, so much so, that the rest of the group applauded her when she matched Zritz' power in their final exchange.

'We will all improve quickly if your practice sessions

continue to be such fun, Zritz,' she said.

'Good. It will prove vital to pass on messages quickly, I'm sure of it,' Zritz replied.

* * *

'So, how did your day go?' Jayak asked of the others.

'Fine, ' said Klara, 'Though I didn't expect to end up directing others, it was a bit hectic at first.'

'There's nobody who could lead healing better,' Dayx said, 'They need you and you'll do a great job, so don't be soft, love.'

Alleri rolled her eyes, 'Well, while you two spent the day pining, some of us were working. You too, eh, Els?'

Yes, and I did enjoy sending, although Zritz says I won't be there long.'

'Why, did you offend him?'

'Alleri! Stop teasing Els,' Jayak said.

'I'm not offended,' Els spoke up quickly, *'I'm getting used to you lot. Actually, Zritz wants me to try all the groups, so I can extend my skills in all areas.'*

'So talented,' Jayak laughed.

'I don't know about that, but I can do different things and I suppose it'll help to be prepared on all fronts.'

'It certainly will. Also, practical experience in a range of areas will soon help you move through the magic ranks here.'

'Oh, listen to the sorcerer,' sniffed Alleri.

'I'm only being realistic. Els has gifts and it would be a shame to waste them.'

'And L'ra would be displeased,' Klara said.

Els looked around at her friends. They nodded in agreement with Klara's remark and even Jayak refrained from joking. How do they all know this and not question? How can they trust this L'ra is real? Els thought back to Kyrria and the others at the temple. Why can't I believe as they do? she mused.

'Els? Come back from wherever you are,' said Jayak.

'Are you all right? Do you miss Sorab?' Klara asked.

'Sorab? He's fine. Though I cannot bring him to lessons, he is always waiting in my room. He is happy enough there, jumping around in the fabrics. The food here agrees with him, too.'

'And you?' asked Klara, 'Or is it very different from what you are used to?'

'I don't know what I'm used to anymore' Els said. *'But I like most foods here. They are certainly spicier but more interesting for it. The only things I really miss are the berries.'*

'We have berries here,' said Alleri.

'Not the same, though,' Els smiled. *'At home in Garrtron, there were all sorts. Big juicy purple snaffleberries that you can't stop eating, tiny reemoberries so sharp your teeth squeak.'*

'Still, some of our produce is appetising, too?' Jayak asked.

'Oh, of course. I think whlan is a much better meat than any in the North. Even your chicken is more tender, perhaps it is the sun.'

Later, as she wandered back down the corridors to her room, Els was still pondering the differences of the South. Thoughts soon fled from this topic, however, as she heard Sorab's low mumbling from her room. Opening the door she found the room strangely light for the time of evening. Gods, but I have no staff or weapon, thought Els. Then she remembered how strong her mind was and gripped the door handle firmly. As she entered, the light surrounded her, bright, but not blinding; it made everything in the room somehow clearer than it should be. The room hummed gently and Sorab lay in a corner, crooning softly now. Els followed his gaze and took a cautious step towards a beautiful mherl, much larger than any natural one, curled in the centre of the floor. Its eyes glowed a bright green as it turned to look at Els. As she knelt beside it, the creature grew, fur turning to skin, hair and fabric. Soon, a beautiful dark woman stood before her, a serene expression on her face.

Els was amazed and yet she knew no fear. It did not cross her mind for an instant that this could be an enemy, she simply knew she was in the presence of good. The woman smiled at her.

'It has been a long time, little one. When I last saw you, it was not yet in you to see. Now you are grown strong enough to help others.'

'Who are you? How do you know me?' Els asked.

'I am the goddess L'ra. Don't look so shocked.' L'ra laughed, a golden chiming. *'You have learnt of me yet not known me. I know you well, so I show myself to you now, that you may know me also.'*

'Why?' asked Els

'Because you must see the truth. Before the Demon Lords come, all the warriors of this world must be secure in order to understand what they defend. You do not know enough.'

'I'm no warrior, you must have mistaken me for another,' Els said.

'No warrior? Why, who fought her own tribe for freedom? Who battled bandits with a barely trained weapon? There is nobody better equipped to fight the Demon Lords.'

'Why should you care? I don't even worship you. There are plenty who do who you could count on to help to fight a war.'

'But none like you. A long time ago, I helped your mother – in return for the kindness she had shown me. I gave you the powers you have. Yet even I am amazed at how comfortably you use them. I am glad to help.'

'Then I am meant to use my...powers?' Els asked.

'Of course, this present time more than any other. I see your destiny, Els. Remember, whatever concerns you, you can always speak to me. Go into this war with my power in you.' L'ra waved her arms in blessing and was gone.

Els sat for a time, stunned. Sorab crept onto her lap and gave her a quizzical look. *'Don't ask me who that was,'*

Els told him, *'I'm not sure what to tell you.'* Els realised she was shaking from her experience. From my proximity to a goddess? One who knows me? Can it be? Els knew there was only one person to go to for answers.

It had been a while since she had used her powers to transport her spirit but Els remembered the advice of her friends and teachers. Lying back on her bed, she shut her eyes and breathed gently, imagining herself back at the temple of L'ra. Slowly, Els flexed her hands and murmured the incantations of spirit flight. Though her body remained on her bed, eyes closed as if asleep, her spirit was projected across the desert to the building she had grown to know well. As she envisioned the temple, so she saw again the friends she had met there: Rayth, her stern look hiding a friendly soul, quiet Plarina with her dark eyes, Skrella and Roro with their gentle explanations. Most of all, though, she remembered Kyrria, so calm in her awareness of herself and her world, so dedicated to the service of her beloved goddess. Yet all the time possessed of a sense of humour one would expect to find in a merchant or a stranger. It was this friend her spirit raced towards.

All at once, the spirit-Els found herself in the small South-Eastern room she knew so well. An amused Kyrria turned from the wall-table she was working at.

'It's good to see you, Els, but really, a written message would have sufficed.'

'Not this time.'

'The danger is present? I heard Nahvib made his fears public but I had no idea .'

'It's not the Demon Lords, not yet. No, it is another unexpected guest I have to talk to you about. L'ra.'

'You saw her. And this from a girl who once doubted her very existence,' Kyrria tried to look severe.

'I cannot explain what I saw, or felt.'

'You saw a woman called L'ra?'

'Well, yes, but...'

'She appeared in a vision? Did she use a mherl form

53

first?'

'Again, yes. And by the way, you could have told me she uses mherls.'

'Oh, I knew she would show you that some day. Really, Els, can you doubt, in your soul, that the woman you met was the goddess?'

Els closed her eyes for a moment, thinking back. The woman had been beautiful, the shape change a marvel. Then there was the way L'ra had spoken of Els and her mother. The being was filled with more than great knowledge – a generous love towards humans, a sympathy with their endeavours. None of these things convinced, though. Els' conviction came now from a clear belief she could not attribute to any one thing. The whole thing was a miracle and so she answered her friend with confidence,

'I have no doubt, no,' Els told Kyrria.

'Good. Then stop shaking and sit with me,' Kyrria's grin was a knowing one. 'It's a shock at first but you soon -' She was interrupted by a knock at the door. 'Timo, what are you doing? I know Roro and Skrella are at the palace, but they could be back at any time.'

'I know. I didn't want to come to your wing at all, I know the rules. Plarina's nowhere to be seen, though and I'm supposed to be guarding with her.'

'Have you asked Rayth?' Els suggested.

'I've tried her already, she's no idea either. 'Tis like Tadir himself has swallowed her.'

'I doubt you'll find her in the earth, Timo, calm down.' Kyrria put a hand on his shoulder. 'There's no more you can do. Take your watch alone. If Plarina fails to turn up soon, it'll only be her own folly that betrays her.'

'Where is she?' asked Els, once Timo had gone.

'I wish I knew,' Kyrria responded grimly. 'Twice now, I have known her to be missing. I suspect Rayth knows of more occasions. I'm beginning to think she is seeing a man.'

'But that's forbidden. Would she be so stupid?'

'You'd think not, but she's been very distracted lately.

54

Besides, she was young when she came here, she could be finding that difficult.'

'You mean she's not had your chances to experiment,' Els grinned.

'Els! Thank you very much. Mind you. It's true, I suppose. I don't regret my vows, maybe I would have otherwise.'

'Rayth's been here a while, though.'

'Yes, people do it, it's just harder for some.'

'Well, I have a few things to think about myself now,' Els said, *'I ought to be getting back, really.'*

'Yes, your friends will miss you. They sound like good people, I'm glad.'

'I don't forget my friends here, you know. Maybe next time, you could visit us.'

'Yes, good idea. I think I'll take a horse, though and make it official,' Kyrria laughed.

Bidding her friend goodbye, Els clasped her hands and began a different incantation, this time imagining herself back at the palace. Again, she seemed to fly across desert, this time, towards her home. The building no longer felt intimidating, but strong and welcoming in its grandeur. Back in her body, Els picked a puzzled Sorab off the floor and hugged him. *'Poor Sorab, how much I have confused you today.'* Putting him on a cushion, she closed her eyes once more, only this time to fall into a deep sleep.

* * *

'Morning, sleepyhead,' called Alleri from the dining area.

'Hello,' sent Els, going over to find Jayak and Cyru at the same table.

'You must have been really tired last night,' Jayak said, 'We called round to see if you wanted to try a new drink Cyru bought, but there was no answer.'

'To be honest, I wasn't asleep the whole time from when I left you,' said Els.

'Company?' asked Alleri, smiling.

55

'*Alleri! There's no need to ask Els what she was doing,*' snapped Jayak.

'*Well, I suppose I did have company -*' Els replied.

'I'm off to practise, I'll see you lot later,' Jayak cut in, abruptly striding out.

'*What's the matter with him?*'

'Possibly a tiny bit jealous of your visitor?' suggested Alleri.

'*I didn't even say who she was. And why should Jayak be jealous?*'

Alleri and Cyru exchanged glances.

'Well,' Cyru began, 'Perhaps you should have mentioned it was a female friend quicker.'

'*Would that make a difference?*'

'*L'ra give me strength! You think Jayak takes such an interest in all new pupils?*' Alleri demanded.

'*But, well...you're all my friends. Jayak doesn't treat me any differently. He doesn't. I mean, he can't.*' Els was shocked to catch the thoughts uppermost in her companions' minds.

'Els, when I was angry with you and you got scared, didn't Jayak sort everything out?'

'*Well yes, but he'd do the same for any friend, surely.*'

'*Jayak is a sorcerer. He seldom has time to spare for those new to magic.*'

'Yes, sometimes he has little enough time for us', Cyru snorted. '*Arrogant as an Easterner.*'

'*I don't understand,*' Els frowned.

'*You do feel for Jayak, though. I mean, it seems you like him,*' Alleri said.

'*Yes, but this is all too strange. First, L'ra visits me to tell me she gave me my powers, now you say Jayak has feelings for me. Am I blind as well as mute? Or am I crazy?*' Els ran then; she wanted no more questions or answers. In her room, she could be safe from them.

'*Sorab, Sorab, only you are the same to me. Why must others be so confusing?*' Casting her mind through the floors below, she listened for Cyru and Alleri's thoughts.

Dismay and guilt were prominent, yet a central feeling of helping both Els and Jayak remained. This, they were explaining to others. Ah, yes, Dayx and Klara had joined them. But Jayak had not returned. Els knew she could find him, seek his real feelings. He would realise she was there, though. So she didn't dare. Angrily, she used her powers to throw objects around the room, causing Sorab to retreat under the bed. Why must I aways do it wrong? she raged. Why can't I just get along with my family, get a boyfriend like everyone else? Thud! A hairbrush hit the sink. Why do I, instead, leave my family, make a friend of a goddess and hurt one of my closest friends when all I want to do is…Here, she began to cry.

There was a tapping. *'Sorab?'*

'Els?' Only Jayak sent so clearly. What do I do? Well, L'ra proclaimed adventure a virtue…Els opened the door.

'Els? Is it true?'

'That was going to be my question,' she said, wryly.

'We ought to talk, but I see your thoughts so clearly now.'

'I know, there's no need.' But already his arms were around her and she found herself responding to his touch with a passion she hadn't dared to hope would be reciprocated.

'Jayak.' His name was a bright mental cry as, kissing him fervently, she undid his cloak.

'Wait, one thing first, love.' He laughed then, and she wondered how she had waited this long. *'My apologies, friend.'* So saying, Jayak transported a puzzled Sorab out of the room. *'Sorry, Els, but I can't have him here with us now.'* The look he gave her then took her all in, from her small feet to her light hair. Suddenly, Els didn't mind looking, being different. Jayak was different to her, but she wouldn't swap his dark eyes or curling hair for any other. Not when he looked at her with those eyes and gently swept the hair back from her face. *'I didn't know if I should love you,'* he said *'You were so new, still are. Probably,'* and he unhooked her cloak, reaching quickly

for her tunic, *'I shouldn't be doing this now.'*

'Do you hear me argue'? Els pulled him nearer, unbuttoning his clothes. Soon, their clothes lay with the cushions on the floor, while the two of them lay together in Els' bed. Now, neither voice nor mind commanded them. Only their bodies, Els' lithe limbs and Jayak's strong ones, showed their feelings. This, though, was more than enough.

Chapter 7

The next morning, the pair were met by a smiling Alleri, Dayx and Klara.

'All made up, is it?' Alleri grinned.

'I'd say so, there was a definite shift in elements on your corridor, Els,' Dayx added. 'Ow!' he said, as Klara dug his side with her elbow.

'We've made up. Everything's well, thank you,' said Els, trying not to look smug.

'Wonderful,' said Jayak with a brazen grin. *'So good of you to ask.'*

'Marvellous!' Alleri said. *'Now I've got two irritating couples around.'*

'Come on, you know you love us really,' said Els.

'True, I don't know who is more foolish.'

'Students, wizards, sorcerers.' Durrew clapped his hands and quickly gained their attention. 'Today, now that you are trained further and prepared better, King Nahvib wishes to speak to you.' A ripple, vocal and telepathic, spread and settled again.

'It is good to see you.' The king walked onto the main stage.'What Durrew, Pocack and Zritz tell me is encouraging,' his gaze swept the audience. 'Sadly, it needs to be at such a time. In Jhrik-ansi, several people have died or been driven mad by Demon Lords. Others joined them, looting temples and wrecking homes purely to test their powers. I call on your aid.'

'You have it.' was the answering cry, universal in its vehemence.

'This I know. I have spoken with many people and chosen a group to go to the area around Jhrik-ansi with me. The rest must stay here to keep communications open.'

'Or heal any...injured,' Klara said.

'You are most astute, Klara,' Zritz agreed, 'This, too, may be a crucial task.'

'Those who leave, however,' added Pocack, 'have but one hour to ready themselves. Jayak, Vanya, Casti, Reynon, Aashi, Memrob, Ikki, Els, Dryn, as there are eight gods, there are eight warriors here. Go now.'

Els looked at Jayak, stunned. *'Me?'* she queried.

'No, us,' he said.

'Hello, Els,' said Vanya, *'Now we put Zritz' lessons into practice, eh?'*

'Yes, we had better pack,' Els agreed, *'Speaking of which, Jayak, where's Sorab?'*

'He's in the stables. I thought he'd be happy enough there. I can fetch him back.'

'I'll just walk over, actually, conserve my energy,' Els said.

Walking over to the stables also gave her time to think. This is a war, now, she thought. We know and they know. I go to Jhrik-ansi to find and kill Demon Lords, to intercept thoughts and seek the damaged. The idea seemed mad, yet she could not run from the necessity. Still, she thought, I have Jayak with me. She smiled, thinking of how clear he had made it that they were together. Daydreaming about her lover, she nearly walked into the stable boy currently at work.

'Oh, Els, um, hi,' stuttered Brin.

Els grinned, unable to speak to him, she tried to reassure the youngster she had often seen at work with his beloved horses.

'You want a horse?' he asked.

Els shook her head. They would need horses to get to Jhrik-ansi and she didn't have one of her own. She shrugged, holding her palms open.

Brin seemed to make a decision, 'If you're looking for a horse, I can show you them. I'm sure I can find you something.' His shyness was forgotten, now. Almost dragging Els along, Brin led her into the dark stables. At first, Els was hardly aware of anything. Then the smells of the place and the curious thoughts of the horses came to her. Through the gloom, she made out the shapes of the

60

beasts, huge yet quiet as they contemplated this stranger.

'What about this one?' suggested an excited Brin. 'Oh, she'll be just right, she's beautiful, er, I mean... she's small, you're quite light, I,...anyway her name's Audcy.'

Els gave Brin a wide smile and gently, hesitantly, patted the little brown horse. *'Audcy?'* she called. *'You have a beautiful name and, truly, you are a beauty.'* The horse whinnied softly and gazed at Els with her honey-coloured eyes. *'I am to ride with you. Together we will run.'* Els reached her arms around her new friend's neck and stroked the soft brown hair. Though Audcy was lithe, she was no doubt strong on her slim legs.

So engrossed was Els, she didn't hear the firm tread of the king behind her, followed by the others.

'Ah, Els, you've beaten me to it,' he said.

'Your m,majesty,' Brin, stammering the words, bowed low. 'I only showed Els the horses, she came for a look and I, I thought sh,she might like to see some possible m,mounts, s,s,so I w,went and...'

'Well done.' Nahvib clapped a hand on the stunned Brin's shoulder. 'If you pass a fraction of your love for these beasts onto their new riders, you have my heartiest congratulations, boy.'

'Er, thank you your majesty,' said Brin.

'And Els, you seem to have found your mount straight away.'

'Only on Brin's recommendation, King Nahvib, but I would be glad to ride her, now I know Audcy,' Els said.

'Well, she is the one I had chosen for you.' Nahvib said. 'Where is your mherl? Will he travel, too?'

'Sorab?' Els called to the mental presence she could feel near her. *'Sorab? All of these people are friends.'*

Suspiciously, slowly, Sorab crept from under the largest horse's hooves until he saw Els, whom he ran to eagerly.

'Good, my Clarenz does well not to squash the little thing,' said Nahvib.

'Why your interest in him?' asked Els.

'They're lucky,' broke in Reynon, the moody young man from a town further South.

'Well, that's a superstition, really. Still, the creatures make good company, I'm sure you'll agree,' the king answered.

'Yes,' Els said, *'Sorab has been a great friend to me already.'*

'You make me jealous,' said Jayak. *'Come, your majesty, where is my fine horse? I too would like a friend who cannot answer back.'*

'Jayak! Thank you very much.'

'Don't argue now. Indeed, Jayak, there are mounts for us all.' Nahvib smiled. 'Yours, Jayak, is the star-marked one to the left of mine. His name is Krin.'

The black horse was as dark as King Nahvib's Clarenz, as dark as Jayak himself, but for the grey star on his forehead. The king seemed to have matched horses to people very well. Vanya's grey mare had a mane to match her rider's hair and stood as patiently as the sorceress. Casti's white stallion whinnied and nickered in tune with Casti's absent whistling and tapping. Reynon's reddish-brown horse was quiet and watchful. Memrob and Ikki, twin brothers, had a pair of piebald horses, Val and Erin, as alike again. Aashi, a stout woman born and bred in Istalan, would be proudly carried by the sturdy Krett. Newly proved a wizard, Dryn was ecstatic with his dark brown, white-socked Heti. Nahvib himself was clearly proud of the huge, pure black majesty of Clarenz. 'Brin,' he called, 'Saddle up these horses, load our packs for us and we ride thereafter.'

'Yes, your majesty.' Hurrying about, Brin nevertheless took no short cuts in preparing the horses for the journey ahead. As the king and his magical team prepared packs, the stable boy diligently checked water and saddles, packed food and tablets should illness strike the creatures.

'Well, love, looks like we're off. At least we make our journey together.'

'Yes. I don't think I could stand to be at the palace,

wondering what was happening to you.' Els shuddered.

'Don't worry, we'll be safe.' Jayak put his arm in hers briefly before they made to follow the king.

King Nahvib rode proudly in front, Clarenz stepping with dignity across the courtyard and over to the palace entrance. As the others rode in pairs behind him, Els and Jayak the second couple behind Vanya and Casti, they became aware of the noise from the crowd gathered at the palace's outer archway.

'Good luck,' they called.

'Arram bless your animals.'

'Thank you,' the king said. 'We make this excursion on behalf of you all and ride bravely for that reason.'

The crowds spread far beyond the palace walls and even at the temple of L'ra, those priests and priestesses not currently occupied hurried to enthuse their magical allies and their beloved ruler. Sorab peered out of Els' cape.

'Look. Our favourite!' he said.

'Els,' Kyrria cried, running over.

'Kyrria, good to see you before I go.' Els said.

'You too - and Jayak.' Kyrria grinned at him.

'Hello, Kyrria. Glad you approve,' said Jayak.

'I didn't say that,' she replied, 'But take care, both of you. *Els, there is danger, tread carefully.'*

'Of course. I'm not rushing anywhere. There's no need to be afraid for me.'

'I think of you often in my prayers.'

'Farewell, Kyrria, we'll be back soon enough.'

'Let it be so.'

As Els and the others made to move off, the king halted them. Skrella and Roro themselves had left their normal time of prayer and meditation to send off Nahvib's party.

'Goodness,' said Ikki, 'We are big news.'

' Yes,' agreed Memrob, ' I thought this was a short trip, not a grand expedition.'

There was a hush, then, as Roro and Skrella came down the steps. They walked in silence past the riders until they reached the king. Each of them held one of his hands and together they spoke,

'L'ra, may you protect your loyal followers. Lead this king, a noble one who hears you well, into safety with his friends. Help them escape the evil in the land and prove powerful instruments of good instead. Let adventure go rewarded, we pray you.' So saying, they then let go King Nahvib's hands and walked back to the temple without a backward glance.

'You heard them,' called the king. 'Let us help L'ra and ourselves. We go to bring peace to this land. May we seize the best opportunity to do that.'

On they travelled, skirting the temple and heading East. As they passed other towns, supporters welcomed them and many offered refreshments. Moving on, though, the dwelling places became smaller and more scattered. The group finally rested in an area near some trees, this at least providing them with wood and some shelter.

'It's been ages since we've seen buildings,' said Memrob.

'You're right, brother,' agreed Ikki, 'We've seen only smaller places recently, and the last village was a little while off.'

'We're not all city bred.' Reynon said, 'Some might see nothing wrong with a little quiet.'

'Maybe we all see a strangeness in our journey here,' the king said. 'Lack of homes, quiet, these are just symptoms of the oddness I feel here.'

'Well, strange or not, fire grows and dinner cooks as well here as in Istalan,' Aashi interrupted. 'The company, however, is all of our making.'

'Very good, Aashi, let us eat.'

The food was certainly as tasty as that Els had grown used to and by the time she had eaten her fill she was ready to sleep. Trying to listen to the talk around the fire, Els felt her lids begin to droop.

Do I bore you, dear?' Jayak asked, his firm mental 'voice' a welcome intrusion.

'No,' she replied hastily, *'Not you, never. I am not used*

64

to riding, though, especially over such a distance. That and Aashi's fine cooking; I fear I must bore you, I'm so weary.'

'You couldn't.' Jayak took her hand. *'Just being together like this seems bliss after so long wondering how you felt.'*

'Yes, it took us long enough to get here.' Els smiled. *'But it is worth it.'* Leaning against Jayak, she realised how lucky she was. The future was scary and unknown, yet she faced it with so many people who cared about her.

The group talked for a little longer before it began to get too dark for any to stay awake. As they slept, they were largely unaware of the forces gathering about them. In the now immediate town of Jhrik-ansi, a grey cloud seemed to mutter as it broiled about the townsfolk; many now dead, wounded or crazed with fear. This fog appeared to mock all about it.

'These people were no challenge. All who are of any use to us are joined, or will be...these who come to help are merely a second course. Aid? They neither have nor bring none...naught can protect...We see new allies...'

In the camp, Jayak woke up shivering. To his relief, he found Els still asleep. 'Can't sleep?' Vanya whispered from her own bundle of coverings.

'No. How long have you been awake?' Jayak replied.

'Just a few minutes. I heard a noise and decided to find out what it was.'

'And?' prompted Jayak.

'Only Reynon. Seems he sleepwalks.' Vanya pointed to the other side of the camp, where Reynon could be seen wandering back and forth.

'Is this right?' Jayak said.

'He does no wrong, others walk at night,' Vanya responded. 'Let's see if we can return him safely to bed, then we will both sleep better.'

Reynon, however, was less than keen to return with them. 'Dark, too dark. Out there, dark things....out...don't want...no it's not...too...dark...' he muttered strange things and was oblivious to his two companions. Vanya and Jayak exchanged worried looks.

'You think this is normal?' hissed Jayak. 'Nobody else does this, plus he's got hardly any more training than Dryn, and half the power. Nahvib must have been mad to take him, I know I wouldn't have.'

Vanya's eyes flashed at the hint of insult to their ruler, yet she scarcely raised her voice. 'Then you would not have chosen your girlfriend, either, I take it?'

'How dare you criticise Els. She is more powerful than Dryn and Reynon put together.'

'Yet she has little training and she also has her oddities, the lack of voice, an unknown background.'

'You may make no slur upon her background, that is well told and received. Take back such comments.'

'Jayak, Jayak, calm yourself.' Vanya sighed. 'I have every faith in Els myself. It is only that I would show you what an injustice you do Reynon, and our leader, by allowing no-one else to make the same exceptions you have. Do not let arrogance blind you.'

'What's the matter?' A confused Reynon stumbled towards them, awake but unsure of his surroundings.

'You were sleepwalking, that's all. There's nothing to worry about, is there Jayak?' Vanya looked at him closely.

'Indeed not,' Jayak said.

'Good. We'll get you back to camp now, the others will be up soon.' Vanya escorted Reynon gently back to camp.

'I still say there's something wrong,' muttered Jayak, but he, too, went back to join his friends.

It was not long after their return that the others began to wake. The dawn was scarcely rising but everyone wanted to make haste and reach their goal as soon as possible.

'Praise Tadir that the earth sleeps us so well,' the king said, following breakfast.

'Praise Arram for our fine horses. Last of all, the highest of praises to L'ra as we go about our business today.'

'Praise be to Tadir, Arram and L'ra,' they all cried.

66

Then they rode. Brave and strong with the knowledge of what they must do, they made little time of the remaining ground. The land flashed by all too quickly and they soon found themselves in Jhrik-ansi. The town looked like it had been blasted by an extremely angry god or goddess, so total was the devastation. Few houses were still standing and those that were stood so strangely it appeared almost as if they had melted. The wind howled ominously, blowing broken possessions and bones alike in a horrid whirling motion that nevertheless compelled those watching.

'By all that's good, what can we do here?' Ikki had never looked so serious. Even Aashi looked shocked and Casti's tapping had taken on quite a frantic rhythm. Els looked about her, aghast at the inaction.

'Do we come so close just to stop? There could still be people in there!'

Half-scared at her boldness, she started off on Audcy without waiting to see who followed her. Sorab's warmth gave her hope: he at least, was not going to run away. By the time she had entered the town and dismounted she realised there were plenty of hooves to be heard behind her.

'All right, my dearest, now you've shown us the way, let's get moving.' Jayak's tone was half mocking but Els guessed he must secretly be proud.

Together, they began to search the houses. The sights they met were awful. Bodies lay smashed, like discarded dolls. Anything in the dwellings was broken beyond any repair. Worst were the words daubed upon the walls, words so sacrilegious Els tried not to look. The writing, however was too terrible to ignore. Large letters written in blood proclaimed the might of the Demon Lords: **NO RULER BUT THE DARK POWER. HRAI IS KING BEFORE NAHVIB. ALL GODS AND GODDESSES BOW BEFORE THE WANDERERS. VENGEANCE! THE LAND TURNS DARK WITH BLOOD.** These and other similar sayings sickened Els horribly. Suddenly, a distant cry made her turn.

'Help! Oh, by the goddess, someone help me!'

'None can help! Not against the Demon Lords. Join us or perish.'

Els was stunned that the voice could be heard in her mind, as well as by her ears. She did not want that voice in her head, creeping across her brain like a disease.

'King Nahvib! All of you. Come quick!' She sent a mental image of the next house, where she could feel the sick presence and the frightened victim. Dashing there, she met the terrified gaze of a young woman cowering from a dark figure. The figure turned to meet Els.

'At last, I find more powerful souls to join me. This town has been lean in its pickings.' It appeared to be a man, yet so swathed in dark shadows few features were evident.

'You do not take this soul. Nor any other.' Els shook with fear and rage but gladly felt Vanya's steadying hand upon her arm. Sorab looked at Els, then ran to the woman on the floor.

'This is not your victory. Go foul thing. We use our strength and that of our gods and goddesses. Begone!' Vanya cried.

'Begone!' The others shouted. *'By all that brings good. L'ra! Cala! Tadir! Raz! Myrrine! Arram! Ellari! Gax! Help us now!'* As they shouted, the group raised their hands and the invocation brought power through them. Raw energy swirled from their fingertips, even Nahvib's hands bringing gold glowing power upon the enemy. Els and Vanya though, were clearly strongest, from them the creature shrank furthest. Seeing this the others shifted their energies to join their aim, melding all they had to beat it. Shrieking, the thing fell to the floor.

'You...will not win...others come..' The creature hissed malevolently as it shrank into itself and disappeared.

At first there was a shocked silence.

'You killed it!' cried the woman, breaking their reflections.

'Yes,' said the king, 'And now we must take you back to Istalan. You will not be safe here.'

'Thank you.' sobbed the woman. 'My name is Karryn. I lived here with my parents until,' she broke off, crying bitterly amidst the ruins of her former home. Sorab gently licked her face.

'You were lucky to survive this,' said Jayak.

'Yes, what happened?' asked Memrob.

'My parents were outside, it caught them first. I hid when I heard all the noise. At first I watched from the attic window but when I saw my own friends and neighbours turning to dark creatures, killing my parents and others. I ran to hide down here. I thought I could block the door with the furniture.'

'But you couldn't?' asked Ikki.

'One was already there. I kept close to the floor. I didn't want to see its face. When it came in, it seemed I could read its foul thoughts there. I knelt down here and prayed to the goddesses that they would help me. I thought that I could hear L'ra, Cala and Ellari telling me not to fear.'

'Truly, those we worship are there in times of need.' The king bowed his head, honouring their protectors, and the others followed suit, Karryn as well.

All were quiet and thoughtful as they walked to the horses. Their encounter had frightened them and they were deeply saddened that Karryn was the only one to be saved. Yet, they also felt a happy surprise that they had been able to accomplish her recovery, despite such a terrifying foe. As they reached their horses, the air began to shiver about them and they braced themselves for further attack. Yet it was not a Demon Lord, but L'ra herself who appeared, standing before a ferocious fire. They all fell on their knees but L'ra beckoned them up. 'I congratulate most of you on your mission here.'

'We all participated,' said Aashi.

'But sadly, not all did so with pure hearts.'

'What?' Memrob gasped.

'It is with sorrow I tell you that one of you is already a

victim of the Demon Lords. There must be a test of your integrity. This fire must be walked through by every one of you who came today. Karryn, I bless you, for I know your soul is innocent, so bravely did you resist your attack. One of your saviours, however, was too interested in the power coursing through you all to care about anything else. Such a corrupt one will not be able to walk through flames of my making without admitting this and cleansing themselves. I go now, but heed my warning.'

She left them, only the flickering jade and gold flames attesting her presence.

'You all heard her. We must do as she says,' Nahvib instructed.

'No. Not fire,' Reynon shuddered and moaned. 'I would do anything else, only, not fire, please.'

'It must be him,' Ikki said.

'He's weaker in power, it makes sense.' his brother agreed.

'I accuse nobody. That is not my place,' sighed the king, 'Perhaps Reynon is corrupt, perhaps he fears fire.'

'I'll talk to him if you like,' offered Jayak, trying to ignore Vanya's ironic glance, 'Maybe I can find out.'

'Very well. The rest of us make the test now. Any reservations you have, expel them. Maybe we can all pass through.'

Els grinned at Jayak as he walked to a safe distance with the frightened Reynon.

Typical of Jayak, she thought, I bet he manages to bring Reynon out of it, too.

King Nahvib passed through the fire first. Confident as they all were in their ruler, every one of them sighed with relief as he made it, untouched, to the other side. Els took a deep breath, remembering all Kyrria's words about L'ra as she walked through. The flames were bright and towered above her, yet she felt no fear, only calm. The test was only to aid them and she knew she had used the power lent her purely to help. She stepped through to meet Nahvib who gripped her hand as much in gratitude as to steady her. One by one they went safely through, Dryn finally turning to greet Jayak and Reynon.

'Your majesty, I have spoken to Reynon and he was indeed ill. Yet we prayed to L'ra and I believe he is well now. Should we still take the test?'

'There is scarcely need if you are whole. Reynon, how is it with you?'

'I, feel weak still, but no longer afraid.' Reynon was pale but he held his head high.

'Very well then. I suggest we make the journey back quickly before any other ill thing seeks us.' The king rode off with Karryn on Clarenz with him and the others close behind him.

'Well done, darling, you saved Reynon today,' Els smiled at Jayak.

'I felt I should at least try. He's not a bad kid, really,' Jayak answered, trying to ignore the amused look on Vanya's face. She was the last one to leave Jhrik-ansi and the fire died behind her.

Chapter 8

Some hours later they reached the palace, where joyful crowds greeted the returning fighters. King Nahvib rode proudly through the gates, the exhausted Karryn still clinging to him. His brave subjects followed, tired yet triumphant in this first battle against evil. Els felt she could hardly move but, like all of them, she rode with her head high and her soul joyful at their success. Sorab perched on her shoulder, looking around at everything going on. As they reached the crowds, the king faced his magic folk and his smile spoke of more gratitude than words could express.

Durrew, Zritz and Pocack hurried to meet them, checking their colleagues over for signs that they might need Klara's healing skills. They also cast an intrigued eye over Karryn. The king dismounted and met his people. 'My dear subjects.' he began. 'You see us returned intact and with a survivor. We appreciate your concern and your presence here is a pleasant welcome indeed. Yet I must request that you disperse shortly, for we all are weary and in need of rest.' There were a few grumbles at this, though most of the crowd applauded the king and cried that they would be back another day. Gradually, they made their way back to their homes and the rest of the king's group stumbled off their horses, who Brin and Bataz, the head groom, were waiting to care for.

Also waiting was Nahvib's valet, Sousk. A quiet man, he walked over purposefully, 'What do you need, your majesty?'

'Ah, Sousk. Good to be back.' Nahvib greeted him. 'You see we have a survivor of Jhrik-ansi, this is Karryn. Could you inform Matzi to set a room up and care for Karryn. She is to be my guest during her recovery.'

'Certainly, your majesty. Pleased to meet you, Karryn.' Sousk bowed and moved off briskly to inform Matzi and carry out his own duties.

'You don't need to. I'll be better soon.' Karryn protested.

'Nonsense.' said Nahvib. 'You are drained from your ordeal and I will not let such a heroic subject struggle by on her own. Let me help you.'

'All right.' Karryn managed a smile as Nahvib helped her down from Clarenz. She wondered if he realised his moustaches were twitching? King Nahvib's moustaches were still struggling to remain still a few days later, when he asked Karryn how things were going.

'Very well, thank you, your majesty. Matzi is most zealous in her duties, indeed, all your staff have been very friendly.'

'I rather gather you have acquired a fan club as well. Sousk mentioned some visitors you had this morning.'

'Yes, they were very kind, but I hardly knew what to say.' Karryn laughed. 'Three women came up with a basket of goods. It appears they have premises in the city and wanted to help me out in some way. It was very embarrassing. They kept going on about my bravery and everything. Still, I'm grateful of their aid and yours, your majesty.'

'Karryn, please, you need hardly address me as such. After what we've been through together, I think you can use Nahvib, the same as the rest of my friends.'

'I'd be glad to...Nahvib.' Karryn said, twirling her hair around her fingers.

'Come in,' sighed the king, breaking off his chat with Karryn to answer his door.

'Your majesty, I have a message for you,' announced Drayk, his Chief Minister.

'Yes?'

'The message reads...' Drayk fumbled with the scroll in his hands, 'To His Majesty King Nahvib of Sytrannia, Favoured Follower of L'ra and Emperor of Grateful Subjects. Many thanks and felicitacious wishes on your endeavour against our common foe. May Raz also heap Bounteous Blessings upon you and aid you with his Fiery might to Smite those who dwell in Darkness. We kindly request your Noble Presence at a Grand Meeting of us all, that we may beat these demons between us.

Your beholden friends:

Queen Ashla, Empress of Zaritt, Overseeress of Southern Maidens, Ruler of the followers of Raz;

King Azabar of Izk;

King Vistar of Akrin;

Queen Lidynne, of the Prophets of Gax;

King Sedryk.'

King Nahvib groaned slightly. 'Ashla! Drayk, kindly alert the other ministers to this and send a reply. I will go, I must.'

'You may enjoy it, your majesty.'

'I probably will, it's just that Ashla is a trifle long-winded at times.'

'You know her well, your majesty.' Drayk left, smoothly exiting the heavy doors.

'What on Rima is the Overseeress of Southern Maidens?' asked Karryn.

'One of Ashla's more interesting titles. She works very hard for her country, she is a good Queen. It's just that there has to be a ceremony about everything. Her league of Southern Maidens is a sort of glorified women's club.'

'Pardon?'

'Oh, I've nothing against women working together, Ashla does a great deal for young mothers, women looking for trade promotion, all the rest. But she feels such a sisterhood needs a title to reflect its moral nature and making herself its 'overseeress' gives it a sense of dignity. The league itself has benefited many but I don't know why it must be so grandiose.'

'You are very friendly with Queen Ashla, though? She must think a lot of you, too, her letter suggests so.'

'Yes, we get along well. She's a pleasant change from her father, he was always taking offence, we could hardly move without him causing a fuss. And I like her husband, Prince Griorg. He's just built a new smoke room and I know he's desperate to show off his new pipes. Now *that* is a good reason for attending this meeting.'

* * *

A week later, King Nahvib was reminding himself of his words on his way to the capital of Zaritt. The coastal route to Kreab was poorly kept and the royal carriage swayed precariously past the cliffs. Drayk looked at Zritz, clinging onto the carriage's furnishings, his face paling considerably.

'Perhaps we ought to raise the issue of road maintenance while we're there.' said Drayk.

'It might not be a bad idea.' agreed Nahvib. 'Takka is a good driver. I pity those who travel without her.'

'I praise Tadir for making our lands border Zaritt's,' agreed Zritz, 'I'd hate to come from further out.'

'Yes, I wonder if we will see Queen Lidynne at all?' Nahvib laughed.

Fortunately, they soon arrived at Kreab castle intact. This was a very different royal home to Istalan's palace. Built by Ashla's great grandfather, it had been made to last. Thick brown walls and four squat towers gave the impression of a large toad. The heavy portcullis rattled slowly upwards to let them in and the three Sytrannians were glad to see some light from the courtyard.

'There you are! My dear Nahvib!' Ashla called, running to hug him.

'Ashla, how good to see you!' King Nahvib somehow managed to mutter, as the queen nearly crushed him.

'I'm so glad to see you. We'll have dinner tonight, then meet properly in the morning. It seems Queen Lidynne will be late this evening. Such a way to come you know. But do come in, Griorg's been simply dying to see you.'

The three men walked in through the ornate hallway, marvelling at the hangings and pottery.

'Every time I come, there's something else in here,' Drayk said.

'Impossible surely, every inch must be decorated,' Zritz

argued.

'I know, but she's stuffing things in somehow.'

'After her ancestors' starkness, I think Ashla makes an admirable change,' said Nahvib.

'You not planning on turning Istalan into a fashion show, I hope?'

'No, Drayk, I'm not that keen.'

'Good. I don't believe our budget would suffice.'

'His Majesty King Nahvib of Sytrannia!' announced the queen, throwing open the doors to the dining area. 'Slayer of demons, Saviour of innocents!'

'Do we have to call you that?' whispered Zritz.

'...Accompanied by His Excellency Lord Drayk, the First Minister; and Renowned Zritz, Highest of Magi, Celebrated Tool of the Gods.'

The three men walked into the room, wondering how they were to live up to their announcement. Drayk, who had visited with the king before, soon found his foreign counterparts and was talking politics while they waited to be seated. King Vistar, listening to King Azabar, suddenly noticed Nahvib. 'King Nahvib! How are you? Congratulations and all that.'

'King Vistar, King Azabar, hello. I don't believe you've met Zritz, my chief magus?'

'A pleasure, Zritz.' Azabar shook his hand rather violently.

'Good to meet you, Zritz, your presence here is a welcome addition.' said Vistar.

'Did I ever tell you what happened to my previous chief magus?' asked Azabar.

'I don't think so,' King Vistar said reluctantly.

'Well, it was a funny incident really, rather peculiar...'

King Azabar was still telling his story when the dinner bell sounded.

'Thank the gods.' whispered Vistar. 'I hope Lidynne hurries up, she has more patience with that bore than I.'

'I couldn't agree more,' Nahvib said, taking his seat between Vistar and the Zarite First Minister.

Thankfully, Queen Ashla and Prince Griorg had plenty to say themselves and Azabar hardly got a word in. They skilfully introduced their guests and quickly led conversation onto the latest news and gossip across the kingdoms. King Vistar was congratulated on the birth of his third son and all agreed to visit Queen Elaina as soon as possible.

'For you're both young, you know and I'm sure you could do with some advice.'

'And who better to give it?' called a new voice, as Queen Lidynne at last made her appearance. 'My dear Ashla, Griorg, splendid to see you. I seem to be in time for dessert as well. Excellent.' The queen's broad smile radiated good nature and she hardly looked a woman who had just completed a journey of great length and danger. The same could not be said for her First Minister, a thin man who still shook. His ruler looked at him sympathetically, guiding the man to a seat. 'Ashla,' she began, 'Couldn't you take a look at your roads sometime? I doubt I'll be able to persuade Dekkomas to come another time otherwise.' Dekkomas smiled nervously, as Queen Ashla looked a little upset.

'Why don't we deal with it in the morning?' suggested Nahvib. 'We could put other mutual issues on the agenda after the main discussion?'

'That seems fair enough, Ashla?' Lidynne replied.

'Yes, good idea King Nahvib. Let's deal with everything on the morrow.'

'Well, enough of business for now then,' said Queen Ashla. 'We've had a new smoke room put in and I know I'm not the only one to partake. Ladies, gentlemen?'

'Yes, why not?' said Lidynne, 'I hear you get a much better range of flavours over here. What are you doing, Taheya?'

"I'll join you a little later, your majesty,' smiled the Izkan First Minister. I'd just like a chat with Queen Ashla first.'

'Of course, my dear!' Ashka cried, 'Is everything all

right?'

'Yes, just a few things I'd like to clarify, being new in the role and everything.'

'And to such a king! An admirable man, but really, how do you put up with him...' Ashla led Taheya off, talking away. Prince Griorg took the others to the smoke room, where the finest pipes had been brought from all over the South and some from even further afield. A large room, the queen and prince had seen fit to enlarge it to fit in more tables and chairs, all heavy but comfortable, for few people could pay only a brief visit there. Small tables held different pipes, some delicate and covered with intricate script, other, heavier pipes of strange, dark wood. There were several books on the shelves, but these were punctuated by vials of different liquids, as well as glasses for those who preferred drinking to smoking. 'Come in!' called Griorg. 'What will you have first? I've been saving some new ones, you know.'

'I'll try the Western amethyst, if you have any.' laughed Nahvib, 'I've been desperate to try it and it's impossible to get hold of.'

'Yes, tell us your secret,' grinned Lidynne.

Queen Ashla and Lady Taheya soon joined them and it proved a late night for all.

* * *

Back in Istalan, the night was much quieter. Most of the bars had closed an hour ago and stars glittered over a relatively calm capital. Even at the palace there were only gentle bursts of laughter to show that some of the young people were still awake.

In Els'room, there was also laughter. Curled up on her bed, she and Jayak had somehow stopped kissing long enough to have a proper conversation. Well, they'd tried to, but Jayak had reminded Els of a joke he'd played on Cyru earlier and they both kept giggling at the thought of their friend's face.

'…if he could only have seen what he looked like,' Jayak wiped tears from his eyes.

'Oh, you are awful. Poor Cyru,' said Els.

'You're laughing!' Jayak pointed out.

Under the bed, Sorab uttered a low growl, lashing his tail. For a while, Els and Jayak stopped talking again. Sorab hissed, but did not try to communicate with his mistress. When after a time, Jayak left, Els reached under the bed and scooped the mherl out.

'What is wrong with you? You're lucky one of us didn't throw you out!'

Sorab grimaced, *'He's always here. Sometimes I need to talk to you.'*

'Oh, Sorab,' Els sighed, *'Jayak's special to me, we're in love, you can't expect me to be with you all the time. But I'll never forget how we saved each other in the North you do know that, don't you?'*

'Yes, of course,' Sorab muttered, *'Maybe, you go his room sometimes?'*

Els hugged him, *'Yes, all right. But you'll always have a place here.'*

'Thank you,' Sorab said and jumped up on the bed. Only when Els had fallen asleep did he also drift off.

* * *

While Els and Sorab dreamed, those in Zaritt were in the great hall ready for the conference. True, many had dark circles under their eyes and King Azabar was clutching his head rather frequently. Being unused to smoke rooms, he had made rather a fool of himself the previous night and, as a result, was much quieter than usual. This suited the others well, and Ashla opened the meeting with vigour.

'Dear friends, the main item on the agenda: The Demon Lords; Secondly: Transport; Thirdly: Industry; Finally: Meetings/Celebrations. I wish to open the first item, The Demon Lords, with a hearty message of congratulations to King Nahvib, a worthy ally.'

'Hear, hear!' echoed Prince Griorg.

'And the same to all who helped him!' added Taheya, to which Zritz looked pleased.

'Thank you. Of course, it makes our task easier to know that we have your support. Similarly, any we can offer to others in distress, we give,' said King Nahvib.

'Good point, your majesty. Has anyone else had any problems that suggest the Demon Lords in their own kingdoms?' There was a silence at first and Taheya felt she had been too bold.

'Come on!' shouted Queen Ashla. 'Well, I shall venture first if you are all too proud. We have had five deaths we believe are due to this menace.'

'Five!' King Azabar was astounded. 'Well, I'm sure there's nothing going on like that in Izk.'

'Two, that we know of, your majesty,' coughed Taheya.

'By Tadir, I knew none of this!'

'You were given a report, King Azabar, I handed it to you myself.'

'I know of three in Akrin,' interrupted Vistar, hastily. 'I feel I should have been more vigilant, but Elaina was very ill with this last child of ours and that has taken precedence lately.'

'Don't apologise,' Queen Lidynne laid a hand on the younger ruler's shoulder. 'Myself and King Sedryk have watched all our children grow up, yet we still failed to spot this menace. Let us not waste time in placing blame.'

'Quite correct, Lidynne. The thing to do now is to make sure we can attack it,' Queen Ashla said.

'Yes. Perhaps King Nahvib and his advisors could tell us what helped them?'

'Chiefly, I have to say, the gods.'

'The gods?' Azabar looked incredulous. 'So we pay our alms and visit the temples and it'll be okay? Well. I'm sorry, but I don't buy that. My people are very pious, I'll have you know, but that doesn't seem to have stopped two deaths,' he scowled at Taheya, 'In my own kingdom.'

'It is not about duty alone.' Nahvib sighed. 'But the gods

are there to help us if we act with them in mind. L'ra is the goddess of adventure and you know that has been important to myself and all Sytrannians for some time now. We did not merely sit and pray our way out of trouble in Jhrik-ansi, I can assure you, King Azabar.'

'Certainly we helped ourselves.' continued Zritz. 'I know how hard my people of magical capabilities worked to practise their skills. Any who say that was easy are welcome to train such skills in a matter of weeks themselves. Yet every one of the eight who accompanied our king would acknowledge the help of their gods was crucial to their victory.'

'Yes, our skills were great. I was followed by two sorcerers amongst other powerful team members, but we all felt what we had was enhanced when we called upon the gods at a desperate time.'

'We must also remember,' pondered Queen Lidynne, 'That it was that fellow, Hrai's, going against the gods that brought about all this badness in the first place.'

'So, you would say,' Queen Ashla tried to bring some order to the table, 'that we should ask our gods for aid and practise the skills we have?'

'But also communicate our needs and any developments.' Drayk added. 'If we had not been notified of Jhrik-ansi's plight so soon, Karryn may not be with us now. Perhaps earlier calls for help would have saved others. We must be vigilant as to signs of distance, pre-occupation, in those we know. If we fear an outbreak, there is no sense in hiding it, we must contact surrounding kingdoms.'

'Yes, give them a fair chance to protect themselves.' cried King Azabar.

'Or help their neighbours,' cut in Amsala, The Akrinian First Minister.

'To that end, I propose we contact the kingdoms on the East and West. They may also have news and their proximity could be important.'

'Those immoral swine! Have you heard what goes on in

the East, Ashla? They don't even fear Raz there.'

'They may have different ways,' said Ashla, ignoring Azabar's snorts. 'However, if a wave of Demon Lords crossed the Myrrine Straits, I'd rather be ready for it.'

'What about the North?' asked Vistar.

'Interesting point? Any action up there?' said Lidynne.

'Not the last I heard,' said Nahvib, thinking of Els.

'They really are different,' agreed Asha.

'Still, you don't know what defences they have,' Lidynne said.

'I say we leave them for now. If we fear it is spreading North, we contact them. Let us hope it doesn't come to that. Agreed, then? Messages to Eastern and Western kingdoms?'

'Agreed.' The vote was unanimous, though Azabar still looked doubtful.

'Well, then, with all these messages between everyone, I suppose we'll have to sort the roads out quickly?' Lidynne smiled.

* * *

'Good morning all.' cried Zritz the next day, greeting his students.

'Well, it can't have gone too bad, he seems happy.' said Alleri.

'Wonder what the gossip is, then.' added Jayak.

'Maybe,' sent Els, *'he'll tell us if you two shut up.'*

'Excuse me!' Jayak said mockingly. *'I'd say you got out of bed the wrong side only I know perfectly well you didn't. I'm kidding, dear, cheer up. Are you all right?'*

'I don't know. I feel sort of, worried, but I'm not sure why. I thought it was because of Reynon, but I saw him chatting to Cyru this morning and he seemed fine, I just feel a little uneasy.'

'You're bound to. I feel weird just being back here, studying again instead of calling on gods and dealing with Demon Lords.'

82

'Yes, maybe that's all it is. Thanks, Jayak.'
'Always a pleasure, my love.'

Els smiled, then sat forward to see what the magi were going to say.

'I'm pleased to tell you,' Zritz announced, 'That yesterday's meeting was greatly successful. All the Southern rulers are preparing in a similar way to us and Queen Ashla is sending messages to the Western and Eastern regions as we speak.'

Not the North? Els wondered.

'The East?' Alleri said. *'Why bother?'*

'Because, Alleri, Dayx, we need allies, not further enemies. And if you will send so loud, I can hardly help but hear you.'

'Well!' Alleri was still in shock in the canteen at their inter-lecture break. *'Is this what the Demon Lords do to people? Zritz laughing at me and Easterners trusted to help?'*

'Why this hate towards the East? I came away from my continent to escape such intolerance, I didn't think you were like that here.' Els admonished.

'Ah, Els. the East is not just different, it's evil,' said Jayak.

'Really?' asked Els, scared by the way the faces around her had suddenly become so serious.

'We are forgetting Els doesn't understand,' Klara said.

'True. I'll tell you the story of the East, then,' said Alleri. *'It was centuries ago, now.'* she seemed to be sending for dramatic effect, Els thought, amused, but interested nevertheless. *'The people in the East had been worshippers of the same gods as us in the South and West, yet over time, they had forgotten many of the old customs, and few gave true respect to the gods.* Sorab growled and Els gently scratched his neck to calm him. *People were cruel to one another, the cities were in disrepair, children roamed the streets. Not only their own people and places were shown no respect. Neither were air, water, fire nor earth around their lands.'*

83

Her friends gazed at her in fascinated horror as Alleri continued the tale.

'The gods of the elements were particularly angry, and Tadir himself came down to the Eastern city of Nimiana. He showed himself to the king there and his high priest. Ten feet tall, brown-skinned and clothed in layers of different plants, he represented all the good that was on their land. Angry, he raged against the leaders for their waste. 'My land is burned! Unfarmed where it should be used, and overburdened where it should not. Cities of steel and stone alike shadow where there was once grass. What food you do harvest goes only to the rich. Yourselves!' In a terrible fury, Tadir caused a dust storm to rise, so rapidly whirling that it tore down the Imperial palace and the temple, sucking them into the earth. 'These are no longer places of council or worship. They have become refuges for the wealthy to plot further ways of draining the life from the land. You treat this continent wisely from now, or I will destroy it as easily as I did your homes today.' But they didn't listen.'

'Not that arrogant lot!' Cyru added.

'No, not them. The king was furious at having his palace destroyed, but he and the high priest were much more interested in rebuilding their homes and replacing their luxuries than heeding Tadir's words.'

'Even though he was a god? Is, I mean,' Els added hastily.

'That didn't matter to them, only their wealth. All the Easterners just wanted to make all the profit they could, never mind that there would scarcely be any land left for their grandchildren. A few months later, after having watched, hoping for a sign of change, Tadir attacked. He came with Raz, the god of fire, and their devastation was awesome. Tadir opened up the volcano in the centre of the continent and Raz boiled the fire within to a still hotter temperature. Then they turned it loose on the land. Sorab chittered and shook his head. *Lava ran across the land, spreading in all directions. Nearly all the Easterners were*

killed. The few survivors are said to be descended from the last remaining true worshippers, and those who tended their land well. Lava and ash covered four fifths of the continent and until recently, was unmanageable. They are said to have better rulers now, and to have improved life there, but you still wouldn't catch me going there. Or trading messages.'

'Still, they'd help us if it is against the Demon Lords, they wouldn't want another disaster if their land is so devastated already.' Els said.

'I'd like to think so, I'm just not convinced,' Alleri admitted.

By the next week, they all felt the wisdom of Alleri's caution. Rulers from the three Western kingdoms had sent a message declaring their wishes for alliance and desire to meet Southern leaders as soon as possible. The East, however, remained silent.

'Perhaps they didn't get the message?' suggested Klara, but even Dayx looked doubtful.

Further problems also occupied the Sytrannians. The daughter of one of the royal ministers was found using an ancient text to try and summon Demon Lords, claiming one of her friends had already done so. Her father, Nobleman Zachari, offered to resign, but Nahvib would have none of it. 'You can try and help us sort out this mess, but don't blame yourself for the actions of Zacharette.'

'Els! Jayak! Klara! Sorry to interrupt, Durrew, but I need these students for a while. Bit of a problem.'

'Certainly, your majesty.'

'So, you see I need some help.' the king said, having explained his problem. 'I want you to see if you can identify which of Zacharette's friends has had contact with those monsters, then we can set about the process of healing.'

The three magic students were taken with Nahvib and Zachari to the main school in the city. It was a plain enough building on the outside, grey stone and a gently sloping slate roof, but inside was painted various shades of green. Zacharette and her group of friends were in a small, mint green classroom on the second floor. The headteacher strode across the room to meet the king's party. 'Your majesty, honoured colleagues. So sorry to bother you with this business. You have no idea how surprised I was to find Zacharette in the common room engaged in...black arts,' she said.

'I'm am equally horrified myself, but hope to solve this riddle now,' said Zachari, casting a sad look towards his daughter.

All six girls looked innocent. Wide-eyed, some teary, it seemed as if it was all a strange dream to them. Yet Jayak and Els sensed foreboding and hate beneath the dreary expressions and set their receptive powers to finding it. Klara, waiting, felt as if she, too, was being tested, so potent were her friends' gazes.

'I can't find it, it's moving,' Jayak said.

'I'll put my full force onto it,' Els offered.

'No! You're only backup, I'm the sorcerer.'

'There's no need for that. Find it yourself then,' Els retorted, hurt.

'I can't. Everywhere I look it moves away. I can't catch it.'

'Use all your power, it should be frightened. It can't have much of a grip yet, if it's so interested in a bunch of schoolgirls.'

'I can't do it, by all that's sacred. Stop going on at me!'

'I will, then.' Shocked at Jayak's fury, Els clung to her objective for security. *'I do this with the strength of the goddess L'ra.'* she thought, as much to comfort herself as to scare the Demon Lord present. Slowly, though, it dawned on her that what she said was true, L'ra was there to help, and heighten Els' powers. *'I am stronger than you. Now leave the child and go from this place.'* As she spoke, Una, a slight girl in the centre of the group, fell to the floor, writhing. *'Leave her! Out!'* Els cried, hurling all her mental fury at the thing that felt so hideous, its creeping thoughts trying to attach itself to her, now. This proved its

undoing, it could not grip Els' mind and maintain hold on Una's. *'Begone forever!'* Els shrieked, hurling it out of them both, quickly shielding those of them in the room without the capability to do so. *'I will return with others!'* cried the monstrosity, as it faded further and left.

'Well done, Els...Jayak. Klara, I believe I can put Zacharette and Una in your capable hands, now.' King Nahvib said.

'Yes, and I'll check the others over to make sure they're not affected.'

'What was that all about?' Els asked Jayak.

'I just couldn't do it, okay? Leave it at that.'

'No, I'm not going to leave it. You're supposed to be my lover, never mind a colleague. Is that the kind of support I should expect?'

'I'm sorry. It's...You're the novice, you know? I suddenly couldn't get near the thing, but you were straight in there. I'm not used to any of my friends, or girlfriends, beating me. I think I was shocked.'

'Well, you certainly shocked me,' Els said, somewhat mollified, though.

'I didn't mean to, you just blew me away a bit. I'll try and go with you next time. Forgiven?'

'Course you are. Don't be getting jealous though. Gods! There's plenty of things you do better than me, you silly thing!'

There were three similar incidents that week and the couple worked more successfully after that initial upset. Els also felt better working with Arak, Vanya and Khanie; it gave her and Jayak less pressure. The work was gruelling and depressing, but they felt they had prevented the Demon Lords from getting a strong foothold. 'Maybe that's why they were in Jhrik-ansi.' said Jayak. 'Perhaps they feared the higher populated areas?' At the very end of that long week, King Nahvib called a public meeting in the city's main square. *'What now?'* groaned Els. *'I don't think I have the energy for another attack.'*

The king's proclamation, however, was entirely

different. 'You all know Karryn.' he said, indicating the young woman standing shyly at his side. 'I have much admired her since that terrible day in Jhrik-ansi where she showed strength and courage few can match. As you know, she has been staying at the palace while deciding where to move. Recently, we have decided that won't be necessary. Karryn and I are to be married in a month's time.' Beaming, he placed an arm around his fiancee's shoulders. Karryn, then, came forward to address the crowd. 'I am extremely happy.' she said simply, struggling to get the words out while smiling at Nahvib. 'Both deeply happy to be the wife of this man, yet also excited at the prospect of becoming your queen. I have been a proud Sytrannian always and, after the battle, I hope I can help in the city as so many people here have aided me.' The crowd began to cheer, then, all the women who had visited Karryn convinced she meant their contribution particularly. Jayak hugged Els close to him, and Alleri, unseen in their mutual joy, gave the pair a strange glance.

Chapter 9

The joint meeting of kingdoms was also held at Zaritt. King Azabar protested that it was unfair and Izk would make a far better location, but Queen Ashla correctly pointed out that her country was nearer for the Western contingent. Azabar was somewhat mollified by the promise that the next meeting would be able to take place in Izk. The other monarchs were happy to let Ashla host the event and looked forward to meeting their Western counterparts. This meeting was to take place at noon and any festivities would only take place afterwards. Recent outbreaks of Demon Lord-related attacks, coupled with the uncertainty of support from Western rulers, meant business would have to come first. Such thoughts occupied King Nahvib as he packed papers and selected his best travelling cloak. 'I will see you tomorrow, dearest,' he told Karryn, poking his head around the door to her suite, 'Matzi will take care of everything you need.'

'Wait.' Karryn sat up in bed, her night-clothes rumpled, but her eyes alert. 'I wasn't asleep. I knew you were going soon, I couldn't sleep. At least let me kiss you before you go.'

'Only too happily, dear,' said the king, 'But it's not as if I shall be gone for long.'

'I know darling, but please take care on those roads.'

'Of course, I'll be back in no time.'

Soon enough, the king was on his way, this time with only Takka and Drayk to keep him company. The desert roads he passed along were dotted with few cacti and Nahvib wondered when the rains would come. Still, the roads were clean and smooth; they made good progress along them. As the Sytrannian ruler saw the cliffs loom into view, he groaned. This was soon cut off, however, as he saw men bustling about the uneven surfaces. 'Workmen, your majesty!' laughed Takka, 'It seems her majesty Queen Ashla has been as good as her word.'

'Tadir and Myrrine be thanked!' Nahvib exclaimed, 'An improved route to aid travel by earth or sea. Queen Ashla has indeed been busy.'

The roads were far from finished, but it was clear work was being carried out and progress made. The bumpier sections still required a settled stomach, but Nahvib, Drayk and Takka found they were easier to endure when punctuated by better laid sections. They reached the castle in slightly less time as a result and were much more composed on arrival. The queen's groom took their horses and the king made his way in quickly, for this time, even Lidynne had beaten him there, along with her First Minister.

'And here is King Nahvib now,' announced Queen Ashla to those assembled in the drawing room. King Nahvib, may I introduce my guests from the Western continent?'

'Indeed, Queen Ashla, I would be most honoured.' King Nahvib smiled at the strangers.

'Firstly, I present to you, King Eneb of Liance, with his First Minister, Lady Rona,' she indicated the pair. The king seeming quite happy next to Lidynne. 'And this is King Yacconi of Rucilia, with his First Minister, Lord Amar.' The ruler of Rucilia was a thin, grey man, who looked extremely severe, but his minister smiled at the new arrivals. 'Lastly, but not at all the least, King Ep of Cassal and Lord Winnalio.' The last pair could almost have been brothers, sharing chestnut hair and bright blue eyes. After shaking hands with the Western rulers, King Nahvib and Lord Drayk seated themselves between the Lianch and Cassase parties.

'We seem to have had much the same trouble as you,' said King Eneb. 'To be honest, it was quite a relief to get your message.'

'Indeed,' agreed King Ep.

'Have you all had the Demon Lords invade your people, then?' asked King Nahvib.

'Not I,' said King Yacconi, 'But my subjects are rather

better taught of their gods.'

'Or it just hasn't got as far as Rucilia yet,' objected Lady Rona.

'Possibly,' conceded King Yacconi, 'But it has to be admitted that my country is – currently – untouched.'

'For those of us who are infected, what can we do?' asked King Ep.

'Well, make sure you have healers, in fact all people of magical skills, on alert,' Queen Ashla said.

'It means you can deal with things quicker, chuck the rot out before it sets in,' put in Lidynne.

'Yes,' King Azabar looked at King Yacconi, 'I wasn't convinced at first but it has helped us deal with cases that could have been overlooked otherwise.'

'Well, I heard it was all about behaving properly towards the gods, and my subjects have always done that,' the Rucilian king explained.

'I thought that too, just make sure it is worship and respect, not mere duty. That is an easy trap to fall into and I would not wish another to witness the consequences of it,' he shuddered slightly.

'You have seen this in practice?' asked Lord Amar.

'A sufferer was brought to my attention and I saw one of my sorcerers try to aid him. Sadly, he was unable to do anything, the corruption was too far gone. I know how easy it is to think it won't affect you or yours. I urge you, King Yacconi, think carefully about defence.'

'I carefully consider all my actions, I assure you.'

'My friend meant no disrespect, dear King,' Lidynne added quickly.

'No, I'm sorry if I have caused any offence. It is only that I fear for others having seen what the Demon Lords can do for myself,' Azabar apologised.

'Yes, I can see you mean well. Certainly I will try and share defences with my Western colleagues if that will help,' said Yacconi.

'We would be most grateful,' King Ep said, fervently.

'A gracious offer, many thanks,' said King Eneb.

'Would it be an idea to pool resources?' asked King Nahvib. 'I have many people of magic who are currently less occupied. It would make sense for us to send aid where it is needed most.'

'Why should you do so? What if you need them? I don't understand where you would gain by this?' said Azabar.

'Must every action have a selfish purpose? Surely our Sytrannian friend is merely making a generous suggestion?' countered Lord Amar.

'Just the most logical suggestion, actually,' admitted Nahvib, 'If we make regular contact with each other, we can send the best of our experts where they are needed. I will happily send experienced magi or sorcerers to any other country, but I would also expect the same kind of help should disaster occur in my realm,' he looked rather pointedly at King Azabar.

'And by discussing the problem, we could help decide who is best able to deal with it,' King Ep realised.

'Yes, healers could be selected based on previous dealings with this trouble, those with a particular kind of magic according to the strength or type of Demon Lord or victims, would be best chosen from a wider range. Hmmm. It may work that way,' King Yacconi stroked his grey beard thoughtfully.

'Are we decided?' Ashla asked, 'Queen Lidynne, you haven't commented yet.'

The Lykrosian queen failed to answer, though, as the door burst open and a short, dark man entered, pursued by two guards.

'Gods above! An intruder!' cried Azabar.

'An Easterner, from the look of him!' shouted Vistar, causing several of those present to recoil in horror. The man would not stop, however, until he reached Queen Ashla, where, gasping, he rested.

'I mean no harm,' he stammered out, 'Please believe me.' He cast frightened eyes at the guards behind him. Ashla hesitated a moment but waved them away. She turned to the newcomer as a footman found a chair for him. 'Well, if you mean no harm, you can give your name and purpose here.'

'Stec, my name is Stec.' Seating himself, the man regained some composure. 'I'm the Calanese First Minister. I got your message.'

'There was no reply,' Queen Ashla said.

'I had no chance to. I see how little regard you hold the East in.' Some of the rulers looked embarrassed. 'Sadly, I am forced to agree,' the little man drooped somewhat, 'Hardly any believe in the Demon Lords. Even the legend of Tadir's punishment is dismissed by most as unfounded.'

'But not by your ruler?' said Prince Griorg, trying to remember who was on the Calanese throne.

'Queen Wertle believes nothing and no-one. Only those who flatter her ego, court painters, ladies in waiting, these are the kinds of people she occupies her time with. When the message came, she laughed, as did Prince Alzin. I couldn't convince them to come, or even send anyone. Two of my fellow ministers, Abrim and Saluna, agreed with me, so they told the queen I was ill while I made my way here. It was tricky, but I had to come. We can't have another disaster, we'd never survive.'

'Have you had similar problems to us?'

'I think so. There have been suspicious deaths, but I have little information. Wertle won't publicise anything negative: even as her First Minister, I don't get to hear everything.'

'Well, you are here now,' Queen Ashla smiled at him.' If you give us what help you can, we shall do likewise. Are there others you could persuade of this urgency?'

'A few, Saluna and Abrim have some friends in the small towns who agree with us. I don't know what help they would be, but I will try them.'

'Good, once we share our thoughts, we should be stronger.' Ashla, Nahvib and Lidynne told Stec what had happened so far, with Ep and Vistar joining in at times.

'So, we are all organised, then?' asked Ashla, finally.

'Looks that way, now,' said King Ep, with a friendly smile in Stec's direction.

Suddenly, there was a **whoosh** and the very air about them altered. It wasn't a noise, indeed, all sound seemed to drain from the room. When the strange change had shaken them, Lidynne was the first to raise her head and look around. At the front of the room, the gods themselves had gathered, amassed and obviously unhappy. The four gods of the elements, Raz, Tadir, Cala and Myrrine stood together, different in every aspect, yet united in their disapproval. Arram barely glanced at the humans, more interested in the small animals which rested on his shoulders and in his pockets. Ellari's gentle old face was sad, but the tall, lean Gax stood angry beside her. L'ra herself looked deeply disappointed and the absence of her usual smile was most worrying. As chief of the eternals, however, it was she who strode forward.

'Is this how we fight, then?' she demanded, 'A handful of our people and only the barest of agreements?'

'The Easterners fail again,' commented Tadir, severely.

'Please, I came,' said Stec. 'There may be only a few in the East who believe, but we will strive towards good.'

'Too few, what punishment should we exact this time?' Tadir turned to his friends, 'Myrrine, perhaps a tidal wave this time?'

'No,' Myrrine waved an admonishing hand at the earth god, 'We cannot punish what good there is, we should help those who work with us.' Though she was still, water cascaded endlessly over her body and her sapphire eyes whirled.

'But what good do they do, so few? Besides, I demand to know why the East is not all here. Does this one really try to persuade his friends?' Raz literally blazed down at Stec.

'You ask nothing about the Northerners. Are *you* really trying to persuade all men?' Stec replied, bravely remaining still in the face of Raz' blistering heat. The others gasped, Azabar clinging to Taheya's robes. Truly,

Raz was a fearsome sight, the fire god's body pulsating with flames so fierce that those present tried to shield themselves from the heat. Stec, however, moved not a muscle. His white knuckles betrayed his fear, yet his face was more full of anger. Everyone waited, unsure as to whether Raz or Stec would first with their fury. In the midst of the tension came a tinkling laugh. Queen Ashla, aghast, searched the faces of her comrades to fund the foolish culprit.

'It's not funny,' she hissed, her gaze still darting about.

'Oh, but it *is*.' The laughter came from L'ra herself.

'I don't think so,' said Raz, but his eyes were no longer spitting fire.

'Why, Raz, this man is right. We are all cross with human failings, but what of our own?'

'True,' said Ellari, gently. 'We have made no effort yet to persuade others of this cause, yet we berate those, like this Easterner, who are trying to defeat the menace.' She smiled encouragingly at Stec and he felt strangely reminded of his mother, though he had not thought of her in years.

'And this Easterner has courage, audacity. I like that.' L'ra looked directly at Stec. 'I hereby proclaim you the first chief priest of mine in the East.'

'But I have no training, I - '

'You have all the training you need. A life spent persuading others of the true gods, the strength of spirit to aid your fellow man, even those who live far away and differ from you greatly. The rest of your life is to be spent in educating your people and fighting these demons. For my part, I will make contact with the North and lend aid to those rebuilding your continent. A bargain, Stec?'

'Yes, L'ra, I will serve you until the end of my days,' Stec said.

'Calan must find a new First Minister,' Lidynne said.

'Yes, probably just a pawn of Wertle's.' Stec frowned, 'I'll try and talk to Saluna and Abrim, though, see if we can engineer either of them into favour.'

'It's already a dirty business, Stec,' said Ep.

'I have no idea what you're talking about,' replied the ex-minister, doing his best to look pious.

'I have underestimated you,' said Raz, peering down at the man from behind fiery eyebrows.

'Yes,' agreed Tadir, 'it is not often a man survives trying to fight with elementals, but today, I am glad you did. It gives me hope that there are still easterners who keep the faith with all their might.'

'Maybe we will even have luck in the North?' suggested Cala.

'Let us go and see,' said Arram, 'If nothing else, I would like to check they still treat their animals well. Which reminds me, King Nahvib, my thanks for keeping your horses healthy while in Jhrik-ansi.'

'Why, Brin and Bataz would have frightened me nearly as much as you, had I allowed injury to any,' Nahvib laughed, a little shakily.

'We will go to the North,' said L'ra, 'but not like this, all in a group. We will allow these people to choose a delegate to explain our urgent mission, but such a person must be so chosen that they have the support of all the gods. They may need it to win over their Northern brethren.' As suddenly as they came, the gods deserted them.

'It would take a remarkable person,' said Drayk, slowly.

'Do you know someone?' asked Ashla.

'There are many with great talents who fought at Jhrik-ansi - '

'– Ashla, you are very kind, but there is no reason it should be someone from Sytrannia,' said Nahvib.

'Other than Drayk's reason? Come, Nahvib, don't be too modest,' argued Ashla.

'If your people fought as hard as is said, surely one could be chosen to take a message,' King Yacconi remarked.

'I would find it hard to choose just one of such a brave

group,' protested Nahvib.

'Your magi could help. A joint decision would work,' Drayk argued.

'Isn't there anyone in mind? I'm sure you can think of someone,' said Stec, with a knowing grin much like that of his goddess.

'I'm sure I can. I'll have to,' sighed King Nahvib, 'Well, something to keep us busy on the return journey.'

'Come on now, some time with the pipes before you go,' smiled Prince Griorg.

'Ah yes, we don't have them in the West. We're all looking forward to trying it,' said King Eneb.

'Don't be too hasty, my friend,' muttered King Azabar ruefully.

Sure enough, both Eneb and Ep were massaging sore heads in the morning. Surprisingly, King Yacconi was amused by the previous night's activity, despite having been unsure about it at first. 'Excellent hobby, your Royal Highness, must try to get it going in Rucilia,' he declared.

'Please, call me Griorg,' laughed the prince, 'It's always a pleasure to find someone else who really appreciates it. I look forward to next time.'

'Perhaps you will visit us next?' suggested King Ep, 'I will have a few pipes ready, though I won't have quite your array of flavours.'

'We meet on business first,' frowned Ashla.

'But your husband's incentive will draw us all back,' said Nahvib.

'He is right,' agreed Taheya, 'But maybe next time we will discuss progress too.'

'Well, I shall go and discuss the issue of a messenger, perhaps then I will be the next with something to report,' announced Nahvib.

'Farwell, dear Nahvib. At least we now know the gods wish us well, too,' smiled Ashla.

Before long, Nahvib, Drayk and Takka were once more negotiating the Zarritian roads back to their own land.

'Do you really have ideas about who to send?' the king

asked Drayk.

'Well, I could think of a couple but I'm sure Zritz and the others will have a clear idea.'

'Yes, it is not a decision I want to reach alone,' said Nahvib. He felt strangely calm inside, even though he had not yet made a decision as he very much wanted Zritz, Pocack and Durrew to discuss their ideas first. An inner quite lay over him, much like the time he had first met L'ra. He had faced death, then, an agonising end via starvation, but a part of him had known it would not come to that. Now he also felt some knowledge at the back of his mind, a sense that the right choice would be made.

Back at the palace, he desperately wanted to see the magi, to end the anticipation and feel that sense of the right thing being done. However, he knew L'ra's protection enabled them to make their move all in good time and besides, Karryn would be worried. Indeed, when Nahvib entered her room he was nearly knocked over by her. 'You're back!' she exclaimed with relief. 'Did it go well? How was the journey? What are the Westerners like?'

'Calm down, my love. The journey was fine, Ashla has begun to improve the roads already. It's still uncomfortable in places but a lot less dangerous. The Westerners seem friendly enough, though King Yacconi – the Rucilian ruler – took some convincing as to the urgency of our situation. But the other kings, Ep and Eneb, are much more jovial. Oh, the Easterner was a fine fellow, too.'

'The Easterner? What Easterner? You were attacked? And you wonder why I worry!'

'Karryn, dearest, there was nothing to fear. Stec is a good man and even when the gods came, it all ended well, no-one was injured.'

'The gods came?!'

After that, Nahvib found Karryn needed to hear everything, but it was very pleasant to be with her again and time flew as he told the whole story of his recent trip.

Karryn listened in amazement and held her fiancé's hand tightly, glad to have him back safe. Nahvib realised with a start how much he enjoyed this. He was not missed as a ruler, or even a friend, but someone who meant much more. This was a new sensation to him but he found he liked it and was equally pleased to see Karryn again. 'Next time I go to such a meeting, I think I will take you,' he declared, 'then neither of us has to worry.'

'Would that be allowed, though?' Karryn asked.

'When you are my queen, I see no reason why you should not accompany me. Lidynne often brings Sedryk,' the king said.

There was a knock at the door, Nahvib groaned. 'Enter!' he called.

Sousk came into the room. 'Durrew wishes to see you, your majesty. He desires to discuss the meeting and our future plans,' he announced.

'Let him in,' Nahvib said, 'thank you, Sousk.'

'Your majesty,' Durrew bowed, 'I believe we have a few things to talk over.'

'I see Drayk has been talking already,' the king said, dryly.

'He just felt we ought to know the events that took place. It was rather monumental, if half of what he says is true. Besides, I think he felt it would be better if he explained and left you to greet your dear lady,' Durrew nodded graciously in Karryn's direction.

'Well, I do appreciate his concern and yours Durrew, but now I must speak about our decision with you and your colleagues. Are they outside?'

'No, but eagerly waiting in our office.'

'I shall come at once.'

'Very good, your majesty.'

'Spare me, Durrew,' laughed the king, 'I have enough to worry about without titles, you know that.'

In the office of the magi, Zritz and Pocack sat sipping tea, the picture of relaxation.

'Cake?' enquired Pocack, innocently gesturing at the

plate on the table.

'I hardly come for the refreshments,' grimaced Nahvib, 'But yes, I'd hate to offend.'

'Anyway, after all those meetings at Ashla's place, you must be used to such luxuries,' joked Zritz.

'Seriously, we must choose a messenger for the North – and quickly.'

'But carefully, we must not be too hasty,' Durrew said.

'Well, who can we put forward as initial suggestions?' said Pocack.

'Aashi? She is a good traveller and able to protect herself,' said Zritz.

'Vanya is a sorceress, her power is stronger.'

'Jayak purged the evil from Reynon, he is also strong and would readily accept the task,' said Nahvib.

'Readiness to prove one's strength is not always an asset,' said Durrew, seriously, 'Myself, I would opt for Els.'

'Els? She is barely trained. I know you are her tutor, but do not let that blind you to her limitations,' said Zritz.

'I realise she is young, but she is powerful beyond the abilities of her peers. Even Jayak, older and more experienced as he is, will be left behind by her soon.'

'It means going back to her own people, though, is that wise?' said Pocack.

'She is very strong,' said Nahvib.

'Absolutely, her training is also in many areas. She cannot fully handle the elements yet but all other areas are easy to her,' Durrew agreed.

'I didn't actually mean her magical power,' said the king, 'She has an inner strength, she dealt so well with all that happened in Jhrik-ansi.'

'True, we didn't see that,' Pocack said.

'I honestly can't think of anyone else – excuse the joke – I would rather have fought the Demon lords with. Jayak was strong, Vanya was wise, but Els' power went beyond all that.'

'Let us wait a few days,' said Zritz, 'I think you may

well be right, but let us have a few days to be sure of our judgement.'

'Four. My mind is made up, though,' said Nahvib. It was as he had known it would be. As surely as he had known he could fight the illness on that fateful journey as a young prince, he knew Els was the one for this task.

Els herself remained oblivious to the speculation surrounding her. Daily she continued to practise her skills, sometimes under the watchful gaze of Durrew, sometimes informally with her friends. There, too, she was busy. Knowing Alleri and the others well, now, she played a greater part in their activities. Jayak moaned that she hardly ever spent time alone with him, but, in truth, Els spent much of her time racing from studies or social events to be with him. Klara noticed this and asked her about it when Els left a party at Cyru's, thrusting an angry Sorab at Alleri as she went. 'Why do you race off again, Els?'

'*Jayak wants to see me, I said I'd be at his soon.*'

'Can't he meet you here? Why does he have to see you alone?'

'*It's not like that, Klara. We see little enough of each other anyway. Sometimes it's nice, just the two of us.*'

'Of course, Dayx and I always find time to be alone together, but we also mix with others. Don't let Jayak take you away from your friends.'

'*He isn't. We both want to spend more time with each other. Jayak's not taking me away from anyone.*'

'How many times have you been the one to suggest being alone? How many times has it been him?' Klara regarded Els sadly. 'I love you both dearly, but you,' she touched Els' shoulder briefly, 'You deserve more than jealousy.' Klara walked back then to where Dayx, Cyru and Reynon were waiting, leaving Els very confused.

Jayak, jealous? Klara's words seemed ridiculous. How could Jayak be jealous? He was the sorcerer, the envy of his friends, not the other way around. As for being jealous over Els herself, why, with his dark good looks and quick wit, there were many young women in Istalan who would happily be in her place. Els hardly thought there would be men queueing to accompany her if Jayak had not chosen to be with her. Yet, if she was honest, it *was* nearly always his idea to spend more time together, less time with their wider circle of friends. Els realised she enjoyed the company of others more than he did. But then, she had been deprived of such friendship in Garrtron, perhaps she was revelling in something Jayak had grown out of. After all, he was those few years older, maybe that explained everything. Still, this explanation did not entirely convince and it was with brooding thoughts that she made her way to her lover's room.

All that vanished, though, when she opened the door.

Jayak's room was slightly larger than her own, so he did have better opportunity to entertain. Even so, the efforts he had gone to were impressive. His wall hangings were richer than hers, true, but she knew she could not have hung hers in such a graceful arrangement. The rich reds and purples in the heavy fabrics were only a part, however, of the brightness which Jayak so adored. Candlesticks of red and gold held tall, delicately carved purple candles, illuminating the room just enough. The embroidered table napkins Els knew to have come from one of her favourite shops in the city and Jayak had folded them into the swan shapes she so wished she could make. A large bowl of fruit sat in the middle of the dark wooden table and pleasant smells came from the covered dishes beside it. As Jayak rose from the table to welcome Els, his long berry-red robes framed his powerful body in deep folds.

'Els! You look wonderful tonight,' he sent.

'You too, the room is beautiful and you look...splendid.'

'Well, myself and my room only try to reflect your own glory.'

'Glory? Really, Jayak, you do exaggerate.' But saying that, she ran to his arms to hug him tightly. The others can say what they like, she thought. Jayak loves me and I him,

102

there's nothing wrong, he's do anything for me. Klara is only jealous, just because Dayx doesn't have Jayak's talent.

'Come, let's eat first, darling.'

'Yes, my love.' Els took the proffered dish to find tender chicken, delicately flavour with the Southern spices she adored. The evening passed well, the two of them talking over dinner in uninterrupted peace. They talked of many things, what they knew of the current political events, fashion, food, the growing popularity of ground couree petals as an alcoholic substance, but none of these in relation to what others thought, only their own views mattered. Later, relaxing in bed with a subtle Lykrosian wine – for Jayak was yet to be convinced by couree – Els thought she could hardly be happier.

In her healing class, the next day, Els felt less than happy when she saw Klara. She had not meant to speak so harshly the previous night, but the words had been said and she didn't know how to correct things. Still, she remembered how glad Alleri had been to patch things up when they had argued, perhaps Klara would listen. As the other students filed in, Els sent her mind out to the gentlest presence that belonged to the best young healer Sytrannia had.

'Klara? I...I'm glad to see you today,' she thought, hesitantly.

'Me too. How did it go last night?'

'Great. I mean, it was good.'

'I'm glad, really. Don't sound so guilty.'

'I can't help it. I feel like going over to Jayak's last night caused trouble between us. I actually had a wonderful time with him, but that isn't worth us falling out.'

'I was concerned over how busy you are, how you try to please all, you know that. But that doesn't mean I begrudge you spending time with Jayak. I want it to work. It will not cause trouble, though, I would rather not speak of your time together at all than lose your friendship.'

103

'Oh, good. Friends then?'

'Of course.'

Els was very pleased to have made things better, though she still wished Klara wouldn't talk about her and Jayak as if something was wrong. Why, L'ra herself could not find a happier couple, Els thought. Still, Klara was that used to helping those in distress, she probably didn't know when people weren't. The two young women remained together for the class, cheerfully comparing notes and commenting on what Zritz had to say. They left together and managed to find Alleri, Dayx, Cyru and Jayak in the lecture room before the lecture on mind-guarding was given. Els sat between Jayak and Alleri. Jayak had his arm around Els and Alleri turned to smile at her on occasion, but there was no room for speech, this lecture was a serious one.

'The ability to guard the mind against Demon Lord attack will be crucial,' said Pocack. 'It is of no use having highly trained men and women if they only end up confused or even fighting for the enemy.'

'Guarding your mind is like using a blindfold, only it is your very self you must cover and you must remain functioning. Think too hard about your guarding and you will barely be able to use your powers. Give your mind a barrier like a fog, a delicate, yet impenetrable cover and you will be able to use your full powers whilst confounding those we strive to work against.' As Pocack pointed out the instructions all were to take for practise, Alleri stood to go and the others began to move to join her. Pocack, however, waved her to sit, the others falling sheepishly back into seats alongside her.

'I appreciate you are keen to leave and practise, Alleri,' Pocack sent, impishly, *'However, we are not quite done and I think you and your friends would like to stay.'*

'As you say, pardon my haste,' Alleri replied. Pocack, however, only answered with a near smirk as Zritz and Durrew came in to join him. The assembled students, from the lowest apprentice to the sorcerers in the group,

flinched as they saw all three magi together. *What does this mean? Trouble?* Anxious thoughts flew across the room in waves. The initial concern subsided, however, when everyone paused to notice their superiors were smiling. Zritz, in the middle, came forward to get his audience's attention. 'Fear not,' he said, 'For today is an occasion of joy. We three come to announce the attainment of wizardry for three of those amongst you. If Durrew will do me the favour of calling those who have accomplished the level, Pocack and I will present each with their cloak. Durrew?'

'Gladly!' the broad man was hopping from one foot to the other while waiting. 'Alikx Menazz-al-Shiban.' The young man who ran down the steps was about Jayak's age, but just as glad to be a wizard as Jayak no doubt was to be a sorcerer. He took his brown cloak with joy and shook hands with the magi despite some trembling. 'Sandovahn Hakkali.' He was slower down the steps, but also clearly excited and Els remembered him from Dayx' birthday party when she saw his squared hat. Like his headgear, his cloak was made of different coloured squares, with which Sandovahn seemed delighted. 'Els of Garrtron.' Durrew announced and his eyes danced with glee.

'I?' was all Els gave, but with so much force, all those receptive in the audience heard her and giggled at her confusion. *'You!'* all three magi sent and there was no hesitation in their answer. Jayak, momentarily stunned, roused himself enough to help her out of her seat and Els made her way carefully down the steps the two men had walked before her. It seemed to take forever, at times she felt there could be no end to her descent, but in reality, it only took her a matter of seconds to reach the bottom. 'Congratulations!' said Durrew and Els fought off tears as she accepted her cloak, a beautiful garment of jade with a golden trim. 'Jade seemed right, somehow,' said Durrew, 'And King Nahvib himself suggested the gold. I don't know why, but it feels it is the right choice for you.' The other two magi looked on in agreement, yet there was

105

something more in Pocack's blue eyes.

Later, at the celebratory party, the king himself came to congratulate the new young wizards. Els, Sandovahn and Alikx were also pleased to make each other's acquaintance and to share their new happiness. 'Well done, Els,' said Cyru, 'Knew you could do it. Those Demon Lords had better watch out for you.'

'We all knew it,' sent Klara and her gaze was kind.

'It's a shock, but I am glad. I thank you all, without my friends here, I could never have been deserving of this. And you my love.' She turned to Jayak but he had walked away alone to the darkest corner of the balcony. *'Jayak?'* she sent, but his mind was guarded.

'Leave him,' said Alleri, *'You know how he gets.'*

Puzzled, hurt, Els left Jayak and went to dance with Alleri and Klara to one of the popular drum songs of the city. She knew Jayak couldn't be jealous of her, but whatever it was that was troubling him, it was probably best to let him sit it out until he was ready to share his concerns with her. If she had been able to read his thoughts, it may well have spoilt her night.

How can it be? She is young, far younger than I was when I made wizard. Why? And they always ask what she thinks. Why must she be so powerful and me hardly reflected in that? I cannot bear it. Sometimes I want to...

At the port, unaware of all such concerns, Pocack sent a letter with his majesty's seal to the Kingdom of the North.

Chapter 10

'Karryn? Karryn, are you awake?' came a pleasant female voice.

'Umf?' was, however, the only reply.

'Karryn! It's Matzi. The dressmaker is ready for your fitting, remember?'

'Today? Coming, Matzi.' Karryn ran to let in her maid, though the description hardly gave credit to the many roles Matzi took on. Alarm clock, too, thought Karryn, ruefully, running a hand through her tangled hair. Tying her overgown on and pulling her hair into a rough knot, she let Matzi in. 'Sorry!' she said,'I have no idea why I'm sleeping so much, I can scarcely rouse myself these days.'

'Ah well, best you get some sleep now afore you're married.' Matzi winked.

'Yes, well.' Karryn blushed. 'Anyway, you say the dressmaker is ready for my next fitting?'

'It's only next week, dear, there is scant time left to prepare.'

'True,' Karryn said, slowly, 'The time has come around quickly.'

'No regrets, I hope? I mean, I erm...' Matzi's voice trailed off, she feared she had said too much already.

'Not about Nahvib!' Karryn laughed and her maid knew her feelings to be genuine. 'I love Nahvib deeply, I cannot wait for our wedding in many ways. Being a queen scares me a little, for it is a great responsibility, but I know with the care of my husband and the guidance of the gods I shall be safe. The only sad thing is that none of my family will be there, they will never know the man I have grown to love.'

'Maybe they do.' Matzi said softly, 'I don't profess to know everything about the gods, but I believe our loved ones are cared for beyond this realm. Those who serve their gods are surely rewarded.'

'I hope so.' Karryn said, wistfully, 'Thank you, Matzi.'

In the office of the magi, preparations were also under way.

'The dark blue? Or the sage green? I really don't know.'

'Honestly, Pocack, you're worse than any woman. Anyone would think you'd never given a woman away before.' Zritz said.

'My daughters were different, they had very definite ideas about what they wanted me to wear.'

'I can see why.' said Durrew, 'Just be glad you have family to worry for you.' Pocack and Zritz exchanged looks at this. It was not often that Durrew compared his lifestyle to theirs as family men, but it was more painful at such times as these. There had been no woman in Durrew's life since his wife died at a fire in the palace ten years ago, with no children to ease the pain.

'True enough,' said Pocack, 'Besides, it is Nahvib who must worry the most about his attire.'

'He has decided upon an outfit, I hear. He seems remarkably calm about the whole thing.' Durrew said.

'I think he has long felt the need for a wife.' noted Zritz, 'Ruling a country must be a lonely job at times and the need for an heir is, of course, always a concern.'

'Karryn is a good choice for queen, I'm glad Nahvib didn't rush into anything earlier for the sake of an heir.'

'No, agreed Pocack, 'Especially when you think of some of the choices he had...'

'That lady from the Eastern province!' Durrew shuddered.

'Lady?' Zritz snorted.

'Ah, well, at least we know he has made the best choice now,' said Durrew.

Durrew's views were shared by most Istalans. There were a few who muttered at her lack of noble blood, but most of these were jealous families who felt one of their daughters would have been a better match. Besides, it was hard to argue against a woman whose faith and courage had saved her from the worst evil in all Rima. Indeed, many a poet within the city had made himself popular with ballads about Karryn and King Nahvib fighting together. Karryn's genuine warmth had done her more favours than even her quiet grace and delicate features, for her kindness was much appreciated by palace staff, whose opinion carried more weight with the average Sytrannian than that of any number of nobles'.

Truly, the royal wedding had made a great impact on all King Nahvib's people, but none more so than the subjects in his own city. The news-sellers were most grateful. Business had risen sharply in what was already a competitive area. King Nahvib's gardeners had been busy sculpting the palace grounds and the chefs' recipes were practically a state secret. Local inns were even more full than usual, with people ready to gossip about the change in their king's life. The King Mahtid, named for Nahvib's father, promised free drink throughout the ceremony and a pipe tasting was to last through the night. 'It's what he'd be doing if he wasn't with the fair lady' was how the innkeeper, Lars, put it. Dressmakers had transported material from other countries to supply all the nobles invited, but even the commoners who would line the streets from the temple of Lr'a to the palace were preparing their best.

'The problem is what colour to choose.' Kyrria moaned.

'That all depends on who you are going to be standing with.' sent Els.

'Jayak getting uppity again?' Alleri asked, exchanging looks with Klara. The four young women had been elected to decorate the temple, but they had taken a break from floral arrangements to discuss their own preparations. Els grimaced. *'Uppity doesn't cover it. He's been so strange lately.'*

'Jealous.' Kyrria decided. *'He's so used to being the talented thing round here, he can't handle it now you get more attention.'*

'What makes you so sure? How do you know that's the problem?'

'I might be a priestess now, but you know that wasn't

109

always the case. Kyrria answered. *'Every boy I went out with was jealous of my previous boyfriends, none of them could stand that I knew other men. Then, when I dropped them all for a life of service to the goddess, nothing changed. They chased me as much as ever, it just meant they were jealous of L'ra instead.'*

'Yes, ' agreed Klara, *'You may not have old boyfriends to make Jayak jealous but the friends you have and the respect they give you, all these are things that Jayak expects for himself.'*

'He'd rather not have to work for it, though, so I don't think he sees your efforts, only your triumphs.' put in Alleri.

'How serious are things, Els?' asked Klara, seeing the obvious pain on her friend's face.

'Not good.' acknowledged Els. *'We're not talking like we used to and when we do, I feel like I only make things worse. We still have good times together, but less often now. I don't know, maybe it's just all that's been happening, we've both been through a lot lately.'*

'Everyone has, don't let that be an excuse.' Alleri warned.

'Absolutely, if it isn't working out and Jayak won't even try to resolve it, you might as well end it now, rather than later.' sent Kyrria.

'But it's not that easy. I love him, even if he is being difficult right now; that isn't a reason to stop being with him.'

'Do you love him?' Alleri asked her, *'This is the first man you have known like this. You came here not knowing anyone, half scared of yourself and Jayak made you feel special. I think now you know your powers and have your own friends, he doesn't like it. Let it drag out and Jayak might just drop you for the next talented apprentice that comes along anyway.'*

'Thanks a lot.' Els tried to smile but failed.

'Besides, you could fare better, what if you met someone who was less arrogant, more caring, someone

110

who would understand the many demands on you? Klara suggested.

'Maybe you're right, I just don't want to be hasty. I'll talk to Jayak before the wedding, see where things are going and make a decision. I can't let it overshadow the ceremony, I want to enjoy that, not spend it worrying about my own romance.'

While the young women were contemplating men, clothing and the like, the magi had moved on to government matters. Pocack and Durrew were discussing the political implications over a cup of tea when Zritz burst in, out of breath and clearly excited. 'A reply!' he gasped, waving a paper at them.

'To *the* letter?' Durrew asked, disbelievingly, 'So quickly?'

'Gentlemen.' Pocack chided them, *'I think this is better as a private conversation.'*

'Yes, sorry Pocack. I can scarce believe, but the North seal is upon it.' Zritz said.

'Does any other know of this?' Pocack asked, carefully guarding, as did his colleagues.

'Only Drayk, he was on his way to us when I bumped into him, only the four of us know it has arrived.'

'Very well, I will open it then.' Pocack solemnly broke the seal and shared the contents of the message:

'Magi of the South,

Long as I have ruled over the kingdoms of the North, I never expected to see such a day. A letter from Southerners and asking for help! I near choked upon my luncheon at the scandal – that you blasphemous foreigners should request our aid. Was not splitting our peoples apart enough? Must you not only ignore the teachings of Bronv himself but directly oppose his schemes? My head reeled at such indolence. However, such a noise as that which I made gasping at yout news brought my advisors. Once assured I was well, they insisted on reading your message for themselves. They were surprised and amazed, but not as angry as I was. They pointed out that your account of

111

the Demon Lords matched well with signs and portents from Cridf and Old Lok. Besides, they asserted, the need for help came with the offer of aid. One of my advisors, Lord Cranff, said that Cridf had answered his prayers with the knowledge that help would come from an unexpected quarter. Perhaps even the unholy Southerners were being prompted by our gods. By all means send an ambassador to further explain yourselves, maybe we can discuss the situation to aid us all. Though I warn you, come bringing war under the guise of peace and I will destroy you all. But come as allies and we of the North welcome you. A fortnight's time?

His Majesty,
King Hurburt VII

'Well, of all the arrogant...' Durrew could scarcely believe the reply.

'Typical, really!' Pocack laughed out loud 'Only a Northerner could give such a message and expect us to be glad.'

'We should be actually, at least he agrees we may be of use to each other.'

'Oh indeed we should, it's just the manner in which it is said. That we are to be grateful, while all the time he looks down on us as 'blasphemous foreigners'. Raz give us strength!'

'I suppose we must tell his majesty?' Zritz said.

'Yes, you are right, as ever, friend. I will go, only give me a moment to compose myself.'

'Poor Nahvib,' sighed Durrew, 'Mere days to his wedding and he must be disturbed by arrogant foreigners and hysterical magi.'

'I'm sorry, Matzi, I've no idea where the flower girls are. Aashi brought her girls a few minutes ago, but I don't know where they are now. Try my sister, she may have got them together, she was muttering something about flowers.'

'I was muttering nothing, brother dearest.'

'Nubira! Thank Ellari! Where are the children? The flowers?'

'Nahvib, stop fretting. I just showed the girls to their rooms and reminded them a little of the procedures for tomorrow. Everything is in order.'

'Easy for you to say. Most of the guests are yet to arrive in Sytrannia and I have no idea how some are going to get along. People have come from all over.'

'Only because they are eager to share the happiness of your majesty and my lady.' said Matzi, 'They come to enjoy themselves, surely.'

'Exactly. Come, brother, all will be well.'

'I hope you still say that when leaders from every nation meet. Even Queen Wertle has sent a representative. How will my people react to an Easterner at the feast?'

'They'll mostly be glad it's not Wertle herself. A great many of us will be keen to see her new chief priest, he sounds an interesting fellow.'

The king was about to reply when a sturdy knock at the door stopped him.

'Come in!' called Nubira and the now somewhat more composed Pocack appeared in the doorway.

'What is it man? 'Tis hardly like you to shuffle in so. Don't tell me, you've invited the Kings of the North and sat them all next to Azabar and Yacconi?'

'There is only one Northern king, Your Majesty, but though he is not a guest, I have a message from him. *A reply to our earlier note.*'

'*I see.* Nubira, Matzi, if you could check whether Zachari and Horik's daughters are here yet, I'd be most grateful.'

'Very well.' Nubira looked a little startled but she and Matzi left, nevertheless.

'What does he say'? Many emotions were evident in Nahvib's face and it was well that Pocack had felt them already.

'That we are infidels, lunatic strangers, practically –' Pocack began.

113

' – What? So there is no help from that quarter, then?'

'Ah, do not jump to conclusions, dear king. Suspicious the Northern king is, but his advisors appear less so. They have encouraged their king to accept a visit from our emissary and to find out more. I'll wager the king is as scared of the Demon Lords as us and has sense enough to check all offers.

'At least he has some sense, then. I'm not sure I am that keen on his outlook but this problem is bigger than one kingdom. I suppose we had better inform our representative.'

With Pocack's words, Els paused in discussing outfits with Jayak.

'What is it, dear? Are you all right?'

'Of course, darling, it's only that Pocack wants me.'

'Now? I wish they would leave you some time to yourself.'

'Me too, but I will hurry back. Jayak?'

'Yes?'

'The green looks great on you and I'll think about the pink. Like you said, we'll look good together.'

'Great, see you soon.'

'Pocack?' Placing her hand on the door, Els bade it open and was more than a little taken aback to see King Nahvib seated with the magi. *'Your Majesty.* She knelt for a moment before sitting down with the group. *'Is it more news about the Demon Lords?*

'Not as such.' Pocack told her. *'Yet there are things you must know about our fight and your place in it. Many things have happened to us and those others who fight our enemy, even in other lands. You understand how important it is to communicate our knowledge?'*

'Of course. There is no adventure to be had alone, L'ra teaches us that.'

'It is necessary, therefore, to share our wisdom…at all costs.' Zritz said quietly.

'Els, have you ever met the king of the North?' Durrew broke in.

'No. Why should I? I lived in a village, it was of no interest to the king.'

'Well, shortly you shall meet him. We sent a message to King Hurburt –'

'Ridiculous name!' snorted Nahvib.

'- Declaring our wish to send a representative, an ambassador, if you like, to explain our views on the Demon Lords, to agree some kind of battle plan, a proper system of aid.'

'A good idea, but why does it need my approval?'

'Yours was the name we gave as a representative. Tomorrow, you will once more cross the great North Sea.'

'Me? Tomorrow?' she shook violently at the news.

'Be calm, Els.' Pocack's mental voice swept over her like familiar waves kindly lapping a shore. *'In answer to your last question, yes, it must be tomorrow if you are to make the meeting at the designated time. As for our choosing you, it was a joint effort. All those in this room agreed it and L'ra also gives her blessing. Indeed, I believe your coming here has led up to this as part of your role in this fight.'*

'Certainly,' added Nahvib. *'I am neither magus nor priest, but L'ra spoke to me as clearly as on the day I was first tested. We all know this to be right.'*

'You may, how do I? I would have to stop at Garrtron first, you know that. How can I face my people? I may be a Northerner by birth but they will scarcely see me as such now. I can't even talk to them. Think how hard this would be. Explaining to King Hurburt is the least of my worries, quite honestly.'

'Els, think of your powers.' Durrew hastened.

'Dear child, think, as I did, of your faith.' Nahvib said, laying his hand upon her shoulder.

'It will be hard.' Els finally gave.

'But not impossible.' countered Pocack.

'I go then. For, as you say, this is in the hands of those

stronger than I. L'ra gave me courage, I will not fail her. Yet let me go to tell my dearest one, there will hardly be time before I leave.'

'Very well, tell Jayak the good news we trust you with, then get some sleep before tomorrow, as I must.' King Nahvib sighed. Glad though he was to have the war underway with some kind of plan, he looked forward to the hour he would be out of this hubbub and in Karryn's arms.

Equally preoccupied with thoughts of her loved one, Els hastened back to Jayak's room. He, however, failed to notice her entrance. Stretched out on the bed, he appeared to be far away in a dream. He twisted around in his sheets, muttering about flames and faces. After some futile shoving, it was Els'mental laughter which woke the sleeping sorcerer.

'Love, how long have you been there?' he sat up hurriedly.

'Only a few moments. Why, you silly thing, there is no shame in being found sleeping!'

'I know, it does just seem daft, though. Especially in the afternoon like this.'

'Well, we've both been busy. And it seems I have work yet to do.'

'Oh, those old buzzards come up with more chores, have they?'

'Chores barely covers it.'

'Yes? Darling, what's wrong?'

'Jayak, tomorrow, after the wedding, I must be away for a while...to the North.'

'You can't. I don't understand, why do you want to go back there?'

'It's not that I want to, I simply must.' Els took a step back. *'I have the power necessary to show people the horrors we must avoid, as well as knowing the people. I am the only one who can speak the truth there. Besides, the gods will have it so, I know L'ra wishes me to go.'*

'Well, I don't!' Jayak's mental tone was

116

uncompromising.

'It's not about either of us! Why is it always be like this with you?'

'Oh, it's my problem now, is it? I suppose I should like my girlfriend spending every minute she can at work or prayer, rather than with me?'

'Jayak!' Els held up her hands. *'How can you be jealous of such things? All that I do, I share with you. I want you to share my joy and, yes, some fear, at this news. As I am glad when you show your strength, surely you can be pleased for me?'*

'No. I need you. They can send someone different.'

'They can't and they won't. I won't force another choice on them. Jayak, I am going, I will not fight with you over this, it is too important to be overthrown by your petty whims. I have given up many things for you – and seen little return of late – but this is one thing I cannot drop. I would rather go with your support though, because I love you!'

'I won't give you my good wishes for this. If you go, you journey alone and selfishly. All this is a means of showing everybody your power, it disgusts me. I don't even know if I want to see you when you get back.'

'Don't say that, please.' Els began to cry.

'I don't know what to say, I just don't. It seems you would choose the fun of an adventure over time with me.'

'It is only you who makes me choose between you and the gods, there need be no such conflict between us if you would only listen.' Els didn't look back at Jayak, she fled the room before her tears overwhelmed her. Back in her own bedroom, Els held Sorab tightly, her tears falling into the mherl's soft fur.

'Oh, Sorab, why doesn't Jayak see the opportunity before us all? Why can't he help me be part of it? Can I repair the damage we have done each other tonight? And other nights, other arguments. I can't bear this pain.' Some time she sat there, pouring out her concerns to Sorab. Gentle as the creature was, she knew she had to talk

to a human friend, one who would know something of her trials. Strong now and swift with her power, she sent her thoughts across the city to the temple.

'Friend? Kyrria?'

'Ah, Els!' Realising the pain in Els' tones, Kyrria straightened up out of bed immediately.

'I should not be surprised,' she sent, 'All night I have dreamt of you, I have hardly had a peaceful half-hour.'

'Kyrria, I've had such a dreadful row with Jayak, I think it might be over between us.'

'Do you want it to be?'

'I don't know. He was so horrible, but no, I can't stop loving him, not just like that.'

'What did you argue over?'

'King Nahvib and the magi have decided I must go to explain our attack to the North. I don't know how, but they believe I can use my powers to do so.'

'Then you will be able to. Nahvib may not be a magus but he has a sense of what must be – his encounter with L'ra has been the shaping of his life. The magi know your powers and Nahvib has confidence in you, it will happen.'

'I wish I had your faith.'

'My faith!' Kyrria's chuckle echoed like mental ripples across the desert. 'Dear Els, the road to my faith has been a winding one, you will find your own way in that. Yet you know as well as I do that L'ra is real and the will of the Eternals must be done.'

'I know, I will go. I am just fearful at seeing my people again and now I must worry about Jayak as well.'

'Fear not. I shall pray for you on your journey and as it worries you so much, for Jayak too. He is my friend because he is yours and I promise I will see him come to no harm.'

'Thanks Kyrria. Well, let us both get some sleep before tomorrow.'

'Indeed, it promises to be a great day.'

* * *

'We causeth some trouble, but ist such enough to distract them?' Quivviam said.

'Most probably. We soweth doubts in their minds, we stir up friend against friend, reminding them of old wounds they hath…or those they imagineth. I think we can prevent their unity, give it time, though, my dearest, it taketh some planning.'

'Yes.' The female chief of the Demon Lords paced around the ornate table on which lay a map of the lands below. Her robes rustled eerily as she did so. 'Nevertheless, we must deal with Els, she payeth too much attention to her goddess yet, despite our best efforts to distract her. Then there is this priestess. I did not think this Kyrria wouldst be such a great companion to Els. We have people to deal with, Xanesh and I favour being very harsh on them. Very *cruel*.' She smiled, silver glinting beneath her hood.

'Feareth not, my dear.' her partner sniggered, a sound like the wind smashing against long-dead bones. Remember who we whisper to in Sytrannia's palace. Our time will come, even swifter than you might hope.'

* * *

The morning of the wedding day dawned at last.

King Nahvib threw back the covers and ran to the windows. He could just feel the slight warmth of the early sun as it stretched lazy fingers over his kingdom. Nahvib sighed, satisfied at the simple glory of the country he was now to share with his queen. In all his joy, Nahvib looked the very image of his father, though the gods were the only ones to see it that morning.

By the time Karryn woke, the sun's rays had crept further on. Startled at the light in her room, she turned away from it until it could no longer be ignored. Then, tensing like a cat, she tentatively pulled back the covers.

119

Groaning, she stretched into a sitting position and rubbed her eyes. So, she thought, today is the day. With a contented smile, she lowered herself to the floor, ready to face a day unlike any other.

In the kitchen, Nubira faced Matzi over two large mugs of tea. 'Well, in a few minutes, we must wake the girls, put dresses on, check the flowers and generally make everything run smoothly from now 'til day's end. But let us have these first few moments to ourselves!'

Els woke from a sleep so deep she hardly knew where she was, banging her head against the wall when Sorab clawed her into consciousness.

Jayak slept on past all his friends, in a dreamland where no problems could leave him powerless.

Alleri woke, checked her wedding gift was on the shelf ready and promptly went back to sleep.

Cyru rose slowly, but made his preparations carefully, for he had planned all he needed to do.

Lars checked his bar and larder were stocked. For, as he told his wife, 'You never know what these foreign guests might want.'

Upstairs, his guests began to stir. 'Brace yourselves,' said the first one up, 'You don't know what these Southerners might serve us.'

At the temple of L'ra, Skrella and Roro had risen early to pray together. They had already had breakfast but were still early enough that the other inhabitants of the temple lay asleep. Their office was as tidy and tranquil as ever, so the two of them sat in soft chairs at peace.

'Gods, goddesses, hear our prayers.' began Skrella, 'Help us to act on your will, to play our rightful part in all that is unfolding around us.'

'As my sister in the faith says. Above all, we praise you and thank you for these recent signs of your great power. Help us to guide those you have given great purpose to. On this day, give your blessings to our king and his new queen. May all the gifts you have to offer be shown in them or through them.' Roro's voice took on a deeper tone, pronouncing talents with authority, 'May the Elementals, Tadir, Cala, Raz and Myrrine, make their passage anywhere on Rima easy. Arram, as Nahvib has shown kindness and mercy to all creatures, so let animals be his friends when the need arises. May both the royal couple have the agility and stamina only Gax could lend in the hunt, yet temper this with your compassion, Ellari, and let this shape their heirs. Above all, may noble L'ra infuse them with a spirit of adventure.'

'Yes,' added Skrella, 'May L'ra guide Nahvib and Karryn in saving their land from the Demon Lords, cause them to rise fresh to every challenge. And not just these two, but all who help them. Above all, guide your chosen one, Els. Give her strength in her powers and friends to light her way. And praise you goddess, for all the powers you have lent us thus far.'

'Praise you for all that you give us, all that you show us. Let your ways be upheld.'

The Great Hall was ready. Servants, relatives and friends of the couple had all been busy, for flowers and ribbons festooned the whole place. Every arch and pillar was in some way decorated. The flower girls let petals fall softly at the feet of the noble guests. A small band played traditional Sytrannian tunes, using pipes and delicate stringed instruments. Pale purple and green candles lit the front of the raised stage where Nahvib and Karryn would make their vows. Before the couple made their entrance, their guests were making enough of a stir. Queen Ashla and Prince Griorg were received with many smiles and some people clapped, for the queen had been a regular visitor even before Nahvib was king. King Azabar and his family were greeted courteously by many fawning noblemen, but Zritz and Durrew, coming behind him, took more of the attention. King Vistar and Queen Elaina smiled warmly at the crowd and all were pleased that the young queen and her children looked so healthy.

The bulk of the minor Southern royalty followed them and the crowd began to mumble again, until their Western allies entered. Then heads craned to see the kings of Rucilia, Liance and Cassal with all their entourage. Many commented on difference in dress, but similarities were also duly noted. King Yacconi's lack of family was apparent and caused the older Sytrannians to remember stories of his career as a soldier. Everyone settled in their seats, expecting a pause before the arrival of the royal pair. The guests were not all in yet, however, when people gasped in amazement at the sight of the short-haired man in orange clothing closer fitting than anybody local would wear.

'Guards! Danger!' shrieked Lady Caree, but noblewoman Orlanda hushed her.

'Danger? Goodness, *friend*, we must watch out!' cried King Sedryk in mock horror, linking arms with the stranger he had arrived alongside. Lady Caree was unconvinced and rose to challenge the newcomer. Nobleman Lins, however, beat her to it, 'Honoured guests, it gives me much pleasure as Foreign Minister to announce each one of you, but none more so than our newest ally, Stec, the Eastern priest of L'ra.' Muttering grew again but the tone was less dubious and Stec made his way into the hall with a brief smile.

'Come on, Lins, where's the official welcome for me?' said Sedryk, at which everyone laughed.

'Why, Sedryk, I fear you have lost your novelty,' Lins replied.

'Yes, it'll take more than a late entrance to get you noticed now.' Yacconi said.

'Huh,' Sedryk murmured beneath his breath, 'I'll see you at the pipes later.'

The exchanges and explanations eventually died down and at last everyone turned for the entrance, which required no comment.

King Nahvib was every inch the monarch, from golden crown to the jewel-studded white sandals made to match his robes. As everyone stood and applauded his entrance, the king smiled so brightly he seemed to reach every one of his subjects. Proudly, he strode towards Roro and Skrella on the candlelit stage. For a moment, he stood alone and only the odd nervous cough or jangle of jewellery broke the silence. He didn't have to wait for very long, but it seemed everyone in the Great Hall held their breath with him. When at last they exhaled, it was with a gasp of admiration. Karryn's attire was simple enough that it showed her natural grace to every advantage. Her gown reached to the floor, a brilliant green which spoke of hope and fertility. The wide hem and cuffs were embroidered with gold thread, the neckline decorated with tiny yellow byeera stones. Karryn's rich brown hair was made into several minute plaits, each fastened with clips of finest jade, fashioned by jewellers under the king's own direction.

The serene grace of Karryn was well matched by the calm strength of the two men who accompanied her. On her left side, Pocack's steady walk and floor-length grey robes were enough to show his might. On her right, Drayk also wore grey, though his light, loose tunic was open slightly to display his slender chain of office. They moved as one towards the stage where Skrella and Roro waited with King Nahvib.

'Hail, representatives of L'ra!' cried Drayk and Pocack together.

'Hail, servants of King Nahvib!' Roro and Skrella replied.

'It is our pleasure indeed to welcome you and Karryn today,' continued Skrella, 'For this day is one of joy, where two people join in happy union and a new queen is made, to love both a king and a country.' Smiles and comments passed amongst the guests, but neither Nahvib nor Karryn saw anything beyond the small stage. Roro led the ceremony, 'By what right do you invest this marriage?' he asked, speaking to both the men in grey.

'By the right of the council.' Drayk said, his voice reaching even those furthest from the little group. 'Karryn is honest and takes on both new roles with genuine commitment. May no man give argument for the army and the noblemen of this country support her.'

'By the right of magic.' Pocack declared, his voice low with the gravity of his words, 'Karryn knows the true path of magic and seeks not false power. May no man give argument, for the magi support her.' A glow appeared to illuminate Karryn then, but Pocack gave no sign of knowing its origin. Their parts done, he and Drayk turned to the remaining pair, seeing their eyes already on the waiting coronet and headpiece.

'Now, we ask, by what right do you invest this marriage?'

'I, Skrella, chief priestess of L'ra, declare this marriage to be the will of all gods, none more so than our goddess. Karryn has the caring nature of Ellari, but the fighting strength of L'ra. Karryn,' pausing for a moment she looked fully into Karryn's brown eyes as she placed the gold circlet upon her head. 'In the name of L'ra, goddess of all adventures, I pronounce you, Karryn, wife of King Nahvib and Queen of all Sytrannia.'

Roro could barely lift the woven gold cord to Nahvib's head for laughing, for shouts of joy were already echoing across the Great Hall. Yet the noise died enough for his speech, for the whole occasion would be unfinished without it.

'I, Roro, Chief Priest, declare this marriage to be the will of L'ra and all the gods. Nahvib may hunt enemies with the swiftness of Gax, but it is the courage and resourcefulness that only L'ra can lend a mortal, which makes him the man we celebrate with today. In the name of L'ra, goddess of daring, I remind you of the burden you bear as the ruler of Sytrannia. Today, however, L'ra seeks to reward you with the beginning of further adventures – I pronounce you Karryn's husband!'

The Great Hall erupted then, claps and cheers heralding this new age in Sytrannian history. Their hands together, their heads close, nobody could tell what the royal couple were saying to each other. Every guest, however, saw the way the eyes of each never strayed far from the face of the other. Making their way along the length of the hall, the king and queen stopped to shake hands and greet people. 'Long Live Queen Karryn! Hail King Nahvib and Queen Karryn!' called those inside and outside alike.

At the reception, it was clear that Matzi and Nubira had been busy. The palace ballroom sparkled and the food provided demonstrated the very best the South had to offer. Unfamiliar smells also hinted at ingredients specially shipped over from the East or West. After the meal, Nahvib and Karryn began dancing with such unthinking grace, it was clear no guest would get a word of sense from them.

'A 'thank you' or 'Glad you came' will be our best conversation tonight, the poor man's lost to us now.' muttered Sedryk, 'It'll be nights in front of the fire and the pipes all forgotten.'

'Come now, your majesty, is Queen Lidynne so provoking?' smiled Dekkomas, King Sedryk's First Minister.

'Dekkomas! Why do you politicians move with such stealth? True enough, you spot the lie in my words, I would not be without my own queen, you know it.'

'Still,' said King Yacconi, 'Having recently learnt to enjoy some of these Southern pipe flavours, I hope I am not about to lose the better part of my companions?'

'Indeed not!' Prince Griorg cried, 'The minute festivities are done here, I believe a certain innkeeper holds his own celebration…'

'Go, if it pleases you, but by the gods leave Azabar out of it.' Lady Taheya begged.

'The inn is a safer place than his current one.' said Drayk, pointing to where Azabar was slopping his drink onto the table whilst guffawing at his own jokes with a Western noblewoman.

'Queen Xyami doesn't look very pleased,' Sedryk realised. 'I suppose somebody had better rescue the drunken fool.'

'Pipes soon, then?' Prince Griorg asked.

'Out of the cook pot and into the flames,' groaned Taheya.

Azabar was rescued from immediate embarrassment by his friends and the politicians' attention was soon diverted by the many new faces they saw around them.

'Awful lot of young people here.' said Dekkomas.

'That'll be down to the magi, they'll want their youngsters to mingle,' Lord Bik said.

I wouldn't want it any other way.' said Nobleman Zakkari, 'Those people of magic have given every effort to support their monarch. I myself have been in need of their services when it came to this new menace. Not me personally,' he corrected hastily, seeing the look on Azabar's face. 'But my dear daughter was in danger at one point, children being more impressionable, you know? I mean to say, she's fine now.'

'Speaking of talented youngsters,' Taheya moved on, 'Where's this Northern sorceress we keep hearing about?'

'Yes, ten years old and killing demons, they say.' Bik told her.

'She sixteen, almost seventeen, for a start,' laughed Drayk, coming over with Stec and brimming glasses of Zarittian wine. 'Her name is Els, she came to visit from the North and has stayed for tuition. She has not destroyed any evil ones but has been instrumental in their defeat. And for pity's sake, don't go saying she's a sorceress, she's barely been made wizard and you could upset all sorts of people with that kind of chatter.'

'And her talents come from the goddess L'ra herself.' Stec noted, 'So don't be upsetting her, please.' Though he smiled, there was caution in his words.

'How is this new life treating you, Stec?' enquired Vistar, 'Must have been a huge shock.'

'I am well, my friends felt the greater shock. I had quite a reputation in the council and my purpose is rather changed now. But I am happier, thank you for your concern. And Vistar, fear not for Elaina's health, she has

126

come through an ordeal not to be repeated, I am sure of that.'

'Thank you, Stec.' Vistar said, looking a little dazed.

'Well, idle talk is all very well but I am determined to greet some unfamiliar faces myself. Who's with me? If I can enter the party with an Easterner, I'm sure I can leave it on the arm of a Northerner!' Sedryk strode away with Vistar, Dekkomas and Stec at his heels.

'He had better not even think of it.' Queen Lidynne said, walking over to Taheya, though her smile showed she had no real fear for Sedryk's intentions.

'Does he ever stop, your majesty?' asked Taheya.

'Seldom, Lady Taheya. It's true, I can never guess what his next exciting idea might be. But I have never met a man so generous of spirit as my husband and I am yet to spend a boring day in his company.'

'Why, you stole my very words!' said Karryn, pausing momentarily in her dancing. 'Though I may not have had as long to enjoy my husband's company. You have stood here too long, however. The musicians play one of my favourite tunes next and we must all dance. I see Nahvib is waiting for me, but there must also be gentlemen willing enough to partner you two.'

'I really don't know.' Taheya hesitated.

'As Queen of Sytrannia, I would be deeply offended if you hadn't danced at my reception.'

'I will and you will.' Elaina insisted, 'Anything that raises menfolk's thoughts above wine and pipes cannot be a bad thing.'

'Hmm, very well.'

The musicians played skilfully, it was a melody not often heard, yet many felt able to dance to its beat. Married couples twirled gracefully to the music's broad sweeps, strangers keen on new company let dancing take the place of introductions. King Nahvib and Queen Karryn held the attention of most and made sure they swept by enough officials to satisfy everyone. Every participant delighted in movement to the strings played so expertly by Sytrannia's musicians and Lady Taheya soon forgot her reservations as she danced with Lord Bik.

Els was one of the few oblivious as the music started, for, true to his word, Sedryk had descended to find out what he could, bringing his somewhat embarrassed companions with him.

'Els! I hear so much about you! Is it true you helped defeat the enemy in Jhrik-ansi?'

She shook her head helplessly and looked to Jayak in desperation, *'I can't send to him! What do I do?'*

'Oh, now you want my help. Can't you do everything with your amazing powers?'

'Jayak, I know you're cross, I want to sort things out, but later, please.'

'Later, she says. But when you want something, it must be now. You weren't exactly thinking of me when you insisted on wearing that cape to the wedding.'

'What on Rima! It's my new cape. The jade was King Nahvib's own idea. I thought you'd be pleased to be seen with me wearing it.'

'It would be a miracle if anyone could see me at all with you showing off so. All that jade and gold.'

'Jayak, what is it you want me to do? How am I supposed to please you?'

'Like you want to! Oh, I'll play the devoted lover for these fools, but I'm far from happy, Els.'

As suddenly as the outburst had come, Jayak returned to his usual smiling self.

'My apologies, King Sedryk. Els communicates only through the mind, but I am happy to translate that she is pleased to meet you and your friends.'

'She wonders, how many people of magic do your own lands have?' interrupted Alleri, casting a concerned glance at Els as she read her mind and felt the after effects of Jayak's comments.

'Well, not as many or as talented as here, of course,' replied Sedryk, 'But we are training more every day.'

Els smiled and Jayak relayed her ideas for helping new

recruits. The men from South and East were hesitant at first but soon warmed to this young girl who smiled and gestured where her mouth, and their minds, failed them. Before they knew it, Cyru, Drayx and Klara were also telling their stories and Jayak was amusing the kings with his jokes.

'Perhaps you could visit Akrin sometime, both of you, give us some ideas with the magic.' Vistar offered. Jayak stiffened at the mention of travelling together but Els was sure Vistar didn't notice. Stec, however, missed none of it.

'We really ought to dance,' he said, 'It would be rude not to.'

'You're right, Stec and I must find Elaina, too. Come Vistar, Els, you all dance?' King Sedryk said. Els nodded, but it was Alleri's hand that Jayak took and she found herself without a partner. In that moment of waiting, she realised how beautiful the music really was, aching strings heightened by haunting piped notes. Something in the song reminded her of home and she felt tears prick her eyelids.

'Soon you will be there.' A quiet voice and gentle arm penetrated her lonely thoughts and she turned to find Stec at her side.

'How do you know?' she asked, unthinkingly.

'I cannot read all thoughts, not yet, but our goddess has been generous in her gifts. If this reminds you of home, perhaps your thoughts are better there than with that young man. Yes, the emotions behind his speech made strange contrast with it, you are not to pursue that argument now. L'ra wants you North, it is a simple truth that you must go. But it is not a punishment, rather an opportunity.'

'Have you got the gift of prophecy?'

'In honesty, I have used this knowledge given me little enough to tell, yet. But what is there in my head is so clear. I feel a curtain has been removed and I see a part of the world as it really is, not as it would be perceived. Jayak may fool the casual observer, but not those who seek the true way. I don't know what your future holds but I do know you will resolve nothing until you have been back to

129

the North.'

'Thank you. I felt I was going mad for a minute. Kyrria says much the same as you, you must meet her.'

'After this dance, my dear. For a little while, you will dance with me and only the music need concern you.'

'I'd be glad to.'

Els took the Easterner's hand and followed him across the crowded ballroom. Forgetting Jayak, as Stec had said, she thought only of the music and the goddess who had placed her there with it.

Chapter 11

Els packed slowly. Whenever she sat down to organise her things, Sorab reached a paw up to stroke her face, realising how reluctant she was to leave. Putting her things together, Els could not help but contrast this voyage with her journey to Sytrannia from the North. Then, it had been hasty, a grabbing of nearby articles and a quick goodbye to Cam, the one person sorry to see her go. Now, however she had so much more to leave – Alleri, Klara, Dayx and Cyru. Not to mention Jayak. Just when they really needed to spend time together and sort things out, she must rush off miles away. Kyrria, she hoped to contact despite the distance, but even that was far from certain.

Besides, she had grown to love Sytrannia itself. The desert landscape, which had once seemed so bleak, now struck her as peaceful. The swishing of robes and tinkling of laughter in the palace would be sorely missed. And why now? Well, she knew all the answers to that, but it was hardly fair. She wanted to live in Sytrannia under the new reign of King Nahvib and Queen Karryn. She wanted to be there when the three magi determined new tactics, or discovered the latest movements of the Demon Lords. Alleri, Cyru, Dayx and Klara would all be finding new homes outside the palace, for terms of apprenticeship and long-stay magicians' study were coming to an end. Those who had begun the fight against the enemy could no longer make claim on the king's home in quite the same way. Some of their rooms would be filled by youngsters from all over Sytrannia, some amongst them the next to be apprenticed. With a start, Els realised she may know few faces at the palace on her return and all her friends would have moved on in one way or another.

It wasn't just the fear of what she would leave, either. She had no idea what kind of welcome she would receive on returning to the North. The thought of seeing people like Liv and Bronv-Grii again made her stomach tense.

131

What of her family, though? Part of her longed to see them, but she felt she would not be able to bear it if their meeting went badly. How could any of them cope with the memories of what had gone before? Her birth itself had been the burden of her mother's life, she knew that. The Festival of Fair Voice was meant to be a joyous occasion, yet even there she had brought shame to her family.

But the goddess willed it so. There must be no argument. Deciding she must face this now, if she was ever to do so properly, Els put down the bundle of clothing she had already carried up and down the room three times and knelt on the floor, holding Sorab.

Goddess L'ra, hear my cry! she began, *Though I am yet new to your purposes, let me be guided by your will in all things. If, as so many of your followers tell me, it is your desire to send me Northwards once more, then let this be clear to me. If I am truly to address my people in your name, lend me your power to do so. Help me not to think sadly of what I leave or fearfully of what I may face, but to undertake this task with a glad heart. Praises to you, noble L'ra.*

As she finished her prayer, the strangest of feelings came over Els. At first, she sat up, expecting to see L'ra in the room, the sense of her presence was so strong. The goddess remained neither visible nor audible, yet Els couldn't doubt that the being she knew was with her. No words were spoken to her, no signs were seen.

Nevertheless, Els was wrapped in a feeling of the deepest peace she had ever known in her life. *'Of course,'* Sorab sent, *'She heard you.'* Els hugged him.

Jumping up, she threw her clothes into one of her bags and began packing in earnest.

By the time she came to leave, her friends had gathered in the courtyard to say goodbye. Els embraced each in turn with vigour, though not with tears. Cyru promised to look after her remaining belongings. Alleri said she would try to find accommodation for Els' return, 'Because you will return.' she insisted. Her final hug was painful in its grip and Els felt in that instant how Alleri's humour often hid her fears. Only Kyrria said what all were thinking, 'No Jayak, then?'

'No. He wouldn't even open his door. I fear it is all over now,' Els frowned, *'But I am resolved to go now. Perhaps when I return we will be together again, I don't know. That, however, is another day.'*

'It is. In the meantime, I will pray for you both. I meant what I said before, I will let no harm befall him, I promise you that. Maybe there will be a resolution to all this when you return.'

'Maybe.'

It was the new queen who had the final goodbye.

'Be brave, be strong, dear Els. You are the hope of this nation and much more beside it. Our faith in you is strong, your journey will be blessed. Takka is ready to take you to the port. Nai-kin awaits you there. Take care, adventure be with you.'

'Thank you for all you have done for me. I hope my people greet me as willingly as you did when I came here. The goddess keep you safe until I come back.'

Then she turned and left with Sorab and Takka. Once she turned back, a last glance to see if any other had come to say goodbye, but the hallway was closed behind the group, so she set off in a brisk walk with Takka and was quite calm by the time she reached the port. Nai-kin showed her his boat, introduced her to the crew, explained their route and told her where she would sleep, but to Els it was all a blur. Sleep was the only part that mattered to her and that bit came easily enough.

Jayak, however, was far from sleep. Though he sat on the most comfortable chair in his room, surrounded by luxuries few of his friends could afford, Jayak's mouth was set in a snarl and his forehead was creased with frowning. Leaning to look out of his window, he clenched his fists so hard his knuckles turned white,

'Why?' he raged, 'Why is it allowed so? By all my

133

powers, I will not be defeated so!'

He raised his hands above his head and made a low incantation. At first, his voice was a low rumble that was barely audible, but it throbbed with the powers which went into his spell. As his fists punched the air above him, his hair fell from its loose knot and tumbled to his shoulders, billowing, as his cloak did, with the energy radiating from him.

Then he cried out sharply, 'Azikiban, Arramitah! Gonnihiah ah jex van nyi!' His words would have sounded strange even to a native Sytrannian, being ancient words of might that few had ever had cause to use. Yet it seemed they suited Jayak's purpose well. At the seventh time of calling, blue flame formed before him and he smiled for the first time in several days.

The flame was an icy blue and hovered directly in front of him, flickering without substance. Gradually, a face appeared within it and Jayak sighed with satisfaction.

'You are unhappy with events?' enquired his friend.

'Are you not? Jayak's eyes narrowed. *'Els is lost to us and the plans of these believers thwart us still.'*

'Can we not follow these fools? Dog their efforts at every stage? Your power is strong, you summoned me in this form much more quickly than I could project either of our physical forms.'

'True enough, but to the North?'

'We do not do this on our own strength. You forget, we have allies stronger than any of their friends. Kings, priests and the like are no more powerful than the worthless gods and goddesses they worship.'

'Yes, let me call upon my one true friend. I will show these do-gooders they should have appreciated my magic while they had the chance to benefit from it.'

'Surely with Quivviam and Xanesh on our side, revenge will be ours.'

'It cannot be otherwise. All who have wronged us, kept us from true power, will feel the force of what we have now. How does it go with your enemies?'

'They suspect nothing. All around me are so caught up in their pathetic little lives they assume everyone thinks as they do. But you see the same thing at the palace, I tell you nothing new.'

'No, but it is good to hear you have the same story. There can be no end to this but the destruction of these idiots. And yet...' He paused and rubbed his head in confusion, for an instant looking like his old self.

'What? You cannot shrink from the task now.' the summoned face said.

'Nor do I want to!' He shook his head and the kind, confused Jayak had vanished again.

'We must leave each other now; I would no more be caught like this than you. We must act fast, while those around us are still more occupied with feasting than fighting. There are others we could add to our number, some whose powers would be of much use.'

'Yes, and some whose absence would go undetected...for I feel our new friends grow hungry.'

'And we must keep our new Lords happy. Praise be to our new rulers! Let this world soon become their state, so we can govern with them!'

* * *

Els awoke to the smell of chicken cooking and for a moment thought she had better hurry to the dining room before the best of it was gone. Then she heard waves slap against the boat and realised with a start that she was already that much nearer to her homeland. Sorab jumped about excitedly as she got dressed and Els put her clothes on quickly, for fear of getting scratched. She hadn't wanted to wear her apprentice's cape, it seemed to her as if the sailors would think she was showing off, but Nahvib had insisted she take it with her.

'Put it to good use!' he had said the previous morning, so she didn't want to ignore his words now. Stepping out onto the deck she was glad of it, for the wind was cold.

135

'A good morning to you!' Nai-kin exclaimed, 'Oh, it may not feel like it to you now, but the wind is in our favour, we make good time.'

'Goddess be praised!' said one of the men, raising his mug.

'Els, tea?' Nai-kin asked.

Els nodded and smiled, hoping Nai-kin and his crew could understand her thanks. Once again she wondered how on Rima she was to communicate her crucial message to the people of the North. Her people. But were they really hers anymore?

Nai-kin returned with Els' tea and an assortment of breads and meats for breakfast. Els had scarcely though she would be so hungry, but the food disappeared rapidly as he briefed her on their advances.

'We made good progress yesterday. Oh, yes, it was a whole day you slept and nothing this lot did could wake you. Mind you, not saying they didn't try.' The captain looked at his younger crew members witheringly but none of them seemed perturbed.

'Come on, Capt,' said Dri-angk, an attractive dark-haired young lad who was probably yet to start shaving, 'It was only the one sail fell in and you like to be kept on your toes, I know it.'

'Know this, Dri,' said Hrikki, the solid second, whose grey hair and wrinkled skin spoke of rather longer experience at sea, 'If it'd been one sail in a storm, you'd have been in the sea quicker than it takes Af to brew the tea.'

'Thanks, Hrikki, I'm sure Dri doesn't plan on repeating his many mistakes.'

Nai-kin sighed, 'But the gods are with us for sure, we are nearing quickly, for you can see we left the icebergs far to our right.'

Els dropped Sorab from her lap and strode to the wooden rail to check. True to Nai-kin's description, the icebergs fell behind them, untroubled by their passing.

'Of course, you must remember the ice flows. I hear

you had a few adventures there last time.' Nai-kin smiled.

'We sailed through, You were so brave,' Sorab smiled.

'Not bad for an untrained sailor,' Hrikki grimaced, 'Might be able to show these boys a thing or two.'

'Well, no time to argue it. You can see, Els, we are past halfway now, so me and my lads here'll press on a short while, make the best of it while the wind's with us. You want more tea, go see Af, he may have something for the mherl, too, but keep it out of the kitchen.'

'Yeah, Af's plain funny about animals, reckon he's scared – ow!' Dri-angk found out too late that Af had come to say hello and collect his plates.

'It's a matter of hygiene, as you should know. But then, who'd expect an animal like you to understand that? Yes, Els, please keep Sorab in your cabin unless you're holding him, but I'm sure I can find some scraps. Come and find me when you next get bored.'

'Won't be too long, I shouldn't think. This is a long trip for a girl used to the city. Still, no crazy magic yet,' muttered Hrikki, not so quiet that Els didn't catch his words, however.

She didn't react though, but took Sorab and settled in her bunk for the next few hours.

Determined to prove Hrikki wrong, she sat down to cast her eye over the notes Nahvib and the magi had given her. The points to be made to King Hurburt and his advisors were very clear. If she could only begin some kind of communication in the first place, she knew she would be all right.

The notes on magical talent were rather more interesting, however. Reading through the notes over the long days at sea, Els realised how much she had learnt in the past months. Fire power was now a power she could use with some accuracy. She didn't think it was likely she'd need it, but she was a long way from the uncontrolled demonstration with the bandits; now she could better use what she had. The other elements were, as yet, a mystery to her, but one she looked forward to unravelling. Walling, the power to block forces, was another thing she had some ability with and one she feared she may need in practice. Her people may attack her, much as she hated it, it was a possibility she had to face. They may not want me back, she thought; they may not even recognise me. Thinking this, her hair fell across her lap and she realised it was both longer and lighter than it had been when she left Garrtron. The months she had spent in the South had greatly changed her.

And what of her family? They too, might have changed. Cam and Reesa were no doubt an accepted couple, perhaps even married now. Bronv's Sal must have had their baby. Lissal was probably much the same, but even of that she could not be certain. As for her parents, they would no doubt look much the same, but what had changed inside? Had they forgotten her? Tried to? Or did her parents spend sleepless nights contemplating Els' whereabouts? She had no idea.

For the next few days, she pondered these matters. Sometimes she stopped to see Af, sometimes she only spoke to Sorab. Twice, she used walling to protect their vessel against violent wind, sudden storms so dramatic even Hrikki didn't comment on her use of magic, while Dri-angk's arrogance vanished in a fit of vomiting when he saw lightning streak the sky. Els, however, was unwavering from one situation to the next. Asleep or awake, in prayer or contemplation, there was no direction to her thoughts but the one they must all work towards. Those among Nai-kin's crew who had mocked the slender Northern girl who would sail with them found their objections flattened with the strength of her spirit. It is their will, she thought, why is our path so mysterious in the face of that? Though none could hear her wisdom, there were some among the crew who sat with her when she prayed. Not one amongst them could read the mind of his fellows, yet the Eternals heard many prayers that said the same thing. Thanks was given for the journey thus far, along with pleas for the ship's final passage. So they passed the storms that dogged them and found a calm so peaceful that even Sorab gave thanks.

So it was that twelve days from leaving Istalan, Els awoke to shouts of glee from every sailor.

'Ah, my love!' beamed Nai-kin, crushing the young girl in his grip. 'Thanks be for your prayers and powers alike. For, look, the land of the North meets my ship this morn!'

Els steadied herself on the mast before she turned to follow Nai-kin's gaze. But when she did, the emotions she had up until now touched so tentatively hit her like a wave. A sudden fear swept over her, for now there was no going back. It seemed only hours since she had left her friends at the palace, she couldn't be here already. But the fear drained from her as the boat came nearer to shore. Without even thinking about it, Els was first off the craft and was running to the grassy bank before Nai-kin and his crew had even moored the boat securely. As her boots touched the land, Els felt the welcome crunch of leaves underfoot and realised with a piercing joy that she had arrived in autumn.

She whirled around then, arms laden with bright, crisp leaves to scatter them, smiling, at Nai-kin's feet. Her hair fell loose and swirled about her with her cape and long skirt. Stopping to steady herself, she looked at her Sytrannian helpers to find even Hrikki was amused.

'Not so bad to be home, then' he said; but his tone was more gentle than usual.

'May its people be as ready to recognise her,' Nai-kin added. 'Let's get that one over with first.' He threw Els her knapsack and she caught it swiftly, striding ahead to lead the way. Sorab ran and jumped alongside her.

'*Home!*' he said.

'*I know,*' she sent, '*It really is.*'

If it hadn't been for the others, she would have run, for her feet knew this land and hurried her on towards her purpose. The green hills were fertile, fading flowers giving way to ripe fruits or red and orange leaves. Els realised the

139

bandits must have moved on since the spring and wondered where to and how they had done so. How much had occurred in her absence? She had missed the feast day of Fess, the only Northern goddess, and Fess was She Who Finds and the bright revealing light of the sun her biggest gift. But what sunshine Els had found in Sytrannia, what new things she had discovered there!

They paused just once for a hasty supper and Els smiled to see the weather-beaten Hrikki pull his coat tight against the Northern wind. She relaxed as the wind – breeze, really, she thought – tempered the rays of the sun. Sorab curled up on her and snuggled comfortably into her skirt. *'Back now!'* he sent. *'For now,'* Els told him cautiously, though she knew she felt almost as happy as him. Perhaps it was the difficulty of communicating with the sailors, or the restrictions of the boat, but Els felt a great relief to be on land again; she wanted to run the remaining lengths to Garrtron.

She didn't, however. Nai-kin was aching and muttering about land-dwellers. Af was complaining about the Northern food they would soon have to suffer and Hrikki was telling anyone who would listen that it was unnatural to live amongst so many trees.

'Can't see a k- blessed thing,' he moaned.

'That's probably the idea,' Dri-angk said, casting nervous looks at the dense forest about them.

Els though, remembered the forest with delight. It might be frightening to those unused to its depths but to her it had been a refuge in a time of need, so she felt only safety in the greenery wrapped around the little group. She made a brisk path between the trees, heading North-West to her old village. They didn't say anything, but the Sytrannians behind her marvelled at her knowledge of the forest, amazed that she barely paused to find her way. In and out of the people, Sorab scampered, occasionally jumping onto Els' shoulder to share his observations with her.

It was perhaps a thousand-length to cut the corner of

the forest, so dusk was falling as they left the last trees to step out into the cleared area which was all too obviously inhabited. Distant smoke would have alerted anyone to the presence of the village, but the sailors had noticed Els' face first. Her eyes lit in recognition and, shaking, she set her knapsack in the ground and paused a moment to take in a view she had once thought she might never see again.

Then she turned, gripped Nai-kin's arm once to show him her purpose and was onwards, snatching up her belongings as she marched towards the largest wooden house in the centre of the village. She rapped the staff of her knapsack upon the door in a strong rhythm and she waited. Standing there, trembling staff in hand, prized mherl on her shoulders and dark Sytrannians at her side, she knew she made a spectacle for any Northener. Yet her eyes were those of her father and his father before him and the knock she gave was the Garrtron passknock, none could argue that.

These, and many more thoughts besides, ran through her mind, but though she shook with a violent heat, the moment had passed, the deed was done.

The door opened while she stood there still and Bronv-Grii looked out with wary eyes.

'Els? With Southerners?' he regarded her thoroughly, taking in every inch of her features and clothing alike.

Els didn't answer him, after all, Bronv-Grii had made a point of knowing she *could* not, every day of her life. But the village elder hadn't finished his speech. No doubt he had noticed the crowd of villagers gathering behind him, just as Els had.

'I heard they were sending someone,' he said, challenging her. 'But I scarcely would have thought that it would be you. I don't know why Southerners should want you, which is up to them, however, what on Rima makes you think we would want you?'

'Yes, why don't you go back?' someone called.

'What use are you here?' another added.

'Stay with your darkie sand-lovers if you like it so

much!' one cried, causing Nai-kin's hand to move to his knifebelt.

'Show weapons if you wish to leave in pieces,' Bronv-Grii warned. 'We are peaceable enough but this is our land. Show your purpose or leave.'

'The Southerners don't know why they are here!' a young man called, work-axe still in his hand.

'Maybe Els can tell us!' a woman laughed and Els felt sure it was Liv, though she could not see to be sure. Scanning the crowd, she saw many who had laughed at her, thrown stones during Bronv-Grii's teachings, left her out of their games. Some faces she remembered only too well from the Festival of Fair Voice, those whose cries had hounded her from the feasting without even the conviction that Bronv-Grii had felt, only seeking to cast her strangeness from them, to make themselves look right in the face of their people. Not all were hostile, though. Cam stood, near the back of the crowd, looking over those in front with a curious smile on his lips. Hwym craned forward, confused to unexpectedly see the girl who had changed his life as quickly as she had left it.

Only one moved and that was Mavri. Slowly, yet without hesitation, she stepped towards the daughter she had lost, had feared for so many times since her tragic, silent birth. Mavri stood at the front of the crowd, oblivious to its sudden hush, as she reached out her hand to Els.

Els took her mother's hand and the grip between the two was firm, strong in the love it carried. That wasn't all. As Els held Mavri's hand, she found she could pick up her thoughts clearly, the relief at seeing Els well, fear and confusion as to what she was doing back in Garrtron. Above all, her love and the overwhelming knowledge that this time she would not desert her daughter. Remembering her abilities, reminded now that her powers could work as well on Northerners as any other people, Els extended her thoughts throughout the crowd. Some, like Liv, Lissal and Degra, were violently hostile, angry and afraid at what they saw as Els' intrusion. A few, most notably Mavri and Cam, were happy to see Els, keen to find out what she had been doing while away. The majority of the villagers, however, were less clear in their thoughts. Confusion was the predominant feeling – Why is she here? What does she plan to do with us? To us?

For a second, Els paused, trying to take in all that was happening, struggling to find a way through it. She thought she could, if she summoned all her power, speak in their minds for a short time, but would they listen and respond well? Or would they fear her still more? A shaft of light fell across the clearing then, one of the last, as the sun was fading fast now, dusk giving way to dark. Its golden ray reminded Els of L'ra, the purity of power which Els' own cape spoke of. Following the light, Els looked to where it shone on a group of very small children, too young to be bothered by the concerns of adults. They had an instrument, a small drum with strings attached to the top, which they were trying to play for themselves. Their noise was untrained, yet the sound was sweet enough in its wild patterns.

Then Els knew. *'Thank you goddess, that you show me what to do.'*

She had bent her head as she praised the goddess, but she lifted it now and raised her right arm high above her head. Some of the people ducked, fearing an attack, but Els only smiled.

And then she sang.

At first, her song had no words, but every villager put their hands to their heads amazed, as a humming began within. Els may have had neither voice nor instrument, but none there could doubt the song was hers. She smiled again and the notes built to a fine melody as she sang words of happiness, of community, of home. In her calm mental tones, she sang of her new learning in the South, the coming fight between Demon Lords and those who fought for the forces of good. And the people listened. Her words were in their minds, there was no way to ignore them or the powerful things they sang of. Finally, Els finished the song by telling them how and why she had returned,

'...though I have travelled to far-away lands,
To see the dark ones laid low.
My powers are such I use them for all,
To aid the people I know.'

She stumbled then, but Nai-kin and Mavri caught her between them and sat her on a rough seat near the children. Els clutched her head, her demonstration had drained her. Not that it mattered, for most of the crowd were clapping and several were in tears. Liv had stomped off bitterly and Lissal dragged Roga off in great haste, but it was Bronv-Grii himself who ran to fetch a cup of water for Els.

'The gods challenge us every day,' he sighed. 'I know, why couldn't I have said that while you were still here? But I had no idea of such gifts.'

'Pity none of us looked. Yes, myself included,' Gron muttered, but his hand on his daughter's shoulder was steady.

'I should have known, I should have believed her.' Mavri said, bringing Els food. 'There was this woman you see, Els -' But Els stopped her, placing her hand on her mother's arm. For she had already read the story in Mavri's mind and knew that the dark stranger was L'ra. So that's what she meant when she said she had given me my gifts, Els thought, at once amazed and amused by the goddess' work.

The small family group was interrupted by the arrival of Hwym. His blue eyes serious, he gave Els a small book. Looking at him warily, Els opened the book. Inside, the pages were blank but Hwym had laid on the top a small wooden pencil.

'I just thought, if you are going to be here for a bit, you could use this,' he stammered; pale cheeks flushing red for an instant.

Els smiled gratefully, relieved there was no bad feeling

144

for the last time she had tried to communicate.

Cam laughed aloud and thumped Els on the shoulder. 'Better start writing, sis, it sounds like there's a lot you've got to explain yet!'

Chapter 12

'I tell you, Woh-Luhn, that's the way of it. I'd not have believed it myself, but for it happening in front of me.'

'So you say, but what of all that you've told me about her allegiance to Southern gods?'

'I don't know exactly how her powers work, but they work. And her intentions are good, every note of the song spoke it. She has to be aided, no gods will stand in her way. I'm not to be talked out of it, though don't think I haven't tried myself.' Bronv-Grii sighed, rubbing his forehead tiredly.

Five days Els had been back in Garrtron now. Five desperate days for the village elder while he had tried to work out what to tell Woh-Luhn, the elder of Burret Onri, Garrtron's nearest neighbour. They would need his help to get to King Hurburt. Each day that he had waited for the elder, he had passed in prayer and careful watching of Els, searching against all hope for a sign that she was a fake, a tool of the evil ones, feigning powers for reasons of her own, anything that would disprove her claims. But five days Bronv-Grii had watched and waited in vain, his gods silent to his cries. As his hopes faded, he had began to accept what he knew in his heart to be true, that Els had been sent and must be allowed to fulfil a destiny he had too long worked to spoil. It dawned on him that he was now the one who must convince others of her truth.

Sighing at the weight of such punishment, Bronv-Grii turned back to the sceptical Woh-Luhn.

* * *

'Els? How are you doing?' Hwym joined her in the clearing, crunching the leaves underfoot.

Els paused a moment, then searched her skirt's pockets until she found her notebook. **Well enough. Do better if I knew what B and W were saying about me.**

'Can't be all bad. You made yourself clear to Bronv-Grii. Most people are with you. I am,' Hwym spoke earnestly, blue eyes flashing through the pale hair which flopped in front of them.

Els smiled, **I'm glad someone is** she wrote.

'Well, I suppose it's about time I did help, instead of treating you like a problem.'

You never did that.

'What about the Festival of Fair Voice? I let you down, you can't pretend I didn't.'

We don't need to talk about that. It's in the past.

'It happened. I think we should talk about it. We need to.'

I don't. Sorry, Hwym, no dragging up the past. Let's just be friends, all right? Els scrawled, underlining the question.

'All right,' Hwym said raking his blond hair with his hand in frustration, but bowing his head to avoid further argument.

I wonder if he knows what he looks like? Els thought, all confused and hurt. Is he really so upset that I won't discuss what happened? He's certainly more charming than I remember, so how could he possibly be so shy? She bent her head to hide a smile then, but catching hold of herself, felt suddenly ashamed. What am I doing looking at Hwym so closely anyway? Goddess knows, I have a boyfriend already, awkward though he may be. I don't need to think about Hwym's hair, even if it is quite the palest shade of fair there is.

See you later. Going to find Cam. She wrote quickly, leaving before she could stop to see a response in the blue eyes whose gaze she could feel upon her. Stop it! she told herself and hurried off home.

The first person she met at her parents' house was Degra, idly tuning his lyre outside.

'Oh, it's you.' he sniffed. 'No, don't get your pencil out, I'm not interested. Mum and Dad wanted you, I'm supposed to pass that on. They're at the elder's. Maybe they've decided if you're worth sending to the king. It'd suit me, get the place back to normal.'

Els pulled a face, but didn't stop. There wasn't any point in arguing with Degra, he always had all the answers. Or at least, he always used to have. She smiled at that, perhaps she could knock a few old thoughts out of the townspeople's heads. Bronv-Grii would no doubt tell her.

She knocked on his door loud and hard, a more confident Els than the one who had arrived the previous week.

'Els, glad to see you.' Bronv-Grii swung the door wide, inviting her in.

Inside, Woh-Luhn looked a little surprised to see such a welcome, but rose from his seat to greet Els himself.

'So, this is Gron and Mavri's infamous daughter,' he began.

Els gritted her teeth at the implied insult and smiled warmly. Her parents were also present and she didn't think they'd appreciate her blasting Woh-Luhn with a mental attack just now.

'Bronv-Grii and I have been talking about you...and your new information.' Woh-Luhn said, as if bestowing a huge favour by this attention.

'*And?*' Els asked, enjoying the shock Bronv-Grii tried to conceal at her approach to the conversation.

'We feel that we should convey you to King Hurburt's castle at once.'

'Though your allies' wishes remain unclear, we cannot deny a desire for good akin to our own,' Woh-Luhn added. 'Of course, we still seek to advise your friends as to their foolishness in ignoring the true gods, but while such information you have corresponds to that our gods offer us, we must accept they work their way in you and those you consort with.'

'*Thank you. When do we leave? What about my crew?*'

'We leave this afternoon, I think we all agree that delay could be dangerous,' Woh-Luhn said.

'Yes, the time we've already wasted would have been

well spent elsewhere,' Bronv-Grii added. 'As to your companions, Els, they will be well cared for here. Cressa and Maimish have offered to look after them, their house lies too empty for them with both daughters married now.'

Els stifled a smirk. It didn't look like Liv would be visiting Cressa for a while, not with Nai-kin and the others taking up space in Cressa's family room. Not such a bad thing for Cressa and Maimish, though.

'*I'll get ready then,*' she sent to Bronv-Grii and Woh-Luhn without a hint of her former nervousness.

Come, Mum, Dad. Time for lunch before I go, she wrote, gently taking her mother's arm.

'Back here at a quarter after the one. Not a stroke later!' Woh-Luhn cried, but Els had already departed. Her father was the only one to turn his head, with such a glare that Woh-Luhn retreated into his fellow elder's house quite hastily.

Els, in comparison, took a leisurely walk back with her parents. Lunch went well: though neither Degra nor Lissal would come and share food with Els, Cam was happy to and even Bronv made an appearance, intrigued by the sister he had long considered dead. Reesa also joined them, for there were only a few months until she married Cam and there was nothing the two did not share. They talked about the wedding preparations and filled Els in on what other events of importance she had missed, such as the arrival of Bronv and Verys' firstborn, little Bren.

'He should know his famous aunt, it's too bad Verys and her brother are at her parents' now, I wish you could meet him.'

I don't know about famous. But I'd like to see Bren and Verys. Next time.

'Must you go again, when you've only just come back to us?' Mavri asked.

'Yes, we have had little time to right the wrongs we did, to speak to you, now that we know how,' Gron added, sadly.

Els looked at them before she raised her pencil. She

149

shifted Sorab on her lap. If they were going to think I'm mad, they would do so already, she thought. **The goddess wills it so. L'ra, whom you know already.** She waved the pencil accusingly in her mother's direction.

'You know this to be true?' Bronv asked.

'Look, I know it sounds blasphemous, but...I know it is so, yes.' Mavri avoided her eldest son's gaze, as if she might thereby invite the wrath of the god he was named for.

'Mother, I trust your knowing. It can't be for nothing you and Els have such similar accounts of this woman, this L'ra.'

'Perhaps this goddess exists as well as our own?' Gron put forward, though he looked far from convinced by his own answer.

'Certainly, L'ra's existence need mean no threat to our gods. The words of the elders have proved true over many years. Surely, this trip to King Hurburt's can't be wrong, for neither Bronv-Grii nor Woh-Luhn would allow it to go ahead if it were so.'

It may be as you say, brother. Time passes, though, I must find out what I am to do when I see the king. It's time to leave. Goodbye.

Els hugged each family member present, each one tighter than the last. Her father held her awkwardly, it was a long time since he had felt anything binding towards his youngest daughter. He was ready to start anew with her, but such connection still made him uncomfortable. Mavri was last to take Els in her arms and would have pressed her advantage longer, if time had not been against them all. When she at last released her daughter, holding her at arms' length in front of her, she didn't cry, but held her gaze.

'I love you. Come back soon.' Mavri smiled then, 'I know you will, I needn't fear for you anymore.'

Els nodded, they had both communicated all that was needed, so she waved and strode across the town to Bronv-Grii's, her cape swishing with her movements.

'Ready?' said Woh-Luhn, 'It's a long ride you know. You can ride?'

'I have everything. And yes, of course I can ride. How do you think I saw so much of the South? Or didn't you listen to my reports at all?'

'I was only checking. This has to be done properly. However, I have made one concession to your ways.'

'My what?'

'Be calm, Els, I'm sure Woh-Luhn means nothing by it.'

'I mean, Bronv-Grii, that I ought to be given some credit, as the senior elder present, for directing this voyage. I could have made things very difficult, you know.'

Could have? Els could hardly believe what she was hearing, but managed to bite her tongue. What had he done that was so great, provided the horse? Even that was scarcely a match for Audcy.

'Your sailor friends persuaded me this was of some worth to you, possibly instrumental in your magic? I don't usually approve of such creatures, but, as your way in this seems to be to break every rule and be allowed it...' Woh-Luhn indicated Sorab, who joyfully jumped onto Els' shoulder.

'Thank you Woh-Luhn, I'm grateful.'

'Enough arguing, both of you. We leave this quest from my town and I will not be accused of delay.' Bronv-Grii mounted his horse with a skill born of practise and the others followed swiftly.

The road to King Hurburt's castle was treacherous and took the three travellers' minds off any conversation. Leaving the tall trees of Garrtron they passed through some meagre grassland, which Els had never seen before. Birds and plants she had not heard of before existed amongst the grasses and shallow water, but they had no time to stop and examine them; Woh-Luhn led his companions at a demanding pace.

Even he had to slow down a little at the hills, however. Though not as high as the mountains on the North's

Eastern coast, these Western hills were high enough to deter all but the most determined visitors. Rocky, uneven ground meant the horses had to pick their way over the hills with great care and Els and Bronv-Grii were grateful when Woh-Luhn decided to stop for the night.

'It may be still light, but not for much longer. Bronv-Grii, help me gather some branches for a fire, the cold here is said to be quite harsh come evening.'

'Gladly. Els, stay here and keep guard over our equipment.'

'Yes, you could find the food packages and start on a meal whilst you wait. They're in my bundles, I believe.'

'*As you wish.*' Els kept her head down, she didn't think she could carry off the humble expression Woh-Luhn would be expecting if she faced him right now. Fine, I'll do the cooking, she thought. I'm a qualified wizard with conflict experience and I'm asked to tend the cookpot. She sighed inwardly, I suppose everything isn't going to change at once.

Barely twenty minutes passed before Bronv-Grii and Woh-Luhn returned, but in that time alone, the temperature had dropped noticeably and Els was shivering, cape pulled tight around her.

'We came as fast as we could, but there doesn't seem to be a lot of firewood around here,' Woh-Luhn said.

'*Bandits?*' Els suggested, remembering the scarcity of plant material where the bandits had surprised her before.

'Unlikely, so close to the king,' Bronv-Grii said.

'True, but best take turns to keep watch tonight, all the same,' cautioned

Woh-Luhn.

'*Better keep ourselves warm if it's going to be a long night,*' Els sent her mind out to the pile of branches, confidently found its central energy and let her mind free it. She had the pleasure of seeing Woh-Luhn jump backwards in fright, while Bronv-Grii, smiling slightly, lent in to warm his hands. Woh-Luhn recovered himself and offered to take first watch, with Bronv-Grii following him.

Their turns passed without incident and by the time Bronv-Grii came to wake Els, she had slept a few hours quite soundly. Casting her receptive powers out around her, Els soon realised there was nothing within the vicinity to fear. Even Sorab left her side and went to hunt small animals, sensing there had been few people near enough to lay any traps recently.

Left in peace, Els reached out again with her powers, further and further until a mind like a bright and gentle light shone out at her.

'Kyrria? Kyrria?' Els pressed again with her powers, a gentle but insistent presence in Kyrria's mind.

'Els? Are you really here? From there?!'

'Well, it sounds as if you are the one who doesn't know where she is! Yes, I have reached the North and found I still like it.'

'Your parents?'

'Glad to see me, as are most, although several still mistrust me. You should see the way they regard L'ra here, it is like a cloud is upon them and they cannot see.'

'Or will not. Have you met the king?'

'On my way, tomorrow I think, weather being no object. Oh, to have Dayx' powers now!'

'Be careful what you would wish for. Another's gifts are never a replacement for one's own. Speaking of which...'

'What? Kyrria, I fear from your tone what you want to say, but don't keep from me what I will only find out later.'

'It's only Jayak. He's been... sort of strange.'

'How?'

'He barely talks to the others, Alleri's really worried. He seldom comes out of his room unless it's a magus asking. Maybe he's missing you, he might not want to admit it to the others, he knows they think he treated you badly.'

'I hope that's all it is. You don't think he's ill?' Els asked.

'I don't know. When he bothers to attend training or conferences, his power is as strong as ever. At times, it seems to be growing. It's just that he seems to sleep so much, he doesn't interact with people as he used to. He does still socialise with his friends, but his mind doesn't seem wholly with them.' Kyrria tried to explain.

'Perhaps that's because he's working on his powers. Maybe he's trying to prove something. I know he needs to feel he has a strength to offer in all this.'

'Maybe. It might even be he's physically sick. There's been a few people ill in the palace.'

'Really?'

'Yes, even Karryn seems under the weather, you know, lethargic. King Nahvib's a bit worried, reckon there's something going round. Cyru is the only one in classes without a sniffle or some sort of drowsiness, so Durrew says. It's not what we need right now.'

'Well, keep an eye on Jayak, please.'

'Of course, I'll honour my promise, you know that.'

'Yes, I don't doubt you'll keep him from harm.'

'How difficult will that be, just keep him from anything that would dent his pride.'

'Don't remind me! I had better try and contact him, but I think I'll deal with King Hurburt for now, give you a chance to talk to Jayak first.'

'Thanks. And the times you've wondered at my vows regarding men. I think I took the easier way. Anyway, I must rest. This is too great a distance to talk at such length. I shall be of no use to anyone tomorrow. Speak to you soon, dear friend.'

'Here's praying it'll be with better news between us. Goodbye for now.'

Els came back to her surroundings to find Woh-Luhn getting up for his shift.

'Are you all right?' he asked. 'Has there been any trouble?'

'None. I just spoke to an old friend, rather a long way to shout, you might say.'

'Oh, I see. This young man of yours, I suppose?'

'As it happens, it was a female friend, but I will be contacting Jayak at some point.'

'I suppose he follows this L'ra also?'

'As is common in Sytrannia, he does adhere most closely to L'ra of all the gods, as do I. You would argue this?'

'Not now. My focus must be on meeting King Hurburt for the moment.'

'Until the morning, then.'

Come morning, Woh-Luhn spoke no more of his feelings about Southern gods, but pressed on with the journey. They ate a good breakfast and Els insisted they provide the same for the horses, the memory of Arram's words still strong. The other two grumbled at this delay, but the horses appreciated it and made good speed across the remaining part of the trail. Eventually, the hills grew less steep and the three travellers could see Norrlans Castle in the distance. Heavy brown stone, crumbling in places, it was nevertheless well protected by a deep moat, not to mention the hills on every side. Icy winds swept over the trio and they made their way to the gates with haste.

'And what is your business with His Majesty?' enquired the guard. Six guards stood watch outside the castle, wearing mail from head to toe, yet Els could not remember the last time the Northern lands had been at war.

'My business is with both His Majesty and his advisors. It is a matter of national urgency.' The last, Woh-Luhn pronounced in a hushed voice, no doubt expecting the gatekeepers to understand his importance.

'Shouldn't that be international?' Els sent. The guards were no more impressed than her and looked at Woh-Luhn with great suspicion.

'National urgency? Who are you to say what is urgent enough for the king's ears?'

'Well, actually, I'm a village elder, I - '

'Right, that makes it fine, I suppose. Honestly, Aybri, I don't know what these peasants think.'

'Truly Gathrun, you'd think they put themselves on a level with us.'

'Listen, you fools, this is urgent.' Woh-Luhn stamped a foot in disgust.

'I can assure you my friend is correct, we must see the king. We bring news from the South,' Bronv-Grii explained.

'The South, I've heard it all now!' laughed the largest guard.

Els, tired of such antics, stepped forward with two scrolls. One, the original letter to the magi, clearly bore King Hurburt's seal. The second, a reply, bore the mark of King Nahvib and carried his plans for further action. As soon as they saw them, the guards dropped all playfulness.

'Why didn't you say you brought the delegate? That's who we were told to look out for.'

'I could hardly get a word in edgeways with your japing. No regard for authority, I shall be forced to inform His Majesty.' Woh-Luhn strode forward, hurrying the guards as they let the party through the foreboding portcullis and into the castle proper.

The three were brought to the king's drawing room, a chill room with little to brighten it. There, at the head of a long table, sat the king. Els was aghast. She had expected someone taller, smarter, wiser-looking maybe, but certainly not this. King Hurburt was a shortish man, yet nearly as wide as he was tall. His robes were stained and tattered, his beard didn't seem to have been brushed that recently.

'Ah, so you are the delegate?' he looked straight at Els, who was shocked to find his pale blue eyes quite piercing.

'*I am.*'

'Oh, so you're one of those? I'm not that surprised, though it's been a while. You didn't learn it around here, I suppose?'

'*Hardly. What do you know about magic?*'

'Enough. Magic was my life for a while, even this place was built using it. It had become too much of my focus

156

however. The resultant energy used caused an explosion outside, killing my wife and youngest son. I haven't been too fond of training people in the old arts since then.'

'I don't use them for myself.'

'Never? Then you are a rare creature. It's too easily done. But let us not argue now. I believe you have plans for me?'

'These are yours. But what about your advisors?'

'Advisors? You mean my son and my nephews? They won't agree to these, I will deal with them myself.'

'But, I thought it was you that didn't see the sense in dealing with foreigners?' Woh-Luhn shook his head in confusion.

'What about your comments in this letter?' Bronv-Grii added, indicating the first scroll.

'Once, I felt like that. My powers gone, I felt I had been punished for doing something different, I retreated to old ways.'

'You decided to hold back developments?'

'For a while I halted any progress, yes. But I soon saw everything had stagnated, nothing new was made or discovered. Bandits fought us with new weaponry while we cowered, afraid of our ignorance, but more afraid still of knowledge.'

'What changed?' Bronv-Grii asked.

'I gained a new advisor, Cranff. His father was a priest of Old Lok, one of few left. He saw strange things in the future, at first I thought he was mad. Then events proved him right. There was my eldest son's theft from my vaults. I could never have foreseen it, but Cranff knew. I'd sworn he would be proved wrong and die for his treason, but he never faltered. He knew he was right.'

'Why do none of your people know of this?'

'After years of living in the dark? Will you tell me Els' abilities were appreciated from the start?'

Bronv-Grii and Woh-Luhn exchanged guilty looks.

'Exactly. There will be fear, panic, if any of this comes to light too soon. Yet, Cranff and I knew we must act. So we do, but in such a way my true feelings are not known, an uprising is adverted.'

'Sure! Cover your back first and foremost,' Woh-Luhn snorted.

'It is more than that. This continent needs much work, but it must be slow. A rebellion now would mean civil war and that we can ill afford. No, it is better my relatives and fawning advisors carry on playing their part, while Cranff aids me in the real work. That letter was sent to King Nahvib and his magi precisely because it portrays me as the buffoon my advisors must view me as. Where I speak of a word from the gods, I blame it on different courtiers, so they might each blame the other, but never look to me.'

'A dangerous game, Your Majesty,' Bronv-Grii said.

'Particularly so when one lives it every day. Yet, day by day, I give a false sense of inebriation and slothfulness, while arranging favourable appointments and looking to future needs.'

'Speaking of which...'

'Yes, King Nahvib's papers. Let me see. Cranff, is that you?' Footsteps were heard down the hall and a slight, wiry-looking man appeared, brown hair curled tight at the neck, wrinkles just beginning to show.

'Your Majesty.' Cranff took a seat, gratefully easing himself into it. 'I have just been discussing your complete imbecility with dear Prince Niil. It quite taxes me.'

'And he still thinks his clever theft quite undetected,' King Hurburt sighed, 'Still, more important things must be seen to. Take a look at these papers, Cranff. They look perfectly reasonable to me, but can we get them through council?'

'Give me a minute, King Hurburt, I will find a way.'

'So, you have seen signs of this dark menace here?' asked Bronv-Grii.

'Oh, indeed, all too horribly,' the king admitted. 'One of my sisters suffered hideously, she's completely mad now. I had to tell the others it was because her husband died of a sudden illness, that the grief was too much. The

158

truth is, they were in some awful pact together with one of these Demon Lords.'

'Why would anyone do that?' Els asked.

'I haven't met one, but all the reading I've done on the matter suggests they ensnare some victims with promises of untold power, whatever evil appeals to the individual,' King Hurburt said.

'But doesn't that limit their success? I mean, only great wrongdoers could fall for such nonsense,' Woh-Luhn argued.

'Then you are beyond any price?' Cranff laughed. 'I tell you, these demons know their territory well. They see human failings all too clearly. Most scholars believe they persuade their victims that people are treating them badly, then make the gaining of power seem the best means to get back at people, revenge the perceived injustice.'

'The evidence is there before us. On the Eastern coast of our land, a group of bandits overran a town, destroying all men, attacking women and children alike. The damage was unspeakable...and complete. Yet these bandits numbered thirty at the most. There was more than luck to this,' the king insisted.

'In these Western hills, lovers out for a peaceful walk in the hills, old warriors retracing past victories, many have been the small groups lost out there, only to be found mutilated, or wandering, gibbering with madness,' Cranff told the horrified guests. 'We are especially concerned by the proximity of recent attacks. These hills have seen more problems every week and the attack on the king's sister brings this danger into the castle. Your Majesty, I think these papers should be signed. I can deliver them, if need be.'

'There is none other I can trust. I'll tell the council I am dissatisfied with your work, make it seem this posting to the South is to be rid of you a while. Els, I will send Cranff with the people who would be of use to him back to our allies with you. Are we all agreed?'

'Yes.' Bronv-Grii pounded the table. 'At last we take

action.'

'Certainly,' said Woh-Luhn in a small voice. 'We had better return to our homes, brief the people as need be.'

'Only those who must know. I will remain in communication as often as possible, but I am limited in sending messages,' King Hurburt reminded him.

It was a long ride home. The day was sunny and the journey easier downhill, so Woh-Luhn decided they should not stop. Apart from this discussion, he was almost silent, shocked by what he had heard. Bronv-Grii was similarly thoughtful, but stopped to talk to Els occasionally. For her part, Els found this quite companionable, perhaps the journey had been as important for her guides as her. All three spent the trek mulling over what had passed that day and the curious arrangements of their ruler, so the return soon passed and they were back in Garrtron before nightfall.

Els ran into their house to reassure her parents she was returned without harm. She longed to tell them the remarkable truth, but instead she spoke of the king's failings, his advisors' need to explain things, how any agreement was arranged by those around the king, only gaining his grudging permission.

Cam and Bronv asked her many questions, while Mavri bustled about making a meal for Els. They were still talking well past dusk, but Els knew there were still some things she must do before she could rest.

I have to send a couple of messages. A long way.

'Oh of course. I expect your young man will be worried. Will he want to meet us soon, or does he hate us? I don't know what he must think of all you went through.'

He doesn't hate you. Really, I don't know if he would visit. We're taking it easy at the moment. Can it wait?

'Yes, dear, just, I'd like to meet him. It sounds as if he's very special to you.'

Well, I wouldn't say that. It's not that serious right now.

'Tell that to Hwym, the time you spend talking about this Jaik,' Cam cut in.

Jayak. And what's it to Hwym?

'Oh, I'm sure you couldn't guess?' Cam grinned.

Brothers! Els underlined heavily before taking herself to her room. Peace at last she thought. Now I will try to reach Jayak, serious or not. *'Jayak, Jayak.'* she called, at first to no avail. Then, tentatively, she caught a reply.

'Els? I can hear you. It's so far away, I didn't think. How are you anyway? How did your people react?'

'Better than I expected. I'm sorry I couldn't reach you before, I've been so rushed.'

'I've missed you, you know.'

'Really?'

'Lots. I wanted to talk to you, there's so much I want to tell you.'

'Then tell.'

'I forget now. I had all these things to say, they seem to go as soon as I want them.'

'Never mind. I do love you, Jayak. I just have to be here right now.'

'I know. I wish you were here though, it's so lonely without you.'

'What about the others? Talk to them.'

'They wouldn't understand, I...'

'What's wrong? Look Jayak, everything went well with our king today, if that can happen, anything can. This thing is going to be defeated. We can sort things out, just as soon as I'm back there, we can get things back to how we were.'

'I'm sorry, I don't share your optimism. You have no idea...'

'What? What about?'

'It doesn't matter.'

'Look, if you can't talk to me, talk to Kyrria. I won't lose you just because you can't cope with our problems right now.'

'Does any of it matter? There are things bigger than us,

more powerful. Els, you don't see what can be, you won't look to the future.'

    'You won't let me. Gods! Jayak? Jayak?'

    But there was no more reply. And my mother wants to know how serious he is! Cam teases me about Hwym! I was just enjoying what I had with Jayak, why must it all change? Els fell asleep deciding to send to Kyrria in the morning, but her sleep was tormented with dreams of Jayak's words.

Chapter 13

While Els lay sleeping amidst uneasy dreams, it was morning in the South and there was no rest for the magi. Their three faces were serious and the guarding was cast so strong that only one possessed of sorcery would recognise even the presence of their room.

'So? What would you have us say?' Durrew began.

'There are difficulties within the kingdom, within this very city. We must tackle these. That is why I ask for this conference now. I nearly asked King Nahvib, it is still his city but I think he has enough to deal with,' Pocack said.

'With Karryn being so ill? That is precisely why he *should* be here to discuss this. Rima alive! The trouble is within these very walls,' Zritz shouted.

'Zritz, calm yourself, there is nothing to be gained by needless panic,' the chief magus admonished his colleague.

'What makes you say this, Zritz? You seem so sure of your words,' asked Durrew.

'Half those studying the magical arts fail to attend classes. I haven't seen Reynon at a healing test in a week and he's one of the best, after Klara. Our records show that Cyru's the only one with complete attendance this month! The queen is dangerously ill and King Nahvib is distracted beyond measure by his wife's sickness. All events come together at such a critical time as this, yet you do not see anything to suspect? I feel I am the only one in Istalan with eyes!' Zritz cried.

'Queen Karryn is ill, yes, but hardly in danger. Given what the woman has been through not so long ago, I do not wonder her health must eventually suffer. I appreciate your concern, Zritz, but I have no fear for a speedy recovery,' Pocack insisted.

'Yes, but Pocack, you have to see what Zritz means about timing. Neither an epidemic nor a frightened king is what Sytrannia needs right now. Might it not be an attempt by the Demon Lords to confound us before they do battle?' Durrew suggested.

'I hear what you say, but I don't think we should rush to conclusions. There could be entirely separate causes for events at the palace right now. We mustn't let our imaginations run away with us.'

'But if we fail to act, how could we reverse such activity when it has run its course?' pleaded Zritz.

'The students are restless, some appear vacant. Even Jayak and Alleri are hardly themselves, I'm really worried,' said Durrew.

'Don't take offence, Durrew, but is this a sign? Couldn't it just be the end of a hard year taking its toll? Not to mention the excitement of the fight fading into a time of waiting? It could just be that everything is a bit of an anti-climax now.' Zritz suggested.

'No!' Durrew looked furious at Zritz' comments. 'I know my pupils better than that. Something has affected them much deeper than mere frustration. If only Els was here.'

'You know that could not be,' Pocack said.

'I know, I just think her friends need her, maybe she needs them, too. The gods know, we sent her on a desperate errand.'

'Kyrria's report was good, we should expect Els back fairly soon. In the meantime, let us act cautiously. It won't do to start rumours at a time like this. I say we ask Drayk what information he and the Council have, talk to the students and try to find out how serious Karryn's illness is. Agreed?'

'Agreed,' Zritz said.

'Agreed,' echoed Durrew. 'But let me deal with the students. I have met personally with those most deeply affected, particularly Els' friends. I feel a duty to them.'

'Very well. I expect a full report by the end of the week. I say we present the findings to Drayk, whatever the position regarding His Majesty might be.'

In the temple of L'ra, everything was as peaceful as

always. Skrella and Roro were interviewing prospective novices, some priests and priestesses were showing such guests around and the remaining inhabitants were left to their own devices. Arrok was scouring ancient texts for clues to defeat the Demon Lords, with Plarina and Timo working for him. Kyrria and Rayth, however, preferred to work in the fresh air and had taken to the gardens. They made good progress with the sowing and weeding of new vegetables and their quiet laughter kept the old priests cheerful while they worked with the animals nearby.

It was the familiar chiming laugh of Kyrria that alerted Jayak to them, as he walked into the gardens.

'Kyrria?' he called, gently, knowing how peacefully the temple folk lived.

'Jayak! Good to see you, come and help.' Kyrria indicated a hoe.

'Very well.' Jayak joined them in their preparations, somewhat bemused to conduct a conversation while weeding, but putting it down to the seriousness of Kyrria's duties. 'No Plarina, then?' he asked.

'Inside, working with Arrok, why, did you want her?' Kyrria wondered.

'Hardly! Just used to seeing you three together, that's all. Anyway, what's Arrok doing that's so much more interesting than vegetables?'

'Books, lots of them,' Rayth groaned. 'Old stuff, they're looking for something on this menace. Apparently, someone wrote down a prophetic word from L'ra, but it all happened so long ago, no-one's been able to track who even mentioned seeing it, never mind writing it. Anyway, it's supposed to tell us how –'

'That's enough Rayth! You know what Roro and Skrella said.'

'Come on, Kyrria, it's only Jayak.'

'I know, but an instruction from Skrella or Roro should be taken as an instruction from the goddess. You know the third rule as well as I. Sorry Jayak, but it has been made quite clear we aren't to talk about our part of the fight to

165

anyone outside, even if it is a friend.'

'That's fine, I understand. Things are fairly tight at the palace, too. Can't be too careful.'

'True enough. Speaking of the palace, any news on Karryn?'

'No, she's much the same. Everyone one else seems to have shaken this thing off except her.'

'What do the magi think? I mean, I don't want to worry you, but, have they thought it might be more than physical?' Kyrria suggested.

'Kyrria, you expect me to tell you when you can't let any secrets out? Be fair!'

'All right. Besides, our prayers are with her, I know L'ra must reveal her will in all things. But, if you didn't come to tell us anything, why are you here?'

'I can't just visit my friends? Just wondered if you'd heard from Els, really. I spoke to her yesterday and she appears to be coping well, despite being amongst those barbarians.'

'I've spoken to her as well. I agree, things are going well. Did you tell her you missed her?'

'Sort of.'

'Jayak! She can't read your mind over that distance and shouldn't have to.'

'I need to see her face to face. I'll make it all up to her next time I see her.'

'Just don't dawdle when you do. One thing this menace shows, there's no time to be wasted.'

'True words, Kyrria. Well, I'd better return, Alleri keeps going on about meeting for games, I think it's probably easier to humour her once. Maybe she'll let me alone after that.'

'Your friends only want your company, Jayak. There is no wrong in that.'

'I know. Goodbye for now, goodbye, Rayth. Say hello to Plarina for me.'

Once Jayak had gone, Kyrria turned to her friend, perplexed.

'I'm sure I don't know what he wanted,' she said.

'Well, Els isn't here, he's lonely. Jayak just wants to talk to the next best thing, her friends.'

'That's what I thought, but he hardly talked about Els. And if he really wants to be close to her friends, why does he hold himself so far from Alleri and the others? It just doesn't make sense to me.'

'Well, that's the way of men, Kyrria, they can't make their minds up. Let's be truthful, Jayak only decides he really needs Els' company when she's gone.'

'Well, Rayth, I hope that's all it is.' Kyrria's face, however, looked far from convinced.

If they had but known it, the two young women were not the only ones to feel some confusion. In Roro and Skrella's study, the chief priestess looked less than happy herself. Sifting through notes on the recent interviewees, Roro paused when he saw his old friend's face.

'Tired, Skrella? Skrella?' he called.

'What? Oh, Roro, yes, indeed I am.'

'Is that all?'

'Well, mostly. It's just…Oh, it sounds silly.'

'No, go, on.'

'Well, I feel there's something missing, something extra L'ra's waiting for us to see, only we can't see it. I just sense there's a new height to be reached, or a new depth.'

'A new depth? What on Rima can you mean by that?'

'I knew it sounded foolish. I feel like there's something we can't get to grips with now, but L'ra wants us to use. I just don't think it's all going to be pleasant. I can feel some hard times coming, Roro. I think we will need our strength more than ever, soon.'

'Well, we have each other's strength to unite. Not to mention the people we've trained here, young and old, men and women. They all have talents and courage.'

'Yes, but are they all strong enough? Some of them are still so young, Roro, so untried. Sometimes I'm afraid. There, I've said it. I worry for them. I worry for this temple, this city.'

'Then we need to trust L'ra's guidance. Do you want to pray, now?'

'More than ever,' Skrella said, with some relief. 'I won't be able to focus on any more applicants until I do.'

* * *

Els, happily far removed from her friends' problems, relaxed in the centre of the village with Hwym, Cam and Reesa. The sun was a pleasant warmth on them only occasionally broken by a sudden flurrying wind. The songs of many birds, excited over the local berries, filled the air. Els noticed Sorab's mouth was already stained with purple juice. For long stretches, none of the young people moved or spoke, but simply lay soaking up their surroundings.

A week had passed since the meeting with King Hurburt and Els had almost begun to relax amongst her people. She had shared lunch at Cressa and Maimish's place, along with Nai-kin and his crew. The Southern sailors seemed to fill the wooden house, but Maimish seemed to be appreciating the male company after years with a wife and two daughters. Sytrannia's finest boatmen were also not without musical talent and Maimish had proved very interested in their assortment of pipes and flutes.

'This is as nothing to the king's collection, you should see that. It'd make your eyes fall from your face, yes it would!' Dri-angk had announced, with his customary confidence.

'Don't get ahead of yourself, Dri,' Nai-kin had warned him, while Hrikki had contented himself with glaring at his shipmate.

But neither Maimish nor Cressa had taken offence. Slowly, yet steadily, their interest in these dark strangers had grown. For their part, the sailors had satisfied some of their curiosity about these people who lived amongst so many trees and discovered they were not all as dreary as they had expected. True, no Southerner was ever going to enjoy t'por meat, any more than the Northerners would ever accept shoulder length as a suitable hair arrangement for a man, but these differences were cause for amusement in the main, only those such as Lissal or Liv would try to make more of it than that.

So, it was with pleasure that Els saw Nai-kin approaching her and her friends. Or it was until she saw Bronv-Grii and Cranff not far behind. She closed her eyes, frustrated by the break to her peace. *Sorab!* she sent, *leave those berries and come here now.* As the creature hurried over, she felt herself begin to relax a little.

'It's all right, it's probably nothing,' Hwym suggested, trying to comfort her himself.

Cam and Reesa nodded, but by the time the three older men had grown near, it was clear there was something amiss.

'Els, we need to talk to you,' Cranff said.

'Alone,' Bronv-Grii coughed, looking pointedly at the others.

'No!' Cam said, 'Why should we go?'

'He's right,' put in Hwym, 'We're her friends, we have as much right to know what you want with Els as the three of you have to use her abilities.'

'It's not like that. Hwym, you have to see beyond this desire to protect your friend. It's about more important matters than you need to know of and Els is keen to work with us,' Bronv-Grii insisted.

'So you say. How do we know you don't just want us out of the way so you can pressurise her into doing something you want? Besides, if it is all for the greater good, we should know what is happening. We could be useful ourselves.'

'Yes, Hwym's right. Why should we just allow Els to be sent off and act like we don't care,' Reesa agreed.

'She's been shoved out once, it won't happen again.' Cam said, eyes glinting in the sun.

'Fine, you've made yourselves clear.' Bronv-Grii

sighed. 'I suppose we will be collecting a force of people for this battle, you could be useful.'

'Battle?' Hwym gaped.

'Are you sure they are ready for this?' Cranff asked.

'Who would argue them out of it?' Nai-kin countered, then both Cranff and Bronv-Grii were silent.

So, what battle do we fight?

'A battle on the Eastern side.'

Not the West?

'No. It appears the trouble in the hills there was merely a diversion from the greater evil brewing,' Cranff admitted.

'What kind of evil?' Hwym asked.

'Every kind. Mental attacks disable the people whilst physical attacks show this time the Demon Lords mean to punish those who won't turn to their ways.'

'How, exactly?' asked Cam.

'Sometimes with magic, the ground tearing up, swallowing people, or their sorcerers hurl magical fire at victims, paralyse them if they don't get killed,' Cranff said.

'Worse still, however,' put in Bronv-Grii, 'Is the way they use people to fight, like warriors with no minds of their own, against their own folk. The Demon Lords have so possessed some that they will torture and murder family or neighbours. By all accounts, it's horrific,' he shuddered.

Looks like King Hurburt has a civil war on his hands after all, Els looked Cranff in the eye. **When do we start?**

Cam and Hwym smiled at each other and Reesa took Els' hand.

'Not you, Reesa, this is no place for a young girl... unless she has specialist talents like Els, of course,' Bronv-Grii added hastily.

'Reesa, I think Bronv-Grii's right,' Cam said.

'What? You'd let your sister go, but not me? Cam, I'm only two years younger than her,' argued Reesa.

'Two years that could make all the difference in a battle

170

situation. Reesa, I want to be marrying you in the spring. I won't risk losing you in this. I wouldn't let Els go if she couldn't protect herself.'

'So I have to wait while you go off and get injured, possibly killed?'

Stay with our mother. She likes you.

'All right.' Reesa sighed.

'Then it's decided. Els, Hwym and Cam, you will make the trek through the hills to the Eastern woodlands. Nai-kin, are you coming or not?' Bronv-Grii asked.

'I'm taking my crew round the coast to the Eastern sands. That way we fight them from two sides.'

'Couldn't we ask the Eastern kingdom to support you?' suggested Cranff.

Unlikely. I could try and reach Stec, but he's nearer the South than us and his queen isn't about to help in a hurry.

'Very well, then. Nai-kin, take your boat along the coast. The rest of us will take the land route. I've rounded up some young men willing to fight and we'll take the greater part, but a few can join you on the boat,' Bronv-Grii said.

'What about the men the king sent?' Cranff wanted to know.

'What, all fifty of them?' Bronv-Grii snorted. 'They can come with us too.'

'Those are the troops the king trusts. The fact that he sends them at all shows how seriously he takes this.'

'Oh, fair enough, Cranff. I'm just not sure how good our chances are, I'm not used to this,' Bronv-Grii said.

'Then get used to it,' Cranff answered him. 'The gods are with us if we only dare it so.'

'Huh, but which gods do you mean?' muttered Nai-kin to himself.

'Actually, wouldn't it be an idea to take some of the king's men with you, Nai-kin?' said Bronv-Grii.

'I can't take many more on, but yes, some expertise would be appreciated,' Nai-kin said.

'Five of Garrtron's leaders, five of His Majesty's

171

commanders,' decided Cranff. 'Hopefully, one hundred men from Burret Onri and its surrounding towns will meet you near the coast. We don't really know how large a force we must fight against. Reports have mostly come from those who escaped the devastation and they are extremely traumatised by what they saw.'

'Woh-Luhn has men in preparation already. They'll meet us on the way over. Probably eighty, his town is a fair size,' Bronv-Grii said.

'And you've had thirty training?' asked Cranff.

'Training, since when?' Hwym wanted to know.

'Since last night, further out into the woods,' Bronv-Grii told him. 'I wanted to know what kind of might we had before I dragged Els into it. Anyway, I spent a night besieged by dreams of terrible magic taking its toll on the battlefields, I had to bring Els. I think Bronv wishes it so.'

'Well, you young people had best go tell your parents you're leaving. Bring any weapons or food they can spare you and be ready in ten strokes, we leave not a stroke later,' Cranff strode away, leaving the others to scatter behind him.

Hwym moved off for his parents, while his friends made for Gron and Mavri's. Els and Cam rushed in, Cam babbling their news in a scared hurry at their parents. He stopped when the expected argument did not come.

'You must go,' Mavri declared. 'The gods have looked after you both this far in your lives. We must trust them with your safety another time, that is all. Besides, it is not as if it is …a surprise, we have had a …little time to get used to the idea.' She struggled with this last bit, tears falling despite her understanding of their situation.

'How did you know?' Cam asked, astonished.

'Come on, my son, it was not so long that I fought in the bandit wars. I may be too old to go on this campaign, but I still recognise the sight of soldiers training when I see it. Your mother and I knew from this morning, we assumed you'd tell us when you felt ready,' Gron said.

We only just found out. We have to go soon, now,

172

really. But the three of us, Hwym too, we'll look after each other.

'Yes, and you leave Reesa to look after us,' Mavri said.

'Go with our blessing, send word if you can, though,' Gron said. 'Here, Cam, take my axe and dagger, may they serve you as well as they have me. Your brother has my sword, this is a proud day for us.'

'Bronv has the sword?'

'Hardly be Degra, would it now? Reckons his musical gift is a greater thing and he'll stay here to keep morale high! Just you make sure you're back to tell him of your triumphs before too long,' Gron chuckled.

Hugging each other, promising safety and blessings to all, the group separated. Reesa stood solemnly beside Mavri. Els and Cam ran to meet the others. Bronv-Grii was inspecting his men as if he was the king's chief commander, but was notably cheered by Cam's contribution. He ran through lists of targets, descriptions of what Demon Lord-possessed might look like, then they moved off.

Initially, travelling was easy and talk amongst the group frequent. By nightfall, however, they were all feeling the price of their efforts and were gladder than any of them would have imagined possible by the view of Woh-Luhn, ready to greet them at the beginning of Burret Onri, the town he had led for twenty-six years now. His town was all lit up and women bustled around with food for the warriors, clearly Woh-Luhn had made this matter a priority to his people. For the warriors' part, they were relieved to eat and get rest for the night, knowing the next day would bring harder travel still.

In the morning, it was Els who awoke as soon as she heard Bronv-Grii and Woh-Luhn up and about. Her companions took a little longer. Fearing they would never wake, Els banged on the slim, hastily constructed partition between their sleeping area and the one Els shared with Macie, the only other girl on the journey.

'What? It's still dark!'

'Ow, who's there Hwym? Aargh, I can't see a thing.' Cam grumbled.

Smiling at their confusion, Els poked her head round the flimsy wooden board.

'Els! Goodness, I know you're keen and all that, but we'll be no use training for a while yet.' Her youngest brother complained.

'Then you think our enemies will leave their attack until lunchtime?' Woh-luhn shouted. 'Get up! Els and Macie, I'm glad to see you standing. I was ready to strike the drum to summon all to the day's first training. Then you get to eat!' He marched off again, leaving Hwym and Cam to hastily throw some clothing on and join their peers.

Training was as vigorous as they had dreaded. A long run was followed by exercises designed to stretch every muscle, so that the group were in great need of their breakfast by the time they got it. A hearty grain soup was accompanied with slices of meat and cheese, the best meal the soldiers were to see in some days. Woh-Luhn had his most experienced warrior, Cuhlm, train the majority of his force, but allowed Els the same time to practise her skills. 'I don't have a teacher to lend you, but perhaps the time will be of some use in testing yourself,' he ventured.

'Yes, I'm grateful. I haven't practised my skills enough lately. Thank you.'

'It's for the cause of all, don't thank me,' Woh-Luhn said, taking himself off.

Can he ever be happy? Els wondered, but wasted little time on him. Practise time had been in short supply with all that had occurred since she returned to Garrtron, now she would have a chance to see how lazy she had got. At first, she was slow, but daily she made improvements. By the end of the second week, her family and friends complained about how much time she spent in honing her skills.

'We hardly see you between our training and yours,' complained Bronv, for the first time showing he missed his sister.

Do you know how hard this is? Els cast fire out in a large ball overhead, not straight, but turning, falling to the right of her friends and a startled Sorab.

'All right, we don't need a demonstration, point taken,' Bronv said, hastily, glancing at his clothing to make sure nothing was burnt.

You're fine. Only because I practise, though, aim doesn't get that good by accident. Els wrote. **Can you even imagine how hard it is to prepare for getting into sick people's minds, spying out the evil in any we come across, trying to banish it? It's not easy.**

They left her alone after that, even Hwym saving his questions until a time when they were all resting. He had often tried to broach the subject of the Festival of Fair Voice, but Els would hear none of it. Hwym found he could talk to Els of many things: despite all that had passed between them, they could share their fears for their country, their people. Els happily spoke of Sytrannia knowing that Hwym didn't see anything wrong in her relation with the folk there, but rather, was fascinated by tales of a people who seemed so exotic. Mentioning the past, however, always made Els distant and Hwym dreaded doing this, seeing in her expression at these times that of the lost-looking girl who had been so cruelly abandoned that day.

'I love how you bring your whole family along, too,' smiled Macie.

Hardly all of them. And Hwym's not family.

'So, what is he? Boyfriend? Because it's really slow-burning if that's not the case.'

He's only a friend.

'Yes? You're mad, he's lovely. I'd sing for him myself if I thought he'd listen. But I didn't think that mattered with you any more?'

It doesn't. He's just not what I want, that's all. Anyway, I'm with someone back in the South, if you must know.

175

'How have your parents not killed you? My father only let me come because I'm so fast in combat, Woh-Luhn says it'd be sacrilege not to send me. And I was surprised enough at that. So, how did you get hold of a Southern man?'

It's a long story… Els began, but Macie didn't seem to mind and their shared stories made the awful journey go a little faster. It was amazing how much they all talked to each other. But a true companionship had sprung up and the more they communicated, the easier their troubles were to bear. Their support had seen them through a treacherous pass across mountains, a river infested with leeches and the grim dwindling of their rations when, three weeks from their departure, they saw the edge of the Green Forest.

The forest was so named for the multitude of different greens which could be seen, leaves of every hue apparent. Birds flew overhead, twice as large as the chickens which populated every Northern yard, bright red and yellow in colour. Joyously they flew above, twirling in the sky like fire, happy to entertain, so it seemed.

A horrible scream rent the air and the birds disappeared like vapour.

Els and Hwym looked at each other, as more screams followed.

'It begins!' cried Woh-Luhn and led the way forward.

Chapter 14

Els and Hwym were first behind Woh-Luhn. Macie and Cam were not far after them. Their young regiment followed the elder closely into the heart of the battle. At Woh-Luhn's instructions, Bronv's group took a route North of the others. Of the remaining warriors, one group came almost alongside the youngsters in support, while the other scouted to the South, aiming to come round in an arc as reinforcements.

Els covered her ears at first, trying to block out a noise unlike any she had heard before. She soon realised the futility of this, however, as the mental wails hit her. Confused, she turned this way and that, wanting to help one victim, then being mentally deafened by the torment of another. She wondered which to deal with first, for the unguarded, violent anguish of those controlled by the Demon Lords was just as bad as that suffered by their victims. Reeling, she struck onwards, clutching the spear she had been given by Woh-Luhn. Sorab, shaking somewhat, huddled in between Els' tunic and cloak.

Silently gesturing, Woh-Luhn and Carlor, Cuhlm's second, showed their warriors where they must be. Carlor pushed forward with Macie, Mandh and Glin, along with others renowned for their strength. They were followed by Els, Hwym, Shvarn and all those who would be more able to use speed to support their fellows. Cam and Ilsorn brought up the rear with Woh-luhn and those he considered strong enough to hit their enemy in a second wave to finish them.

'Els.' Woh-Luhn whispered, 'I place you in the centre to relay information, we need to know what we are up against so we know how far to push our resources. Let me know of any developments at all – threats to our men, victims in need of attention, medical, spiritual or even magical if you feel it is appropriate.'

'You place great authority upon me, Woh-Luhn.'

'You don't feel you can do all this? Look, I only want your best effort. Anything that you bring will give us more information than we could ever hope for by ordinary means. But don't overstretch yourself. Give me a, what do you call it, shout? I'll get someone to you if they try anything to counter you, or even if you're tiring. This battle will no doubt last many days, don't try and resolve it in one fight.'

'Thank you.'

'It's not for your benefit, I want this menace dealt with,' Woh-Luhn said, gruffly, moving off.

The rest of the group moved on as well, Carlor having given the warriors their instructions. Walking forward at a brisk, but steady pace, they clutched the weapons, ready for the action to come. They did not have to wait long. Through the trees came a small clutch of possessed warriors.

'Rarrgh! Death to the foe! Let our lords reign! Aiyh!' The enemy screamed, relentlessly heading to fight the force that was obviously far superior to them in power. Faces contorted with hate they launched themselves at the warriors, flailing axes before them.

Carlor, Macie and the others in front had their own weapons ready and their stout spears inflicted wounds quicker than most of the axemen could strike a blow. The shouts of Carlor's team rallied their friends and the middle and tail sections were keen to show involvement too. Ten of the group of corrupted were killed and many injured by the time Cam's wing brought up the rear.

In the midst of all the shouting and slashing of weapons, Els was the only person listening. Reaching into the minds of the fighters, she found little of their humanity left. Tortured thoughts of the wrongs others had done them and the new life promised by the Demon Lords instead, chilled her to the bone. Just rarely, in between the largely horrific mental images, she found those with glimmers of their old selves retained, though anyone feeling such memories was fighting it, not doubt informed to do so by those who governed them now. These men with remnants of real emotion, some attachment to family, friends, and honour for their gods, filled Els with a sense of desolation, that someone could fall so far, led astray by misguided desires. She thought for an instant of Jayak and what Klara had said about his jealousy. But in the melee of the battle, the thought was lost.

The nearest axeman to Els looked set to attack Woh-Luhn, but Els saw in his mind his real intention, to kill the first of the younger fighters coming his way.

'Woh-Luhn! The one near you is to aim for Ilsorn!' she called, hoping Woh-Luhn would not be too involved in the fighting to hear.

Woh-Luhn obviously heard her, though, for he turned to defend the young fighter who hailed from his own town.

'Ilsorn! An attack to your right!' he shouted.

Turning to heed his leader's words, Ilsorn moved from the position that would have meant certain death. Still the axe fell, cutting Ilsorn's shoulder in its strike. Livid at the damage to his friend, Cam swept in to deliver a fatal blow with his own axe. Shvarn ran forward with Cam to finish off the remaining warriors, whilst Hwym guarded the injured Ilsorn, standing alert with his spear. The weapon was as slender as its owner, but had a tip filed to a deadly point, made of the best metal in the land. Twice, Hwym had to use it, but neither attack caught him by surprise. Swiftly he showed the deranged fighters there was more to war than sheer strength, confidently dispatching them.

It seemed hours they had fought, but in reality, a single hour had not yet been reached when Woh-Luhn called them to order, this battle won.

'I am pleased, but we rest now before we press on any further. We should all eat and Ilsorn's wound must be dressed.'

'That is all the congratulations we get?' asked Shvarn. 'We fought well and all but these two prisoners,' he indicated two defiant warriors, 'have been killed. Is this not success enough for you?'

'This is but a beginning,' said Carlor. 'The force sent to fight us here was just a small one, probably sent to test our strength before a greater onslaught. If we are to win, such courage and might as you showed today must be sustained. Do not think we are not pleased, we are. But it doesn't end yet.'

'As Carlor says. Feel proud of what you have done, but look to what must be done next.' said Woh-Luhn.

'From the minds of these men we hold, I know Carlor is right. Greater numbers will be thrown against us, including those able to use magic. The Demon Lords have no respect for human life, they will gamble men on beating us here, seeking to prevent us attacking them elsewhere.'

'Thank you, Els,' said Woh-Luhn, quickly relaying her information to the rest of the group.

'Els, I must thank you most of all,' Ilsorn said, propping himself up with his good arm.

How painful is it? Els asked.

'Very,' Ilsorn grimaced. 'Still, but for you I would not be here to complain about it. I owe you my life.' He tried to smile, but couldn't quite. Instead he lay down again, Hwym helping him lower himself to the floor.

'We all need rest. Macie, help me patch Ilsorn up before he gets infected. Els, maybe you could get some dinner brewing.' said Woh-Luhn.

'I'll help, Els.' Cam said.

'Yes, so will I.' Hwym quickly offered.

I'm fine, thanks. Els replied, going to get the cooking things.

Hwym shrugged and seemed happy enough trying to take Ilsorn's mind of his injury. While Macie aided Carlor in applying ointments and sewing the shoulder up, Hwym talked away about music, family, the way the war was progressing. Both Ilsorn and Hwym sang as their highest musical expression and had much to share. While Ilsorn's shoulder was being sewn, Hwym began to sing. Unplanned, unpractised, Hwym's melody still managed to sweep across the little crowd, lifting their spirits.

Distracted by the talk, Ilsorn became calm enough that Hwym could check his wound from time to time without worrying his friend.

If only I had healing. Els said, despondently.

'Don't worry, it is nearly finished. He will be well in days and with a scar to tell tales by. He'll have to learn to throw his spear with his left hand, mind, but that shouldn't be too hard, what with all the physical practice we've had.'

Macie's words proved correct, as Ilsorn was soon back fighting again, only occasionally showing the adjustment he had had to make. It was fortunate that this was the case, for the enemy certainly wasn't holding back in any way, either. Each day, attacks grew more ferocious and two of the younger men on Woh-Luhn's side lost their lives when they failed to check there were adequate forces to back them up. From mental readings, Els knew the other groups had also had fatalities and Ilsorn's was not the only injury. One of the more experienced men in Bronv's force had sustained a serious wound to the back which risked infection and the group furthest South had found themselves nearing the middle of the forest with their friends still some distance behind. Els hastened Woh-Luhn on and the tenth day since they first saw Green Forest brought them right into the heart of it, not a minute too soon.

The Southernmost fighters were in the thick of a terrible battle. Men and women were engaged in action everywhere, desperately stabbing with spears, or thrusting axes in the sides of their enemies. Drawn into the centre of the forest, the density of the different trees left scarce room for manoeuvre and gave little light in which to see those attacking. The chosen warriors of the Demon Lords were much more used to their surroundings and fought hard, pressing their advantage.

'Where have you been?!' roared Cuhlm, as he saw Woh-Luhn and his troops come alongside. 'I sent Jarrod to see where Bahlov's lot have got to. Thank the gods you're here.'

'Where's Nai-kin?'

'Not a sign.'

'The Demon Lords have cast a storm upon the sea, they probably can't get through.'

'Els says it's Demon Lords, they're controlling the weather. How bad are things?'

'Bad enough. I've lost ten good men this morning and the others are tiring. We can't go on much longer, even with yours.'

'Right, I'll send my men in the way that's worked for us so far. Els, you stay here with Cuhlm. See if you can reach any of the others, find out where people are. Let us know where the elemental wizards are, or the innocents who remain in this town, we need to find them too.'

'Of course. Gods be with you, Woh-Luhn – all of them.'

'Later, Els!'

So Woh-Luhn charged off with the others. Hwym cast a backward glance at Els, but she didn't see him, she was already miles away, reaching through the forest with her mind. Cuhlm and his men fought close by, with one eye upon their wizard, but Els hardly noticed they were there. She remembered the first time she had used her powers deliberately, back in the temple and used that calm, clear searching that came from within. She recalled how Durrew had asked them to find certain thoughts he had given them and she used that clarity of inner vision.

The first news she found was that Jarrod had met Bahlov coming to help and had fought off the men trying to prevent Bahlov's passage through. Once beaten, the men left alive sunk into themselves, left adrift from their given task they didn't seem to know what to do. Bronv was on his way down from his Northern post, having been delayed by the freeing of captured villagers. He had also lost men in his campaign, but would arrive within the hour, soon enough to be of use. Though his warriors were grieving their dead comrades, the release of the captives, some of whom were well enough to fight alongside them, had given them a great resurgence of hope.

Els was far more concerned about the fate of Nai-kin and Cranff's forces. Reaching out to sea, she found desperation and fear on the Southern ship. A terrible storm had come and not from any natural source. Fierce waves lashed against the craft and a dreadful wind howled around it. Every man on the ship was involved in repair, mending sails, bailing the decks, fastening tight anything that would roll or topple. Thick grey fog enveloped them, cocooning them from any sighting of land.

'I can't see a thing! How can we sail in this!' screamed Cranff above the wind.

'The instruments won't work, these demons fight us with everything.' added Dri-angk. 'We'll never make it to shore.'

'And what should we do, turn back?' shouted Nai-kin.

Stood on dry land, the last place they would look for aid, Els thought hard. At the moment, the possessed thought they had stopped the sailors, that they only had ground troops to dispatch. They would throw everything they had into finishing off their enemy, which they saw as the two forces led by Cuhlm and Woh-Luhn. If she could do something to stop the storm, get Nai-kin and his crew inland, their unexpected arrival would turn the tide of the battle. How, though? Well, she would have to know what she was fighting. It was not long before she found them, sorcerers using their powers for the dark ones. She couldn't shift the elements in such an extreme casting, but perhaps she could shift those who cast it themselves.

Stay away. Or why not join us; we have all powers to command. The rule of the elements could be yours also. Either way, you will not beat us; we know you cannot harness our skill.

Their slithering, insinuating tone made Els' flesh creep, but she would not be swayed now. For all their words, they were three young men, no older than Jayak and not used to such strength yet. They would not be able to read her thoughts in detail while they had to concentrate on such an unholy storm. Seeing the beams in the hall they sheltered

183

in, away from the fighting, she smiled grimly. It was so like that long ago cookpot, only this time she meant the harm.

She stood tall, her cape swung out its green and gold proudly.

'L'ra. Renew my strength, give us power over your enemy and let good triumph. With your blessing I raise my hand and cast against evil!'

She lowered her head as she raised her hand and thought only of the beams and what they were needed for. At once they fell free from the roof, crushing the sorcerers below. Now we are free to do what we must! thought Els in joy, searching out for Nai-kin and his ship.

'Gods be praised, the storm is over!' Nai-kin cried.

'Where has it gone?' asked Dri-angk, scanning the horizon in wonder.

'Never mind that, lad, let's have the ship moving.' Hrikki shouted.

'The land is right before us, a swift rate o' knots and we'll be there in time!' Nai-kin decided. 'All men to work! Cranff, make yourself useful, get the king's soldiers rowing or helping to take the rigging down. We'll be there to help the others or I'll not sail again!'

'I'm with you, Nai-kin; it's a fool who doesn't make use of a miracle,' Cranff said, like Dri-angk, casting a long look out to sea. But there was no sign of the trials they had undergone and the crew set to work with a new will.

Els set her mind to alerting Woh-Luhn to the turn of events, one final surge and they would finish this battle. Cuhlm, already aware of what was needed, pushed on with his troops. Swept up in the attack, he failed to notice a possessed warrior run towards Els. Only Grint, last of the soldiers, saw the terrible fate rushing at Els.

'No!!' he screamed, running at the possessed man with his spear in front of him.

'Raargh! She must be destroyed!' The man continued his attack and swung his axe at Els.

'Goddess, no!' Els cried turning at the warrior's shout

the memories flooding through her. Her journey with Sorab, the temple, Kyrria, Jayak, working with Durrew, her calling as wizard, Jhrik-ansi, the wedding and coronation. Must I lose all now? she thought, in terror. The axeman was trying to concentrate on Grint's attack and his swing could be not be judged as well as he wished, yet his goal was clear and he thrust his axe hard at the girl he had been trained to eliminate. Desperately, Els threw herself to the ground as the axe came towards her. *'Not now!'* Was her last cry, but so strong that any in the forest who still had an uncorrupted soul must have heard her.

For a few minutes she laid on the ground, unmoving, while friends and allies bustled around her. Goddess, if she is yours, do not take her! Woh-Luhn prayed, incoherently trying to guide the others. He found he could direct them no more, it seemed the heart of their attack was gone.

'Pull yourself together!' screamed Cuhlm. 'I will leave Grint and those two of yours who care for her to keep watch over Els. But we must drive on, for, look, do you see? The sailors and their force are fighting, we must be with them!'

Woh-Luhn turned to look where the soldier pointed. Disbelieving, he looked again. But still he saw the pale clothing of the Southerners through the trees, heard the startled groans of dying Northerners who stood in their path. It cannot be! he thought. Then he heard Nai-kin's rough tones bellowing orders and straightened his back. He paused only to wipe the clotted blood and hair from his spear and marched with Cuhlm, calling all but Cam and Hwym to follow.

Els awoke, the noise of battle still around her. I still hear, I still see, she realised happily. Then I am not hurt, he must have missed. She tried to twist round to get her notebook from its pocket but the pain that hit her caused tears to gush from her eyes. Looking at her right side, she nearly fainted in horror. The axe had cut deep and Hwym was still trying to halt the bleeding from it, which Sorab was desperately trying to lick off her. Following Els' gaze,

Hwym tried to reassure her.

'It'll be fine. I'll bind it, Cam and Grint will defend us. Besides, the sailors are come now, it is nearly over. Soon, we can take you to rest.'

Sailors? Els wondered who he could mean. Losing consciousness, she turned Hwym's words over in her mind endlessly. But of course the sailors are here, we came weeks ago, there was a storm, she remembered, a bad storm. But we came, I sang, they all heard. But why is there still a storm? Why can I not move? Jayak, Jayak, I'm frightened. Delirious she spent three days half in, half out of consciousness, finally awaking to find herself in the hut of the local priest.

'Welcome my dear,' smiled the wrinkled old man before her. 'Seems your brother and friend's special care has brought you recovery at last, though the gods must be thanked for the large part of it. It's a miracle to see such a deep cut result in survival of any kind, much less one as complete as this.'

'Doesn't feel so great. And what's this about special care?'

'Why Hwym and Cam have stayed with you night and day.' Woh-Luhn said. 'They talked and sang and held bandages to your wound. It seems their extra effort has paid off.'

'Then I am healed?'

'Enough to travel back. We are grateful for your kindness, Fewh-Lok, but mustn't stay longer. Our people need to know what happened here and you have great rebuilding to do.' said Bronv-Grii

'Yes, hearts as much as houses,' agreed Fewh-Lok, 'But Old Lok guides our efforts and those of us who remained untouched by the evil will heal our friends.'

'Well, as you say. Though Bronv has been my guide, I know Old Lok is of great might also. We must prepare to leave, but my prayers are with you.'

'And mine. Yet allow me one more word with Els before she leaves.'

'As you shall have it. We ready the boat for her to be taken to it in five strokes or thereabouts. I will send her brothers for her.' Woh-luhn said.

'What do you want?'

'Only two things, for both you must hold to in the times which descend on us now. Firstly, let the prophecy be read right, be sure whom you seek. Secondly, always examine yourself with a clear heart, no matter what others say and do.'

'Why do you say such things? I don't understand.'

'You will. The gods go with you, Els, goodbye.'

Fewh-Lok didn't talk to anyone else before they left. Having said what he had to say to Els, he was content to turn to his people again. Els was much troubled by his words. Between them and the extreme pain still coming from her side, she slept fitfully on the journey back. Cam, Bronv and Hwym were anxious watchers at her bedside, and were relieved to reach Garrtron without further injury.

'She's all right, mother, father,' Bronv said quickly, seeing Mavri's face turn ashen at the sight of Els' bound side.

These people have kept me safe. It looks worse than it is, really.

'I hope you're right,' Gron said, grimly. It was two days before either he or Mavri would let Els out of their sight. They soon had to admit that Hwym and Cam were as caring as themselves, though, so dedicated were they in occupying her time while she healed.

I'm grateful for all your efforts. Els said, one morning alone with Hwym.

'I just want to see you get better, that's all. It's no trouble.' Hwym smiled.

It's just, you know what you said about the Festival?

'Yes. Look, are you sure you're up to discussing this?'

Yes. You're right, we –

'What is it? Are you hurt?' Hwym cried, aghast at the dreadful expression on Els' face.

187

I, no, it's not my side. In my head, the most awful mental pain. Someone's so hurt.

'*Els! Els! It's me, it's Kyrria. Come quick!*

'*What is it? How do you come to shout so clear?*'

'*I'm learning fast. There isn't time to talk. It's Jayak, he's with them and Plarina, they nearly had the prophecy.*'

'*Who's them?*'

'*The Demon Lords!*'

'*No! Not Jayak!*'

'*It's true. Klara and I are trying to save him but we can't expel this without you. He talks to them and cannot be distracted from them - we need you. The magi will fill you in on your journey, but it's chaos at the palace and the temple. If Pocack hadn't come to the temple we could all have been lost.*'

'*Jayak will be all right?*'

'*Not unless you get here soon! Els, this is his life at stake and more if they keep control of him! They're eating away at his soul.*'

'*Gods! I'll be there.*'

'Els what is it? Your face.'

It's Jayak, he's in trouble.

'You're going, aren't you?'

I have to. It's more than just Jayak, it's Sytrannia itself at stake.

'You still care for him, though. Don't you? Don't you?'

Yes! And there's no need to shout at me. I will go because this is what is needed of me.

'What about what you want?'

This is bigger than that. I'll pack, tell Bronv-Grii to send someone to my house, I'll need the ship ready too. Briskly she walked off, ignoring Hwym.

'Do you even care what you're doing?' Hwym shouted, but Els' back remained turned.

Goddess, see me through this. Els prayed, tears falling as she readied herself for her next battle.

Part Two

Chapter 15

Els sat on the shoreline, scuffing her feet in the grey sand. Her parents' words were still echoing in her head,

'Why do you need to go there?' Gron had demanded. 'Sounds as if the problems in the South are of their own making.'

'And how can you solve them, anyway, dear? You're healing yourself. And I thought you'd forgotten all about this Jayak. You and young Hwym seem to be getting on so well.' Mavri added.

We're not. This has nothing to do with Hwym. I don't even want to hear his name again. Els wrote, tearing the paper in her fury and hugging Sorab close to her.

The argument had raged for some time, with tears on all sides, before Bronv-Grii stepped in and asked Els to let him speak to her parents alone. That had been several strokes past and Els had been left alone to reflect on her choice. But what choice was there, really? She had come to the shore because she knew Nai-kin's boat would be leaving with her on board, whatever her parents felt was best for her. It was not her will that mattered, but that of the gods, L'ra above all. If the trouble in Sytrannia is as serious as Kyrria said, well, I must go there, she thought. I have to help protect the temple and King Nahvib's country itself. Then there was Jayak. How could he have done wrong? For all his anger, surely he couldn't have meant harm to others? And injured himself? This was not the proud sorcerer she had left behind, it couldn't be. Still, a terrible chill went through Els as she recalled Kyrria's words. She had to help, what was taking Bronv-Grii so long?

She heard footsteps on the bank, then, occasional branches and twigs snapping. Turning, she saw only Nai-kin and Cranff making their way down the slope.

Where's B-G? What's happening? she scribbled.

'They're still talking to your parents,' Cranff sighed.

'But you're coming, girl, have no fear of that,' added Nai-kin.

'Your parents still don't agree, but Bronv-Grii insists you go. I will come with you, that way, the king can still carry out his plans. He'll say I didn't do enough in battle, left it to the elders. Besides, I think you should go with as many friends as possible, this situation doesn't sound good.'

'Truly spoken, Cranff. I don't like the sound of anything you've told us about Sytrannia, Els. The queen being ill so soon after the celebrations, that's a blow. Well, enough time for chat on the trip, let's get this vessel moving before it collapses.'

Certainly, it was evident that Nai-kin and his crew had played a vital part in recent events, for their ship bore many holes and dents. The Northerners, grateful for its aid, had done their best to repair it, but it still looked a sorry state. The sails were patched and the sides of the boat boarded up to prevent leaks. Its masts leaned at a precarious angle and it was clear the ship would not last much longer at sea.

But this was a journey it must make, for too much was at stake for it to fail now. Full of the weight of their mission, the crew set to work swiftly, Els and Cranff helping where they could. Once the journey was underway, Els was not the only one to be silent. Nai-kin called orders to his men, but didn't need to shout, for many were lost in thought and those who did speak only did so in the most subdued of tones. All of those afloat were wondering what they faced on their return and how they would cope with it. Cranff worried that the Southerners might not understand his contribution, might be hostile to a stranger in their land while they faced internal struggle. Cranff, lost to those around him, thought, how should I convince them I hope to help bring peace? Dri-angk, normally so tiresome, had lost his enthusiasm for pranks, troubled by this sudden news. He wondered how his mother was coping and sent a silent prayer to Ellari, trusting the goddess of children to care for his only parent. What if she's been ill, how dangerous is it there? Seeing the restless people around him, Nai-kin said his own prayer to Myrrine, 'Goddess of water, protect as us we cross your depths, for we must travel far and fast.' Els watched him from the kitchen, feeding Sorab as she observed those on the deck. She had said many prayers to L'ra herself, now all that was left was to trust her.

A week of clear waters and a strong wind behind them brought the sombre company back to Istalan's port. The relief at being home was tangible, but the fear was greater felt. They were so busy mooring the ship that they were all on land before Nai-kin spotted Zritz waiting for them.

'Zritz!' he called. 'We arrive safe and with the enemy's forces diminished in the North.'

'Let us hope miracles can also be worked here – soon.' Zritz said, without the trace of a smile. 'Els, I must see you alone before guards arrive to escort you to the palace.'

'Excuse me, but I am here from King Hurburt, I have come to help,' Cranff said, putting his hand forward. 'Lord Cranff, His Majesty's Chief Advisor.'

'Pleased to meet you, Lord Cranff. My name is Zritz, I'm one of King Nahvib's magi. Excuse what appears to be rudeness, but I must speak to Els briefly alone, before the escort comes.'

'I understand, circumstances precede etiquette.'

'Thank you.' Zritz turned to Els.

'What is it?' she asked, scared by the look on his face.

'Where should I start?' The magus sighed. *'You already know Jayak has betrayed us?'*

'I was told, I could hardly believe it.'

'Believe. His soul is with the Demon Lords, Klara wrestles them for his life as we speak. I'm working at the temple to see if we can save Plarina, but she's at least as threatened as Jayak.'

'When did this all start?'

'We still don't know, they must have worked for many

weeks at bringing us to destruction. Karryn's illness is no doubt their work and a lot of recent deaths and diseases are beginning to make sense. Many are the friends no longer speaking, the marriages disintegrating, most the subtle work of such agents as Jayak and Plarina.'

'Will Jayak recover? And Plarina?'

'None can tell. Long has been their pact with this evil, we have never tried to set one free from such bondage as this. The most important thing is that we have the prophecy, you must know of that before you take a step further on this ground.' So saying, Zritz unfurled a piece of paper from his pocket.

'You have it written down?' Els asked, incredulous.

'We guard it well; it is never the same person who carries it from one day to the next. It must be read only to those who are mentioned within the prophecy or who have been given authority by L'ra. Often, a person fulfils both demands. It is read aloud from this paper that the words be neither corrupted nor mistaken. Els, I have to tell you, choosing to hear this prophecy places your life at risk; the Demon Lords will stop at nothing to get hold of this and prevent it coming to fruition. We have already seen evidence of that.'

'I am ready, I must hear it.' Els sent calmly and stood still, awaiting the words that would show what was to happen, if the will of the gods came to pass. She thought of Fewh-Lok's words and listened well.

"A time cometh, in the sixteenth year of the reign of the eighth king of the House of Vib, that great strife shall fall upon the land of Sytrannia and beyond." Zritz paused to see if Els was following the old text. Satisfied, he read on,

"The gods prevent not this torment, for man makes his final choice over good or evil ways alone, but let him look to the gods and we show a way. If our way is to be heeded and our wisdom chosen, true justice prevails, but only if the path is followed closely. To this intent we place people and portents to guide the way – heed these well:

A warrior unlike any other must come from each

194

continent; this is the step of power. A battle must be fought on each land mass and the gods glorified in its success, this is the step of faith. There are Three Chosen who must all unite in Sytrannia with the blessing of the true gods. If all the battles are won and yet the Sorceress, the Healer and the Guardian do not meet, all is in vain. This is the wondrous final step, which all confusion works to confound."

'It's certainly clear there will be trouble and that we must choose the way of our gods. But how do we know when we are doing this? Why are you so sure I should be told this?'

'The Sorceress?' Zritz looked at her.

'Me? I'm only a wizard.'

'Do you think we have time to arrange the ceremony to declare you have sorcery? You have proved yourself in battle twice and thanked L'ra both times. Your clarity of power is exceptional in one so young – even without the power over the elements; you destroyed those who would use such ways.'

'But Jayak is a sorcerer; I'm not as powerful as him.'

'Look again Els, see how he is fallen and tell me still he has your strength. Half of his undoing has been his jealousy of your talents.'

'But there's so many things I can't do yet, I can't manipulate the elements, you said that yourself. I can't heal, either.'

'Then why do you come now? You come to save Jayak, don't you? You believe you can.'

'Well, yes.'

'I promise you this, save his life and his soul and you will be a sorceress. I will be the first to congratulate you. The Healer, Sorceress and Guardian will be shown us and I know you are both The Sorceress and the Warrior from the North, whether you do or not.'

'But what about the others?'

'Els, I cannot stay now, I am needed to assist Roro and Skrella. Ask Pocack and Durrew, but go to Jayak first.'

195

'Right, blessings to those at the temple. Good fortune with Plarina.'

'Cranff? We should go now.' The guards from the temple, to Els' delight, were Rayth and Timo. Though they were both looking very serious, Els relaxed a little to be protected by friends.

'What did he say?' Cranff asked, bewildered by the strange mood around him, not to mention the alien landscape.

'Things are bad, but we've got a few ideas...I think. How are you Rayth, Timo?'

'The goddess protects us, so we try to do the same for others. It's a relief to see you again, Els, even if I wish the circumstances were better,' Rayth said.

'The same here, Els. We'll probably see you a lot these coming days, we've been shepherding people from palace to temple a fair bit lately.' Timo added.

Els introduced Cranff and the four of them swapped news as they made their way to the palace. Most of what they had to say was frightening to hear, but they all listened intently, feeling they had to know what they might have to deal with. Rayth and Timo shared their fears for Plarina. Since being caught trying to steal the prophecy, she had fought her fellow priests and priestesses with a savage strength, possessed by the will of the Demon Lords. The previous day, Skrella and Roro had persuaded the magi to visit. They had been so horrified by the young woman's transformation, they had left Zritz to work with the chief priest and priestess to rid Plarina of the evil. At the palace, Pocack and Durrew had enlisted the help of their young students where they could, because too many people were badly infected for them to deal with alone.

Els and Cranff spoke of what had happened at Green Forest and the evil that had almost prevailed there. 'Were it not for Els, the sailors might never have made it in time.' Cranff said, heaping praise on the embarrassed Els. Rayth and Timo listened in horror at the news of how affected the villagers had been by the evil, but were cheered to see

196

that a difference had been made.

'Let's hope you can work L'ra's magic as well here,' Timo said, earnestly. For all the sharing between them, Els noticed that Cranff did not speak of King Hurburt's plans and no-one mentioned the prophecy's details. Too many secrets, Els thought bitterly, is this what they have brought us to?

They reached the palace and the guards were clearly relieved to see them.

'Thank you for bringing them safely,' The eldest one said to Rayth. 'We'll take you straight to the king, Els; he will talk with you first.'

'Goodbye. Send any news back with Kyrria,' said Rayth, cupping her hand over her fist in blessing. Why do we only do this on parting? Els wondered, returning the sign to Rayth and Timo. She didn't think of it for long, though, the marked change of atmosphere in the palace held her attention. There had not been as many guards before now, but increased protection she had expected. Inside, however, the mental energy was so erratic she would have gasped. She always experienced a range of emotions when reaching out in a crowd, but here, even in individuals, feelings surged and fell at alarming rates. King Nahvib's strong mental tone was at once that of a commanding monarch seeing success in things achieved, the next, the depths of despair as he vainly tried to rouse Karryn from sleep. Pocack and Durrew's tones could be felt, calming those around, but they also descended into fear and anxiety, burdened by the enormity of the task on their hands. Beyond these clear tones, other feelings on every side of the palace bubbled from high to low as events changed around people. From the attic rooms of the newest apprentices to the butler in the cellar, everyone was asking themselves, what next? When will it stop?

Cyru brought Els and Cranff to the king's drawing room and it hardly seemed the same room she had first met Sytrannia's ruler in.

'I hope you've got some good news,' whispered Cyru.

'Things are pretty desperate. The king's taken all this very badly, blames himself for not seeing it sooner.' Certainly, the room was full of noisy talk, with Pocack, Durrew and Drayk all accompanying the king. It was too much for Els to take in at once but she saw the reality of Cyru's words in the chaos there. They broke off when they saw their guests had arrived.

'Els!' The king sagged with relief, but it was Durrew who greeted Els with joy first before need, 'Thank the gods you're back safe. Kyrria said you were wounded but you look well. It's good to have you with us again, never mind the -'

'- circumstances? I've heard that a couple of times! I've heard a lot about our problems, too, how are we going to resolve them?'

'Let's start with the people we need to help first,' Pocack said. 'If we can help them, we are able to help others.'

'Plarina is already taken care of – Zritz, Skrella and Roro will save her or no-one can,' Durrew explained. 'Myself, Pocack and King Nahvib will wait on Karryn and combine our skills to rouse her. If we take you to Klara and the others, maybe you can assist Jayak, if you are happy to?'

'How can I refuse Jayak aid? You shouldn't need to ask me that, Durrew.'

'Very well, I thought you'd agree. Cranff, if you follow His Majesty, I'll take Els to her friends.'

'Can I help?' Cyru asked.

'No Cyru, thank you but you're not needed for the moment. Come, Els, but prepare yourself for change in all your friends,' Durrew warned her. He led Els along the corridor to Jayak's room. I know where I'm going, she thought, but when he opened the door, she knew why Durrew had led her there.

Three heads turned to meet her shocked gaze and Els couldn't decide which frightened her most. Klara and Alleri leant over the bed, only briefly breaking from their incantations to greet their friend. Turning back, they shuddered with the power of their spells, only speaking to each other in occasional whispers. Alleri had dark circles under her eyes and her curls hung lifeless and undecorated. Klara's eyes were bright, almost feverish with the will to cast away the influence of the Demon Lords in this room. By the window, unused to such intense magic, Kyrria paced. Up and down she walked, praying to her goddess, sometimes in hushed words, sometimes out loud, crying to L'ra for a sign of hope. Backwards and forwards she walked, hair unfettered, the moles on her cheeks standing out stark on skin suddenly pale. She turned to smile at Els warmly, but Els had hardly greeted her dearest friend when her attention was caught by the figure that lay on the bed.

It was Jayak, but she had to look twice to check. The man on the bed before her had lost a great deal of weight. He hardly resembled the vibrant young man who had first attracted her, animated in arguments, passionate in his feelings for her, fierce in battle. Now, he lay wasted while his friends fought to save him. He was still for a while, then rolled around, shouting about flames and power. Just as suddenly, such a fit would subside and he would fall motionless, but for the occasional shaking. Hearing his desperate moans, Els moved towards him. Shocked, she saw his face was a ghastly pale colour, yet sweat drenched his face and body.

'*Jayak!*' she screamed.

'Els? Els? I thought I dreamt you! Gods, you have to help me...I can't fight this thing...on my own. Help me.. No! No! You won't, you won't. Leave me, leave me alone! I don't want to anymore...I ..can't...you won't...be able..to..I have...friends. Aagh! No Quivviam, no! Not that! You can't. I...' His voice trailed off as he fought Klara and Alleri's restraining arms, coughs and awful oaths distorting his features.

'*Can't you do something?*' Els sent.

'Why do you think we called you?' said Klara, looking

at her friend.

'I can't help him alone'

'No, none of us can,' Kyrria spoke, the first time Els had seen her pause in prayer since she entered the room. 'We can only try and pray for the sending deep into his mind, asking for the outcome we desire. That is all.' She continued her pacing and prayer, but Alleri and Klara turned to Els.

'It could be dangerous, you realise that?' Els tried to argue.

'We have to try,' Alleri said, 'We can't just let him go.'

'No matter what he has done,' Klara said, sadly.

'Then what do we do, you're the healer?'

'We try and we pray, like Kyrria says.'

'As easily as that? Don't tell me, we must try. As the goddess wishes, so it must be.'

Els heeded the advice of her friends and joined their efforts willingly, though not without fear. The terror of the Demon Lords lay heavy on Jayak's heart. Every groan, every fit, spoke of this and the air crackled with an energy that was not welcome there. She drew circles on the floor with Alleri, waited while Klara poured powders into and across them, but though the evil energy wavered, it would not fade. For three long days, the friends tried every spell and casting they had been taught and, in their desperation, some they had only dimly heard about. But though they were prepared to give their every strength, nothing changed. Still Jayak writhed in torment while his friends tested their powers to the limit.

* * *

'I only hope the others are having more fortune.' Els said on the fourth day, thinking of Durrew, Pocack and King Nahvib at Karryn's side.

'Why don't we ask?' Alleri suggested and she sent to the Royal Chambers eagerly, glad for something she could do. *'King Nahvib? How does it go with Queen Karryn?'*

200

'It comes and goes, I have hope and then it dies.' Nahvib sounded exhausted himself. 'The magi work their magic, Cyru and Dayx have tried many times but they have made no difference either. Myself, I only hold Karryn's hand and think of how I wish to see it move again, to see her wake from this frightful dream we're all in. How is Jayak?'

'Not great. But you give me an idea, Your Majesty, perhaps a simple answer works as well as magic.' Alleri turned to her friends. 'Nahvib's given me an idea. We cast for Jayak, we fight for him, when did we speak to him? He needs to know we are here for him.'

'How do we do that?' Els was confused.

'Same as we do for any friend, reach out to him, speak to him and touch him. Let's make our presence known to him, make it more real than theirs is.'

'Very well. It sounds a little mad, Alleri, but you're right, we need to fight for Jayak as much as against the Demon Lords.'

Relieved at Els' agreement, Alleri took Jayak's left hand, Klara his right. For a moment, Els was confused. Then, she placed a hand over Jayak's heart and all the wrong he had done her was forgotten in that moment. The three sent deep into his mind, searching for the Jayak they knew of old. They found the terrifying truth in his soul, the war fought there between Demon Lords and the true gods, the torment that raged in Jayak's heart.

'Jayak, hear us, you are not alone! You are meant to be here, with us, on our side.' Els insisted.

'All they have told you is false. They promise untold riches, but deliver only a wasteland for your soul,' Alleri added.

'Jayak, hear where your soul really lies, come back to us, to your former way, that which the gods wish for you,' Klara sent.

They continued like this for some time, the pauses in their efforts punctuated by King Nahvib's frustrated cries at the far end of the corridor. Karryn's recovery didn't seem to be going any smoother, Els thought, sadly. But she didn't give up, she couldn't. This was Jayak, whom she loved, what reason could justify leaving him now, when he most needed her? *'L'ra, aid us, L'ra show us how to aid our friend. Give us strength and courage to save your former servant from his depths,'* Els prayed.

'Let the Demon Lords know failure. Spare this soul to fight against them another day, hear our prayers, noble L'ra,' Kyrria joined in.

The young women around Jayak held him close, reaching with all their power into Jayak's mind. For a long time they heard broken bits of his thoughts, as they had already. Els fought back tears, seeing him so desperate, so lonely. She seized on this, determined to challenge the desperation the Demon Lords had brought him to, *'Jayak! Don't listen to the doubt they bring to you, listen to the gods instead, listen to us.'*

'But... you won't want me any more, none of you... will,' Jayak replied, tentatively.

'What makes you so sure? You cannot know that,' Els sent.

'But I've done so much wrong. Els, I lied to you. My mind was not with you but with Quivviam and all she promised. I kept my thoughts hidden from all my friends, what hope for my future is there?'

'Every hope!' Alleri argued, *'Jayak, we are with you, I am with you. I always will be, all of us will help you if you only listen.'*

'Yes. Hear us. Come back from the place they hold you in,' Klara sent gently, yet insistently.

'I want to. I see them changing. What I remember of their promises is so clouded, so changeable now. But I don't know if I remember what I had before, what I have to return to,' Jayak panicked.

'You have love, mine and that of your friends,' Els said.

'You have power, remember the day you were declared a sorcerer?' Alleri sent, *'I was proud to be your friend. You don't need their promises, you have more than enough*

promise of your own.'

'Yes, yes.'

Feeling Jayak's courage return, his friends sent to this feeling, nudged it into the forefront, fed it their hope and love. He sat up and tried to speak, but fell back at once. He moaned loudly, babbling in fear, but his mind was clearer and they knew he felt the truth on their hearts. He shook his head, *Get away, leave me!* And though his friends had cause to fear his enemy, they rejoiced that he fought against it at last.

'I can't do it,' Jayak moaned. *'I can't fight it anymore. And, some of what they say is true – there will be no place for me in Sytrannia when this is done, how can there be?'*

'There will be, we need you,' Alleri insisted.

'I can't...I'm reaching all I can but... she's blocking me. Every time I try to see you properly, there's a cloud all around you, all I feel is fear and guilt. You tell me not to, but she won't let me forget my bond to them. Help me! Oh, gods, L'ra, help! Els! Alleri!'

'We need help, we need a magus or a sorcerer at least, we can't do this just we three wizards!' Alleri screamed.

'And where would we find a magus not working now?' Klara asked.

'There isn't anything we can do.' 'There must be, we can't let him die, not like this!'

'We won't,' Els sent decisively, *'I'm a sorceress and I say we can do it.'*

'Since when?' Alleri demanded.

'It's not official, but Zritz told me this afternoon.'

'Are you sure we can save Jayak, though?' Klara asked.

'I'm a sorceress, you're a healer and Alleri, you have the most experience with magic, besides, you're Jayak's oldest friend. We fight this with a real strength the way we care for him, know him.'

'We also know we have to for the war that we fight, Jayak is an important part of Sytrannia's magical talent and that must be saved,' Kyrria added.

'Then we agree? Let's use our gifts!' Els sent. Taking the lead, still keeping her hand upon his heart, Els began to cast, *'Fear that clouds, fear that holds, begone! Hate that binds, hate that hides, begone.'*

'Jayak, see, beyond, behind, above, resist your foes,' Alleri added.

'As anger burns, love heals. As guilt cracks, friendship mends. What fear chains, hope breaks. Like children to Ellari, like adventurers to L'ra, come home,' Klara sent.

Thirty strokes ticked by while they continued to cast. Jayak's eyes were open and his moaning subsided, but he was still far from them. Every casting they gave brought sweat out on his face and they knew they were close, yet their enemies would not loose their hold.

'Leave him to us, give up thine foolish hope!' A terrible cold voice invaded their minds and Els knew it was the voice she had heard in Jhrik-ansi. *'He is ours now, thine gods shalt not have this one!'*

'No-one spites the gods!' shouted Kyrria, 'We will not let you.' She strode over to the bed, her eyes bright. 'I lend my spirit now,' she said, placing her left hand on Jayak's head.

'Are you sure?' Els asked, *'Will this work?'*

'I haven't spent the last few days in prayer for nothing, Els. I trust L'ra to know what is right. As you have your skills, I come to this as a priestess and I say he will not be taken, for L'ra does not wish it so.'

The others nodded their approval and set to with renewed strength.

'Too much!' The dread voice of Quivviam cried. *'Leave off, leave off! I am Quivviam, leader of many Demon Lords, I will have my prize!'* She attacked the sources of Jayak's hope, but the four women only cast with further might,

'Out, vile one, Hrai called you, we banish you!' Els sent.

'It is not your time any longer!' Klara added.

'Go! Send this evil out! Jayak, this is not your burden!'

insisted Alleri.

'You are free, Jayak,' Kyrria called, but the attacks of the Demon Lord weakened the little talent she had. Sweat drenched her and she shook from head to toe with the force of what she must do. Yet she did not waver. Once, she looked skywards and murmured something to L'ra that the others never heard. She looked at Jayak, then, a final time. *'Begone from him! You are free Jayak, the goddess banishes your evil. L'ra be praised, that she should send me to do this!'* she said. Jayak sat up with a great start, but nothing was hidden behind his eyes any more. Kyrria staggered and fell into the chair. Alleri and Klara checked Jayak's breathing and found it normal. Though dazed, there was no longer confusion in his mind. Els, however, had realised the import of Kyrria's words, *'Kyrria!'* She sent a shattering mental cry as she rushed to her friend.

'It's all right, Els,' Kyrria said, opening her eyes and smiling gently. *'The goddess needs him more than me.'*

'No, no, Kyrria.' Els sobbed, shaking her friend, but Kyrria's skin was already clammy to the touch.

'You must fight the rest of the war, look to the prophecy,' Kyrria said. *'I kept my promise, I let no harm come to him. Goodbye, Els,'* Her eyes closed, her breathing stopped.

'No!!' Els called. *'Not Kyrria, not this price for Jayak's life!'*

Alleri and Klara gathered round their friend, but Els was oblivious. Tears ran down her cheeks and her fists were clenched white with a despair nobody could interrupt.

'Why, why do you demand this!' she asked the goddess, enraged, and was still asking that question when Pocack and Durrew entered the room.

Chapter 16

Pocack and Durrew looked at each other once in confirmation. The terrible blow to the girls had sent reverberations through the whole palace, so they came prepared for fallout. Pocack clapped his hands authoritatively and Alleri and Klara hastened to hear his words. Durrew went to Els and took the stricken girl in his arms. She sobbed violently and hardly heard a word the chief magus said. Klara and Alleri, however, sought comfort in Pocack's wisdom.

'Els, Alleri, Klara, I'm so very sorry that Kyrria is lost to us. Yet you may be proud of what you did here.'

'What, killing our friend?!' Els sent, fiercely.

'Banishing the evil was what I meant. Jayak is free and the curse he and Plarina wrought upon Istalan has been lifted.'

'What do I care about Jayak? His life is not worth losing Kyrria for.'

'Els, what Kyrria did was entirely voluntary. She knew what she was doing,' Durrew told her.

'She wouldn't do that; she wouldn't kill herself, not for him.' Els cast an angry look at Jayak.

Jayak wrapped his arms round himself and shivered, murmuring quietly. Occasionally he glanced at Els, but her look was so fierce each time that he turned away from the depths of her fury. Confused, he looked from one person to the next, then down at his own hands. Am I really here, without *them*? he wondered, shuddering at the reminder of that which had defiled him.

Pocack sighed. He knew none of today's workings would be made clear speedily, but someone had to begin the healing process. As chief magus, he tried to take that lead,

'Els, I know you are saddened and angry at this loss. I would expect no less, considering Kyrria's role in your life. However, I will not let you wallow in grief; neither

Kyrria nor her goddess would want that.'

'And, Els, I didn't mean she killed herself; all of us know Kyrria would do no such thing, she valued life highly. One day in her company and you knew that,' Durrew said. 'I do know, however, that she played her part in restoring harmony to the palace, knowing that her death was a possible result. She didn't seek her end, but let the goddess decide her fate. Her death must have been for the greater good or Kyrria would not have given it so readily.'

'I won't accept that. What kind of goddess demands such sacrifice? It doesn't make any sense.'

'Why should the words of our gods always make sense? What makes them accountable to us?' Pocack said gently.

'I won't stay and listen to this rubbish any longer; you're all crazy to believe it's all right for Kyrria to die.' Els stormed off, snatching up Sorab and slamming the door so hard behind her that the walls shook.

'She will need her friends around her now more than ever,' Durrew said.

'As will Jayak,' commented Pocack, looking at the two girls.

For their part, Klara and Alleri looked as dazed as Jayak himself. This end was not an event they could have foreseen; yet suddenly they were a part of one friend's death and another's salvation.

'I will go to Els, you stay here with Jayak,' Klara said.

'Very well,' Alleri replied.

Jayak, hearing himself under discussion, rose to remind the others he was in the room and able to hear them. The effort of movement was almost too much and for a horrible moment he swayed. I won't fall, I mustn't crumble now, he thought. Not when they've fought so hard to save me. Whatever they might think of me, at least I am still here to face it, surely that must be my strength? It was unnerving, though, not to see that blue flame before him, not to hear Quivviam's voice in his ear. His confidence wavered for a second, but he made it upright. He would draw from his friends' strength now, not that of any enemy.

'I'm fine,' he said, answering Pocack and Durrew's anxious looks, 'I know what's happened has been dreadful ... and I have a huge amount of responsibility to admit to in that. Nevertheless, if Kyrria's death is not to be entirely in vain, I would like to rejoin my friends in the fight against those who misled me.'

'Jayak, I wish I could accept you back so readily.' Pocack sighed. 'However, we must make sure you are completely cleansed and healed in mind and spirit before we can count you fit enough to practise magic again. Besides, the final say in your fate is the king's. What you dealt in amounts to treason. There can be no question of that.'

'Then let me see the king, I will convince him of my cure or nobody can!'

'Where is the king?' asked Alleri, suddenly aware that King Nahvib had not joined the magi in their hasty arrival. 'Doesn't he know what has happened this afternoon?'

'Indeed he does, but he must deal with his joy before he comes to face his pain in this loss,' said Durrew.

'Yes, today Karryn awakens and brighter than ever. She has no memory of her recent illness; it is as if she merely rises from sleep,' Pocack added.

'How can it be?' asked Jayak.

'Whatever spell you worked upon her has clearly been broken. That, at least, can be counted in your favour.'

'But I didn't cast any spell on Queen Karryn. Not that I remember, anyway.' Jayak couldn't recall any time when he had been asked to threaten the queen but he wasn't sure. He realised he would have a hard time tracking all his misdeeds.

'It'll be all right, King Nahvib will see that your heart is pure again, that you wish no more harm to anyone.' Alleri asserted.

'Let's hope Els is fine. Her grief is so deep; I must go to her.' said Klara.

'Well, when she's calmed down, maybe she'll see some sense in what everyone's telling her,' Alleri answered. 'Right now, Jayak needs reinstating before the next battle looms, I don't think the Demon Lords will let us rest easy on this victory.'

* * *

Els lay sobbing in her room for some hours.

'Els? Stop crying,' sent Sorab, pawing at her gently.

'Kyrria's dead, Sorab. Don't you understand? She was my first real friend and now she's dead. All because of Jayak.'

'But Els, you see your friends now?'

'And who are they?'

Sorab sighed and snuggled in to Els, hoping his company was some comfort even if his words weren't. Els certainly wasn't prepared to listen to any of her human friends. Even after her tears had dried, she kept the door shut on Klara's calling. Several times Els' friend shouted to her, said consoling words to a silent door. After a little while, she went, though Els could hear her whispering to King Nahvib and the magi in the corridor. 'Then we'll leave her for now,' The king said. 'She'll talk to others in her own time.' His footsteps faded with the others' and Els lay on her bed and cried again. She remembered all the times she had cried in the past year, but none compared to now. Lots of times she had missed her parents, doubted her purpose in the South, yet Jayak had always been there to comfort her. Now, the one she had relied on so much was the last person she could trust her feelings to. Every time she thought of the face she had loved so dearly, she saw only the torment of evil upon it and the sadness with which Kyrria had bidden her goodbye. Els spent the evening alone with such thoughts until she fell asleep.

Deep in sleep, she found herself in a dark forest. The trees hemmed her in, but she could hear someone calling far away.

'Help, give them the answer or they will kill me!' The voice shouted, 'Show yourselves or we are destroyed. Where are you all? We summoned The Three. Why do you not show yourselves?'

Els tried to answer, to call that only she was in the forest, but her mental shouts went unheard and the distant voice cried again and again the desperate call for aid she knew she could not give alone. She tried to move towards the speaker, but every move she took she seemed further from the shouts. Around her, strange shadows muttered and she cast anxious eyes about her. Nothing came forward, nothing attacked, but the feeling of peril remained. Sorab scampered near her feet, but human help was nowhere to be seen.

Scared more than she had been by any dream before, Els woke with a dreadful feeling of desolation. No-one will help, she thought, no-one can. So she was not in the best of moods when Alleri knocked at her door.

'I'm coming in, whether you like it or not. I can cast a spell to open this door and I doubt you've the strength left to keep it off,' she shouted.

'Leave me alone,' Els insisted.

'Why? I'm not Klara to be frightened off so easily.' Alleri tapped the door three times and called Els' name. The door opened at once, revealing Alleri in a light cloud of purplish dust.

'Don't make me do that again!' Alleri spluttered, waving the dust out of her eyes. *'Anyway, when are you coming to join us in drawing up plans for the next attack?'*

'Why, so someone else can get killed?'

'Don't be stupid, we have Jayak back now and Karryn and the others are well again.'

'I'm pleased about Queen Karryn. But I can't be glad about Jayak, not now.'

'Els, be fair. Jayak needs help too. This wasn't all his fault,' argued Alleri.

'You're very understanding all of a sudden.'

'He is my oldest friend. Just because he made a

mistake, we shouldn't abandon him now.'

'I don't know how you can say that, Alleri.'

'We need to be in this together. You didn't mind playing at sorceress, now live with the results like the rest of us.'

'There isn't time enough to heal the hurt; that's my result!' Els rejoined.

'Speak to L'ra then. Surely the goddess can make clear what happened here?'

'The goddess? Where was she when Kyrria helped Jayak? She didn't see to her servant's need there did she? I don't even know if I can follow her anymore.'

'Don't say that!'

'What do you want me to do? Pretend I see sense in this? Go and smile at Jayak, welcome him into my arms again? Talk to the magi about the plans for the future like nothing happened? I've lost everything I trusted in, Alleri, if you can't see why, then I don't think we have much to say to each other.'

'Not now, that's for sure. I'll try again when you've had time to think straight,' Alleri said, walking out.

'No amount of thinking will right this!' Els sent behind her.

The argument with Alleri haunted Els, for she could not see how her friends' views could differ so from hers'. She could hear their thoughts so clearly, she was amazed at how quickly Klara, Dayx and Alleri welcomed Jayak back into their group. What about all you told me before? she thought. You told me he was arrogant, you told me he has little time for others. You could see what was wrong in Jayak, only when he kills our friend you welcome him back, treat him like a king. And all the while you look upon me strangely for missing my closest friend. What has happened to us all?

Els found no more comfort in authority; Pocack's stern sendings bringing her to lectures three weeks after Kyrria's death. *'Come now!'* He sent simply, with no room for argument. So Els went to his lecture, but made no

211

effort to learn from her instructors. She traipsed into the hall as Pocack was introducing his subject, causing curious looks all round. Her hair had not been washed since her return to Istalan, her clothes had been picked from her bedroom floor at random and her fingernails were bitten so short they bled. Els had deliberately left her cape in her room and took a seat alone near the back. She ignored Alleri's looks and Klara's coaxing, their sympathy was useless to her now.

Pocack spoke for some time about the power of healing and most students listened attentively. The past months had seen a few friends lost to this dread foe and many wanted to apply a solution. Klara leaned close to hear the chief magus' words, muttering under her breath as she thought through the implications of what was said. Cyru's pen raced over his paper and he was soon borrowing more from Dayx. Cyru had been part of the group who saved Matzi from death, so he sought fresh comfort in the unexpected power healing spells had shown him.

Els, however, made no notes and scarcely heard what Pocack taught. Once she heard him begin on healing, she scorned him for his hypocrisy. No-one healed Kyrria, they only took from her, pounded through Els' head, to the exclusion of all else. Pocack approached her after the lecture before she could escape.

'Tomorrow evening is Kyrria's funeral; I assume you have heard of this already?'

Reluctantly, Els nodded. Half the palace was discussing it, she could hardly pretend she hadn't picked up such obvious news.

'Then you will be there, at the temple?'

'*Why, what good does it do now? Isn't it a little late for Skrella and Roro to decide to take care of Kyrria?*'

'*They had no choice and in your heart, you know that as well as I,*' Pocack insisted, dropping into mental voice to ensure his admonitions remained private. '*Besides, you don't know what good this might do you. Maybe laying Kyrria to rest will provide you with some relief? I can't promise anything, Els, but I think you at least owe Kyrria a proper farewell.'*

'Very well, but I only attend to say goodbye to Kyrria. You needn't think Roro and Skrella will be able to talk me into being happy – or following L'ra any further.'

'Strange you mention the two things together, don't you think?' Pocack walked off, leaving Els with his challenge. Goddess, stay with this one, please, he prayed.

Els forced herself to go about her studies that day and the next, for time alone was resolving nothing. There could hardly be any tears left in her, or so she thought, but a tiny phrase or thought would remind her of Kyrria and they would flow again. Twice she struggled to hold her grief back in Durrew's lessons. Before the first day was out, the back row of his classroom had become her accustomed place, for she gained no comfort from the sympathetic looks of her classmates. Durrew at least left her alone, not asking her questions or following her about as Pocack and Zritz seemed to. His eyes were concerned and his tone was gentle, but there were no questions and she was grateful for that.

So she dragged herself through the hours concentrating on her work and little besides, giving herself no room for thoughts. Only in her afternoon lesson, the last before the funeral, did she lose her control. Tears welled up during the final casting of the wind spell they had learnt. She tried to concentrate, the elements were still forces she battled with, but she remembered how she had prospered in castings, while Kyrria had been unaided. She couldn't cast, just couldn't. Then she cried. Huge tears ran down her cheeks and soon her face was hot with crying. Sorab woke up as Els' tears wetted his fur, but Els didn't even notice. She was lost in the torrent of her anguish. *'Oh Kyrria, why you?'* she sent, not meaning to, but losing control of her talent in her grief. Angrily pushing past the other students she raced out of the building. Her tears blinded her and she ran on as if in a dream until she found herself at the temple.

213

Everything was quiet: she guessed most people were inside, praying. She ducked into the basement, and carefully crept down the corridors, Sorab hugging the wall beside her, until she found the room next to the hospital, the room where Kyrria's body lay. Els stood looking at her friend, remembering the joy and humour they had shared. Part of her wanted a miracle, felt sure the young priestess would sit up and laugh at her confusion. But really she knew this would not happen. Instead, Els took Sorab in her arms and bent down to stroke her friend's hair. Sorab rubbed Kyrria's cheek with his ear, saying his own farewell.

Overcome with emotion, Els left the room in a rush, nearly colliding with Timo.

'What are you doing here?!'

'I needed to see her. What about you? Not praying for her?'

'No,' Timo shrugged, *'Won't bring her back, will it? Come on, I'll walk you back to the gate.'* As they got there, they paused.

'Thanks for walking me back, Timo, I'm glad you were here.'

'That's okay. Els, I'm sorry, I wish I could make it better...'

He touched her face then and looked at her in a way he never had before. Suddenly, he touched his lips to hers, but Els quickly pulled away.

'Timo, what are you doing? You're a priest!'

'I thought...you looked sad and, I thought you wanted to be with me.'

'Not like that!'

The priest took a step forward, but Sorab hissed at him as Els made her way back to the palace.

Neither of them saw the face watching from an upper window.

* * *

214

It was a quiet party that wound its way to the temple of L'ra. King Nahvib and Queen Karryn led the way, wearing their state robes, Nahvib's purple and Karryn's a sombre grey-green, buttoned to the neck. Though both wore their crowns, for this was a ceremony, neither wore any jewellery, nor did their subjects. The magi followed, long robes pinned so as not to flap about, for tonight would take them to the desert where the evening winds were sharp. Els bent her head low as she walked, making sure her cape was secured like her friends'. Klara smiled at her sympathetically. Els tried to return the smile, but it was a feeble effort. Between thinking about Kyrria and wondering about what had happened with Timo, Els could concentrate on little besides. Alleri only occasionally looked her way; she was talking to Jayak, for he was very pale and kept glancing about nervously. Cyru and Dayx walked alongside him as well, all three sensing Jayak's vulnerability. What about me? Els wanted to scream. A tiny voice within her said she could walk with Klara that the others would talk to her if she let them. But Els squashed this voice, these were not words she wanted to heed.

They went in the temple gates and were met by the chief priest and priestess, solemnly resigned to their task. The group were brought to the coffin which lay beneath L'ra's statue, as it had since Kyrria's death. It was open and a few minutes passed in silence while those who had known Kyrria looked upon her silent form. Only one who had known her was absent.

'Where's Plarina?' Els sent to Rayth.

Rayth's large eyes filled with tears, '*We will not be seeing Plarina much now, Els,*' she sent. '*Plarina doesn't recover as Jayak did. They have converted the end of the East wing to a safe room for her.*'

'*A safe room, what do you mean? She isn't dead, then?*'

'*No, I think it is worse than that. Her mind is gone, Els. She rants, tears her clothes, cries bitter curses or descends* into hysteria. Her room is made safe so that she does not hurt herself. The furniture is bolted to the floor, nothing made of glass or resembling string is allowed near her. I haven't been permitted to see her yet. Later they say, but I don't know when that will be. I have heard her though, such cries I cannot bear. Many are the nights I've taken extra guard duty to avoid them. She may not be dead, but I have lost two friends in this.'

'And Jayak lives yet!'

'Only the goddess knows why, but her purpose will be revealed when we need to see, I am sure.'

'I do not have your certainty, only Sorab keeps me going now.'

Rayth turned to listen to Roro, so Els could not be sure what she had made of her comment.

'We will now take Kyrria's body to the desert, where Skrella and I will recite the final prayer. Those who are to aid us, step forward.'

Rayth and Timo stepped forward. As they did, Els saw that their normal clothes had been swapped for jade tunics and trousers trimmed with gold. Rayth's face and the terrible story she spoke had so occupied Els that she had not noticed the temple people wore the only bright colours in the group and she wondered at this. She had time to muse over it as she followed the coffin as it was wheeled to the desert. By now, it was already dark and the torches carried by the priests and priestesses lit the ground as the stars lit the sky. When the small cart with the body was wheeled to the point an equal distance from temple and palace, its bearers stopped. Timo was standing next to Els now and gave her arm a small tug. Els did her best to stare firmly ahead, but could not resist glancing his way. Timo gave her a cautious smile, then Skrella began to speak, 'Goddess L'ra, recognise your priestess, Kyrria, honour her with a place in your home.'

'Mighty are the works she has done in your name.' Roro continued the prayer.

Listening to his words, Els looked again at her friend's

body. She found herself calmed by the peace on Kyrria's face, glad to see her one final time.

'...dedicated in her life, honourable in her death, we give her back to you L'ra and praise you for the gift of knowing her.' Roro finished

Els wept then, tears coursed her face as she realised she had to give vent to her emotions, she could not lose such a friend and not mourn the passing in some external way. *'Are you all right?'* Timo sent, shielding closely.

'Yes, I think I might be now,' Els replied.

Everyone was either crying or offering their own prayers to L'ra, so Timo felt bold enough to take Els' hand in his. Moving quickly away as the mourners left, Els hurriedly shook it off, hoping no-one had noticed. But when the following morning saw most people keen to put recent events behind them, Alleri had not forgotten seeing Els' hand in Timo's.

Chapter 17

That night was Els' first peaceful one in many days. She had begun to believe she would never slip easily into sleep any more, but suddenly she found herself drifting off, without a dream to remember. The same could hardly be said of her old friends, however. Timo fell in and out of sleep. Happy dreams of being with Els soon subsided as he woke, anxious that his leaders might find out the truth.

But the person most wide awake was Alleri. While those around her indulged in dreams or wrestled with nightmares, she sat alert at her desk.

Had she really seen what she thought she had or was she just imagining it? No, there was no doubt about it, she knew she had seen Els take Timo's hand. But did it mean anything? Alleri recalled the events of the last traumatic week. Maybe that was why Els had been so reluctant to spend time with her friends – she had been with Timo! Alleri was convinced she had stumbled onto something but had no way of proving it – yet. She resolved to speak to Klara in the morning. She could be trusted to give her opinion on this new development without sharing it with others. After all, nobody would want Jayak to hear such strange rumours so early in his recovery.

Thinking that made her angry. Here was Els railing against Jayak, blaming him for everything, when she herself was far from blameless. But what should I do about it? she wondered.

* * *

Jayak certainly had enough to think of without any additional problems. He rose in the morning with a crippling headache. The only relief he could feel was that at least this ailment was the result of stress, not any external influence. But he knew it would be some hours before he could relax. Today, the magi, King Nahvib, Roro

218

and Nobleman Drayk met to discuss his fate. By the evening, Jayak would know whether he could remain a practising sorcerer or be asked to surrender his robe. He didn't want to leave his friends now, more than ever he wanted to stay and prove he had changed. But surrendering his robes, being found guilty of treason, this would make his position in the palace, even in Istalan, impossible. How could he leave Alleri and Klara when they were so keen to help him, though? As for Els, could he ever leave her? He knew a part of him would always feel responsible for her fate, no matter what happened between them. Jayak sighed, the palace gardens below him were beautiful this time of year, yet he could not enjoy them.

'Worried?' a gentle voice beside him said.

Jayak turned to see Queen Karryn approaching. She smiled and it seemed beyond belief that she could ever have been as ill as was reported. Jayak trusted his friends, though, for their hushed tones had spoken of a marvel as amazing as his own salvation.

'Hello,' he said, nervously.

'You are concerned, but Jayak, there's no need.' Karryn assured him.

'Easy for you to say, you haven't done the things I have,' he replied. 'My own friends distrust me. Dayx and Klara are cold towards me, Cyru is openly set against me. I have known him since I was a boy, yet he turns from me, encourages the others to ignore me. And King Nahvib believes I endangered your life, how can he be expected to forgive that?'

'He doesn't need to. I know there was no casting from you and the magi will support that.'

'How can you tell?'

'I know it sounds strange, but I never picked up any evil feelings from you. I was terribly afraid for Nahvib, he could almost see his country disintegrating around him. I never feared for myself, though, and you were close to me all that time, living and practising in the palace.' Karryn

219

argued.

'I still fought for the enemy. It was treason and the king can't risk it happening again.'

'What if he knew it wouldn't happen again? I'm certain the magi will argue that as the case. You have strong friends and colleagues, Jayak, don't lose sight of that.'

'Thank you Karryn, maybe I should go and find some of them.'

'Good idea, Jayak. Don't worry, I have every faith in your reinstatement, I have told Nahvib that.'

'I hope he listens. Thank you, Queen Karryn.'

When Jayak found the others they were drinking at the King Mahrib. Alleri, Cyru, Klara and Dayx were gathered together, surprisingly, with Els. Jayak was tempted to draw back when he saw her, but curiosity kept him moving. It was the first time he had seen Els socialising since the tragedy. What could this mean?

'Hello, you lot,' he said, trying to sound cheerful.

'Hear anything?' Alleri asked, ignoring Cyru's foul look.

'Not yet. Although Queen Karryn did stop and speak to me, she's fairly optimistic.'

'Well, that ought to count for something.'

'Anyway, I think I need a drink, anyone want something?'

'Wine all round, day like today,' Alleri suggested.

The others all nodded, displaying glasses already once emptied.

'You too, Els, old enough to drink publicly now?' Jayak asked, regretting his question the minute it left his lips.

'Why has everyone got a sudden interest in my age today?' Els snapped.

'I only asked.'

'Yes, that's what Alleri said earlier.'

'Because I care, I wouldn't want to see you hurt that's all,' Alleri insisted.

'What's that supposed to mean?'

'You've suffered enough, I don't think you should do anything you're not ready for,' said Alleri.

'I'm not going to get drunk. I'm only going to have a couple of drinks with my friends, I think I can handle that.'

'That's the trouble isn't it? We always think we can handle things when we start them, don't we?' Alleri's tone was sharp.

'Alleri, I really don't know what your problem is!'

'Els, calm yourself. We just don't want to take advantage of you being the youngest here, that's all,' Klara said.

'It never made any difference before. I was old enough to win a battle, old enough to be seduced by Jayak, old enough to witness my closest friend's death! What makes anyone here suddenly think I'm too young for anything?!'

'Maybe I shouldn't have come,' Jayak sent, radiating tension.

'Maybe not,' agreed Cyru.

'Sit down, Jayak, get over it,' Dayx told him. 'I know me and Klara just came out for some good wine and companionship. We all need a break from what's happened recently. Don't we Cyru?'

'If you say so, Dayx,' said Cyru, though he still looked far from happy.

'Get the drinks, Jayak, that's what we came for.' Alleri said, glaring at Els.

The conversation was stilted after that, Klara and Dayx trying to keep the talk from flagging but Cyru resolutely ignoring Jayak. No matter what was said, Kyrria's death and the decision over Jayak's fate were both weighing hard on their friends' hearts. When they were just about to give up and go back, Jayak started, hands falling from his glass.

'Jayak, we have made our decision. Meet us in the king's common room,' Pocack sent.

'*Very well,*' Jayak replied. 'I have to go now,' he told his friends. 'They have an answer.' He left the table, but Els took his arm. *'Jayak, I...'* she tried to say she wished him well, she hoped the decision was positive, but she couldn't. The words stuck short, she couldn't get them out.

'*Let the goddess go with you, Jayak,*' Klara said.

Els thought this was strange indeed, how can any gods be with him? she wondered. But Alleri was nodding, even Cyru managed a smile, forced as it was. Els felt alone again, things were suddenly back to how they were when she first arrived in Istalan and the others were discussing L'ra. Is this it, is everything down to this difference? Am I always to be set apart by their culture, just as my gifts make me a stranger in my homeland? She felt like crying out, but even if she could have, who would she cry to? Family were as far away as friends in their own way. As for L'ra, where was she? Did she even exist? She hadn't been there when Kyrria died, or she wouldn't have allowed it, surely?

Els wanted to run from the group then, wanted desperately to be out of this tight-knit unit that didn't include her. She couldn't run out straight away though, that would look like she was following Jayak and she didn't want that. So she sat, suffering her old friends until a decent interval had elapsed. Then she left, her first thought to seek Timo out, see if he still had any consoling thoughts, or whether that was a sham too.

In the royal chambers, Queen Karryn was tidying the flowers her many well-wishers had sent. She straightened the last bouquet and stopped, seeing Els make her way across the courtyard to the palace. Karryn sighed deeply.

'Are you well, Your Majesty? Not too tired I hope?' enquired Matzi, anxiously.

'No, only sad that our young ones must live through so much torment.'

Karryn had seen Jayak arrive earlier, short of breath, his skin a ghastly colour. She wondered if Els knew he was here. Karryn could see Els was also nervous, she guessed Kyrria's death still hung like a shadow over the friends. 'Why must each suffer alone, why do they not go

222

to each other?' she asked her maid, but Matzi had no more idea than her mistress.

But it was Jayak who made it back to the palace first and so it was his fate that was made the clearer.

Enter! sent the magi.

Jayak cleared his throat once and opened the door. He later said it was the most difficult entrance of his life. The three magi were seated on the sofa, to their right, King Nahvib, First Minister Drayk and Chief Priest Roro sat on high-backed chairs. Though they did not glare, neither did they smile and it was with caution that Jayak approached the chair in the centre of the room. He felt as if his legs would melt, but forced himself onwards. The journey from door to the chair provided for him was twelve of Jayak's strides, though it needed all his will to take them calmly.

'This case has been a difficult one to decide. Long and hard we have talked, indeed, argued, until the right decision could be made with the consent of all,' Pocack said.

'The crime was great, as were its repercussions, so you must understand, there is to be no bargaining over the sentence, hard as it may seem,' Drayk added, looking at Jayak most severely.

'Jayak, do you agree to accept the decision of this counsel, without argument, willingly and completely?' asked Durrew, showing more obvious concern for his former pupil.

'I do,' Jayak said, bowing his head.

King Nahvib rose then. Jayak, lifting his head, was filled with awe. The king wore his full robes, a deep purple, lined with a lighter shade. He wore his crown and the many jewels native to Sytrannia were shown to their greatest advantage in it. When King Nahvib looked at Jayak, his face showed some sorrow, but purpose was there and all present knew that his word was righteous in this matter.

'Jayak, it is known that you have betrayed my rule in

undermining the palace, the very capital itself, by allying yourself with the Demon Lords. Furthermore, you have betrayed the calling of your talent in using your magic for the path of evil.'

The young sorcerer nodded once in response. Oh, he wanted to flee more than ever, but he knew he must stay and find out his fate, though he thought he could not bear it.

'Many have spoken in your defence and I am assured you are no longer a threat, indeed that you wish to work again to serve your king and the magi.' King Nahvib continued. 'Ultimately, I am inclined to agree, yet I cannot let your betrayal go unpunished. You will be free to live in Sytrannia wherever you choose, to mix with who you wish. You shall go unheeded in this land and help our purpose if you so desire – if you are able.'

'Thank you.' Jayak answered him.

'Do not be so quick to rejoice. The greatest evil in your actions was your threat to the will of the gods. Yet, through much discussion, we have to accept that the gods must also seek some purpose through you.'

'Otherwise, my sister Kyrria would not have given her life to save yours.' Roro added.

'This is the truth we come to,' Nahvib agreed. 'You must not threaten the prophecy by your life or freedom, so we say you must help us in its fruition and the bringing about of the gods' triumph over the Demon Lords. We hereby decree that you shall practise no magic, great or small, personal or public, until you have the forgiveness of each of The Three. For as it was their purpose you threaten, so it shall be in your hands to facilitate their unity.'

'But, we don't even know who The Three are. I know you believe Els is the Sorceress, but she will never forgive me Kyrria's death! And how am I to ask forgiveness of the two I don't know?' Jayak's head swum.

'That will be your task. Maybe this is why you were saved, maybe you have some insight we do not yet know.

But you must not speak of this condition to any other. If forgiveness was to be given only for the greater purpose, it would not be given with a true heart and neither you nor The Three would benefit from that.' Pocack warned him.

'Very well. I accept this sentence and will seek its answer to the best of my ability.'

'I am pleased, Jayak.' King Nahvib smiled. 'Though your misdeeds saddened me, it was not my wish to lose you if you could yet be saved from such evil. May you find peace along with the truth we all seek.'

A little while later, the magi had almost begun to relax. The trial they had awaited so nervously had passed as they had hoped it might, perhaps now they could look to some hope in this battle. But peace was not yet theirs, as a steady knocking on the door told them.

'Come in Alleri!' Pocack called.

'Is every young person to see us today?' Durrew asked.

'Indeed, it seems our students compete as to who would change the course of our history the most! But speak, Alleri, we know you would not come on an idle errand.' Zritz beckoned the young girl.

'I would speak with you about Els…and Timo.' Alleri said.

'Timo?' Roro asked, confused.

'It's not that I want to get anyone into trouble, it's just…' Alleri's voice trailed off, Why did I come here? she thought, but she knew she had had little real choice.

'You speak as if it is of little import, but your mind is clouded with anxiety. Wait!' Pocack's brows furrowed as he sought the secret Alleri held. *'Gods, is this true?'*

'Yes. I saw them at the temple, when I had to talk to Skrella about arrangements, and then again at the funeral. I didn't want to tell you but…if Els is encouraging someone to break their vows…'

'Is nothing untouched in this kingdom?' Roro cried. 'I will have to deal with Timo at once.'

'I'm sorry,' Alleri said, 'I didn't mean to cause more

trouble, but, Els is confused already. Not to mention Jayak. I couldn't let this carry further on.'

'Certainly not. Karryn will speak to Els, halt this thing now, then we can proceed with that we had already planned. That will be all, Alleri, thank you.'

* * *

It was a subdued and obedient Els who climbed the steps to the auditorium to be made sorceress three weeks later. She didn't look at Alleri. Timo had avoided Els to the extent of practically running away when he saw her, especially when Alleri was around. Although she didn't want the kind of attention Timo had offered, it saddened her to see another friendship slip away. It was you, she thought, I don't know how, but you did or said something. She started to think how this might have been, but soon dismissed that train of thought. Today was about her powers and the next step to be taken with them.

'Els, today we recognise your progression from wizardhood to sorcery.' Pocack announced. 'Great have been your powers in battle and at peace, for the sake of friends and of strangers.'

'We see the talent invested in you by the Goddess L'ra and we acknowledge it now,' added Zritz.

'We call you sorceress, let faith guide your purpose always,' Durrew said. Pocack smiled and stepped forward to give Els her cloak.

'This cloak we exchange for the cape, as you have moved from learning to accomplishment. Yet even we magi must learn still, let faith be the cloak to all things, as Durrew said.'

Thank you,' Els took the cloak, rich jade material showing no golden trim. Then she turned it over and found it was lined with delicate gold thread within. This was a fine gift and its proclamation of her new role overwhelmed her.

'Congratulations!' called Vanya and Aashti, joyful to

find more female company at their level, her shouts soon joined by all present. Jayak cheered as loud as any other. *She deserves such recognition*, he thought, *while I deserve my punishment. How am I to turn such events around, though, without the use of magic to guide me now?*

Try as Jayak might to avoid it, the circumstances created tension amongst the friends.

'When will they let you practise again?' Alleri asked. It seemed she asked but casually, still passing around the pieces for Arram's game. Yet her look was intent and Klara sighed to herself.

'It is not that I am forbidden, more that I cannot practise,' Jayak answered.

'Then what happened with Kyrria affected your powers?' pressed Alleri.

'Sort of, I don't wish to talk about it, Alleri,' Jayak said.

'Els' powers are not affected, though. Why should that be?'

'Maybe because I didn't kill anyone?!' Els sent, shocked.

'So, you are blameless, now?' Alleri asked.

'What do you mean, of course I am! I had no hand in Kyrria's death.'

'And all else that you have done has been of pure intent, has it?'

'Alleri, stop now,' Klara beseeched her friend.

'Why? Why should I hesitate to say what we all know? You used Jayak for his experience, his talent, then you leave him when he has need of aid and take up with Timo. It's obscene that you stand here now and let Jayak take all blame!'

'Alleri, how dare you?!' Els was furious.

'Easily enough. Everything was fine until you turned up. Now it's all messed up and you walk about unscathed, a sorceress while Jayak cannot practise.'

'Alleri, this is not your argument, please, stop.' Jayak

put a cautionary hand on Alleri's arm, but she would have none of it.

'I am not alone in thinking this,' she sent. *'It is just that I will speak what others think. Isn't it?'*

'There is truth in what Alleri says,' Cyru put in, slowly.

'No, don't say it,' Klara cried.

'Klara, you know as well as I that Jayak dealt in no evil before she came here,' Cyru said. Next to him, Sorab hissed and nipped at his ankles.

'Yes!' Alleri was triumphant. *'There was no-one to pressure Jayak before you. We would aid him, but you only sought to compete with his power. No wonder he was driven to desperate measures.'*

'You cannot justify what he did!' Els argued, but she was uncertain now, the faces of her friends were suddenly turned against her in anger and jealousy.

'Neither is there justification for what you did with Timo, yet you go rewarded where Jayak goes punished.'

'Alleri, what about Kyrria's death?' Klara asked.

'If Els had been more interested in her friend's fate than scoring points against Jayak, who knows what may have happened?' Alleri said. *'After all, if you hadn't run off to the North, maybe Jayak would have told you of his errors and Kyrria wouldn't even have been threatened.'*

'I had to go.'

'Why, to get back with your people? You were supposed to be Jayak's lover but you deserted him when he needed you most. No, Klara, I won't stop. Els, you don't deserve someone like Jayak.'

'Is that what this is, envy?'

'That's enough, Els. Alleri is right. Things have been different since you came, and you have little claim on our friendship after all that has happened since your arrival. I'm sorry but perhaps you had best go elsewhere with your powers,' Cyru said, in a voice that left no room for disagreement.

Els looked around her in horror, but no voice rose to her defence. Klara bowed her head, Jayak turned away. He

228

wanted to tell them why he could not practise magic, take the blame from Els, but could not. Cyru and Dayx stood hostile, unmoved. Alleri turned from Els to Jayak, making clear where her loyalty lay.

'I will not forget this!' Els cried, and left the room.

There was no time to cry. I am a sorceress, she said to herself. I must work with my power, even if it is not to be done here. For a long time she sat in her room and thought about what she must do now. Oh, L'ra, where are you in my time of need? she thought. If you are here, guide me through these battles. For it seems I am at home in neither North nor South these days and can trust no-one. She didn't feel any reply, couldn't decide if L'ra was listening, if she was still there. *'She does listen,'* sent Sorab. Els wasn't sure but she knew she must make a move. The clouds of evil gathered day by day and their bursts of malevolence punctuated lives like lightening unhindered. Determined to act she sought out Pocack, for once alone in the magi's common room.

'Good afternoon. Or is it? You look unwell,' he commented.

'I am troubled by the distance between myself and my friends.'

'And that which separates you from the gods?'

'Maybe. As it is, I have decided to leave. I mean to carry on the fight, but not from here, not now.'

'Perhaps it is as well, though you must stay in contact. Where will you go, home again?'

'Where is that?' Els thought of Gartron, her parents still confused, the tension that remained between herself and Hwym, were things any better there?

'Where then, Els, think carefully.'

Els wondered for a time. She didn't want to go far, not to another continent. Yet she must leave Istalan, of that she was certain. Then she realised. There was one place which needed help, which would perhaps welcome such aid she had to offer. Maybe she would find some comfort in the place where everyone was starting afresh.

'I will go to Jhrik-ansi, for I hear they are rebuilding there,' she answered.

'Yes,' muttered the mherl, nibbling Els' neck.

'Hmm,' Pocack considered, 'That could be a good idea. Queen Karryn will also be pleased, she too, would like to see a hope arise from there. Go then, Els, with the blessings of all the gods. May you know them anew in your work in Jhrik-ansi.'

They shook hands and Pocack was the only one to see Els and Sorab as they left.

Chapter 18

Els ran to the stables and gently called Audcy, *'Audcy? Time to travel again, quickly, my friend.'* She saddled the horse hastily, stroking Audcy's mane to calm her. Els did not want to be found by Brin. If she left swiftly, Pocack could spread the news of her departure with more calm than she would manage. 'Mreak?' Sorab called.

'Yes, now if you are coming!' Els told him and Sorab jumped onto her cloak. He sniffed excitedly, seeming to give his approval to her new garments. I only hope they were not given in vain, Els thought. Still, Jhrik-ansi would be a good place to test her powers, if Pocack's words were true any help would be welcomed there. He spoke of a rebuilding both practical and magical, where she could be useful without feeling threatened.

Once Els had left Istalan, she relaxed her pace, much to the relief of Audcy. Without an immediate threat of battle to coerce her, Els decided to save the strength of herself and her horse, for who could tell what awaited them on their arrival? Taking a more leisurely route, she saw the great beauty of the desert. On her previous journey, fear had painted the landscape with shadows, but now the sun was easy to see and the sand kicked up by Audcy's hooves glowed golden. Els realised much of what Reynon had said was true, what some took for bleakness was in many ways splendour. Few houses meant the broad sweep of dunes reigned supreme for several great lengths.

Six days from her departure, Els noticed large, spiked plants dotting the landscape and remembered how close Jhrik-ansi was to the wilder nature of Lykrosia. Deeper into this plantland, Els was shocked to see smoke rising ahead of her. Terrible fears rose in her mind and she approached with caution. To her astonishment and delight, she saw the smoke came from amidst a group of half-constructed houses.

This was Jhrik-ansi already! she smiled and urged

Audcy onwards. Eagerly, she leapt from her mount and offered her hand to a man holding a great bundle of papers. He looked at her hand, at her cloak, then he shook her hand vigorously.

'Welcome Els! I am Vauram, Townsman when the rebuilding is done. For now, though, I am only part of the group sent to rebuild it. I know I speak for the others here when I say your offer of help is much appreciated.'

'Is this the same Els who drove the Demon Lords out?' called one man.

Els raised her hands above her head as if to make a crown.

'Karryn helped?' guessed Vauram. 'Yes, indeed she did. But Els, if you need to speak of complicated matters, Alkar here can hear and send, he trained as a priest in Istalan and only comes here now through the generosity of his goddess.'

Hello Els. Yes, I trained at the temple of L'ra seven years ago. There were fewer of us then, but life was simpler. I remember Kyrria and Rayth when they arrived. Now we live in violent times, though tidings from fellow worshippers bring light to pierce a dark sky.'

'You misunderstand. I studied at the temple, too, but I cannot see light in any sky now. The light you priests speak of has been extinguished.'

'Do not be so hasty to speak of endings,' Alkar looked sad, *'Strange news comes quickly in such times, who knows what new understanding may come to us? For now, let us concentrate on finishing the building work here, there at least, we can both see results.'*

'There I must agree and nothing would please me more. Where would Vauram need us?'

'Help with making furniture, designing town facilities.'

'Thank you both. Planning, to start with?' Vauram motioned to some of the other workers and two came to join him. By the time they were in the central area, eight of them were present to look at maps and lists. The relatives of Jhrik-ansi's victims and townsfolk from nearby impressed Els with their determination to succeed in their rebuilding and banish the ghosts of terror which tried to linger for many.

'We want the houses reasonably close together, we want there to be support for one another in the town,' said Vauram.

'Isn't there a danger of any evil moving straight through the population, though?' warned Pinarv, a wiry man usually found in more manual work.

'There will be no such strike against us, in that you can trust,' Alkar said.

'How can you say that? We cannot afford to be complacent.'

'True,' acknowledged Vauram, 'Maybe we should be prepared for attack.'

'And create doubt for the people who will live here? Such assumption of evil succeeding here will lead to the doubt and fear it needs to strike,' Alkar insisted.

'Then how are we to act against the Demon Lords?' asked Pinarv. 'Forgive me if I seem angry, but ten members of my family died here. No doubt I would have done if I had not married and moved away. I praise the gods that I did not stay here with my wife and children, but would take any measure necessary that could prevent a similar disaster befalling us.'

'Pinarv, I sympathise with your wishes and will act.'

'Yes, surely Alkar is here for more than just talk,' said Garihm, the architect sitting at ease with his maps, a little apart from the group.

'I hope I am, too,' Els sent Alkar, raising her eyebrows and shrugging at the others.

'Most certainly, Els. We all of us want to act; there cannot be a repetition of the disaster that befell us. As Pinarv says, the memory is still fresh; we need to right the wrongs that were done here.' Alkar sat up. 'I propose we finalise these plans tonight and while the labourers build, Els, myself and Pinarv will see that all communal facilities are correctly filled.'

'Why me?' Pinarv asked, shocked.

'You wish to be able to settle here happily, do you not? Then why not set about creating the town we all wish for, take part in the things which arm us against evil.'

'But facilities? Lounge areas and book rooms, prayer rooms and the like, where does this really lead us?'

'You may yet be surprised at what great things arise from the small, friend Pinarv,' smiled Alkar. 'Besides, Els is willing and she is a sorceress. Yet she trusts me that practical help is as efficient in the right time. Do you not, Els?'

Caught, Els nodded. Then she smiled, certainly Alkar was clever in his dealings with people, she had to hand that to him. Whatever these priests were wrong about, she grudgingly admitted Alkar had the same wisdom shown by Roro and Skrella.

As the days passed in Jhrik-ansi, Els' admiration became less grudging. Alkar may have used his input in planning more than building, but he regularly met with Vauram and the two made a formidable team. Daily the one would hurry to the other, Vauram ready to demonstrate a new building technique in practice, Alkar laden with plans for interiors. Els even found Pinarv complimenting the priest as he worked with her in the town hall. They had taken a break from Els' sending packages across to Pinarv when he confided how his confidence had grown.

'I didn't think this was going to work, but it does feel sort of...homely now,' he admitted.

Els nodded. **Feels like people could really live here.** She wrote on a discarded diagram.

'Even where he's blessed the rooms, well, I don't go in for all that praying over a house, but, things have changed since it started. You can tell the places Alkar's been in and I want my house to be one of them, that's a surety.'

I don't know what he's done, but it has made a good feeling come to settle.

'You must believe in the goddess and all that, though,

234

being a sorceress and everything? Word has it, you're the one in the prophecy, if you don't mind me saying.'

The prophecy? You know as much as I do. Els told him.

For all she wanted to avoid it, news of the prophecy was hard to escape. The recent rebuilding in Jhrik-ansi had attracted the interest of those in bordering lands and the Lykrosian queen was not one to sit at home while events unfolded around her.

It was in the gentle mid-morning sun of the last day's building when Queen Lidynne rode over the border to see the work for herself. Her horse was the bay common in Lykrosia, as were those of her three guards.

'Hail, folk of Jhrik-ansi!' Lidynne called. 'I, Lidynne, queen of Lykrosia come to offer support to your rebuilding. I would welcome a tour.'

'Queen Lidynne.' Vauram bowed. 'We are honoured that you lend your aid. To make the border between countries strong in unity is a welcome move indeed, I am sure King Nahvib is gratified by your fellowship.'

'My friendship with your king is a long one. I hope now to offer help as he has so often aided his allies.'

'And in recent times, allies bring strength from the gods,' added Alkar, following Vauram to see Lidynne.

'And praise them in that. Speaking of god-sent help, I believe young Els works with you here.'

'She does. Do you know her, then?' Vauram asked.

'Not as well as I would like, but I spoke to her at King Nahvib and Queen Karryn's wedding and was impressed by her story. Chief Priest Stec was also intrigued by her gifts and his interests are worth following.'

'Yes, how is it going with my brother on the Eastern continent?' asked Alkar, 'For messages from those lands are hard to come by, often the politicians and kings hear more news than we in the temples.'

'Queen Wertle still sees no threat from the Demon Lords. Stec and his good friends Saluna and Abrim raise the common folk's awareness daily. Though, the time will no doubt come when Wertle comes to realise the truth all others are aware of.'

'Let us hope so. Ah, Els, I think you have already met Queen Lidynne while in Istalan?'

Els bowed quickly, as the others had done. **A happy memory. It is good to see you again. How is King Sedryk? Stec?**

Lidynne groaned. 'They bow to me, but they ask after Stec! I shall have some close words with that priest. His reputation goes far further than it should,' She smiled though and Els relaxed. 'King Sedryk is well. He is busy training the army and raising funds for the treasury. Ashla is in regular contact, too. Stec seeks daily to raise the goddess in glory, though the royal family act as if he is not there. And I deal with politics and prophecies. But how are you, my dear?'

Well enough, missing friends.

'Yes, this war has been hard on many in that account. Yet it seems your work here has been productive, you are surely all proud of that?'

Yes. I came here with Pocack's approval and have learnt a lot under the instruction of Alkar and Vauram.

'Good, I am glad. However, it is only fair to tell you that Pocack and I are not in agreement, perhaps I do not find his approval as assuredly as you.'

Why?

'I hope there is no ill will?' Vauram was as concerned as Els.

'Not at all, only a professional disagreement. But let's see this new town of yours before we get onto anything more serious.'

Vauram and Alkar exchanged glances, but moved to lead the queen's party around the re-built town. Queen Lidynne commanded her guards to leave their horses tied up and survey the town on foot. As they dismounted to join their ruler, Els noticed the stoutness of the Lykrosians compared to the Sytrannians. Lidynne's guards were certainly worthy companions to the queen. Their bulk alone made them worthy guards and it was clear Lidynne appreciated their talk as well, for they commented freely on what they saw.

'Who lives in this large house? It is a great cost for one family alone, is it to be shared?' one wondered aloud.

'This is the Town House,' explained Vauram, amused. 'Here, everyone will have the opportunity to find out about their land and spend time together.'

'Have teachings on the gods,' Alkar added.

'In a sense it is a family house, we hope to unite the town as a family of support and care that will withstand external pressures,' Vauram said.

'And internal ones? For sometimes the strife is greater when it comes in the heart of friends,' Lidynne suggested.

'We hope to counter that also. The temple plays a part as well, of course.' Alkar smiled, 'Let us not forget that.'

'The prophecy wouldn't let us, even if we tried to forget the gods' will,' argued Vauram.

'Yes, but so much depends on how we read that, doesn't it?' sighed Lidynne.

'Ah, I think I see where your disagreement with Pocack lies,' said Alkar.

'You do, indeed,' Lidynne looked unhappy. 'Can we sit somewhere? I have things to say to you, Alkar and I fear what would happen if we are standing while we discuss them.'

'You may trust me not to draw weapons over a difference of opinion!' exclaimed Alkar.

'But raised voices grow further if the stature is likewise raised.' Lidynne said, 'I have learnt this in the past week.'

'Then let us be the first to use the new Town House as it was intended, to discuss and to learn. Come, Lidynne, you need not fear our dissent,' Vauram said.

'Vauram, I appreciate your generosity, you are truly your king's subject. Guards, leave us now. Fear not, I am in good company here.'

Els also made to leave with the guards' dismissal, but

Lidynne caught her hand. 'You must hear this, too, my dear, come along.' Els was surprised at the force of Queen Lidynne's invitation, but hurried into the newly built building alongside the queen, Vauram and Alkar, remembering Sorab just in time.

The mherl gave her a reproachful look, but soon became distracted by this new building. As Sorab sniffed and pawed at everything, Els and Lidynne looked around with an equal curiosity. Though Els had helped in the planning and worked with Pinarv on wall hangings and wooden furniture, this was the larger of the two discussion rooms and she had expected more tables and chairs. Obviously, Vauram wanted people to be able to relax during meetings, for the green cushions sat well on soft floorings. The wall hangings included the necessary maps, but these were broken up with scenes from different parts of Sytrannia – ships in the port, Istalan Palace, Turtle Desert, the Akrin Gate. A small kitchen contained enough stores to make drinks and simple snacks. Vauram, determined to show the visitor a fine Sytrannian welcome, busied himself making juices and fetching fruit. By the time they were all settled with refreshments, the Sytrannians were ready to hear what the Lykrosian monarch had come to say. A greater purpose than touring had clearly brought her there.

'You may not like what I have to say, certainly your king and magi do not, but I bring what information I have to my friends and they make of it what they choose,' Queen Lidynne looked troubled, but her voice was clear.

'Carry on, you can speak your truth here and be heard,' Vauram said.

'Ah, but truth as I have is not easily accepted,' Lidynne paused, twisting her rings absent-mindedly. 'Well, I will tell it as I told it to Nahvib and we will see if the result is the same. Two weeks ago, I had a dream, a visitation from Gax, I am sure.'

'And the hunter god does not bring visions lightly,' commented Alkar.

'Neither was this a gentle word,' Lidynne said. 'I was in a forest, lost and needing aid.' Els sat up, startled. 'I knew help was out there, but that I must ask for it from the right quarter. Voices called, but none I felt I could trust. I wandered, lost, for some time, until I saw figures around me. Grey figures loomed from within the trees, real people, yet their identity was hidden. Each called out to me that they could help, but I had to decide who spoke in truth, who could lead me out from this dense forest. I took the hand of one figure and he, she, I don't know which, led me a long way, until I could see sunlight through the trees. Then the figure left me and others came. I chose again, but this figure was different. At first it led me towards the light and my hopes grew. Then it turned a corner and the sun had gone, we ran deep into the forest. I was dragged on, the creature insistent, but my fears rising. Suddenly the figure left me and I knew I was helpless, knew I would never leave the forest to find that sun. I awoke in a sweat, more frightened than I have been in a long time. Why? I asked and a voice in my mind answered, 'Because there is the danger of a wrong choice being made and you must halt the wrong path.' You can imagine my trepidation, but I realised at once the bearing this had on the prophecy and I quickly sent word to King Nahvib that I was coming to meet with him.'

'I take it he didn't hear it too well?' Alkar suggested.

'Not exactly. Oh, he wasn't angry, but he made clear his objections. I met with Nahvib and his magi and told them my story. I explained I feared they had the wrong person in mind and were endangering the prophecy.'

'Who do they feel fulfils the prophecy, then?' asked Vauram.

Lidynne cast a wary glance at Els, 'I cannot reveal too much, not when you are here, I'm sorry,' she said.

Why ask me here, then? Els wrote.

'I feel you must hear this vision. I cannot tell you who the other candidates are, for you must know you are regarded as the one they call The Sorceress. If I were to reveal those who may be your companions in protecting our world, it would influence your actions and risk altering things which are yet to come.'

You are so confident I am The Sorceress, why does everyone keep calling me that? I was only made *a* sorceress recently. There is no reason why I should necessarily be *The* Sorceress. Vanya and Aashti are Sytrannian sorceresses of great repute, there must be several like them in lands like yours?

'Not as many as you would suppose,' Lidynne sighed. 'We have not invested in training people of magic as much as your ruler, there King Nahvib has the advantage over most of us.'

'Do not be too hard on yourself, Queen Lidynne,' Alkar said, 'King Nahvib's attitude is much influenced by his teenage meeting with L'ra. He has had the wisdom for training given him. Perhaps the other wisdom you bring is as important.'

'May the gods will it so. In them, we have to trust,' Vauram said.

That's another thing. I don't speak to the gods. The goddess I thought was mine was absent when I needed her most. How can I, as far from any faith as Nahvib is close, be one named in prophecy?

Alkar and Lidynne laughed.

'Els, the gods are never straightforward in their methods,' the queen said.

I know that if anyone does.

'Then don't forget it! Kyrria's death was traumatic, I know. Yet who would have expected Karryn to survive, or this town to have been devastated and resurrected in so short a time? The gods will choose the people they need to complete their victory, be assured of that,' Alkar explained.

Even if we don't want to be a part of it?

'Even then.'

'In the meantime, we need to be alert to developments and seek the way of the gods in all things,' Lidynne

240

argued.

'What does that mean, practically, though?' Vauram asked.

'I think we need to keep our options open. We need to cast wider for our three candidates, make sure we find the right three. That's what I told Nahvib, or tried to, anyway.'

'The other thing you all seem to have forgotten is that we deal with a two-part prophecy here,' Alkar reminded them.

'What do you mean?' Vauram was disbelieving.

'Well, Queen Lidynne has told you of the Three Chosen, but little of the former fulfilment.' Alkar said.

'Then you hold all that true?' Lidynne asked the priest.

'Of course. There must be a warrior of unique type on each continent. And that warrior shall fight a battle and thank the gods. When these battles have been fought, then we can look to mobilising our Three. While we still look to see three of the four battles fought, we have time to carefully assess those who may be Chosen, as you were saying.'

'You may be right.'

You say the other three. Where was the first one? Els asked.

Alkar smiled, leaned back on his cushion. 'You have little faith, yet much strength, my friend. I would guess reasons for that, only I know you would like none of them!'

'Explain, priest, leave us guessing no longer.' Vauram shook an admonishing finger.

'When Els was still in the North, there was a call to arms. She was part of a force made up of Northerners and Southerners, sailors and soldiers both. They fought in Green Forest, in the heartland of Northern trees, pressed in on all sides. Demon Lords had caused Sorcerers to come, yet Els and her people fought, bringing defeat to these evil ones. Els was wounded, unsure of where she would go next. The first thing she did when the fight was won was to give thanks to L'ra. Look as unconvinced as you like, Els, you are the Sorceress-Warrior *and* one of The Three Chosen. Where the others come into it, I do not know, but Queen Lidynne is right, we must look beyond obvious answers. Be open, Els, who knows what may yet come to pass.'

Well, I have nothing to lose waiting here and seeing what comes up next.

'Then make yourself comfortable in Jhrik-ansi and we'll all be available to further developments – goddess willing,' said Vauram with a wink.

The sky had darkened by the time the four of them left, Lidynne to her guards and the journey back over the border, Els and the others to their nearer homes. Els felt hopeful; though she did not see any sense in Alkar or Lidynne's words, their efforts seemed to point to an end, even if it was far away now. The light was fading over the desert, but it only brought out the stars and who knew what they had seen in their recent revolutions.

Chapter 19

It was a week after Queen Lidynne's visit that a message came from Stec. He hoped to be in Jhrik-ansi soon to bless the new town and express his solidarity with their efforts. Alkar was ecstatic at his letter. Though he had not seen Stec, he was interested in this foreign brother. One who felt as he did about L'ra, yet had experiences and learning so different to his own - how much they would have to talk about! In his joy at such an opportunity, Alkar was often to be found at prayer or studying works giving word on L'ra's nature. Vauram complained he had lost his best worker, but all saw how he looked on Alkar with understanding, not seeking the priest unnecessarily. The townsfolk also sympathised with Alkar. After all, his seemingly ineffectual peace had caused much change in the short time he had taken responsibility for Jhrik-ansi. Pinarv, like many of his friends, was so taken with Alkar that he had pressed the priest to stay in Jhrik-ansi, though Alkar had only waved him away without answer. Vauram had said nothing, only waited and hoped that Stec's arrival would lead to a decision.

Only Els wished the letter had never come. The last, brief time she had spoken to Stec, he had spoken of L'ra and of Jayak. Then, she had thought his words on Jayak harsh, but those relating to the goddess true indeed. How quickly times had changed. Now she knew all too well how untrustworthy Jayak was, but the goddess' betrayal had hit her as an unseen bolt. Talking to Stec again would be the same as talking to the Southerners she knew, he would press her to accept the goddess' will in all things and she would resist, citing the damage done by Kyrria's death and the break-up of her friendships.

She noisily dusted around Alkar when it was her turn to tidy the Town House, but he acted as if she wasn't there. Smiling to himself, he prayed in silence. If Els was going to rediscover her faith, it would not be done by his efforts.

Meanwhile, Els clanked bottles of cleaning oils and swished cloths to no avail, growing angrier by the minute.

'I hope this priest will cause no more trouble, we need to extend the stability we have, not splinter with our nerves,' said Vauram, as he and Alkar made their way through the market stalls which had begun to flourish again.

'Don't you trust us any more?' Alkar grinned.

'Not you, I know what you're capable of. We're all grateful for the results of your labours.'

'Thank you.'

'This Stec's still an Easterner, though. It'll take a miracle to make me welcome one of them without caution.' Vauram sighed.

'Don't ask for miracles lightly.' Alkar said. 'The goddess always listens.'

'I won't complain of that,' said Vauram.

The days following Stec's letter passed slowly. Vauram was torn between caution and curiosity. He wanted to meet this Easterner and make up his mind about him before his people began to ask too many questions as to his role. Vauram had promised the townsfolk protection in this new home, and he wasn't going to let anybody jeopardise that. Alkar spent more days pacing the Town House than either Vauram or Els would know. Sometimes praying, sometimes dreaming. A part of him feared for this meeting. What if Stec was untrustworthy? What if he just wasn't someone he could befriend? But the greater part of Alkar hoped for more, expected more to come from one whom the goddess had chosen, even met with in person. So he trusted, but the waiting was hard. Els fought cobwebs, shelves, cushions in her cleaning, for all these things were there to fight, Stec was yet to come. The townsfolk grumbled and muttered about the foreigner to come, 'What will he eat?' 'Why's he coming anyway?' Vauram kept the talk vague, he didn't want to commit his own opinion too soon. The nights were sleepless for the new town leader while Stec made his way across the

Myrrine Straits and from there to Istalan and in turn to Jhrik-ansi.

On the tenth day since the letter, Stec arrived. Though he had come from Istalan, no-one had really expected him to have an escort when they considered how tightly resources were stretched. But the priest had been fortunate. Perhaps his adventurous journeying went rewarded, perhaps it was luck, but Stec was guided well by Timo.

'Greetings to you, fair people of Jhrik-ansi!' called Stec. 'Some of you it is a pleasure to know already, others I hope to make a joyful acquaintance with. Come along Timo, I see Els.'

'Certainly, noble Stec,' Timo tied up the horses with haste and skipped along after Stec, his quick, light steps easily catching the older man.

'Els, I am so glad to see you well. Blessings from the goddess to you.'

'Thank you,' Els sent, against her will almost, but Stec's good nature was hard to reject.

'I would like to meet Vauram and Alkar next, though they must show themselves to me: I am ignorant in current affairs and the news in my own country is lamentably thin when it can be found at all,' Stec said, casting his eyes across the gathering crowd.

'I am Vauram,' said the leader, stepping forward. 'The care of this town rests on me. We have eagerly awaited your arrival and have many questions.'

'I have also heard a great deal about Jhrik-ansi, but what I see here scarcely resembles the tales I have been told.' Stec looked about with interest.

'It's not as it once was.'

'That I was told. Yet I had not expected such a transformation to be possible so soon. I would ask with more wonder how you did it, if I did not already know.'

'Then you do believe the goddess approves our rebuilding of a place where such evil took place?' Vauram asked Stec.

'Come, come, Vauram!' laughed Alkar, pushing past

eager townsfolk. 'You cannot trick a priest of L'ra with questions. That won't work with this fellow any more than it did with me.'

'Then you must be Alkar? It's my great pleasure to meet you at last.' Stec bowed briefly, while raising his hands. Alkar returned the greeting common to L'ra's worshippers happily.

'Come, then, good priest, Stec. Let us show you our highly functioning Town House, unless Vauram insists on leaving you out on public display, that is!'

'No, Alkar, I am the first to admit when I am beaten. Let us all go, Els as well.' Vauram indicated the sorceress lingering nearby.

'Of course. I would hardly suggest keeping one of King Nahvib's most worthy combatants from any talks.'

'Must I?' Els asked.

'You'd best do what he says,' said Timo.

'And why would I take advice from you?'

Timo avoided Els' eye, and instead reached down to scratch Sorab. *'Maybe because I've got to know Stec. I'm sure he wants the best for you.'* He forced himself to look at her, *'We all do.'*

Els was about to reply when Stec turned to her, *'This is no more a matter of argument than the advice I gave you when we last met. Let us all go. At once,'* Stec was resolved.

'Very well,' Els did her best to sound grudging, but fought to guard the thumping in her heart. Maybe Stec would impart strange news as Queen Lidynne had? She couldn't tell, but was secretly glad to be invited once more to hear the words of those who knew more than her.

Their walk from the borders of the new town to the central Town House was a lengthy one. For one thing, the town had grown quickly in the last month and large central houses now fed out into smaller, sprawling collections of buildings. Those planning the designs had been careful to place houses near enough to lend support, whilst retaining the space that would lead to comfort and stave off

246

unnecessary tensions. So, the clusters of houses were well serviced by young trees and areas where children could play. The few stalls initially brave enough to try and trade had been pleasantly surprised by the number of people returning to 'Jhrik', as many now called it, so the guests had to wind their way round a thriving market as they drew closer to the middle of town. It still had an unfinished air and men were fixing unforeseen damage to the crucial water pipes, but people were there now, people who lived and breathed where that itself had once seemed impossible. Stec stopped many times to crane his short neck at new sights and the Sytrannians became convinced poor Timo would run into him. Many were the townsfolk who wondered at Stec in return, looking at his orange garb in amazement. Even Alkar wondered that he did not boil wearing such tight clothing, but paused in criticism as he suspected he would be no better prepared were he to wander Eastwards.

Els called Sorab to her just as he getting rather close to a food stall and then they entered the Town House. Stec peered round the rooms with great interest. As they reached the common room, he studied the paintings attentively, eager to learn more about this new land the goddess had brought him to. Timo hung back until the others goaded him forward.

'Don't fight them, these people know what they want,' Els sent, *'They want us here, there's no need to fear.'*

'I'm glad to hear you saying that, from what Rayth has said, I thought you had enrobed yourself in fear and anger?'

'Timo, don't you start on me.' Els bent down to pick Sorab up.

'Els, I am as concerned as Kyrria would be to see you unhappy. Though I cannot deny you look much better for your excursion out here'

'Thanks,' Els smiled, she had no fight with Timo, he was a victim of events as much as she.

'Come, children, Chief Priest Stec must exchange his

247

news today or not at all,' Vauram said, ushering people towards the cushions.

The group moved over and put their cushions into a circle. Stec looked serious for a moment. Then he caught Alkar's eye and the pair of them smiled.

'As my brother says, I come as a chief priest.' Stec said. 'It is not out of curiosity that I visit – well, not that alone. I have been sent for a reason. L'ra has spoken to me and I come here to bless this town.'

'I sense a 'but', for you have led up to this point with great caution.' realised Vauram.

'You are not a man to be fooled and I respect that. It will not change my mind though. I will bless this town, offering L'ra's protection, *but* I will not bless it while it is still called Jhrik-ansi. That is my condition, as it is L'ra's. She will give this town and its people full support if they only turn from what has gone before and look to a change here.'

'What name do you desire?' Vauram asked, stroking his chin anxiously. If the desired change was to be made a reality, he knew who would make that public.

'For the new name, I am happy to let you decide. L'ra only wants you to demonstrate the change of attitude to the greater population of these Southern lands. How you do that, she lets you attend to.' Stec reassured him.

Vauram and Alkar looked equally thoughtful at this. Timo watched with interest, it was a rare honour for one so young and unimportant to be brought suddenly close to the world of politics. Els refrained from sending, she wanted to hear Alkar's choice aloud, for surely the decision would be his?

Yet Vauram spoke first, 'Why, there is hardly a decision to be made!' he realised. 'As it is the Goddess of Adventure who protects us, so we should also show our commitment to her. I suggest we name this place L'ra's Town in her everlasting honour, I dare anyone here to move against this!'

'Fret not, dearest friend, all here will gladly stand with

248

you on this decision.' said Alkar, happily.

'Indeed, a noble choice. I am glad indeed I left this in your hands.' Stec said.

'All happy. A good name.' said Sorab.

'Yes. Now I am glad Timo and I were invited,' Els sent.

Stec looked pointedly at Els, but she refused to return his gaze. Let him provoke her all he liked, he would gain no victory over her, she thought. It pleased her that they had decided on a name for the town and united behind that, for she was fond of them all. However, fondness aside, she was not about to let Stec harass her with his views. The goddess had left her life, that she believed and further than that, she was not about to analyse.

Such gloomy thoughts were far from her mind the next day, however, when the whole town congregated at the Town hall for the official blessing.

Stec walked proudly to the entrance to building and turned to face the crowd.

'Great is the praise I bring to you people in your efforts to fight evil. But higher still are our praises to our goddess of adventure, noble L'ra. To this end, we cast behind us the name and memory of Jhrik-ansi. Instead we herald a new age and a new heart for this town – I proclaim it L'ra's Town, blessed and protected now and for evermore!' he laid his right foot on the step to the Town House as he spoke. The door flew open as he made his proclamation. At the same time, the sun rose from behind a cloud, glowing a bright gold above the town. Sorab jumped. The townsfolk, no longer Jhrikansians, unsure of their identity, but hopeful all the while, cheered and cried with joy. Their home was no longer a place to be abhorred, but one of hope, honouring L'ra. Many hugged each other and the more enterprising new merchants had already begun to sell wine, sweets and peppered chicken pieces to the revellers. Els jumped about as much as those around her. Indeed, they moved so much she couldn't have avoided it. Whatever the reason for their elation, she felt as excited as all these Sytrannians.

249

Her joy was short-lived, however. In the middle of the excitement, Els tried to wave to Stec as she jumped, for he was far from her and surrounded by well-wishers. Reaching high, she suddenly felt a terrible pain in her right side and fell back. She stopped herself from falling the whole way and steadied herself on the ground, stunned by the sudden pain. Those in the crowd nearest to her were strangers and no doubt thought she was drunk or over-zealous in her celebrations.

'What is it?' Sorab cried, pawing at her gently.

'Don't worry, I'm fine.' Els said, hoping she was right.

Examining herself carefully, she found the injury from the Green Forest battle was weeping and sore. She feared she had ruptured the healing wound with her buoyant attitude to the re-naming day and cursed her lack of foresight. But it was a long time since the battle and much had happened since then, how was she to remember old wounds when fresher ones hit her the hardest?

She wondered though, how those distant allies were faring in their own fights now. Were Macie's family reconciled to their daughter's bravery yet, was Bronv-Grii still trying to persuade Woh-Luhn of the good in Els and her allies? Most of all, she thought of Cam and Hwym. Both were more than comrades in this desperate war and news was yet to reach her of them. Cam she thought would fare well, her parents welcomed his vigour in the way he attacked their foes and they respected the bond he had kept with Els through good times and ill. As for Hwym, did he think of Els, did he even remember the wound he had held together?

When thinking of that terrible day, Els was mostly glad that the events had been comparatively short, for she could not have borne much more pain, emotional or physical. Really, though, what has changed? she thought, I still bear this pain in my side, just as the knowledge of Kyrria's death lives in me daily. Strong as her powers were in many ways, she wished she had Klara's healing now. Gods, she wished she had Klara with her now! All these people were friendly, sure enough, but they didn't know her! If any could heal, they would scarce know how to start with such a troubled one as she. Klara's hands were gentle and her face was calm, she had remained the most unruffled of all of them in the room that terrible day. I want a healer, Els thought, I want a healer now, but who can help me?

Much as she feared loneliness, help was at hand. Stec and Alkar came swiftly to her aid, easing her from the sand gently and propping her up with sacks of produce. *'Thanks, now I feel like a potato or some such thing,'* Els sent strongly, though her teeth were gritted.

'Stop trying to brave everything out, you should have told us!' Stec scolded.

'I'd forgotten, it is so long ago now, many nights have passed since and events to shadow the battle which gave me this wound.'

'You speak of Green Forest?' asked Alkar.

'You have heard of it?'

'Yes. Not many details, but it is famed round here for being a battle fought with Southerners working alongside Northerners and with a sorceress trained by our magi. Some here refuse to believe it and think it is a tale of the council's fabrication, made to support the fiction of Northern allies.'

'When will they accept us?'

'Who can tell that?' Stec sighed. *'I am an Easterner and must daily prove I am not of evil blood, how they will warm to your cold and distant people, I don't know.'*

'It is hard, but not impossible,' laughed Alkar.*' If someone had told me a year ago that I would be sat talking openly, even cheerfully, with a Northern sorceress and an Eastern priest, I would have fetched a healer, concerned for their mental health! Yet look where I find myself.'*

'Well said, brother,' Stec agreed. *'How can we say what cards the gods have yet to play? A year has changed much, it is true. Not only you, Alkar, but Karryn, Nahvib, Jayak, Vauram, all of these people and myself, of course,*

would look to the future months with expectations, for we have already been changed by this fight which now consumes our lives.'

'Well, maybe you are correct, but let's get Els inside before she falls over. I wouldn't mark today by a tragic accident, you know, Stec,' said Alkar.

'Hello, I am still here you two!' Els sent, feigning anger. *'You might treat me like a sack of vegetables, but I do feel a little more than them.'*

'Yes? Then use that brain and power and learn when to accept help. Come on, Stec, take her legs.'

'Thanks, I appreciate you thinking of my dignity here!' Els protested.

'Send as hard as you like, we know you are hurting and we will get you some rest, whether you like it or not,' Alkar said.

Els tried to argue, but her side hurt more when she tried to sit up. Her grey face was further evidence of the pain and her head began to ache with the effort of sending whilst in distress. Stec followed Alkar's directions and took Els' legs, as Alkar supported her head. Vauram and Pinarv, seeing the situation, moved to part the crowd and calm the curious looks Els received going into the Town House.

'Don't feel they're being hostile, Els. They care about you now, you're part of the rebuilding as far as they're concerned,' Alkar told her.

'I know, it'd just be nice to blend into the scenery for once,'

'Now, Els, be honest! When were you ever going to do that?' Stec confronted her with a grin. 'There's been plenty of easy ways out that you've chosen not to take.'

'Thanks a lot. Gods, put me down before something else gets broken,' Els gritted her teeth again, but mercifully, the two priests had got her into the common room and were able to set her down upon some cushions.

'You call on the gods, maybe it's time to do that in earnest,' Stec said.

'Yes, which ones?' Els challenged.

'Don't you two fall out now!' Alkar frowned, 'We need unity now, not conflict.'

'True, but I won't allow this girl to make a mistake we could all pay dearly for.'

'Stec, you said you weren't going to speak of this.' Alkar warned.

'No, I said I wasn't going to speak out unless necessary. It's necessary now, Alkar, can you dissuade me of that?'

Alkar hesitated for a moment. 'No, I suppose not. Speak on, brother, though I pray none of us lives to regret it.'

'What are you both on about?' Els stormed, *'I thought you two were helping me here?'*

'We are! But you and the rest of this world!' Stec said. He stood up, then and shook his head. 'Ah, L'ra, why do you choose one so untrained to do your bidding,' he sighed. 'Els, you must raise your sights beyond survival towards a greater goal.'

'Why, because I am a sorceress?'

'No, because you are *The* Sorceress,' Alkar declared, his voice grown more serious with support for his fellow priest.

'Yes? Can you prove that to me, or do I just have to accept your delusional plans for me in this war?' Els raged.

'Proof? You witness miracles and are given talents beyond the understanding of many and yet you dare ask for proof!' Stec shouted.

'You cannot make me do anything. I have fought hard to get myself away from ridicule and judgement and I will not relinquish such change now,' Els felt power flow through her veins, extending past her body to the room itself. Paintings shook, plants wobbled in their pots, but the priests remained unmoved.

'You have choice, we only seek to show you the wisest of your options,' Alkar said softly.

'You are The Sorceress, we know that. All of Rima might wait on the decision of kings and magi over the Healer and the Guardian, yet we priests know who the Sorceress is and ask her to begin to play her part in full,' Stec said.

'And what part is that?' demanded Els.

'How am I to tell? It is not I must speak with the goddess, I have asked and received enough revelation to last me many days,' Stec laughed, 'Els, you do not know what a life I led before, but while I was a politician, I thought I was happy, I knew where I was aiming. A successful election, a good decision from Queen Wertle and I was content. But the goddess called me and I have never looked back. My life is full of challenges, yet the blessings are also huge. I can only urge you to open your soul to L'ra once more, if not for yourself, for the greater good.'

'But I cannot see that there is anyone there to speak to my soul. I know you disagree, but understand how my life has been changed if you can,' Els pleaded, *'I called on L'ra once with a louder cry than I have used in any situation and there was no answer. The one time, Stec, when I would have received hope or instructions with gladness, yet no aid came my way. I will not go calling a goddess I do not believe in. How do you suggest I overcome this? Do I even have to?'*

'What action would be of use without faith?' Alkar asked.

'Do not try to fight on in this battle on your strength alone. Look at Jayak, would you risk similar destruction of yourself and your friends?' Stec demanded.

'Oh, I suppose he would have been all right if he had only followed the goddess more loyally? Do not link me with Jayak so idly, my situation is entirely different. I will help you all and gladly, but on my terms,' Els insisted.

She was tired and her side still hurt but she was determined not to let this argument go against her. I value my independence too much to go chasing something I can't see, she thought. After all that's happened, why can't they understand that?

'There lies the way of confusion and torment. Tread very carefully, Els.' Stec warned, 'Meanwhile, Alkar and I can only pray that the decision on The Three becomes apparent soon enough to guide you.' He swept out then, Alkar close behind him. Els stayed, her distress at his words consigning her wound to distant memory.

* * *

'They work on her, Quivviam, she remembereth how she felt,' Xanesh groaned.

'Nonsense,' answered the other great Demon Lord, 'She does not believe them. They don't exactly offer to help, more trouble is all they bring.'

'Then why does she listen at all? I try to cloud her mind with arguments, but she only shares them with these priests, we will lose her to the goddess again if we are not careful.'

'Yes? She has not forgotten the pains her friends inflicted on her, she has nobody to comfort her beyond strangers and old men. One more trial and she is ours again, I am sure of it!' Quivviam's robe glowed with power as she turned with great thought to her map of Rima.

Chapter 20

'So, you still speak to me, Nahvib?' Lidynne asked her old friend, bemused by the summons she had received so soon after their last argument. So hasty was her exit from Jhrik-ansi, she had passed Stec on his way there. Neither had paused to speak, however, merely raised a hand in greeting and a wry smile at the haste they were both brought to, before riding onwards.

'Lidynne, it would take more than a disagreement to rid me of so long a friend – and ally. I would gladly hear of Els, too.'

'She is well cared for by her friends and colleagues in Jhrik-ansi and yet I fear she cares not enough for herself.'

'She is hardly used to doing so. There has been little time of late for any of us to care too much for self.'

'So you say, Nahvib, but neither can any of us shake off our responsibilities. As you and I have people to protect, doesn't Els have a responsibility to those her talents could assist?'

'Yes, indeed. But you fear too much, Lidynne. Perhaps the Proclamation of the Three will spur her on – and others alongside her.'

'You are ready to declare?' Lidynne asked.

'Almost, I would show Ashla when she returns from Izk. Then we make it public. For now, I would also be interested to hear your views on our decision, though I fear you will not be overly happy.' King Nahvib passed his ally a small piece of paper, folded in half. 'See what you think,' he said.

Queen Lidynne looked at the Sytrannian monarch a moment. Then she unfolded the paper and read the three names it held, noting the titles they were now given. She frowned, fiddling with the trim on her dress.

'You don't agree?' King Nahvib sighed deeply. 'Which one is it that offends you?' He stood then and his voice was suddenly raised.

'I cannot tell.' Lidynne replied, sadly. 'In my dreams I am only given warning that the wrong person guiding along any path brings danger. It is not given to me to find the correct Three, I only know when I see a name or face that promises what it cannot deliver. Nahvib, do not be angry, for I tell you one of these choices at least would be false and their role would turn to smoke in the height of our need.'

'You think I let the magi guide me too easily in all this? I fought that last name, yet they brought me round!' Nahvib shouted. 'The joining will take place on Sytrannian soil, do you not see the power in those names joined, do you not see the logic?'

'I am influenced by neither power nor logic. Find me the faces and names the gods look on with satisfaction and I will show you clarity.'

'There is no-one else to look at. These are found fit to fulfill the prophecy and I will not let you turn us from this course. I have every faith the other Southern leaders will support me, and my own people.'

'You are probably right, but what will happen when one is in need of spiritual healing and finds only a healer of physical power? When one relies on the protection of a guardian who is misguided?'

'Lidynne, you go too far!'

'No, I only wish I could go further. I will find my priest, Tanvi, see if he and Stec will seek the true answers with me.'

'You have little time. Do not come back here with changes, for our minds are made up!' snapped Nahvib.

'So I see, yet I go in peace and hope to return the same way.' Lidynne bowed before her friend, but Nahvib turned from her in anger.

* * *

It was not only the mortal rulers who grew tired of waiting. In the Paradise Realms, even the gods were ready to take action.

'You have hinted, L'ra, but surely they now need more help,' argued Gax.

'You need to trust my timing...and the people I have chosen.' L'ra replied.

'But how can you allow your people to be guided by bearers of false prophecy?' Gax said.

'I will not disclose the prophecy outright. These mortals should seek it with glad hearts. When they discover it for themselves, they know they have the power to win this war. I will not take everything from them by doing it all for them.'

'Rightly spoken. Only, a clue surely wouldn't be unfair, especially now while our enemies look to make mischief against the land of elements. It would please Tadir and the others and raise their people up before the final battle.'

'Very well, I will give the further evidence that Lidynne and Sedryk seek. If they cannot not find the three, they will at least be rewarded for their efforts when they find a warrior in another fight. Come on, Gax, if you wish me to do this, you must help me.'

'And these Sytrannians gladly walk your route to adventure? L'ra, I don't know how they still follow you!' Gax laughed.

* * *

Sedryk was brought to the courtyard one morning by the sight of an Eastern soldier drawing up at the castle gate. The man was panting hard, both he and his sand-coloured horse were drenched in sweat. Hastily, Lykrosian guards helped the exhausted man from his horse before he fell. King Sedryk tried to force a drink of brandy between the rider's lips, but at this he tried to stand up and spoke for the first time.

'No time to stop, drink. My name is Saalbi. I am a friend of Stec's – that's if he is still alive.'

'What? Man, there are things you do not jest with and

Stec's life is one of them,' Sedryk held him by his collar.

'As I know well. Five days ago I left the priest to find aid, for the enemy has taken Volcano's Gorge and we cannot afford another land rupture there.'

'Is this what they plan?'

'As the gods witness me! Stec heard strange sounds and his sleep was interrupted by odd dreams –'

'– curse the power of dreams!' muttered Sedryk.

'– when he arose on the third night he saw the area around the volcano was studded by lights. He sent men to investigate but none returned. Two days more and the volcano was surrounded by Demon Lords and their followers - whose ranks swell every hour. Stec sent me to collect his allies. "Visit Lidynne and Sedryk, and Vistar if you can." he said. I have been true to his word. I first reached Akrin and met King Vistar. He is gathering his forces and leaving on his largest ship as soon as he can manage. If you would help my lord Stec, I beg you to follow.'

'I will, but first I send a message.'

'Your Majesty, there is so little time.'

'And this will take none. Tanvi, send a mental word to Els. Ask her to meet us at my border with Akrin, bringing Alkar if she can. The rest of us ride now, though you, good Saalbi, ride behind my captain. Stec must provide new horses if he can, the rest we trust to the gods.'

It was a restless party that met where three great countries bordered. Lidynne and Sedryk's men were confused, yet excited by the determination of their rulers. Many years had passed since Lykrosia had been at war, so there were soldiers keen to put their training to good use. Sedryk's eyes sparkled when he saw the small group from Sytrannia ride close. Tanvi had done well, for he brought Els, Alkar and fifty of the L'ra's Town men ready enough to fight to keep terror at bay. 'You came, then?' Lidynne asked the young sorceress.

'For my friends.' Els was pale and clearly tired. Sorab stil looked confused, as Els had only had time to tuck him

into the large pouch in her tunic before rushing out. Still, she held her head high.

'Then we fight together,' smiled Sedryk.

'Has King Nahvib approved the sending of forces Eastwards?' asked Alkar.

'His were not asked for. He neither approves nor disapproves, therefore. I consider you men free enough to make your own choice. For Els, I am sure my old friend would not begrudge myself or Stec the lending of the only one we agree on in the prophecy.'

'And she is proved the Sorceress-Warrior in the Battle of Green Forest.' remembered Alkar. 'Yes, Sedryk, we'll take this and see what this next battle wins us.'

'Spoken like the best of my men!' said Sedryk, beaming 'I like this new kind of priest that springs up all over Rima. To Akrina, men, for I will not let Vistar beat us to the battlefields!'

Indeed, by the time the Lykrosians and their friends set sail on the waiting ships, they could sight King Vistar's distinctive sail, a green reemoberry bush blooming against a blue background. The young Akrinard ruler nearly fell off the deck when he turned to see it followed by those carrying the mountain eagle of Lykrosia. 'Hail, Sedryk! Let friendship serve to further our strength!' he cried, waving and calling to his crew with joyous shouts. Yes, this sort of expedition may do him good, thought Sedryk. Happy were the hours from home to the East, even across the plains of Myrria, for these offered no more struggle than they did cover. The soldiers made good progress without overtiring the horses that must serve in battle.

But when they reached the central and largest country, Calan, they stopped in horror. Saalbi had not exaggerated. The ground Tadir had once ripped apart had clearly been restored under future generations, particularly with the rise of the new priesthood. But the enemy obviously sought to subvert this and was recklessly plundering the precious earth in every way. Ground was torn up for the pure joy of destruction, men and those that looked like men but no longer were, paced the ground and led animals over it that were never meant to live in such a climate. Worse of all were the fires, though. Men were quite deliberately starting small fires at regular intervals -dividing Calan by length and breadth so that Rima itself seemed to cry out at the hurt. On any land it would have been hazardous enough, but on land like this, every flame brought closer the wrath that could issue forth from Volcano's Gorge.

'What can any man hope to do here?' said Sedryk, suddenly afraid he had brought his own and other people on a fool's errand.

'Only his best, anything less will fail,' Alkar spoke and many of the Lykrosians turned to look with curiosity at this priest who dared speak so to their king. 'Sedryk,' Alkar continued, 'Stec has called us, we come to bring aid. That is what we will do, have faith.'

'You are right!' Sedryk raised his right hand high, commanding all to listen. Els reigned in Audcy close behind the king's first company. *'Listen well, Audcy, who knows what is planned for us?'* she patted her horse's neck, causing Sorab to cheep in alarm, but kept her eyes on Sedryk and Vistar, who brought his own men up to meet his ally. The two monarchs regarded each other a moment then Vistar smiled sternly at the gathered Akrinards. 'Hear King Sedryk well, we fight as one nation today.'

'King Vistar speaks well! The nation of good to ward off this evil! Stec calls us, we must answer with the gods' own justice. We ride on to Calan's capital with haste to bring this foe nearer its end!' Sedryk swung his sword high above his head and urged his horse on.

It was probably only a half hour that it took them to reach the capital, but the destruction and terror made their passage seem much longer. The Calanese farming communities had obviously borne dreadful attack and mutilated bodies were often found being wailed over by women and children now hungry and homeless. Trees had scars left by fires and some had arrows still buried in their bark. Approaching the city, they met several people in wagons coming their way.

'Don't go there! We left just in time. If the smoke bearers don't get you, the volcano will!' A man called, eyes rimmed red with exposure to the ash.

'Aye, look what happened last time it went up. It'll take more than a foreign army to put everything out now, arms or no.' one old man explained.

'And we come with more!' returned King Sedryk. 'A priest of L'ra and The Sorceress no less!'

'Oh, and I suppose you believe in supernatural warriors to be found in battle, aye?' The old man shouted.

'You don't find any unless you look!' cried Vistar and rode onwards.

'Well, we're all about to ride down and find out for ourselves, one way or the other. We've faith in this fight, why don't you join us and see the truth of it?' Lidynne asked.

'Ah, you're all strange in the head if you think you have a chance.' The old man shook his head.

'I'll come!' called the younger man from the first wagon. 'Don't worry, mother, least one of us stays to protect the old city.' He turned to the kings, 'I know how to handle a blade, my uncle had a smithy and I spent many years training with the arms he made.'

'Well, if this man brings faith and swordsmanship, the least we can do is find him place on a horse. With you for now, Tanvi?' Vistar suggested.

'Certainly, Your Majesty.' Tanvi waved the young Calan over.

The new recruit invigorated spirits somewhat and it was a proud fighting party that made its way into Sky City. The gate was open, panicked guards had fled, yet the city within was untouched as yet. Tall, pale blue turrets showed the Calanese palace and many of the surrounding buildings echoed its tall, thin imagery. The current queen might owe little allegiance to the gods, but many remembered the goddess of the air. From distant memory of the times when Sky City was built, Cala had arisen, as had L'ra, back to the public mind with the words of Stec and those like him.

And there was Stec. Gathering fallen goods, sending people into groups, the priest was busy and moved swiftly. He only looked up when he heard the thunder of hooves on the city's stones and then he put down his bundles and waved to his allies. His back was bent and his face grey, but glad.

'Hail Queen Lidynne! Hail, King Sedryk! Hail, King Vistar!' he cried. 'Happy is the day a goddess answers prayers so swiftly. Friends, our allies have come, we may yet turn the tide. All still able to fight meet in the courtyard, so we can decide our plan of attack.'

The courtyard was full of people, but Stec's fellow priests had begun to group them according to any experience of fighting or healing, and a few with magic were present. Palace courtiers were also to be seen amongst the crowd. 'Where's your queen?' asked Sedryk.

'Fled at the first sign that this trouble was serious,' Stec grimaced. 'I don't know what that will mean for the country, but let's deal with one problem at a time.'

After some discussion, Stec, Lidynne, Sedryk and Vistar agreed their plan. Vistar would take most of the soldiers on horseback to the Eastern side of Calan, hoping to fight the enemy and extinguish the fires there. Sedryk and Lidynne would take the remaining riders and five hundred foot soldiers to the Western side to do the same. They hoped this would give Stec, Alkar, Els and the remaining men on foot enough time to reach the centre of Volcano's Gorge in order to prevent disaster there and tackle the Demon Lords wielding this evil.

They rode out with great strength, the armouries of the palace had been drained and all soldiers wore heavy mail and the pointed shields of Calan. Most brought their own swords, though some had taken those made by Calanese smiths, or knives made with equal skill. Others had snatched what they could, scythes from local farms,

263

arrows used by the city guards. Even Stec carried a great axe, though he wondered what would come to pass if he were called upon to use it.

The first to actually see action were Sedryk's troops. They met their enemy first and found them well prepared. The Demon Lords amongst them were few, but the servants they held under their power were many and knew no other wish than the desire to fight. The initial wave of riders was met by few foes on horseback, but many soldiers on the ground who slashed at horses' legs, bringing their people down, vulnerable to attack. Many riders were lost in this way until Sedryk commanded those on foot to join. They were prepared to fight sword to sword and their shields were easier to maneuver than the Demon Lords' whose were of hexagonal shape and a heavier wood, making them powerful but slower. The sounds of screams and the ringing of metal on metal dominated the air. People were lost on both sides, but Sedryk urged his forces on, 'We fight to be free of this burden!' he cried, 'Look on these creatures and do what you can to protect our lands from such burning eyes.' Truly the enslaved people's eyes were bright with an unnatural light and the allies shuddered at the thought of letting such evil gain control.

King Vistar's forces fought with an equal might, though it was hours before they reached their destination. As King Sedryk was rallying his soldiers, Vistar was beginning the attack from the East side of Volcano's Gorge. Here, the enemy had clearly realised help would come late, if at all. Fires burned tall and the cracked earth running to the Volcano seemed to welcome them. 'Riders to their warriors, those on foot to the fires!' Vistar cried. Many were lost trying to put out the fires, but riders soon drew the attention of the enemy soldiers along the gorge's banks. Fires began to die, but Vistar saw the Demon Lords had kept their high lords away from harm – a dark cloud of them was gathered close to the volcano itself. I hope Els and the others know what they are doing, he thought. But he had no time to wonder further, only to draw his sword and race his horse at the people whose faces showed no emotion, only a bitter drive towards destruction.

For many hours both sides waged a deadly war, hoping against hope that their efforts would be enough. Sedryk witnessed many of his people die, but in the distance he could see the flames of the East going out, then being relit. We seem to be gaining though, he thought, amazed, come then, Vistar, we shall meet in the middle yet! As both sides continued the battle, the Demon Lords grew confused. Where their strange powers and determination had won the fear of the families and townsfolk, here were people who did not bow to the might of them, or even their masters. As Sedryk and Vistar progressed past enough soldiers to get nearer to the middle of the battle, their enemies wondered that they sought out the Demon Lords fearlessly. When Vistar had killed an enemy captain and Sedryk's captain chopped his left hand off to escape the grasp of a Demon Lord, the ranks of evil had begun to tremble.

Els and her colleagues had no idea that the battle had turned in their favour, they only noted with calm how they had been able to use the confusion and noise to reach the centre of it all unharmed. Then they turned towards the centre and flinched with horror. An icy feeling of terror took a grip on Els as she surveyed the ring of Demon Lords around the volcano.

'There must be thirty' she sent. *'We will never stop them.'*

'We have to try.' Stec insisted.

'And quick, they begin to cast.' Alkar noted.

He was right. The Demon Lords' cloaked figures rose even taller as they began an incantation. *'Cala neyr-norr! Ak allmyn corryllihn! Tadir Rima crin! Ak alvakknyt! Myrrine kyp dran nyee! Raz takk alfnva! Sanv yayk! Ak Hrai-ak! Arryn ya Xanesh krii! Quivviam bryk-laan mazn kria!'*

'What are they saying'? asked Els.

'You really don't want to know,' Stec said, grimly.

'Mostly they challenge the elementals and sneer at the destruction of their people and land. They also follow the commands of Xanesh and Quivviam– they glorify these leaders, seeking victory here to earn their rewards.'

'They seem assured of such victory.'

'We shall see. While the three of us have power, I cannot promise them an easy path to it.'

'I think we should each aim our powers at one of the High Lords in this ring and attempt to break their will that way,' suggested Alkar.

'Then we'd better start soon!' cried Stec. 'I'll tune my talents on the figure this side. Alkar, the taller one on this side. Els, I'd like you to channel your powers on the Demon Lord in the centre here.' Stec indicated the clouded figure whose eyes burned green through the indistinct shape that was his face.

'Him? He's the one in charge of it all!' Els was shocked.

'Exactly and you're the only one of us who is actually trained in your power,' Stec argued. *'Make use of the powers bestowed upon you, now if you ever will!'*

Els grimaced at his words, but sent her mind deep to where she saw all her strength. He will not overcome us, they cannot, she said. She felt her powers rising. She raised her hand and the earth beneath the Demon Lord's feet cracked. She smiled, but the Demon Lord merely laughed and stamped his feet over the ground. It reshaped at once, leaving Els stunned. She tried fire, but no flames even grew. *'Fire, take your own revenge on this evil, burn, burn Demon Lord, as you have made the landscape.'* She felt the rage, the heat, but it vanished before it met the Demon Lord and his cruel laughter mocked her. Stec and Alkar were having a little more luck, their cries causing their Demon Lords to sway and falter, halting their own spells. *'Cala, hear us, let the winds buffet them loose from their friends! L'ra, give us strength, give us aid where our own power is not sufficient!'* Determined, they stood ground despite the piercing glances of the Demon Lords, the voices in their heads, which spoke of despair and misery.

'Bow at our command!' added Els, *'Give up this land!'* But her cries became increasingly desperate, as they went unheeded.

Stec and Alkar looked concerned, Els had made no difference to the central High Lord and that left the main link in the human chain untouched. *'Not working!'* cried Sorab, trembling against Els. The Demon Lords felt strong enough still to press on with their plans and began chanting. The sounds were harsh and the magic behind them was completely evil. The small fires still burning along the Gorge leapt into high flames and ran to unite into one central flame at the Volcano's base. The Demon Lords laughed, anticipating the destruction to come.

'We cannot let them win! I will continue to push on with this one, you take the other!' Stec called to Alkar. 'Els, try with yours, he is the strongest, we must break this chain now!'

'Go! Go back to your own realms, leave us. Our good magic defeats your evil.'

But her cries went unheard, for she addressed them only to the wind. To either side of the volcano, Vistar and Sedryk's forces paused, seeing the growing flames. 'Gods! Raz take your power from this flame!' cried Vistar, as all on the battlefields fell to the ground, covering their heads with their shields. Only the priests continued to hope. 'L'ra, come now, as we call you in our time of need!' shouted Alkar, relentless in the face of the evil high lords.

'Why won't it work!' shrieked Els, a cold hard mental voice taking her over. She felt the power flood through her. She shook, the power was so violent, so strong. She tingled all over and couldn't remember the last time she had felt like that. If she had had time to think, perhaps she would have remembered the bandit camp in the North. But she didn't stop to wonder, so the power flowed through her with nowhere for it to be sent to. Stec turned to her, but too late. The force fell back on Els and she was struck to the

floor by its power. 'Els!' the priests cried as one and ran to her side. But there was no answer, only the trembling that still ravaged Els' body. Then Stec turned back to the circle of evil and saw that the flames stretched high, bright against the darkening sky. 'L'ra, hear us now, send us a sign that we can turn this evil tide to your good!' The high lords' coarse laughter filled the air, but Stec continued, 'Noble L'ra, we call on you, for our skills fall short, though we know your might never fails us. We fight this war in answer to your commands. I, Stec, ask for your aid, for only you can turn this black day to one of hope. Hear us L'ra, show us your answer!'

Chapter 21

Stec looked at Els in horror for a moment, to have the Sorceress fall in battle, what could this mean? But he didn't have time to think about the situation, L'ra had blessed him in this battle and that was knowledge he could act on. He and Alkar had prayed, they had to act on the promises of the goddess now, hard as it was.

Thinking this, Stec drew his gaze from Els to the Demon Lords. Despite their sudden increase in might, the Demon Lords had stopped and seemed undecided as to their next move. Stec and Alkar exchanged confused looks.

'Why have they stopped, they could surely defeat us?' Alkar asked his brother priest. But the enemy didn't look like it was about to end the war with a final blow. In fact, as they wavered in their confidence, the fires they had set began to flicker and shrink, where only moments before they had been growing.

'It only matters that they do hesitate, I don't care why!' Stec cried. He realised the truth of his own words, he didn't know what had happened, but neither did he care. He had asked for power and an answer had come, to fail to act on it was impossible for him. Stec moved forward and it appeared to Alkar that the Demon Lords nearest trembled, though they outnumbered the gods' people ten to one.

'You can attack one, defeat one, but we come together, you will never defeat *us*!' Stec cried.

One brief glance upwards, as if in prayer and he stepped forward. He strode up to the central Demon Lord with a terrible calm and swung his axe. There was no rush to his blow, no panic. The hefty blade fell once, bringing the High Lord's head with it. Then the Demon Lords were revealed as powerless in the face of an enemy who didn't care what they threatened; only what his gods delivered. The High Lord's body fell to the ground as his head did and he disintegrated into smoke. Suddenly the power was nothing and the body unravelled along with the spirit it had contained. Stec heard Alkar gasp behind him, but the noise was only a part of the background, he was victorious and he knew it.

But the victory was not his alone. Stec bowed low, lower than was normal in Southern prayer, much less Eastern.

'Thank you L'ra that your majesty is lent to us today. I, Stec, claim this victory on your behalf! Blessed is the day when Volcano's Gorge was won, for we are all brought a step nearer to the final victory.' He swung his axe again, strong and proud. It struck only the earth before him, but the remaining Demon Lords fled at the sight of his action, disappearing into the air above Calan.

Then the flames died completely. Their sudden disappearance brought a pleasant cool wind to the area and relief swept over the Eastern priest. Cries of surprised joy were heard from the Western side of Volcano's Gorge to the East. Sedryk and Vistar shouted thanks to the priests and Els, unaware of the troubles they had been through. Men previously held by Demon Lords mostly staggered about in confusion, though a few left the scene quickly, eager to join their masters. Southern and Eastern soldiers put down their weapons, there were no longer any men left worth fighting. Stec pulled his axe back out of the ground. This is the axe that felled a High Lord, he thought, in wonder. There was blood on the blade and some on his hands and arms. I did this, Stec said to himself, I did what had to be done. He smiled at how obvious it had been once he knew it, how his stride had carried him easily over the ridges, how the blade had fallen right. Then he heard Alkar make another exclamation and turned, remembering the friend who had followed him into victory.

Then it was Stec's turn to gasp, for his friend was no longer alone. Alkar had left his post near Els and walked a little way to greet newcomers from the West. Stec quickly realized the group approaching Alkar were allies. Not only were their weapons loose in their hands, but he recognized Alleri and Klara amongst the five people. They were excited, Alleri waving her hands, seeming to question Alkar; Klara listening quietly, searching her skirts for something to use to help her sick friend. The other three people were unknown to Stec and he wondered who had sent them. The oldest of the group wore trousers and a tunic closer to Stec's own clothes than Alkar's in design, though the colours were not as bright. Two young men, dressed in a similar style, followed him. One walked calmly and confidently, light brown hair held off his face in a rough cord, a knife at his belt. Though taller, the other young man was more nervous, his blond hair as roughly raked up as his friend's was smooth and controlled. This last stranger continuously looked around him and shifted the bundles at his back. Not weaponry, thought Stec, for the stranger carried a spear openly at his side. Then Stec saw the flute poking above the journey bag and his confusion grew.

'Alkar! Who are these you hail in battle?' Stec cried, approaching with arms held out in a gesture more of wonder than concern.

'Why, Stec, the goddess surely sends strength from all quarters.' answered Alkar, laughing with in joy. 'Hail, not only your old friends from the South, but new ones from the North!'

'From the North? Then I welcome you gladly, for you have travelled far to come and help us. I am High Priest Stec, priest of L'ra.'

'I am Bronv-Grii, Elder of Garrtron, I instruct people in the worship of the Northern gods,' Bronv-Grii replied, proudly.

'Then you are Els' Elder, surely?' Stec realized.

'Yes, I have been fortunate enough to have fought with her, an honour I see you claim for yourself in this battle.'

'Much is said about Els,' said the brown-haired young man, 'But though you speak of her as an ally, I don't see her at your side. Where is my sister?' The youngster

271

stepped forward, but Bronv-Grii held him back.

'Patience, let us ask these priests before we rush into our situation. Chh! You boys will run at all your duties. Besides, they do not even know you, yet you seek to tell them what they must do. Be fair.'

'Still, I can see the young man's anxiety is with cause. You say you are Els' brother?' Alkar said.

'Yes. Sorry, I didn't mean to be so quick to speak, only she left in a hurry and that doesn't normally mean good news. But my name is Cam and I serve willingly alongside Bronv-Grii, I come to offer any help I can. Like him, I fought in Green Forest and we triumphed there.'

'As I did.' said his companion. 'My name is Hwym.'

'Are you another of Els' brothers?' asked Alkar, remembering that Els had mentioned more than one.

'No!' Hwym laughed and Cam with him. 'Though I have no blood relationship to Els I would walk many miles to help her as a friend.' Hwym avoided Cam's eye as he said this.

'I see,' said Stec. 'Well, I am glad indeed to meet those loyal to one I also consider a good friend, but the news from the battle is not all good.'

'Els is all right, though?' Hwym asked.

'Hard to say. She has fought with magic at a very high rate of power and hadn't had the best preparations for it.'

'Els always trains hard, you can't mean she was slack in her readiness?' Cam asked.

'No, I would never say that. I could be the whole of the night in explanations if I was to make this truly clear to you.' Stec scratched his head.

'There's been trouble at the palace, that's why your sister came back.' Alleri answered Cam. 'We were in a dire situation, still are, if we're honest.'

'Els helped, she saved the life of Jayak, a friend of ours,' Klara explained.

'Jayak? Yes, we've heard of him,' Hwym grunted.

'He owes his life to her,' Klara explained, 'Only Els' power could bring him back from the hold this evil had over him.'

'Then why isn't he here? Isn't he grateful for all she has done for him?'

Klara and Alleri looked awkward. Alleri rubbed her forehead confusedly and Klara scuffed her feet in the hot soil.

'Yes, why isn't this Jayak here?' Cam demanded. 'Hwym's right, Jayak does my sister little honour ignoring what she has done.'

'He isn't ignoring her!' Alleri cried, 'The gods know, it's all he could do to get near her after Kyrria died.'

'Kyrria? We heard much of her, too.' Hwym said. 'How much has passed since Els came back here?'

'Much, and the strain on her has been great. That's what I meant by being ill prepared, Cam, Hwym,' Stec illuminated, 'Anyone would be less than ready in a situation like this.'

'If that is true, how did you wage war on these Demon Lords so successfully?' asked Bronv-Grii, 'For, though we come to give aid, I see we will be chasing the soldiers who already flee, the main work is already done.'

The group looked around then and everything they saw confirmed the Elder's words. The Demon Lords were gone, the robes of their dead High Lord lay on the ground, scared and confused Easterners ran scattered across the valley. And the fires were out. What had threatened disaster was no more, indeed, it had become a victory.

'And you won this with two men and an injured sorceress?' Even Alleri marvelled at the battle's end.

'No,' said Alkar. His voice was quiet but he spoke with assurance, 'Not two mere men. One mere man, but one the Priest-Warrior. Don't look so shocked, Stec!'

'But…how can you say this?' Stec was startled, tried to shake his head in denial at his brother's words.

'Look at what you did,' Alkar insisted, 'You called on the goddess for help, even when the battle looked most dark to us. You fought with her strength and won. And to her you gave the thanks.'

'Yes. I didn't think of it, Alkar, it was just…right.'

'Of course, some things need no examination, they just have to be done.'

'Like Els in Green Forest,' recalled Hwym.

'Yes, exactly! Today is a joyous day,' said Alkar, 'Long may the Battle of Volcano's Gorge be heralded as the day the second warrior was found. Stec, it is my duty to proclaim you the Priest-Warrior of the prophecy, long may we rejoice in this knowledge.'

'Thank the goddess,' Klara agreed, 'But let's not forget we still have a friend out there who needs healing.'

Guilty, the others followed Klara's gaze to where Els still lay, unmoving, Sorab curled up on her chest. They moved to her with determination. Suddenly they felt a strange mixture of joy and fear. So much had gone their way today, did they really have any right to expect more? Maybe they had. Maybe their work had lifted them from the troubles surrounding most men. That, or the gods had simply decided to smile on them. As it was, Els was just beginning to move a little when Klara reached her.

'Don't send a word,' Klara smiled, 'Let's just get you better, you can tell us all about it later,' she insisted gently.

Klara was soon pulling bottles of sour-smelling oils from her pockets and applying them to Els' head and wrists. The smell was sickly and Bronv-Grii coughed in alarm. Hearing him, Els looked up in amazement, the more so when she spotted Cam and Hwym.

'Don't look so worried, you're going to be all right,' Hwym told her.

Feeling stupid to just watch Klara work, Hwym and Cam helped her move Els to sit up and bound her side wound, which had begun to weep where she had fallen on it. At first, the three worked silently, but Klara wanted the strangers to feel at ease and asked them about their homeland. Soon, Cam was chatting about Garrtron and Hwym retelling the Battle of Green Forest. The three grown men were amused at his detailed recollections, mostly showing Els in a deeply heroic light. At one point,

Sorab left Els to sit at Hwym's feet.

'She's listening, though, she hears it well enough!' Alleri cried.

'Then you're glad at her recovery?' Klara asked.

'Klara! You don't have to ask me that!' Alleri reprimanded her friend. 'I know we disagreed, but, Klara you know it'd kill me to see anything happen to Els.'

'Well, you're both healed today, then, she's right enough now,' Klara said.

'Goddess be thanked,' Els sent weakly.

'And I told you not to do that,' Klara scolded, secretly pleased Els' strength was returning.

'If I don't thank the goddess, now, I can't rest,' Els continued, *'I have fought her too long these past months, but she spares me to fight with her again. I must speak to Jayak, I must try to understand. It's just, I see him and I see Kyrria. I can't bear to think on that last dreadful day for long.'*

'Then don't. Come back to us and let Jayak talk to you when he will,' said Alleri, 'Surely he should be the one to put things right,'

'And who will persuade him? You, Alleri?' Els sent.

'Me? When does he ever listen to me?' Alleri's face was bitter and Hwym looked at her with curiosity.

'What do you say?' he called to Klara. 'We can't all do magic, you know!'

'She's well. If Els can send, she is truly healed,' Klara explained.

'Thanks.' Hwym shook Klara's hand. 'Els is a great friend of mine, you don't know how much it means to see her come round. We are all very grateful for your skills here, Klara.'

'And we are of yours,' Klara said. 'I know this battle is all but over, but I'm sure the king will be keen to involve all his allies in the next one.'

'Yes, this king of yours,' Bronv-Grii cut in. 'When do we meet him? I am sure he will want to know about his new friends here and is probably more than a bit curious.'

'As soon as we finish off here,' said Stec.

'Yes,' added Alkar, 'Let's make certain the East is secure before we allow Stec to train soldiers for the next battle. Though with the Priest-Warrior in charge, I'm sure nothing will be too difficult for them.'

The next two days saw them put the priests' suggestions into action. The first day began depressingly, the allies suddenly confronted by mindless slaves of the Demon Lords' will. Men Stec had once known at court had become violent foes when possessed. Many had to be killed and their deaths brought little satisfaction to those who carried them out.

But Alkar and Stec were sure they should look for hope in the end of the battle and actually began to find some. They rescued twenty men, mostly older men from the cities or towns, whose possession had been recent and who had enough ties to their previous life to enable the priests to bring them back. Klara and Alleri again proved instrumental, using their powers to assist the priests. Hwym, Cam and Bronv-Grii shared their news with the new-found allies, soothing them as they came back to a proper consciousness. Els was keen to talk to all her friends, but Bronv-Grii and Stec agreed she shouldn't overreach herself, restricting her sending. Though they tried to impose limitations on her friends, they both pretended to ignore Els and Alleri's long mental conversations. The two girls talked throughout the day and the entire group was glad of it. Though they couldn't tell what was said, everyone saw them smile several times. Hwym felt himself smile to see Els happy, but he turned before she saw it. It wasn't the time, not now, anyway.

The second day brought the real boost they all needed. Tired and raw, they all moved for their weapons when Sorab gave a sudden cry. Following where he ran, Stec and Alkar were elated to find horses arriving, ridden by men in familiar armour.

'Vistar!' Stec called, 'Glad you're still here to tell the tale in Akrin, my friend!'

'So am I!' cried Vistar, the young king drawing close with some excitement.

'Where are Sedryk and Lidynne? Any news there?' Alkar asked.

'Plenty I expect, but look, they come to tell it themselves!'

Sure enough, the priests and their allies turned to find the Lykrosians approaching from the opposite direction.

'Hail! A new victory and a new warrior, I'm guessing?' Sedryk laughed to see Stec confounded. 'Come, friend, all fires put out and strangers fighting amongst you.' Here he cast a curious glance in the Northerners' direction. 'Couldn't come from anyone ordinary, so I reckon we've found our second warrior. Well, am I right?'

'As ever, Sedryk. Indeed, it seems I am the next appointed to fulfill the gods' ends,' Stec said.

'Glad to hear it. Nice to have a friend I can trust involved.'

Several eyebrows were raised at this, for King Sedryk hadn't spoken to many about his unease over the prophecy, but Stec ignored him and the others continued to clean weapons as if they hadn't heard either. By the time they had all been introduced, the comment had been forgotten by most of the group, though Els and Stec remained thoughtful.

The following morning, they were ready to leave and Stec tried to part gracefully from his friends,

'I must get back to Sky City, see how things are going with Abrim and Saluna, if Queen Wertle has returned or not.'

'Then the warrior leaves us so early?' Sedryk enquired. 'Don't you want to find out who you must fight alongside next?'

'What do you mean by that?' asked Stec.

'Well, I think you should get to know The Three, don't you?' Sedryk pushed him.

'What on earth are you going on about?' asked Stec, confused.

277

'I think he means you should be at the announcement in Izk,' explained Vistar, 'Surely someone told you?'

'To be honest, I've been a little preoccupied lately, what with Jhrik-ansi, sorry, L'ra's Town, and the problems in Sky City. What announcement is this and why didn't one of you tell me?'

'I thought you would have already been told,' Lidynne said, 'The next royal meeting is to be held at Sea's End Valley, over in Izk. King Nahvib's magi intend to reveal The Three there in eight days time.'

'Perhaps Nahvib didn't want too many priests invited. Might find some know more of the prophecy than him,' Sedryk grumbled.

'Maybe it was just an oversight. Anyway, we can all go together, King Nahvib wants these young people here and who can turn the Priest-Warrior back from the meeting?'

'Yes, we can use Stec as an escort, though I fear King Nahvib will think I am making one of my entrances with such a mixed company joining me – no offence, it's a charge that's usually levelled at me,' Sedryk explained, seeing the Northerners faces.

'But Sedryk, you don't think King Nahvib is actually angry with you, surely?' Stec frowned.

'How am I to know? No, I expect not. Who knows, maybe he has changed some of his choices since we last met. I hope so.' King Sedryk scowled and Vistar put a warning hand on his shoulder.

'Come, friend, let's not get upset yet,' the younger king whispered. 'Doesn't do any good to speak ill of King Nahvib now, in front of our new friends. Let's just see what awaits us at Izk.'

'Very well. I wish I had your optimism, though, Vistar,' Sedryk muttered in return.

It was a long journey back to Izk. They nearly choose to make the whole voyage by boat, but where glad they had chosen to change ships for horses later, as the seas were rough enough to put off any chance of sleep on the way back to Lykrosia.

'The straits have never been so foul to pass!' cried Stec.

'I know, let's hope fresh horses are ready, for I want to be at Izk quick and we won't make it unless we race, now!' Sedryk shouted above the sound of crashing waves.

Luckily, horses were saddled ready for the last part of the trip.

'Thank you Timo, Rayth, we'll speak properly later,' Els said, glad indeed that those at the temple had been listening when she'd sent the day they left Calan. She was happier still to find Audcy in the company. **You see, King Nahvib does want us there!** Els wrote to Sedryk, but his face was still grim.

'The note he left in my horse's pack is inviting, but a warning all the same: "Please join us for the meeting if you can, Lidynne, Sedryk and Vistar",' King Sedryk read from the letter he had found. 'I hope you arrive swiftly, but even if you do not, you need have no fear. The meeting will go ahead as intended, I'm sure you understand." Els, it's fortunate he and I are old friends or there would be more trouble over this. As it is, we ride with speed. I will not miss the Proclamation for anything.'

When they arrived, the party was concerned that the sun had already begun to set.

'If it's over, I'll never forgive myself!' cried King Sedryk, riding to the main gate with King Vistar close behind.

'Oh, Queen Lidynne, King Sedryk, King Vistar!' an ornately dressed young girl opened the door. 'And who are your companions?'

'Priests of L'ra and other enemies of evil. Please, let us in!' Sedryk shouted.

'Of course. Hail, King Sedryk, King Vistar and The Company who fight for the goddess!' announced the girl, jangling as her sequined and bejeweled garments banged against each other.

'Glad you could come!' cried King Azabar, hurrying over to greet the kings but jumping back a little when he saw Sorab on Els' shoulder.

'Oh, by Gax' beard, it gets worse!' sighed Sedryk. 'Hello, Azabar, so it's at your place this time. I hope we haven't missed dinner?'

'No, Lord Bik managed to persuaded Lady Taheya and the rest of my ministers that an evening meeting would enable all to attend. So, do tell us all about your recent battles. Are these captives?' he indicated the Northerners with a hushed tone.

'These? These gentlemen fought alongside us. They are Northern allies, Els' people. You do remember Els from the wedding, don't you?'

'Yes, yes.' Azabar looked a little worried, but fortunately, the music began for dinner and the group hurried to be seated.

Everyone was very grand and the palace was quite different to Sytrannia's, so maybe it was this that made Els uncomfortable. She didn't think it was, though. For all that the royalty and politicians around the table greeted each other with laughs and hearty handshakes, there was no warmth, even in King Nahvib' voice or gaze.

'Something's not right. Not them, but not quite right. What do you think?' Els sent Alleri and Klara.

'My thoughts too. Lots of happy faces, but none of it's inside,' Alleri pronounced.

'Nerves? It's quite an occasion,' suggested Klara.

'I hope so, I'll just be glad when it's all over,' Alleri sent.

Throughout the meal, the three girls exchanged similar comments. They had been sat apart from each other and had ample opportunity to speak to different people, but the feeling was the same – most people's bright smiles hid fear and doubt, even from themselves.

At last, King Azabar stood and raised his glass, 'My thanks to you all for attending tonight, but greatest thanks to all who have begun the fight we are all to continue. To all our warriors!'

'To all our warriors!' his guests echoed and Lidynne grinned at the look on Stec's face.

'Most importantly,' Azabar continued, 'thanks to those who have tirelessly worked on the prophecy, scattered and ancient as its clues have been. Tonight, I give Queen Ashla the honour of declaring the identity of The Three, for she has been able to see the answer to the prophecy already, having no interest in it beyond her duty. Her Majesty, Queen Ashla.'

The queen stood up, poised between Prince Griorg on her right and Queen Karryn on her left. Karryn, like many others, was holding her breath, this was news all had waited too long for.

'The prophecy has been examined, tested, analysed and studied.' Queen Ashla began, 'These then, are findings which we come to in confidence. The three are chosen for their abilities and their designation by the gods. I declare The Sorceress as Els, The Healer to be Klara and the Guardian to be King Nahvib. Stand up, these people need to see you together!'

Els stood with the others, dazed by the proclamation. For a long time she had wondered who she was to fight with, who would stand besides her when the final battle came. She didn't know who she had expected, but this didn't feel like the real thing. Els looked around. Klara was more confused still, *'Me?'* she sent.

'Looks like it!' Els replied, but she couldn't be sure. Yes, Klara had healed many times in battle and outside it, had been instrumental in saving Jayak. King Nahvib had proved himself more than just the guardian of his own country as he sought to bring allies together and seek out those with gifts. But something was not right. Els saw that most people greeted the news gladly, but Yacconi's arms remained folded in defiance and King Sedryk shook his head sadly.

'Els? Congratulations.' Els turned to see Hwym next to her and felt a strange twinge. I've hardly spoken a word to him since I awoke at Volcano's Gorge, she realised, and I don't even know how he is, why he came. Some sorceress I am, she thought, how are the three of us going to work together anyway?

'What's the drink like here, anyway? Cam broke in, 'Whatever they've got, I'll find you two some, looks like we'll be celebrating a while tonight!'

'Els? You've gone really pale. Sit down. It's probably the shock.' Hwym sat Els down and she was grateful to be hidden from the view of most of the dancing guests.

Not shock. I knew, just, not sure about it all.

'Well, hey, you can do it. I'm mean, you've got all this magic and look at what happened in Green Forest.'

Thanks Hwym. I know I'm the Sorceress, just surprised a little by the other two.

'Hello, Els.' King Nahvib swept up to the young group. 'I was as surprised as you when the magi first showed me their suggested list, but I trust their judgement. So, it looks like I'll be seeing you back at the palace soon, then?'

'I suppose so. How's Jayak, does he know about this?' Els realised Jayak would probably be shocked to find most of the people he knew included, but not himself. What did the gods want with him? she wondered.

Both King Nahvib and Hwym stiffened at the mention of Jayak.

'I don't think we need concern ourselves with him right now,' Nahvib said, sharply.

'Of course not, sorry,' Els sent. She smiled then and once she had talked a bit with her brother and Hwym, she danced and drank a while. But none of it seemed real. It wasn't right, there was no comfort in this new place the proclamation had brought her to. And she wasn't the only one who felt this way. Lidynne was animated in conversation with Karryn, and the younger woman's reactions were more demonstrative than Els had ever seen her use before. What does she make of the decision to put Nahvib in such a place? thought Els. Doesn't he have enough to do already? Stec came over then and Els realised she had been waiting to talk to him.

'Happy?' Stec asked in an undertone laced with secrecy.

'Not exactly, though I feel I should be. I am formally declared part of the prophecy, along with a good friend and a noble ruler. But I don't feel happy, no.'

'Nor I, neither does Lidynne.' Here Stec changed to sending, *'And there are others, be comforted by that.'*

'What do you propose, a mutiny?'

'Hardly! But I am wary and think we must watch carefully in the days to come. I know you dream, as does Lidynne. Any strange dreams must be shared, perhaps the gods will speak the truth through them – to those who listen.'

'Perhaps. Can you stand up to the royal decrees, though, don't we just have to follow the decisions they make?'

'We're both worth more than that and it wouldn't be helping the kings to follow blindly. All we can do is go into the next stages of the war with our eyes open and pray that the opportunity to fulfill the prophecy comes swiftly. Besides, us warriors have to stick together.'

Els smiled then, at least there was one person who knew where he was heading. Thank the gods, she thought, for I feel all adrift. She looked around Azabar's famed ballroom, seeing only confusion where so many others thought they had found all their answers. Alleri and Klara danced with Cam and Hwym, kings mingled with priests.

Where do I belong? Els thought, Goddess, when will you show me the way home?

Part Three

Chapter 22

Things were very quiet in Istalan the morning after the proclamation. Only those of royal blood were missing, Nahvib and Karryn in their own quarters, Lidynne and Sedryk back home, having declined the invitation to breakfast with them. All the young people were about, though, not to mention Bronv-Grii carefully watching those he had brought. He shared his table with Drayk and the magi, but his eyes never strayed far from where Cam and Hwym ate.

The young Northerners ate at a table shared with Alleri, Dayx and a rather stunned Klara. Indeed, stunned would best describe how most of the diners were feeling; the impact of last night's news weighed heavily upon them. Talk was muted; no-one sure that they should speak publicly about that which had been decided without them.

Unsure of her place in all this, Els slid shyly into the seat next to Klara, causing a few heads to turn.

'Leave them to it, they're just jealous!' Dayx said, hugging Klara proudly.

'Don't know why, they might be glad it's not them,' Klara said.

'Don't be daft, you deserve this,' Dayx argued.

'I suppose so, but why me? There are many others would keep such great company better than me.'

'And better than me, too, but the proclamation has been made, we can't change that,' Els pointed out.

'And why should you, when the gods will it so?' declared Dayx.

'Ah, the will of the gods, isn't it good when we all know what that means?' said Jayak, striding in, with Cyru.

'I hope you aren't about to contest it?' Dayx rose from his seat.

'Peace, Dayx, I come to fight alongside you, remember?' Jayak asked.

'If he should know that, why do you need to remind

him?' Hwym asked, roused from his watchfulness at the nerve of this newcomer.

'Any who know me should trust that, though I realise you do not have that advantage. I am Jayak, sorcerer of Sytrannia.'

'So, you are Jayak? I've heard a lot about you and little of it to convince me as to your intentions.' A glance at Els gave away more than Hwym's words.

'I've also heard a great deal about you, Hwym, but I haven't seen anything to confirm or deny my information until now. Perhaps we should both leave judgement behind until we know each other better.'

Hwym was surprised by Jayak's words; they did not match the image he had of the sorcerer. He was wary, amongst powerful strangers and breakfasting opposite a girl he had once hoped to impress. Finding Els blessed with talents beyond his understanding, he felt the gulf between them widen. Now this man he recognised as a rival was offering him a truce of sorts and who could tell what that could be worth in these uncertain days? He felt the tension in the room, the fear of further fighting. Els jumped as a frightened Sorab clawed her knee. This wasn't the time, maybe it wasn't even the right person. No fights had to be fought today, Hwym knew that.

'Very well.' He stretched out his hand. 'Let us judge each other not by our reputations, but by our actions.'

'I thank you for your kindness, if I can repay you in the battles to come, I will do so.' Jayak shook Hwym's hand.

'That's if they let you fight any,' muttered Dayx.

Jayak pretended he had not heard, but the mood of the group had darkened with his entrance, much as he tried to avoid it. The chair nearest to him was next to Els, but he couldn't pull it out, couldn't ask her leave to sit there. He hesitated until Alleri grudgingly kicked out the chair next to her as Cyru took that next to Els. Jayak was more relieved than he would admit and Alleri turned to Cam before Jayak could try to thank her. So she too, is against me? Jayak thought and he pondered the prophecy sadly.

How could he convince the Three of his changed heart when one of his oldest friends no longer accepted him?

To Jayak, he was the only one suffering these doubts. Els, however, was more troubled than he could ever guess and already missing Queen Lidynne. Though Klara showed some confusion, Els knew she accepted the prophecy readily enough and there were none in the whole of the kingdom who would dare doubt King Nahvib's place in those chosen. Yet someone was wrong, Lidynne had said so and Els knew the power invested in her, had seen it in action.

She may have gone, but Stec lingered a day or two in Sytrannia before visiting Akrin on his way to the straits. Els could seek answers from him, so she left her friends as quickly as she could. The thoughts and fears she had made breakfast uncomfortable anyway, as much as the atmosphere amongst her varied friends and acquaintances did.

She found Stec in the second floor library. It was the smallest of the three libraries within the palace, concerned only with reference works and these mainly dealing with history, languages or works of a holy nature. It was a likely place to find the high priest and yet Els was more than pleased to see him turn and face her. Here was a friend who had fought in battles with her, who had been through changes like those she had. Who better than High Priest Stec to discuss the fears her friends would hide from?

'Els, good to see you my dear.' Stec put his book down on the low table before him and threw another log onto the fire.

'Hello Stec. I'm glad to see you, more than you could guess.'

'Maybe not. With Queen Lidynne gone, you are the only other who agrees with me about the proclamation.'

'That's what I came to talk to you about. This whole thing about one in the prophecy being wrong...'

'At least one. What's the matter, do you doubt

289

Lidynne's words? I know the other kings and Ashla are convincing in their arguments, but her truth is from the gods themselves. Gax rules the hunt, he is never led by a false scent. Do you begin to believe the arguments of your friends?'

What, over those of the gods? Hardly! The gods revealed themselves even when I doubted greatly. No, Stec my fear is one you may have shared with Queen Lidynne, I don't know. It turns around in my mind though and I must know if it does in yours. Stec, have you thought that I could be the one who is wrong?'

Stec looked at her a moment and Els wanted to look away, the priest's eyes saw more than her comment itself, saw the fear and doubt behind her words. Then he laughed, a long deep laugh and Els realised it was a while since either of them had had time for humour.

'You?' Stec chuckled, 'You, the wrong one named?' He wiped his eyes.

'Oh, Els, you are the one person Lidynne and I are both in accordance on. We cannot decide if Klara, Nahvib, or the both of them are those desired by the gods to play their part in this great war. One thing we do know is that you are chosen. L'ra herself has called you to play your part. Of you, we have no doubt.'

Els shoulders sagged with relief. Only then she knew how much she felt the joy of her work, not just the problems it had brought her.

'You know we only say what's true,' Stec said, 'Gods, Els, don't you be leaving the side of good when you are the one strong link we have.'

'One strong link? Scarcely. There are many and lots more powerful than me.'

'Who decides what power is?' Stec asked her. 'That's where Lidynne and I reckon the prophecy has failed. Klara is a strong healer and King Nahvib a strong ruler, but is this what the gods demand? Your young friends come over without magic, yet they play their part. Alkar, Vistar and Taheya all take important decisions yet are ultimately governed by others. How can we decide whom the gods see as important? We can only look for signs and take action when we see them. Time will show us our real allies and our chosen Healer and Guardian, that is all we can know.'

'Thanks, Stec. How long are you staying?'

'Not much longer, I should probably go back tomorrow if I want to stop at Vistar's castle for a while. Besides, you have your friends to catch up with.'

'Yes,' Els grimaced. *'And who are they? Those I can trust are troubled enough by their own problems.'*

'And do you count Jayak amongst those?'

'I don't know where I count Jayak anymore,' the sorceress frowned. *'I had thought I would never speak to him again, yet here we both are, preparing for unknown battles alongside each other.'*

'I think you should see why it is that you must work together, how it can be possible to do so without bitterness. Then you can give proper attention to your brother and your Northern friend. After all, they are in a strange place, just as you once were.'

'Oh, Cam and Hwym can look after themselves. Jayak worries me more. Why did King Nahvib and the magi keep him here, why does he look at me as if he is about to speak and then not say a word? I can't have this confusion before I fight the next battle. You know that as well as I do.'

'Well, we shouldn't speak too much here…there are many with talent and who knows that we can trust everyone? But I'm meeting Alkar in Akrina, maybe we can shed some light on this problem together. Meantime, look out for any hints as to the truth, the goddess loves an adventure, you know that!'

'Yes, seems every day is an adventure of kinds.'

'And don't forget to look out for your friends; they're part of this, one way or another.'

'I'll try, if they let me,' Els said, remembering the strange looks Jayak had cast her way.

Alone in his room, Jayak's thoughts were not that different from those of his former lover, had he known it. I must try to talk to them, he reprimanded himself, I know I must, but... He thought of the dreadful feeling that came over him when he saw his once-close friends. The terrible shame he had felt when Hwym challenged him, the knowledge of how true the accusations against him were and how vain his cries were against them. The way that Dayx avoided his eyes, stuck closer to Klara than ever in his presence. How Cyru, stronger in magic every day, refused to share the ambitions he must have with Jayak, knowing where they had brought him. What did they think he would do next? Jayak felt their distrust, their fear, with every awkward conversation, each made more bitter by the knowledge that he had earnt them.

But Els! His spirit sagged when he saw her turn his way, then turn back, unheeding the need she saw. He knew she was aware that he wanted to speak, could read it in his mind if she dared, but would not risk such contact with one who had betrayed her as he had done. Besides, he was forbidden to.

How then can I seek forgiveness, when the only one I knew to turn to has left my side? Jayak wondered. While the others find joy in the proclamation, am I the only one who has a task so huge to fulfill? What do I do about Els, not to mention King Nahvib? He would say he has forgiven me, but he knows the judgement on me. How can I be sure his words are true? But he is part of the prophecy, as he is one of the Three, so I must trust him. Must I trudge through every battle, unable to fight using my powers, just a foot soldier? Even then, who would be able to follow my instructions, work with me in a fight? Oh, gods, it is not just the forgiveness of the Three I must seek, rather that of the kingdom.

Jayak's situation was most painfully evident in class. Durrew felt tears in his eyes to see his once-powerful pupil have to answer problems with his hands tied by his judgement. The other students gave Jayak little sympathy, scorning the academic way he would mix chemicals where they would cast a spell. The magi all halted the gossiping they heard in class, but once out in the corridors, rumours spread. Jayak had been demoted to wizard and was too ashamed to say, his powers had been taken by the magi, had been lost in his saving. The reality was too obvious and so no-one guessed it.

Truth be told, there weren't many interested in finding it out. Though his former friends would share space with Jayak in the class or canteen, there were few words spoken between them and his well-being seemed of little interest to them.

Jayak began to spend increasing time in the libraries and the offices of the magi. If he had known it, he was tracing Els' footsteps, much to the trauma of their teachers.

'Should we tell them to speak to each other, try and clear the air?' Zritz suggested.

'We can't tell anyone anything, to intervene with the prophecy or our judgement on Jayak would void both of them.' Durrew reminded his friend.

'And what would we tell them, anyway?' sighed Pocack. 'We are as much in the darkness as anyone on Rima.'

'At least we have faith in the prophecy,' said Durrew. 'I mean, you don't believe what Lidynne and Stec have to say?' he asked, fearfully.

'Certainly not! We know the prophecy to be true. That is what guides us. How could that falter at a time like this?' Pocack cried. 'Gods! If we doubt the prophecy, what is left for us?'

'Only faith,' said Zritz. 'That is always left and we will need plenty of that, one way or the other.'

'Yes, it doesn't take a prophet to see that.'

'Enough of prophecy!' Pocack said. 'There is a great deal of work to be done yet and I will not send half-trained wizards or apprentices to do the work of sorcerers.'

'Then you fear the next attack will come soon?' asked Durrew.

'Attacks occur daily, despite our victories,' Pocack said, sadly. 'However, I fear it cannot be too long before the next battle. I think their High Lords will attempt to draw out our best warriors and talented folk in the next fight, before the final battle.'

'Trying to kill the best of our men? Then do we still take all of them into battle?' Zritz asked.

'I don't know yet,' Pocack admitted. 'We must discuss this at length before the time arises. I fear losing people on whom the gods have clearly distributed gifts, yet wonder if we could win the next fight without such talents.'

'There is much study to be done yet!' Durrew sighed.

* * *

Sytrannia's days grew a little lighter and the air stiller in the month that followed. The sun began to reach the palace lawns earlier on the mornings and yet no joyous students sat there in its rays. Everyone was inside, learning, casting, concocting, all for the unknown days to come. Those graduating in this new atmosphere wore their cloaks with quiet pride. There was no grand sweeping of new clothing, only an increased rustling across the floors revealed the level of expertise discovered within this crisis.

Students listened in their classes, there was no laughter at any mistakes made by those teaching, no notes passed. The magi spoke of the new discipline of their pupils happily, yet there was a part of them that missed the carefree times when friends teased each other and magic was as much a gift of fun as of power.

Where were the young people chasing each other in the garden? The giggles of young girls, the jokes of the young men? Flowers decorated the grounds, but there was no-one to see them. Lars complained that his wine lasted too long now, there weren't the young crowds to enjoy it.

One day was hotter than those before it and the bulk of those in the palace came into the gardens, not so much to enjoy them, as to flee the boiling heat inside. Exhausted from study and practice as much as the heat, many sat or lay in the courtyard or on the surrounding grassed area. Still the people outside lay as quiet as the clouds that drifted overhead, not communicating with each other, only waiting, thinking.

'And here is the hope of our future!' rang a clear voice, seeming loud across the stillness. Heads turned, such boldness had been forgotten in the effort of learning.

'Who interrupts our peace?' replied Dayx, though he barely lifted himself off the ground to make his comment.

'I do.' Queen Karryn rounded the corner of the building to face him. 'I, your queen, would like to know what you young people are learning, all stuffed up inside most of the time?'

'Learning? We learn how to fight the battles that will save this country, this planet!' Cyru said, astounded.

'And will you have the energy, the spirit?' countered Karryn. 'You have forgotten how to laugh, how to talk to each other. How can you fight when you forget what you are fighting for?' She folded her arms as they recoiled at her words, except for Sorab, who ran to her. Turning, he bared his teeth, seeming to agree with the queen's words.

There was a stunned gasp. What the queen said was outrageous, yet undoubtedly true. When had they laughed, smiled, chatted, just for the sake of it?

'If you are not careful, you will win this war only to come home to nothing,' Karryn told them. 'Just thought I'd let you know what you were doing before you do it.'

She walked off, leaving a sudden hubbub in her wake. The queen smiled to herself as she heard the noise erupt behind her. This was something to cheer Nahvib up, she thought and ran into the palace happily. In the courtyard, everyone talked over each other, suddenly awoken into arguments and ideas.

'Do you feel the prophecy is enough to save us?' Els asked Klara. She chose her words carefully, yet she had to find out what others thought about the proclamation.

'It needs to be,' Klara answered with equal care.

All around them, others began to pose tentative questions. At last! thought Els, people wake up, perhaps here we will find answers. Stec probably didn't think it would happen this way, but maybe now we will find the other two. She scooped Sorab up to find his heart was racing almost as much as hers.

It was in this atmosphere of change that Jayak felt he could begin his own explorations. Two days after Karryn's rebuke, Jayak decided he could wait no longer. Uncaring who saw him or what anyone might think, Jayak knocked on Klara's door.

'Hello? Dayx?' but Klara's voice wavered, this was not Dayx' knock.

'No, it's me, Klara,' Jayak's answer was soft, but clear.

'What do you want?'

'A moment, just a moment with you, Klara, that's all.'

'All right. Come in,' the healer replied and hesitantly opened the door to her former friend.

'Thank you,' Jayak said. 'I know you must wonder at me coming here, but I have something to ask you.'

'Well, sit down at least, Jayak,' Klara said.

'No. Thank you, but it won't take long.'

'Then go on.' By now, Klara was intrigued, though unsettled.

'I have to ask your forgiveness, Klara,' Jayak said, looking down at his hands, unable to face Klara.

'What for, why me, of all people?' Klara demanded, 'There are plenty you could ask with more cause than me, Els for one.'

'Don't think I don't know that. There's a list of people who I would have accept my desire for forgiveness. But I begin with you. I have abused your friendship, Klara. I took advantage of your giving nature when I laid plans for the enemy. I put yourself and Dayx in danger with my works for the Demon Lords, I jeopardized your very home. I ask forgiveness of you because I know it is yours to give. What do you say, Klara?'

The girl smiled, 'Yes, Jayak, I forgive you.' She held

out her hand to Jayak, forced him to look at her in amazement. 'Jayak, don't look so ashamed. Don't be so ashamed. Haven't we all made mistakes? And there are probably more to be made yet before the gods reveal all. But winning this war is nothing if we can't celebrate it together, didn't Karryn say that?'

'Thank you Klara!' Jayak's eyes shimmered with tears. 'I didn't know what you would say, I know my friends have little cause to know me now.'

'But once we did. Who was it introduced me to Dayx? I will never forget how you welcomed us both, fearful apprentices, to your city. And Jayak, if I can forgive, others will, given time.'

'And what time do we have?' Jayak said, thinking of the others he must seek out and confront.

'The gods give us the time we need – and the places. Look where Els had to go before she heard L'ra again. Talk to her.'

'Easier said, Klara, easier said,' Jayak muttered.

So it proved. Many times Jayak found himself outside her door unable to knock. He saw Els nearly every day in training and was astounded at her progress. One day he thought he was ready to approach her, but as he moved towards her, a slender stream of fire tunneled upwards from her hands.

'Yes, Jayak?' she spoke without turning, knew he was there.

'Nothing, nothing,' he said, feeling the lameness of cold words when he wanted to send, to say everything that had changed in him without searching for words, only connecting with her mind. But Els remained apart, her powers mocking his lack.

Chapter 23

While Jayak was beginning to confront his past misdeeds with Klara, Els sought most of her answers in the palace libraries. She wished Stec were around to help, although she knew he was doing his own work in Sky City. Thankfully, the goddess have given Stec the power to send, but he was still in the earliest stages of using it. Still, sifting through the many books on prophecies kept her occupied for some afternoons. There were small pamphlets written in minute script, thick volumes with paragraph upon paragraph of subheadings, all to search through. Sometimes she would see a title that looked important, only to read the chapter and gain nothing from it. After long weeks of study, she found she had snatched only two relevant indications of the gods' will.

'Stec,' she sent, 'I think I have a couple of things.'

'Really? How clear?'

'Not very, that's why I thought I'd see what you think. Here goes: "Each of the Three will have met already before the final conflict." That's from the Book of the Elementals, so the prophets concerned with them see a general connection in different things to begin with, but still, I thought it was interesting.'

'Yes, after two battles, you probably do already know the other two.'

'Great. I just wish I knew that I know them!'

'Well, it is interesting. What about the other?'

'This is from a funny little book, "Straynge Wayes the Hunt Leadeth and Diverse Adventures upon the Waye."'

'Not one I've ever heard of. Still, carry on.'

'Well, here you are, "Looketh not to thy weapon, rather to thine wielder thereof." Now that means nothing to me, Stec.'

'Surely a warning against being led astray by might, rather than character? That makes King Nahvib seem even more unlikely if you ask me. He has all the weaponry, but *maybe not the character. I mean, I think he's a great ruler of his country, but I think that's because that's the job the gods have given him, not this.'*

'Makes sense with Lidynne's fears too.'

'And Nahvib's hostility – if he isn't one of the Three, a part of him probably knows that.'

'What about Klara, though? She has all the weapons as far as healing goes, herbs, mixtures and all the knowledge. But character? I don't know how well she would cope in battle.'

'Whereas Nahvib would fight mightily in battle, but has little magic. He'd be equally disastrous if he has no god-given gifts.'

'What, both of them are wrong?'

'Could be so, I hope not.'

'Nor I, if we look for two new candidates, it could take forever.'

'Well, one at least is not meant to be present in the final days of the war. I'll share this information with Alkar and some priests and priestesses I can trust. I'll have to go now, this sending still tires me. Carry on your search, but be careful.'

'Don't worry: I'll be very careful who I trade information with.'

Els was remembering her promise the following day, when Karryn stopped her after Pocack's healing class.

'Els? There's a visitor waiting for you in the common room.'

Who waits for me? Els asked, confused.

'I've never met him before, but he claims to have known Kyrria. Gives his name as Sy.'

Sy? What does he want?

'Didn't say. I can send him away if you don't want to see him now. I realise it might be a little strange now Kyrria's gone.'

No. If Sy needs to talk to me, he must have a reason. I'll see him.

'Very well, I'll come down with you.'

Really your Majesty, I'm fine to walk down on my own.

'I'm sure you are! But I'd like to see what this young man wants with you. Nahvib and I do want your return here to be a happy one, you know that. And enough of this 'your majesty' and 'my Queen'! Wasn't I just plain Karryn when we met?'

True. What a long time ago that seems! Well, let's see what Sy wants, it's a long time since we met, too.

Els was quickly reminded of just how long when she first set eyes on Sy. The confident, almost arrogant young man had grown serious in the many months since her arrival on Southern shores. His clothes were brown, darker than any she had seen a Southerner wear and far too sombre for a man used to impressing womenfolk with his fine clothing as much as his expensive gifts. He was thinner too and Els wondered if his social habits had changed as well, for the few times she had passed him in Sytrannia had been in the streets near Istalan's bars and restaurants.

'Hello, Els,' Sy strode forward, held out a hand strangely bare of jewellery. 'I like the robes, congratulations. You've changed a lot since we first met. What is it, two years?'

Almost. Sy, what do you want?

'Why do I come here, without an ounce of magic in me? Yes, I know your queen thought it strange, too.' Sy nodded in Karryn's direction.

'Be fair, Sy. Is this an atmosphere in which we can trust strangers easily?'

'Maybe as much as you can your own!' Sy told her, 'Yes, I can read the papers. It's a poor merchant that doesn't keep up with which way the wind blows these days.'

'Then you're a proper merchant? You have a business already established?' Karryn probed.

'Inherited, since my father died, but worked in since I

can't remember when.' Sy grimaced as he saw Els' sympathetic look. 'Yes, I suppose that's why I came really. Father dying right after Kyrria, it was all too much. Felt I had to talk to someone.'

Why me?

'Well, knew I could get my story out without you interrupting, that's for one!' Sy laughed.

'Sy! That's a dreadful thing to say!' Karryn cried, dismayed. Els however, had already begun to smile.

You're the first to say it like that!

'But not the first to think it, I'll bet,' Sy said. 'You must hear a fair few secrets that others think they can trust you not to pass on.'

Not that many. I can write & send, you know! Though she passed off Sy's comment flippantly, Els thought of Stec and Lidynne. How much longer could she keep their activities secret? More to the point, how would they be able to disclose their answers if they found any? Fear crept about her heart as she imagined what would happen if she and her colleagues were discovered in what many would consider treason.

'The other reason was that you would understand,' Sy paused. 'I knew you must miss Kyrria at least as much as I did. When I first heard the news of her death, I thought I was all right, that I accepted it.'

We all dealt differently with it. Don't feel guilty. Els wrote.

'A part of me does, though. I wasn't bothered about the funeral, reckoned Kyrria would know what I felt, no need to go traipsing out in the desert with all you lot. Not my place amongst priests and magi. So I carried on, made more trips away if anything, threw myself into the business. Made a great deal of money those months since Kyrria's death, didn't shed a tear. Spent my time with my parents, or my customers. Wasn't a day went by that I wasn't busy.'

Then you did better than most of us. Els scribbled with feeling.

'Seemed to. Then one of our neighbours turned weird, started talking funny, wouldn't let us in the house any more. That was really strange. My mother was normally in there all the time, she got on really well with Taykal's wife.'

'Don't tell us, another possessed?' Karryn sighed.

'You guess right. Suppose it's a story you recognise all too well by now. Well, we didn't find out until too late. My father couldn't leave Taykal alone, thought he must be ill or the like. So he went over unannounced one day. Taykal must have been furious to have had his work destroyed.'

His work?

'Oh yes, plenty there was of it as well. Books and potions all over the place. His wife hiding, half-starved in the basement.'

'That's appalling. Brrr!' Karryn shivered, the image all too familiar.

'So there was no way he could let my father report it. We'll never really know what happened but the house was awash with blood when I got there. The only mercy is that I found father's body, not my mother. Taykal fled, but we have heard stories of him since.'

'And others like him, I know. There are many sad evenings ahead of us before children play freely in Istalan's streets once more.'

'And capturing the evil ones is only a part of our solution,' Sy groaned. 'Look how many friends have already been taken from us. What will the gods leave us with?'

In that, we must trust their judgement. Els wrote.

'That's what I've been thinking about,' said Sy. 'It's been driving me crazy, if I'm honest. When my father was killed, suddenly all I could think of was Kyrria. Why did she have to die? What would she say about my father's murder? I didn't have all the answers, but I knew which side she would be on, even foreseeing her death.'

Which she possibly did. Els replied.

Karryn darted a shocked look at Els. It was the first time, to her knowledge, that Els had admitted this. How significant was this at such a time? Karryn looked between the two young people before her, trying to size up the parts they may play in this war.

'Well,' Sy went on, 'I realised I couldn't sit around and do nothing when two of the people closest to me had given their lives in this thing.'

'Maybe not, but beware recklessness. This war is no place for foolhardy heroics,' Karryn admonished.

'And I don't plan any.' Sy added, defensively. 'But I want to be a part of the group that battles the evil ones. And I want to know what Kyrria believed in enough to gamble her life for.'

'You know what you want – answers.' smiled Queen Karryn. 'And that's perfectly natural, who doesn't? But are you prepared for where your questions will take you?'

'Yes!' cried Sy, 'Kyrria was a well-respected friend until the day she died. I must find out more. I must stop these Demon Lords crushing others as they did her. I know many think of me as just her former lover, someone waiting for the chance to get back with her, but it wasn't like that.'

Really? Not even a little? Els questioned.

'No! Maybe others always keep such feelings close, but not I. Besides, Kyrria didn't leave me for another man, she left men behind for the priesthood. You can't argue with that.'

Some would still try to. Els countered.

'I'll leave you children to it!' laughed Karryn, 'King Nahvib will be missing me and I would not leave our Guardian lacking in support just now.'

'Goodbye Queen Karryn.' Sy bowed low. 'I hope I will prove my will to serve Your Majesties is just.'

Bye Karryn. Tell Alleri where I am? Lunch could be late! Els waved goodbye to her queen and turned to face the merchant.

Are you sure your attachment to Kyrria comes from

friendship only?

'Don't try to force your problems onto me!' Sy cautioned.

What problems?

'You don't think the reason you can't see beyond the relationship bonds of a former lover is because of the way you still look at yours!'

What? Wouldn't look at Jayak outside class. scratched Els.

'Oh, of course, gods, no,' laughed Sy. 'Everyone knows you need to sort things out before you fight this war properly. Otherwise your energy is all in fighting each other. Unless you actually patch it up, mind, there're a fair few would bet on that.'

Are there now? The words were few but Els' face spoke volumes.

'Well, can't even the Sorceress have her happy match?' Sy goaded. 'I'm only saying what several think. You need a match who is your equal and who better than Jayak?'

I don't know, but it's not him! The pencil broke and Els threw it to the floor in fury.

'Look, I'm sorry,' Sy was obviously frightened by the outburst he had provoked. 'It's just, looks like everyone knows where they're going except me. I thought you were as focused as everyone else.'

Els shook her head.

'And as far Jayak, it just seemed…You don't like him, then?'

Els shrugged.

'Look, I'm sorry, just came to offer my help. And yes, get some answers. I could be helpful though, I have a lot of contacts. I've travelled, Els. Let me help! Isn't the next battle going to be somewhere different? That's the word in the taverns, anyway.'

Els nodded, there was no point hiding it now. She couldn't decide why the merchant had chosen to come here, but he had already offered a great deal, why try to keep back what she knew. Besides, she had trusted him from that first day at the port and he had led her to the right place from there.

Unable to tell Sy that she had decided he should stay around, Els could only beckon. To her great surprise, Sy came after her. An unlikely sight they made, silently walking the corridors to the office of the magi. Several people turned as they made their way along, for Sy was clearly no apprentice and his clothes didn't match his obviously Southern complexion.

The magi were startled to see Sy, but regained their composure when they saw how keen Els was to support him. Picking a pen off their shelf, she hastily scribbled her recent thoughts: **Friend of Kyrria, fine time to turn up, contacts abroad?**

Although the magi had no place for Sy, like Els, they saw there was value in his trading links and sent him to Drayk.

'He'll be more use there, political connections could be useful – thinking about the East and West,' Pocack said.

'Fairly put!' Durrew added.

'And we hear little news from the North, we can't always send Els there.' put in Zritz.

'True. Maybe Sy's travelling experience would help us there. Cranff and King Hurburt have enough pressure upon them to begin with.' Pocack decided. *'Besides, it just feels right to have him here.'*

So the conversation ended, leaving all concerned somewhat happier than they had woken that morning. Sy was happy to have a part to play in events and the palace officials were more than glad for another willing fighter, however unexpected. Els found herself strangely encouraged by this new arrival. She might not see much of him and it would take her a while to work out Sy's role here. Yet it felt good to have a friend of Kyrria's to talk to. She wanted to talk about Kyrria again, to work out what she would do if she were about now. Would she have been the one to goad the wizards into action as Queen Karryn had done? Maybe so and every day Els missed her friend's humour, the well-timed desire for action which was what had shown her faith. At least now Els could be with one who had known Kyrria well. Perhaps the lonely cloud that had lain upon her for so long had been lifted with the Battle of Volcano's Gorge.

Similar thoughts to those of the young sorceress were tumbling about the minds of all in Istalan. Queen Karryn's words, Sy's arrival and the proclamation had given a sense of unity and purpose back to the city's inhabitants, a sense of momentum that must surely precede an imminent victory.

Then Drayk entered the royal drawing room unannounced and late at night.

'Drayk? You might knock!' smiled Nahvib, and then he saw his First Minister's face. The man was white and he shook badly.

'Gods, sit down! What is it?'

'Get Karryn and the magi, fast.' Drayk said, his voice unsteady.

King Nahvib beckoned to his nearest servant and the others were gathered within minutes. Karryn passed a wine goblet to Drayk and he took the drink gratefully. While he sipped it, the magi and the king and queen watched him with mounting concern. Drayk's face gradually regained some colour, but his hands still shook. When he set the goblet down he looked at his king with an expression of some pain.

'I hate to bear such bad news, but a terrible attack has taken place on the very outskirts of Istalan,' he began.

'Demon Lords?' was Durrew's first question.

'Almost certainly one of their agents.'

'Who was attacked then?' asked King Nahvib, 'All of us are safe, our young people are all in tonight, I thought? Your face is so grave, I know you don't tell me of a stranger being hurt.'

'Which of our subjects has become their latest victim?' Karryn asked, 'We must know, now!'

'Not one of ours, but a friend, yes,' Drayk sadly

admitted. 'One of my advisors found an Izkian horse wandering, riderless, in the desert to the SouthWest of here. Following tracks, he came to the body of Lady Taheya not far from the city's outer borders.'

'Dead?' asked Karryn, horrified.

'Not yet,' Drayk sighed, 'But signs aren't good. She's been badly stabbed in the chest and stomach. She hasn't regained consciousness and so we don't know why she was riding this way.'

'Then send riders to Izk! Let Azabar explain,' King Nahvib cried.

'I have already done so,' Drayk told him, calming now as he realised he had set in place all that he could do. 'I hope for an answer some time tomorrow, our riders will race through the night and travel in a group of three, so they will not be so easily overcome.'

'Yes, why did Taheya come alone?' Karryn wondered, 'She isn't stupid, why ride alone?'

'Unless she had news that could not wait,' Pocack said.

'It must be the case.' Nahvib decided, 'Let tomorrow not be too late to find out.'

'It almost certainly will be, otherwise, why risk such speed and danger to get it to us?' Zritz said.

'Let us hope none of us regret such a brave journey, least of all the lady herself,' Queen Karryn sighed.

'Until tomorrow, there is little we can do. I've sent Lady Taheya to the hospital where they work constantly to restore her,' Drayk said.

'Send the best healers we have, let Klara have a team of her choosing. We will save Taheya if even the slightest chance is given us,' said Karryn.

'Without doubt. Then we meet again in the morning, the ninth hour,' King Nahvib declared, 'Let us pray daybreak brings all the news we need to hear.'

Chapter 24

It was a bleary-eyed group that gathered around the King's drawing room table the following morning. None had slept well, waking amidst fearful dreams of what might have happened in the hours since they had first tried to rest. Durrew looked quite dishevelled, an overcoat hastily thrown over casual trousers and hair untidy. He was incapable of thinking about appearance when tragedy threatened the palace again. Having lost his wife and nearly seen some of his pupils die in recent troubles, the possibilities of this latest disaster seemed particularly desperate. Zritz didn't look much better, tired beyond even his long years. Only Pocack and Drayk appeared ready for action, determined to see through what had passed. King Nahvib looked harried, could he take his country, his continent, through yet another crisis? Queen Karryn sat close, trying to reassure her husband, but her face was also bleak. Rallying students was one thing, averting an evil which had tracked Taheya from the Western limits of the continent, was quite another.

'Well, first the news on Lady Taheya,' said Drayk, looking at the mostly anxious faces before him, 'She is alive.'

'Speaking? Well?' asked Karryn.

'It's too early to say how well she is and speech is jumbled, confused. But even her survival is nothing short of miraculous.'

'Yes, the healers found the wounds she took were worse even than we had at first heard. Many of them had never seen stab wounds go so deep,' Pocack confirmed, 'Thank goodness we had Klara with us or we might never have saved her.'

'As it is, we can hardly depend on her to help us much at this stage,' Drayk said.

'Yes, the enemy has taken a brave ally and left us short of aid in the West,' Queen Karryn said.

'Let us speak bluntly,' suggested Durrew. 'We all know that Azabar is a poor king. We must talk to Ashla and secure our position on the Western shores or the Demon Lords will attack in full strength.'

'Are things so bad?' King Nahvib groaned.

'Worse,' said Drayk.

'Worse, how can things get any worse?' the king demanded.

'News came this morning not only from the royal hospital, but from our riders to Izk,' Drayk explained.

'Then we know why Lady Taheya fled so madly?' Karryn asked. 'There is surely some hope if we can begin to understand why we have been attacked in so foul a way?'

'My thoughts exactly,' agreed Pocack, 'Any news we now have that the Demon Lords tried to suppress must be news we can take advantage of. Let us have it.'

'It's not good, but yes, it is very important,' said Drayk.

'Go, on!' cried Durrew, 'Let us know, so that we can act on it.'

'The news from Izk had come from further,' Durrew explained, 'The West is in jeopardy, Demon Lords infiltrate there.'

'What, even proud King Yacconi now needs our help?' King Nahvib asked.

'None more so,' Drayk said, 'Seems Rucilia is caught in the grip of this great evil. Being Northernmost of the Western countries, her invasion suggests the evil has already swept through Liance and Cassal.'

'Then the Westerners believe the Demon Lords are arriving solely from the Southern end of the continent?' Pocack leaned forward.

'Good point,' acknowledged Drayk, 'They may well have had assistance from the North; we should alert King Hurburt and Lord Cranff at once. I will instruct Bronv-Grii to take a message on his return North. At least he has some protection.'

'Yes. Still, we have to admit that most Demon Lords

probably came over from this continent. There wouldn't have been that many left in the North after the battle of Green Forest I shouldn't have thought?' Durrew commented.

'True, we are yet to see a decisive victory on Southern or Western land,' Pocack agreed. 'Perhaps the time for the Western war has come?'

'That fool, Azabar, why didn't he ask for help earlier? How long have the Demon Lords been growing in his kingdom, getting stronger before they attack the West, along with the rest of us?' Nahvib thumped the table in fury.

'How long, we may never know,' Drayk sighed.

'Yes and as for whose fault it is, that's also irrelevant to discuss now. Let's beat this evil, then work out how to stop it coming back. We don't need to fall out with each other,' Zritz stressed.

'True enough,' Nahvib sighed. 'It just seems we have come so far, only for it to be for nothing.'

'Nothing? Don't say it is for nothing, my dear,' Karryn said. 'We are most ready to defeat this plague and that is worth all the sacrifices we have made. Even Taheya would acknowledge that, or she would never have made such a journey.'

'Queen Karryn is right,' Pocack agreed. 'The students, wizards and yes, even those above them are trained as never before. They have been through some trials, but probably they needed them to be as strong as they are now.'

'Indeed, who would want an untrained warrior in the battlefield, holding his sword well, but unable to use it?' Zritz added.

'Then we must lend the West our aid if we have it in such abundance. Deep in my heart, I know there is no choice, I have to authorize it,' King Nahvib said.

'You don't need to sound so forlorn, King Nahvib,' Durrew challenged. 'We know that there must be a battle on each continent. Surely we should be glad that the prophecy is coming to fruition with increasing speed?'

'You are right. It that case, Drayk, arrange a meeting of the Southern kingdoms in two days time and send word to the East and North. We can't waste any more time.'

News of the meeting spread quickly and while the Sytrannians hastened to ready the palace for such short-notice guests, the youngsters grew confused by recent events.

'What's going on now?' Cam asked Hwym the morning the guests were due to arrive.

'I don't know, something big, or they wouldn't get everyone together. I'm glad we're here to find out, though.'

'Then you won't be going back with Bronv-Grii?'

'Why would I do that? You can't be thinking about it?' Hwym demanded.

'There is Reesa to think about. I have responsibilities to consider beyond my sister,' Cam said.

'I can't believe you'd leave me here,' Hwym was aghast.

'Then come back with me. You don't have to stay here.'

'But I do. Els is here,' Hwym said.

'And? Hwym, I don't want to be cruel, but what interest has she shown you? I'm not overly fond of this Jayak but he does seem to care for Els. Besides, he's clearly back in favour here – and with her, too. Really, how much time has she spent with you lately?'

'More than when we first got here,' Hwym said. His voice was defensive, but then he sighed, 'Cam, it's not about what she does for me, anyway. I love her, Cam, even if she only thinks of me as a friend. And she's still vulnerable here, never mind how powerful she is. I'm not about to walk away just because she isn't attracted to me.'

'Just be careful you don't get lonely out here and end up blaming Els. I know you're mad about her, but it'll be hard to stay around here when she's so occupied.'

311

'I have thought about that,' Hwym nodded. 'I'm not going to sit around. I plan on getting myself signed up if there is a Western war, give Els some support there.'

'How?' Cam cried. 'You have nothing to offer in terms of magic and you don't even know anybody going there.'

'That's not entirely true,' Alleri had heard the young men's voices ringing out in the corridor and had quickly followed them to their owners.

'Oh, hello, Alleri,' Cam replied, embarrassed to be found arguing with his friend.

'Hello Cam, Hwym,' Alleri said. 'I'm going West, and power isn't everything, anyway. After all, it was Kyrria saved Jayak and she had the least magical ability of all of us. Why shouldn't Hwym go if that's what he feels is right? Maybe the gods call him to stay on, even if they don't you, Cam.'

Thanks, Alleri,' Hwym said.

'Hmm. Just make sure you know it is the gods you stay for and not just my sister.' Cam frowned.

'Surely you don't disapprove of Hwym's liking Els?' Alleri asked.

'Not at all. Hwym, you are honest, faithful, full of humour, I have seen all this on our journeys together.'

'I know,' Hwym spoke quietly, 'It is not that you dislike me, rather you feel I am not right for Els.'

'Not even as clear as that!' Cam cried, frustrated. 'Nothing would make me happier to see the two of you together. But I don't know what Els wants.'

'I doubt even she does, at the moment,' Alleri said.

'Exactly. The last thing I want is for Els to be under any more pressure. She's stretched this way and that as it is.'

'And she isn't yet over Kyrria's death, whatever she tells you.'

'She still has that wound too, she isn't as strong as she likes to think,' Hwym grimaced, 'Sometimes it causes her pain and she thinks she hides it, but I know her too well. I see the agony on her face when the pain hits her. I would go to her to help. That's what I want to do. But how can I? I am no healer and I am all too aware how little regard Els holds my mundane skills in.'

'Then she should think on them more, for your observations are right,' Alleri told him. 'I've also noticed the sharpness of breathing, the way she sometimes mishears when the pain holds her concentration more. I did not think any other had noticed, mind, save Jayak and I.'

'Jayak, there lies your other obstacle my friend,' Cam said.

'Hardly!' Alleri laughed.

'But there is so much between them, they were lovers and they share the same power and…' Cam stopped, seeing the pained looks Hwym gave him. 'But perhaps, Alleri, you know something we don't?'

'Little from either Els or Jayak themselves. Yet they are changed, grown different ways,' Alleri looked around to make sure none of her friends were about. 'Besides, they can hardly talk since all that passed with Kyrria's death. Some doubt they can even fight together again.'

'But they must do, it will probably be necessary in the battles that come,' Cam argued.

'I am sure they will, on that I have more faith in my friends than any rumour could challenge. But lovers again? They may have some affection for each other, but nothing more than friendship. Besides, they are not right together, so I would be more hopeful than you are already, Hwym, whatever others tell you.'

'Well, you have decided me!' Hwym laughed. 'For Els, and for the side of good, which protects all our lands, I will travel Westwards if there is the slightest chance of it.'

'Thanks!' groaned Cam. 'You leave me the journey back alone with Bronv-Grii, not to mention explaining everything to my parents – and yours, now I think of it. I won't forget this and I hope the war is ended quick enough that you may come home and pay me back my favour!'

They all laughed, but Alleri was still looking thoughtful

313

when the little group broke up. I suppose I should let Jayak know Hwym is around, she thought to herself, it would be best he knows, whatever his feelings for Els and surely it should be a friend to inform him who stays? Alleri tensed a little with these ideas, but quickly shrugged them off and sent her news to Jayak. I can send faster now, she realised with a shock, perhaps this war tries us all beyond our ordinary measures? It scared her a little, but even more it excited her. Alleri's joy was tinged with guilt that she could be glad in her expanding abilities at such a time as this, but very glad she was, all the same.

The same strange tension hung in the air when King Nahvib gave his magical people the news of the Western War.

'I know there have been many tales told the past few days,' he said, ignoring the apprentices' attempts to look innocent. 'I come to tell you today all that has passed. Three nights ago, Lady Taheya was found brutally stabbed.'

A horrified silence followed the king's statement.

'Fear not!' Karryn cried, unable to see the students' stricken faces and not explain. 'Taheya lives! Though not well enough to tell us much, we feel she will recover in time.'

'Yes,' said King Nahvib. 'Which is why we have taken some of your colleagues out of class lately. Klara and her team have been instrumental in Lady Taheya's recovery. Thank the gods we have The Healer amongst us!'

Klara blushed at this and tried to hide against Dayx' dark cape, but he would not let her. He smiled proudly at her and Klara at last submitted to the applause that lapped around her. King Nahvib and Queen Karryn also smiled, such unity would prove all too necessary on the next venture, and so Nahvib hastened to explain their next move.

'The reason Taheya was attacked was to prevent her arriving her with urgent news,' Nahvib paused for a moment, 'news of the Demon Lords' invasion of the Western lands.'

'Quiet!' Pocack calmed the crowd. 'Let your ruler continue, for time is short enough.'

'Thank you, Chief Magus.' King Nahvib showed Pocack the respect due his role and this formal acknowledgement stunned the students further. Things are certainly serious, Els thought, I wonder what Lidynne and Stec would make of all this.

'The Western lands had little Demon Lord intrusion until recently, but now appear threatened with being overrun. It will not do to let them conquer even the smallest part of this land and so we must send aid.'

'Why? Can't King Azabar sort out his own mess?' called a voice.

'Yes! We don't owe these Westerners anything!' cried another.

'Be still!' cried Queen Karryn, surprising those gathered with her sudden fury, 'Did Els owe me anything when she arrived at the place we now call L'ra's Town? She came from a foreign land, yet who will argue that such help was not a gift from the gods themselves?' The hall remained silent and Karryn sat down, satisfied.

'So!' King Nahvib carried on hastily, before anyone else could interrupt, 'I will choose a group to help save the West, before any trouble overspills to this Southern continent: soldiers, healers, casting wizards and more. When you leave here, you will find a note in your pigeon hole to tell you if you are needed or not and if so, where.'

'Well, we will both be going,' Klara said, grabbing Els' arm in the rush to leave the Great Hall.

'No doubt. But who with?' Els replied. And why? she thought, how have they chosen those who go and those who cannot? She did not expect to find Cam amongst those to go, she knew the Northerners must return soon. After all, how could Garrtron function without Bronv-Grii to lead it? She thought, laughing to herself. But her smile died when she saw Cam and Hwym standing apart, Hwym

clutching his note, stupefied, reading and re-reading it as if there was nobody in the corridors except for him.

Then he turned and found himself looking straight at Els.

'Uh, Els…' he muttered, 'I, erm, they, well…'

They picked you, didn't they? Els asked, impatient.

'Yes, yes they did.' Hwym admitted.

Why? Els demanded.

'I don't know, I imagine they must have had good reason, though, or I wouldn't be here.'

Really? What reason? Name one thing you can do to help! Els wanted to put the pencil down, to stop, but she was angry now. Why was Hwym here? He had no right!

You don't deserve to be here! You have no talent at all.

'Excuse me? I thought it was up to the magi,' Hwym countered.

They can make mistakes too. Suddenly, Els was furious, she wanted to hit Hwym, standing there like he belonged in the South as much as she.

'Els, be calm.' Klara tried to take her arm, but Els shook her off.

'Why? I fled miles to avoid this man and still he follows me.'

'It's not about that, let's concentrate on the war ahead, you're wasting time on all this,' Alleri said.

'Easy for you to say, you go Westwards without anyone tagging along, you have nothing to drag you down with needless emotion in the middle of war.'

'Of course not, you are the only one with worries of that nature,' Alleri said, then she hastily guarded before Els could ask her to explain.

'Els we must all accept the decisions the king and the magi have made, whatever they are,' Klara told her friend, looking tearful. 'They send me and not Dayx, but I cannot see this with sadness, instead I serve my country with joy.'

'But why do they work like this? Is there any sense in the choosing of people in these times?'

316

'Els, we must accept the decisions of our ruler. Is he not The Guardian?' Cyru sent gently, *'You have to work with Hwym if we all go, as much as you do with Jayak.'*

'Jayak too!' Els shuddered. *'Do they choose these men to torment me?'*

'No, because they know who has the skill, the determination of spirit to find victory.'

'And remember, we have a third divine warrior to find in battle, who knows who that might be?' Klara said, *'Stec did not know who he was until in battle.'*

'I don't mind fighting and I will work with anyone they send me with,' Els acknowledged, *'But I will not be followed about by Hwym with that stupid lost look on his face.'*

'Then meet with him as a friend, as we all do,' suggested Alleri.

'Leave the past behind, let's look to an end of this war and the future of Rima,' added Cyru.

'*Very well, I know you are right.'* The sorceress gave in.

'I understand your frustration,' Cyru allowed, *'I must stay here, I only hope I will be able to serve Queen Karryn in some way, as she appreciated my help when she was ill. I would rather be in battle though Els, but we must be content with where the gods place us.'*

'Hello, Els. Seems we all go together.' Jayak came by and waved his note happily at her.

'Gods!' Els sent and swept off with Alleri and Klara close behind.

* * *

'They need greater wisdom, how must they make their way without proper guidance?' Ellari berated L'ra.

L'ra turned her jade eyes on the other goddess. 'If they seek truth in the right spirit they will find the right path.'

'Maybe. But hardly with ease,' argued Ellari.

'Ease is pointless. How can they know themselves or

317

their people if there is nothing that needs seeking?' said L'ra. 'I know you care for them, Ellari, your mothering touch is powerful beyond much else. Yet I think my spirit of adventure leads to truth more deservingly. I know my people and I trust them as they trust me.'

Chapter 25

The preparations were intense and it was not only Els who was unnerved by the events unfolding around her. The magi taught their classes well, yet an element of haste was obvious to all and the lessons were also fraught because of the gulf between those going over to the West and those not.

'I wish I was going with you, darling,' Dayx moaned.

'So do I, but there must be a reason for it,' Klara told him.

'Well, I suppose Cyru is left, at least I have his company.'

'Yes, while I have Alleri and Els with me.'

'And if the group to fight has been chosen with such care, then surely we will win our victory and be home again soon?' Alleri suggested.

'We'll all be glad of that,' agreed Els. *'You're right Alleri, we must work together well so that we can return home.'*

'I go too?' asked Sorab, *'I don't see you here. Always practising.'*

'Of course, Sorab, you seem to keep me safe in battle,' Els smiled, tickling his throat.

'Easy to talk of a united front, but have you seen some of those chosen?' Dayx said.

Els shrugged. *'I only know that I trust the magi and King Nahvib to make the right decisions.'*

'That's not what you said yesterday,' Alleri said.

'Some of the news did take me by surprise,' Els admitted, *'but it was all a bit of a shock yesterday. Then I remembered when I arrived here, being confused by people's roles. But I have learnt to see the people behind the appearances.'*

'A lesson we all need to remember,' Klara said, failing to guard in time the picture of Jayak in her mind.

'Indeed. But can Hwym really be some secret wizard or

something?' persisted Dayx, *'Surely we would know by now?'*

'Like we knew what Jayak was doing? Els countered. *None were closer to him than I, but I still only saw what I wanted. Who knows what skills we may find in our friends yet?'* Here she quickly chased her doubts on the prophecy from her mind, it would not do for any of the others to see them now. *'All I know for certain is that Hwym fought bravely in the Battle of Green Forest. Though no axe man, he fought well with a spear and I probably owe him my life for although I still carry the wound of that fight, I was nearly killed.'* She paused in her sending, this was something she had forgotten in all the excitement of what had happened since. Kyrria's death and her time spent with Alkar and Stec had occupied so much time and feeling that she had forgotten she was lucky to have been alive to experience any of it. And what gratitude had she shown Hwym? Gods, why must everything happening now be so complicated by what has gone before? she thought.

She doesn't look well, thought Alleri. How preoccupied is she by the news we must adjust to? Then Alleri put a hand to her own head, Ellari, heal me, why does such pain torment me now?

'Alleri? Are you all right?'

'Fine, just a bit of a headache, too many late nights with you lot.' Alleri laughed it off, but she was quite shocked; it was not like her to suffer from headaches.

Leaving his sword-fighting lesson, Sy shook his head, feeling as if his hearing was muffled, or his vision blurred. Whatever it was, something meant he could concentrate no longer, but the normally practical merchant was baffled as to what it could be. Something's not right, Sy thought, maybe it's just all the tension round here. I hope so; I won't learn much swordplay as fuddled as this!

Karryn walked into the sitting room as graceful as ever, despite being obviously anxious.

'Nahvib? Dearest, I want to talk to you a minute,' she called.

'Yes, dear?' King Nahvib put down the paper he was reading and went to greet his wife.

'Do you feel this strangeness in the palace?' Karryn asked him, 'I'm worried, I can sense something bringing tension and I fear we could be in danger again.'

'Karryn, Karryn!' Nahvib took his wife's hand. 'You have such a kind heart, dear, you worry too much. We have passed many dangers to reach our current security, in that we can trust now. Any tension is only a result of jealousies over the battle in the West.'

'But Nahvib, I'm not so sure. It's everyone that's affected, not just the young people. And it feels like a cloud hanging over the place, it's like before, when I started to feel ill.'

'You don't feel ill, though?' Nahvib's anxiety was clear, he didn't want Karryn's health risked a second time.

'No. But I fear for the health of others. I know there's danger now, and with you going, how am I to fight it?'

'But, love, I can't stay here because you're scared!'

'I'm not just scared for myself! Look what happened last time we went charging off, sending Els away only for Jayak to be free to cause trouble.'

'But he won't be here.'

'I didn't say I was worried about him,' Karryn cried. 'I told you after Kyrria's death that I didn't believe he was the one to blame for everything, certainly not my illness.'

'Then you're not making any sense. What are you worried about? Darling, I don't understand. I can't stay here just because of your fears.'

'My fears? My fears are for this kingdom, not for myself. You hardly give me credit for thinking of my country, my subjects.'

'Karryn, calm down. Gods! I am thinking of my country when I go to the West, as Sytrannia's ruler and the Guardian of all Rima, I have to accept my responsibilities, I have to fight in Rucilia.'

321

'Why? Nahvib, I know you feel it is best, but something is wrong here. I don't think you have to go to Rucilia.'

'But how can that be if I am the Guardian? Talk sense, dear.'

'If, you say. Yes, maybe you need to examine the prophecy again.'

'Are you saying I'm not The Guardian?' Nahvib's eyes blazed in a way his wife had never seen before and didn't want to now.

'Maybe.' Karryn held her ground, 'I can't think of another way that you could be so wrong.'

'Wrong? How am I wrong? And I question why my wife and queen should think such a thing.'

'How can you not sense the cloud I feel hanging right above us? How do you focus so sharply on the threat from outside and not see the threat within? What kind of Guardian doesn't know the trouble in his own land, his own house?'

'Karryn, I am not about to rewrite the prophecy for your benefit.'

'But that's just it. You didn't write it, you and the others have only read it. How can you know you are right, are you sure? Completely so? Nahvib, I hate to say this but I have doubts and I believe you do, too.'

'I am not the one with doubts!' Nahvib brushed his hands on his robes hastily, 'I know where I am meant to go and you should not question that!'

'Even if I think you are placing us all in danger, if I think you are doing wrong?' said Karryn gently.

'You shouldn't think that! As my wife, you should support me. We have to be unified to lead this country rightly!'

'Lead it into what?'

'Karryn? Trust me. Surely you can do that?'

'Nahvib, don't question me like this!' Karryn cried.

'Then you don't? Karryn, I am…saddened, gods, I'm furious! I need your help, not this whingeing and making excuses for your fears.'

'That's not what I'm doing!'

'Isn't it? Karryn, you disappoint me,' Nahvib turned away.

'Nahvib, Nahvib don't do this now. You say we must be united, yet you turn from my honesty. What do you want? I cannot hide what I believe. Do you wish me ill again?'

'You will make yourself ill if you continue to get hysterical. Speak to me again when you have calmed yourself,' the king spoke coldly.

'Have it your way. But I will not fake my approval, not when the very land is at stake,' Karryn left, before her husband could see her tears.

She fled to the gardens, this time deserted while those talented studied inside once more. Am I going mad? she thought, wiping her tears with her sleeve. Should I accept what Nahvib says more readily? But then she felt that presence again, that low pressure. She was not to know it was shared by Alleri and weighed on Els in another way. A part of her wanted to go to the young women, she was not so much older than them, after all. But what would she say? I cannot speak to them of Nahvib's words, she thought, there is no other I can speak to, none to assess the strange feelings I have. And I don't feel exactly ill this time, only wary, uncomfortable. She sighed deeply, where do we go next? How do I reconcile with Nahvib and still voice my thoughts on the prophecy? She shook her head, only the gods knew; perhaps she would go and see Skrella and Roro.

While others argued or grew weary with pain, Jayak was the only one resolved about his next course of action. Though he was in his room, he did not rest, but stood deep in thought, occasionally moving his hands as if in speech. For the conversation he had decided to hold next was one that might change the course of his life and others besides.

Determined, he walked down the corridors, his feet

carrying him despite his fears. His pace was unhurried, but even, as he walked where his judgement inevitably took him. Jayak's knock upon the door was firm, yet there was no answer. He tried again, but still none and sending brought no more luck.

For an instant he thought of giving up, but only for a moment. When he came out into the furthest reaches of the garden, he saw the one he was looking for and his resolution grew. His heart still beat faster, he could not deny a certain amount of fear, but he knew what was at stake and there was excitement in him too. So thinking, he stepped forward to greet Els.

'Els? I need to talk to you.'

'You are talking to me. What is it? I have had enough of rows and disturbances this week.'

'Me, too, I would rather sort something out than cause further trouble.'

'Sounds good, this is conversation I like, even with you, Jayak.'

'Even with me? Thanks a lot.'

'You know what I mean! I no longer think you will sell us to the Demon Lords if asked, but Jayak, I am not as close to you as I was ...gods, tell me that's not what this is about? For Jayak, I can begin to work with you again, and I am pleased our friendship is beginning again, but Jayak, that is where it ends!'

'I just -'

'- Jayak, I'm sorry, but I don't want to be your lover. Once I had such feelings, but that's not how it is now. After all that's happened, Jayak, even if I did still have feelings for you, I'd be crazy to get involved. I hate to be brutal, but no way, Jayak, it really is over.'

'Actually, that wasn't what I wanted to talk to you about.'

'Oh,' Then Els smiled, shamefacedly. *'I'm sorry. What, did you want* to say?'

'Then you'll listen this time? I want to talk about what happened, with Kyrria, with the Demon Lords.'

'Oh.'

'Hear me out.'

'Very well, can't be any stranger than anything else that's gone on this past month.' She stepped back and let him in, but remained standing with her arms folded.

'I want to explain, first,' Jayak paused, 'And then ask you something. Els, I want you to know that it was my fault and not yours, that I became ensnared in the pay of the Demon Lords.'

'Well, yes!'

'Easily you say it, but I know what others say, I know how you fell out with Alleri and Klara and I should have stopped that, I should have tried to stand up for you.'

'Then why didn't you?'

'I didn't know how, or even if you would let me.'

'Fairly told so far,' Els rested her chin in her hands and looked at the sorcerer expectantly.

'Well, that's one thing. It was my own arrogance led me to seek an evil power and that's a mistake I will not make again. I know Kyrria's death cannot be changed, but no other evil will be the result of my jealousy, I promise you that.'

'I hope you can keep the promise. What is your other news?'

'One more thing, then I will leave you. I recognise what wrongs I have done you and in doing so, I ask your forgiveness for them.'

'My forgiveness? You ask me to forget what evil you did me, to leave it as if it never happened?'

'No! I don't ask you to pretend I didn't do any of those things, just that you accept my need for forgiveness, my intention to do right.'

'Why should I?' Els frowned. 'What good will it do either of us?'

'Much good, I believe, or I wouldn't ask. But I know this issue has weighed heavily on each of us, not to mention those around us. If we can let it go, if you can let go of this burden, we will both be free to do what we must.

I don't want to be always avoiding your eyes for the shame I feel or for you to feel awkward in my company. I want to be on your side again. I want your forgiveness. I need you to put this sad part of our lives in the past where it belongs. Deny me if you will, but I'll ask until you give me your forgiveness.'

'You're very certain about doing this. I could almost believe it is a real desire to do right.'

'Believe it! Els, I know why you hold back from trusting me. The gods know I wish it wasn't so. But please, accept what I say, it is true!'

Els searched Jayak's face for clues and found none to put her off. His eyes shone, but not with any evil intent, just with the passion she had always seen there, right from the day they had met. Though a part of her longed to find fault, there wasn't any she could see right now. And hadn't the gods forgiven her? For though Bronv had made her mother pay dearly for her sin, hadn't L'ra released her from it? How then, could she hold back such happiness from Jayak? And yet, she thought, is it really okay to just let him off?

'I'll give you another chance,' she said, holding out her hand, *'I'm not ready to forgive, not yet. But I'll work with you again and not hold back, I promise you that much.'* Their eyes met as Jayak gripped her hand with a joy that sent a shudder through both of them.

'Els, thank you. I look forward to fighting with you now.'

'Fighting with me? Why, we have only just made up!'

'Don't tease me now, Els,' Jayak laughed, *'I am happier than I have been in a long time, and I'll pray for your forgiveness yet. Besides, you are too strong for me to fight now, everyone knows that.'*

'Why? Because I have grown stronger or because you can't practise magic any more?' Els asked, suddenly feeling bold after their reconciliation.

'Els, don't ask me that now,' Jayak groaned, *'There isn't a simple answer, but I'll explain one day, hopefully*

soon.'

'Well, as long as we win this latest battle, that's all that counts.'

'Yes, at least this latest trouble in the West brings us nearer to the final battle, I suppose we should be thankful.'

'And not for the battle alone, but that there are many like us who fight for the side of good, whatever their skills.'

'Yes and however unexpected. For I hear Hwym joins us, which must please you?'

'Not you too! Leave me Jayak, or we will soon fall out again.'

'And that I wouldn't have,' Jayak grinned, *'Let's go and find the others, bring some happier news to the preparations.'*

* * *

Hundreds of miles across the sea, King Yacconi looked out of his castle at his troops gathered below. They rested now, for they had spent all the morning training under his direction, but though they relaxed, the king could not, tired as he undoubtedly was. How am I to beat this terror? he thought, pale beneath his grey beard. Surveying his country, he thought of all the people out there, ordinary Rucilians who awaited his solution, terrified for their lives... and their spirits.

'What do I tell them?' he asked, turning to King Eneb, who sat quietly at the drawing room table.

'That help is coming? Surely they will be relieved to hear we have allies arriving soon?'

'You think so?' King Yacconi brooded. 'I am not sure. Though these Southern kings – and queens – seem helpful enough, we have never had to rely on their aid until now. How do we know we can actually trust them?'

'We can't, not really,' King Eneb. 'But if you and I can combat this evil, despite all our history, anything can be possible.'

'True, our past has not been easy. But at least you're Western, you understand how the land should work. These Southerners are different.'

'Not so much.'

'I hope they can help us,' said King Ep, arriving from his own preparations. 'My troops are sadly unready for such fierce battle as this will no doubt prove. It has been a long time since Liance was at war and though I lend my aid readily, I am suspect as to its success. I'm thankful indeed that you have the advantage of experience King Yacconi.'

'Experience? Age, don't you mean?' The Rucilian leader laughed dryly.

The other two kings looked at each other awkwardly. They had no idea how they were supposed to take King Yacconi's sense of humour. For so long he had been either an enemy, or the kind of ally who sat unsteadily in the title, that becoming close allies with him was very strange to them.

'It is your experience which brings you fame,' said King Eneb cautiously.

'Or infamy!' chuckled the Rucilian monarch, 'By Gax' beard, I am little enough loved here. Respected, oh to be sure – they have all heard what happens to those who cross me – but I am known for might, not the building of magnificent palaces or the throwing of elaborate balls.'

'But there is pride to be taken in that. After all, who would have the pomp of King Azabar and see their kingdom so despised,' Ep told him.

'Well spoken! Or the decorations and trimmings of Ashla. Gods praise her drive, but preserve us from her furnishings!' cried King Eneb.

'Yes, at heart, I agree with you, otherwise I would not have ruled in such a way. This way is mine and the whole of Rucilia has benefited from it, which is well. But what use is any of my power or experience in the face of this ancient terror?'

'Your people cannot expect a miracle, King Yacconi.

You have chosen your allies well and what follows is in the hands of the gods,' Eneb answered.

'Then I wish I had visited the temple more often!' Yacconi cried. 'For my people have long forgiven my faults, the lack of an heir, the loss of fancy evening occasions, yet now I look at their faces upon losing their country, I know this is a lack they cannot forgive.'

'You talk so much of lack, look at what we do have!' Ep replied.

'Go on, remind me,' Yacconi said.

'Strong allies, good fortifications, trained soldiers, the will of the gods, even warriors from the gods, if everything I hear is true.' Ep reminded him.

'Well, then, to them I will have to trust,' Yacconi frowned. 'This is certainly a war unlike any other.'

* * *

Karryn brooded in the same library Els had used for her research, though her reading was much less focussed. She turned pages listlessly, hardly seeing the words in front of her. If she heard footfall in the corridor outside then she tensed, but all steps passed by. After she had been there some hours, however, she heard steps lighter than those before and the door opened.

'Hello?' Karryn called. 'Who is it?'

But there was no answer, despite the door remaining ajar. Then Karryn turned to see a mherl walking towards her. Karryn was immediately curious, for Els was the only one to own such a pet and it seemed strange that she should let hers loose. The pet was not nervous though, but very assured of its right to be there.

Her right, Karryn felt, she could not be sure why, but she was convinced the creature was female. It came near and Karryn stroked it, the animal nuzzled her gently, softly squeaking.

'What do you want?" Karryn said, smiling.

She relaxed stroking the creature and for a little while

forgot her cares. Even when she came to, remembered why she was here alone, she retained that calm. After all, she would surely patch it up with Nahvib; they were stronger than any argument. What came over us? she thought, It's not like us to argue anyway. I'll be glad when all this is over, we can get back to a normal lifestyle, stop looking over our shoulders.

'Thanks mherl, you've made me feel a lot better.' She shook her head, it was silly to be thanking an animal like it had really done something to help. But that was what she felt, she couldn't shake the idea. When she looked at it, she dropped back in amazement. Its eyes were of the purest green, the brightest jade there could be. Surely not! she told herself, that's all old wives' tales.

But she touched the creature more respectfully one more time, before going to find her husband.

Chapter 26

It was in Sky City that the first warriors set off. Unlike so many of their allies, those leaving the East left in light spirits.

'It's good of you to cover for me,' said Stec to his friend.

'Not at all,' replied Alkar. 'I may not be high priest, but I'm happy to lend what aid I can. L'ra's Town is in the goddess' own hands, I shall do her will here while you seek to advance her ways in battle.'

'Well, I am glad that the goddess lends me such a friend, so I must be the same to the other warriors.'

'Not to mention The Three,' Alkar said.

'Yes,' Stec sighed, 'I hope I am able to.'

'You will help Els just by being there, as to the others, you need to find them first.'

'Hmm. I have a few ideas there, but I'll let the gods guide me in them, because they are clouded still,' Stec sighed deeply. 'This being a priest-warrior is far from easy.'

'Did anyone say it would be?'

'No, you're right again. Well, Alkar, I'll leave my capital and my country in your hands. Saluna will help if there are any problems. Call one of the neighbouring kings if Wertle tries to regain power.'

'I'll be fine, don't worry. Gods be with you friend, return soon!'

'I intend to. The goddess walk with you, Alkar!' Stec tugged at his horse's reins and made off with his army, as Lord Abrim roused them to their mission. They made for the beach with great haste, ignoring the storm clouds chasing them on their way. Great grey clouds buffeted them and the waters rolled violently across the sands, the tide rising with unseemly speed. The skies above were dark and sand blew in their faces, but the soldiers were undeterred. They rode at speed to make their way to the

Myrrine Straits and were in good spirits at their crossing. High Priest Stec and his friend Lord Abrim had no respect for any weather problems the Demon Lords would try to throw at them.

The same was true of the Northerners. Though only Cranff and a trusted group of soldiers were sent to aid the allies, King Hurburt had invested his finest people in the battle and was proud of those who stood before him now.

'Soldiers, I am proud of you today,' he addressed them, 'I apologise that this briefing must come at my cousin's house, far from the palace and the honour you deserve. But Lord Cranff and I are very glad indeed to have such brave troops to fight and save all the land from this menace. Maybe when that is done, we will be able to rule in a new way and give you a place of meaning in our country.'

'Yes, His Majesty speaks true words,' added Cranff. 'All of you men have proved yourself either in the battle of Green Forest or simply in the way you daily serve your king. We have chosen you for your loyalty, courage and faith. You will need all these in the battle to come and one more if today you survive to fight the final battle. We trust that in you and the people drawn from all Rima, this prophecy will be fulfilled.'

'Go, then!' cried King Hurburt. 'Though my people think you disgraced, cast overseas with my traitorous minister, yet I know the gods thank you and will reward you yet.'

It was on the continents nearest to the trouble that doubt came, for there was no excitement of travel or anticipation of something new. Those living in the South and West had only the practicalities of battle to think about and every thought weighed heavy on their minds.

'We must press forward in one movement, throw such strength at them that they cannot withstand our power,' King Nahvib insisted to his doubtful subjects.

'But what if they are ready for us?' suggested Drayk. 'We would be better to go in two or three forces, bringing reinforcements to add to the power the enemy initially thinks we have.'

'Yes, that is the best idea we have had. I think Drayk is right, we should separate and strike from different areas. I thought we had agreed this?' Pocack insisted.

'I don't know. I am just worried that our forces won't be enough,' Nahvib said.

'But they are combined, King Nahvib, you must remember there are greater forces than Sytrannia's alone,' said Zritz.

'My friend is right,' argued Pocack, 'We have Ashla's might behind ours and that is a great force for the other countries' men to fall in behind. And Lidynne tells us she has trained her magical people well, she has great ability alongside sheer numbers.'

'Hmm, Lidynne,' said King Nahvib, 'I just hope her help is loyal.'

'Come now, your majesty, you know all who act against the Demon Lords act together,' Durrew told his king, 'They have to. Whatever Queen Lidynne's and King Sedryk's differences of opinion with us, their support could not be truer.'

'Not to mention our Northern and Eastern counterparts.' Pocack reminded Nahvib, 'After all, the Demon Lords will hardly be expecting them to be fighting alongside us.'

'There you have a fair point. Maybe we could keep most of them for the secondary assault?' King Nahvib said.

'With key people from the South and East to lend experience and guide their attack?' Pocack said.

'It is agreed then,' King Nahvib decided, 'Let us take the battle, and the victory.'

The allies at Rucilia would have given much to hear King Nahvib's words.

'They congregate in the marshes, can we take them there?' King Yacconi asked. 'It is in our very heartland

and yet we have much help. What do you think?'

'If we really have the third warrior to be found in this battle, we have nothing to fear.' said King Ep.

'You're right.' agreed King Eneb, 'if we wait for the arrival, send a main party to head towards the foe with our might, but leave others to come as reinforcements, surprise them with secret power maybe?'

'It's the only way. We'll see in a matter of hours. Let the gods be with us,' said King Yacconi, 'Only with their help will we find our warrior and defeat our enemy.'

Not an hour had passed when the allies arrived to meet the three Western kings at the castle gate.

'Hail, noble friends!' called King Yacconi, without a trace of the hesitancy he had recently felt.

'Goodness, he's older than I thought,' Jayak said.

'Yes, but I suppose he has been around for the great battles,' Sy answered him, 'I mean, my father used to talk about the victory of Lila's daughter and the renaming of the capital from that time, it is little wonder King Yacconi is held in such esteem even now.'

Yes, but neither age nor gossip will prove a man's worth in this fight. Els reminded her friends. The battles themselves tell where our hearts lie.

'Then let our hearts guide us right,' said Hwym, 'For we have a great purpose here.'

Sy looked at Hwym strangely and Els flinched for a moment, embarrassed for her Northern friend. Or is he even my friend? she thought, but she made sure she was with her countryman when the forces were split.

There was little choice, though, if the youngsters were honest. The kings in charge were mighty rulers and there were many others of power and influence among them, not the least Cranff and Stec. When the groups were finally sorted out, Els was both delighted and perturbed to find herself fighting alongside Hwym, Jayak, Sy and Macie and joy welled up further when she saw they were to be led by Queen Lidynne, King Sedryk and High Priest Stec. Their role was to bring reinforcements to the main attack, their group coming last of all.

'There is a lot of responsibility in our attack,' stated King Sedryk quietly, but with such a tone that all listened well, 'Ours may be the final assault upon the enemy, but do not expect to find them readily beaten. They will have fought hard and seen our own men weaken, we have to overwhelm them with a final force so great they cannot counter it. Yes, Stec, what would you add my friend?'

'Only that we must remember we have great talents among us,' He gave a swift glance towards Els and her friends. 'We may respect the enemy's might, for it would be foolish to think our task easy, but we can rest assured in the skill and gifts our gods have invested in us.'

'My friend speaks with great wisdom,' Lidynne confirmed. 'Stec here has been called from politics to a place of worship and investigation of where the divine ones will lead us. His faith is grown large by his learning. However, I would not expect you to follow the teachings of a man whose head is purely surrounded by books. Stec's faith has also been proved in battle, where he was discovered as priest-warrior at a time when the battle waged looked most dangerous for our side. His trust in the gods has been confirmed in the presence of his allies and we know where Stec leads us is into the victory we give to our gods. Let us not look too closely at these Demon Lords' strengths, but rather at our own skills and use them wisely.'

'It is as Queen Lidynne says, we fight on this principle, we win. Simple.'

'Yes, but what about the practicalities of our attack? We're not going to wander in at our own time and hope for the best, are we?' called one grizzled Western general. 'I can fight in faith, but a fight it must be and no more talking is needed to show me what that means.'

'An hour more while King Nahvib's forces travel to meet the enemy head on, then Ashla's warriors are to follow and only then can we bring our might to bear on things.' Stec told the man.

'And when we do, we position the Sorceress near the front,' Queen Lidynne explained, to Els' amazement.

'What?!' was all she sent, but made her feelings quite clear.

Hwym turned around, confused, had he heard Els send?

'You must be near to the attack so that they feel your might,' Queen Lidynne answered the sorceress.

'Don't you think that's putting her into unnecessary danger?' a voice called out. Many turned in surprise at the tones, which were foreign to nearly all present, but Hwym stood his ground. 'Els may be strong but should she really be on the front line? Won't the Demon Lords try to sweep her away before she can do any damage?' the young man asked.

'You have no cause for alarm, much as I respect your care for your friend,' Stec calmed the Northerner. 'I mean to place Els near the front line but not upon it. She will have worthy soldiers placed around her, so that no harm may befall her in battle. Lidynne has already selected her 'close guards', now you know what you are here for.'

'If soldiers are to be chosen for their readiness to fight, you must take me,' called Macie, pushing her way through the crowd.

'Very well,' sighed Stec, but we will take no more volunteers, for we must also cover our other talents – Jayak and Sy, we don't really know why you must be here but accept that your positioning is important. Therefore, we protect you unfailingly,' Stec and Sedryk looked around at this point, they wanted to identify any who might find the idea of supporting Jayak, or unknown fighters, in such a battle a difficult ideal to follow. However, they seemed satisfied and the real preparations soon began.

Glancing about at her friends and allies, Els felt a strange shiver pass through her. Almost two years had passed since she had left her village in disgrace, unloved but for Cam's support. Now, though, people from all four continents joined to fight for the same goals as she did. Not only that, they gladly competed to protect her, to see her talents used well, where others had once only hidden from their power. The goddess is at work in this, she realised and she took up her spear with the same conviction as her Northern compatriots.

Alongside her, Jayak and Sy also armed themselves; swords ready for the slicing and hacking that would no doubt take place shortly. Ahead of them, the middle section led by King Nahvib and King Ep began to move, responding to the sounds of battle that were already to be ahead across the marshland.

But it was King Yacconi and Lord Cranff who led the initial onslaught upon the Demon Lords. The Rucilian monarch led the way, large silver sword in hand and a holy rage in his face. 'By all the gods! You will not oust our good with your evil!' he cried.

Three lines of Rucilian soldiers followed their king with pride and passion. Their swords were as well polished as King Yacconi's and their faces blazed like his. Close behind came mixed ranks of Easterners and Northmen, as the allies now called them. The Easterners used arrows with a deadly skill, for the many newly ordained priests of L'ra had blessed them with powers of accuracy and speed. Cranff's Northmen used the spears they were becoming increasingly famed for, darting in with dangerous blows that could be given much faster than the swords. Behind these three lines, Cranff followed his countrymen with axemen selected from all races, heavy weapons hitting the Demon Lord soldiers, too tired or wounded to dodge them, hard.

They made a good start to the battle, King Yacconi's cries encouraging the soldiers he led. The allies fought well together, cutting a path through their enemies. But these were not the recently changed men they had met in Calan, confused by their powers and unsure of their masters. These people had been long trained in the ways of evil as they had corrupted Azabar's kingdom and infiltrated the West. Many of the Demon Lords' servants here had been with them long enough to forget any other life. Like Sy's neighbour, they were unable to be reached through normal means, no more capable of showing weakness than of showing their heart. They had forgotten what their hearts had once held dear and no longer knew who they were, only who they followed.

Such fanatics fight with an unstinting fury and King Yacconi was beginning to tire as he heard Nahvib and Ep's men come to support him.

'Praise the hunter!' he cried, but he could not waste his voice and returned to the fight quickly.

Cranff moved to close in on those endangering the king, but he took a terrible blow to his left arm as a result. He had no time to notice what had happened, in the midst of the battle he only noticed that his arm didn't feel as it should. But there were so many things to distract from his own troubles. Many of the Northerners had lost their spears and been hewn down, as had several lines of bowmen. Axemen and swordsmen still stepped forward faithfully, trusting their skill and the gods who had invested it in them. But the Demon Lords had expected a hard fight and one of their High Lords, cowled and snarling, released foul-smelling potions and made savage chants upon their foes.

Axemen faltered, swordsmen dropped their weapons, as mists swirled and a dreadful dizziness fell upon them.

'We must fight on!' cried Lord Cranff, 'Whatever they throw at us, we can't fear it or we are done for.' Even as he said this, though, he felt an overwhelming desire to fall down and lie where he fell until it was all over. Then he saw King Yacconi beckon to the men behind him, joyful signals, for the final third was approaching, Queen Lidynne was in sight and even Demon Lords paused in disbelief. But they must know? thought Lord Cranff to himself. They must know our numbers, with all their powers. Ah, he realised, they do not know our conviction, do not know four continents mass against them. I only wish our king was here, that the North was fully armed, he thought sadly, but such doubts would not linger. Though sweat poured from his face and his head was dull now, the Demon Lords could not dispel his gladness and as it flowed through him, so he got up, determined to fight on.

When Els reached the battleground, she was not surprised by what she saw. The terrible smells and sounds were much as she had seen in Green Forest and Volcano's Gorge, though more awful. She knew they would overcome them. Her side ached and her feet slid in the long grasses, but she realised the Demon Lords sought to remind her of weakness and she resisted. They and their people may be fearful to many, but she had strong allies and she had already held back the Demon Lords twice now. The gods have promised a battle on each continent and she knew now she was The Sorceress, knew she must survive and win this battle to be present at the final triumph. But the victory could not be hers alone and so she tried to find where she could help.

Demon Lords quickly flowed to where the new group of fighters came, they were not to be overcome easily. As Els looked about at the different blows being wielded all over the battlefield, she realised that the Demon Lords were trying to separate and ensnare the leaders whose wisdom was so clearly needed by the soldiers. Stec and Lidynne soon found themselves almost surrounded, their key lines of warriors engaged in battle with men beyond all fear. King Nahvib and King Ep fought bravely, King Eneb departing from his line to fight alongside them. The three of them held their attackers at bay but their protectors were being cut down with alarming speed. Lord Cranff was looking worse than ever, but though clearly disadvantaged by his wounds, he still tried to aid Yacconi as best he could. In all the chaos of the battle, only Yacconi never faltered and the Demon Lords pressed a little less closely upon his pack, now centering their attentions on the others.

The allies would have been lost if they had fought by normal means, but their strength was in their faith and their powers were beyond those of normal people - even those trained by evil masters. Els turned her mind to the goddess and sought the power that came from the very depths of her soul. She cast and though her spell didn't kill the Demon Lords outright, it certainly held them off, while they tried to launch their own spells in response. But her powers couldn't stretch much further and she was using all her energy in holding the Demon Lords off.

She searched with her mind for her friends but Sy and Hwym were taking on a band of possessed warriors intent on reaching Queen Lidynne, while Jayak made his way for the axemen who followed two Demon Lords in pursuit of High Priest Stec. Alleri was nowhere to be seen and King Nahvib and the Southern kings with him were desperately warding off their enemies, swords flashing less now where they were grimed with blood.

But one sword still gleamed with the promise of victory and the hand that held it was King Yacconi's. Tall against the skyline, the Rucilian king fought on every side, turning from fighting his own opponents to protect Cranff, whose grave danger he had seen. For Cranff's arm had been hacked from his shoulder and it was clear that he would die shortly if something was not done soon.

'Die you evil things! Die, in the name of Gax!' Yacconi called, assured of his victory in the blessings of the hunter god. In the instant he made his cry, he lunged towards a High Demon Lord and the path of his twisting brought him into Els' view. She heard his cry and saw his movement all at once. There was certainty in his moves and her heart lifted to see it.

'In the name of the goddess!' she called and with a sudden joy saw Alleri answer her with a flame-throwing spell, cast accurately at the Demon Lord pressing upon King Nahvib. The Demon Lords took a step back and Klara held them off with spells of protection while she tended to the nearest wounded. King Ep had lost his sword in the confusion, but one of Ashla's troops threw him a spear and he set about using it with an equal skill.

Els increased her power, drawing upon might she hadn't used in many months, but still the Demon Lords pressed against King Sedryk and High Priest Stec. Their own magic turned the air purple and their evil chants made heads ring, but Els still sought to fight them. I will defeat them, or I will die trying, she told herself.

But there was no need for such a loss. Jayak had seen her need and ran towards her, cutting a path through the soldiers, bodies falling as he went. His cries brought his friends from were they were in battle and they threw their enemies from them, charging for the final fight. Sy leapt to Jayak and Els' defence and they held the Demon Lords attention with physical blows while Els perfected her throwing, calling all her anger into the act of aiming her might at the enemy. Macie and Hwym however, raced to King Yacconi, seeing the need to spread their aid, break the Demon Lords' hold on their warrior, for that was now clearly who King Yacconi was.

Their help couldn't have come at a better time. Lord Cranff was failing fast. Although he still held his sword, he was too weak now to do anything with it and was only remaining standing with great effort. Seeing his weakness, a possessed soldier lunged for him, hoping to finish him off. At this blow, Cranff's blood flowed faster still and he finally slumped to the ground. Yet the soldiers gathered around him, drawing from Yacconi's strength.

'By Gax! We have the hearts of hunters not of the hunted!' screamed the Rucilian king, 'You will not defeat us, not here, nor anywhere else!' He swung his sword boldly and cut a pack of possessed fighters down, along with the Demon Lord leading them. The Demon Lords nearby jumped back in alarm, this fighter was stronger than any of them had expected, worse yet, he called upon a mighty god.

'Yacconi nk grykkniddz Gax acrr gjjhn! Alayyio zykkoy!' the leader cried, harsh shouts sounding more like those of an animal than ever.

His fellow evildoers gathered around him. They followed him to King Nahvib and the other Southern kings, hoping to defeat a weaker victim and then turn on King Yacconi with their triumph. But Yacconi's forces were too quick. They had killed many of their enemy and already turned their attention to the Demon Lords around King Nahvib's forces. Soldiers wielded a mighty array of weapons, stunning the evil forces with their different means of attack. They had destroyed the bulk of the Demon Lords, causing those remaining to turn about and flee.

But they only ran into the way of King Sedryk and High Priest Stec's group, who had no fear left and were glad to chase the enemies back to their friends and allies. Els lifted her hands in confidence and cast a spell only one learned in sorcery could have managed. The fire leaving her hands was trained only on the Demon Lords and burnt the ground beneath their feet. Those who did not move quickly enough were burnt from their feet up, but most Demon Lords moved out of the way and fought Els with their own magic, throwing great spells of despair and confusion her way, with an eerie blue-grey light.

They had forgotten, however, that Els was not the only person of great magical talent to be involved in this battle. Alleri saw her friends' need and looked Els' way.

'Do what you need to; I will confuse them while you act!' she called.

Els nodded once, and began to cast again. As she did, Alleri created a cloud of thick smoke, which lingered around the Demon Lords. Unable to see each other, they created enough spells to cause dizziness and physical blows to soldiers, but nothing strong enough to deter Els. She cast with strength and the Demon Lords swayed.

'Goddess hear me!' Els cried and her casting was awesome. Even her allies held their hands to their ears as her might hit the enemy. Demon Lords swayed, fell and dissolved in sickly grey ash.

The battlefield was quiet for a moment, until King Yacconi and Hwym remembered the dying Cranff. They raced for the injured nobleman, fearing the worst. Macie and Klara followed close behind, Macie covering Hwym and Yacconi from attacks, though these were few now, most men had died with their masters, so strong had been the bond between them.

When they reached Cranff, his face was ashen, his body limp. But Hwym put a hand to him and found him breathing still, quiet, desperate breaths he took, but life was in him still and the allies rejoiced that they had a chance to save their friend.

'Though I am the Royal-Warrior,' said Yacconi, using the divine term quite naturally, unconscious of the effect his revelation brought to the others, 'I would gladly swap that for healing power, for this man has braved many dangers to save me and my land. Yes, even though he wasn't sure of a welcome here. Gods, don't ask us to send this man back to his own land just for burial, let us send him back to the glory he deserves.'

Yacconi placed his hand on the Northerner's temple, praying and muttering softly. Hwym still held Cranff's wrist, whispering prayers to Old Lok while the Rucilian king kept his watch. Macie's spear rested at her side, her attention to the battleground fleeting, her soldier's heart saddened at the loss her friends must surely bear.

But the gods deemed it otherwise. Hwym gasped as Cranff murmured, tried to sit. Though he fell down again, his breathing grew, the colour came back to his face.

'Your reputation is well-earned!' cried King Yacconi, looking Klara's way.

'But I did nothing, I arrived with Macie as you were bent over Cranff. In all honesty, my thoughts were only that a man so injured must be beyond saving.'

'But I am no healer, it cannot be so,' The Rucilian replied, greatly confused.

'Then maybe the gods answer your request, maybe the Royal-Warrior carries such weight.'

'And responsibility, too,' The king said. 'For now I see I must be a part of this battle, the ancient prophecies do reach out even as far as these lands.

'Must you shout so loud?' sighed Cranff, 'I would rather sleep just now, though I can't think why. Don't we have a fight or something?'

'All over and well fought in by you,' cried Yacconi, gladness suddenly making him look a younger, happier man than any had yet seen him. 'Lord Cranff, we will take you to my castle, where you will recover at your leisure. There I will tell you of all that happened today, though I suspect many visitors will interrupt my telling with their own parts.'

Els was as happy as Yacconi when she heard the good news, and joined her thanking of the gods with that of the other survivors. So, she thought, a new battle is won and only the last one is left to find. We will win this. The gods show themselves clearly today. And she hugged Alleri tight, for the young wizard was shocked and gladdened by her own part in the battle.

Jayak was also reviewing the fight. Unwilling to interrupt the young women, he walked back to the castle alongside Sy. Both had taken cuts from spears, but their own skill meant these were only minimal.

'We are lucky we had Klara,' said Jayak, 'I don't fancy Cranff's chances otherwise.'

'Why, what is so special about Klara?' asked Sy.

'Goodness, man, where have you been?' cried Jayak, astounded. 'Didn't you hear the proclamation?'

'No, I was out of town. I heard a proclamation had been made as to those that must be The Three, but I heard many rumours, none could tell me the names with confidence. Why, how does this mean anything to Klara?'

'Why, Klara is The Healer, don't you see?'

'No, no I don't,' Sy said. 'Jayak, don't look at me like that!'

'You don't understand, she must be.' Jayak cried, 'Els is the Sorceress, Klara the Healer and King Nahvib the

344

Guardian. Everyone knows that.'

'Do they? I don't know why, but I already had three names in my own mind,' said Sy, dazed, for he had accepted his list unquestioning, 'In all that happened on my return, Kyrria's death, then my father's, I didn't think to ask anyone. But Jayak, those names together are not the Three!'

'Have you told anyone?'

'No, I didn't need to. Jayak, I don't know why but I am sure I am right.'

'Sy, I wish I could tell you that your list is wrong, but I see conviction in your eyes. I don't know why, but you have obviously been given insight the rest of us don't have. One thing I must ask and I can only say that you must trust me in it. I have to know – *who are The Three?*'

The merchant looked at Jayak for a long moment, but what he saw in the sorcerer's eyes was not to be feared.

'Very well,' He glanced about and drew Jayak near, as he saw other soldiers returning close behind them. Sy whispered the names at Jayak's ear and though the first name brought no surprise, those following caused the sorcerer to stop in his tracks.

'Him? But why, how?' he asked.

Sy however, had no answer to give, 'I only know what I see, I don't know where it comes from,' he said, scared by the knowledge he had, unasked for, yet powerful.

'There is only one thing to be done,' Jayak decided. 'As soon as we reach the castle, we must find Queen Lidynne.'

Chapter 27

In the castle at Lila-Crith-Ak, the mood was joyful.

'A feast, a feast before anyone has to go anywhere!' cried King Yacconi, 'I will not send my brave allies back with empty stomachs, not after so great a victory!'

By the time Jayak and Sy had changed battle wear for evening clothes, the banqueting hall of the castle was crowded and noisy. Huge platters of food were carried back and forth by serving people and the wine flowed readily. Long tables made sure everyone had room to eat, so all who had fought so hard were now able to relax and enjoy the best the West had to offer. Drums and pipes played powerfully to be heard above the noise of talking and laughter.

The young sorcerer was not at all surprised to find Queen Lidynne and King Sedryk at a table with Stec, Yacconi and King Nahvib. There was much laughing and joking, not to mention the retelling of stories from the battlefield. Though most had already begun to be exaggerated already, there was little they could add to the tale of Cranff's heroism.

'It's just a shame he isn't here to tell it himself!' said King Nahvib.

'Ah well, he'll be out here again the minute he's patched up, no doubt ready to tell his side of the story,' said Queen Lidynne.

'Queen Lidynne, could I, we speak to you a minute?' Jayak ventured.

'We? Who comes with you, young Jayak?' asked Lidynne, looking around. 'And what news must interrupt our feasting now?' she smiled at the other kings.

'Good news, more to tell on the prophecy,' Jayak said and the gathered fighters put down their glasses, Stec leaning closer.

'More on the prophecy? Jayak, do you know what you say? This is scarcely the time for wild ideas,' King Nahvib looked at his subject warningly.

'But the ideas I have heard are not mine, I just feel you must hear the news I have. My friend,' here he indicated Sy, standing behind him, 'has news so strong, I feel someone should hear it. When his news countered what the proclamation said, I felt those who had exchanged ideas on the choices to be made should hear it. I particularly felt Queen Lidynne should hear it. Maybe I am wrong, but my feelings on this are so strong, I will not take the chance of leaving information hidden for fear of it being unwanted. Sy can explain his thoughts, you must make of them what you will.'

'Sy? But this merchant is a Sytrannian. And what would he know of prophecy? Still, perhaps Jayak knows something if he ventures to explain to me! Come forward then boy, give your thoughts freely,' King Nahvib encouraged him.

Sy stepped in front of Jayak and faced the assorted rulers and statesmen at the table. King Nahvib was the only one he had seen before, and even that had been at some distance, at his wedding to Queen Karryn. The kings' fine clothing and the different looks of the Western kings intrigued him. The rulers themselves were no less curious, eager to meet this young merchant who thought he had answers where great rulers stumbled. But it was the Lykrosian queen who reacted most violently, for Lidynne left her seat to come and grab the astonished Sy by his shoulders.

'Sy? How can you claim the name of a Sytrannian and look at me with my own face? Is this some evil trick, or should I know you?'

'I don't know what…' but Sy's words trailed off as he saw Queen Lidynne properly for the first time.

Seeing the recognition and surprise on Sy's face, the queen spun him about for the others to see.

'Gods!' was all King Nahvib could offer and the others only gasped in shock. For Sy's features, though younger and masculine, were so like the queen's, it could not be a coincidence.

'Let us be calm.' Stec called, 'Clearly someone is revealed to us here. Maybe this qualifies Sy's words with weight. We must know what it means, true, but I feel sure this is a good omen. Even in the tiredness from battle, when we must see what our losses are, here we have an unexpected gain.'

'But where from?' cried Azabar, 'Gods! We can't have some illegitimate son ruin everything now, we can't afford for Lykrosia to be plunged into chaos now.'

'Whereas we could after all this is done, I suppose? And he is not her illegitimate son!' shouted Sedryk, his hand at his sword's hilt.

'Stop this now! The battle is already fought, why do more damage now? This, the enemy would rejoice to see.' King Yacconi said. 'And you, King Azabar are a guest in my castle, remember that. I saw little of you in the battle, I hardly want to begin our acquaintance over an argument here – or blows.'

'Very well,' Azabar mumbled, but he looked far from happy.

'As I was saying,' continued King Sedryk, with a grateful nod to the Rucilian, 'This Sy cannot be Lidynne's son. The only children we have belong to both of us. Any man who says otherwise is treating his life quite carelessly.'

'I couldn't agree more,' Sy hastily added, 'I have a father of my own, had that is,' he said sadly. 'I did not come to you to seek another. I cannot deny the strange likeness between myself and Queen Lidynne, but neither can I explain it.'

'Perhaps I can,' Lidynne said, quietly. 'Could I ask your father's name?'

'Of course. His name was Amryn.'

'Ah! Amryn, that I should hear of you now!' the queen groaned, 'Too late, I guess, Sy, for you speak of your father as if he is dead.'

'Yes, sadly so. He went to help a neighbour who had

348

been acting strangely. The man turned out to be of the Demon Lords', my father was murdered.'

'Amryn, you never did change, always plunging in! Alone, I suppose?' Queen Lidynne asked Sy.

'Yes, he wouldn't wait until I was back home. For months I have wondered if things would have been different if I had taken an earlier boat, made one less sale before I set off home.'

'No, you will waste your time in unnecessary regrets if you do that. For my brother was sure to die an untimely death, he was always foolhardy. Quick to act and slow to think was Amryn,' Lidynne sighed.

'Your brother!' cried Azabar and most of the people present were equally shocked. Only King Nahvib and Stec looked as if this made any sense.

'Yes,' Queen Lidynne sat back down. 'Sit here with us young man, it appears the gods will test us with story telling as much as in battle. Yes, yes, and you.'

Sy and Jayak sat quickly, the sudden news adding to the many thoughts that already churned their minds.

'Amryn was my twin,' began Lidynne, 'We were very close, so it is both a terrible shock and a great joy to see my brother's face in you. But honestly, I am glad to hear what happened to him, for our parting was not a happy one.' She took a sip of her wine before carrying on, 'We were twins I said, but I was born first and Amryn three minutes after. It is a small matter of time but made a mighty difference as we grew up. Amryn was always hasty, always trying to catch up, to better me. He could charm people into anything and had many friends, but would as soon drop them for more exciting friends, or a new interest.'

'He was a merchant of great influence,' Sy told his aunt.

'I have no doubt, he led me into many things that I'd regret later! But I was the eldest, I felt my responsibility, I abided by my parents' rules more easily than Amryn, tried to study, watched how my father dealt with workers, servants. But then, I was to be queen, Amryn never got over the unfairness of that.'

'What happened?' asked King Yacconi, the feast momentarily forgotten.

'The summer we were sixteen, we argued bitterly. He kept on and on about my inheritance of the kingdom, how unfair it was. Goaded, I rebuked him for his idleness, his picking people up and dropping them so easily. He threw back at me how I was only thoughtful because I feared how people would react to me as a monarch, how he needn't bother with that, so why should he care what anyone thought? He said he had thought of leaving before, but now he knew he had to. I begged him not to, for all his anger, I loved him dearly. I tried to tell him how I would make sure he was respected when I ruled, but he only looked at me with scorn. He left that night and I never saw him again. Tell me, did he keep his chain with the horse and spear upon it?'

Sy pushed back his jacket to display the chain, the gold bright against his cream-coloured tunic. The horse was shown running, the spear across it, as if flying through the air alongside it.

'He gave it to me last year, on my twenty-first birthday,' said Sy. 'When he died, I swore I would never take it off.'

'Nor should you,' declared Sedryk, 'For the chain represents the power of Gax, the hunter god. All Lykrosians give thanks to him, but the royal house of the Irykkians owes him particular allegiance.'

'Now you steal my subjects from me! This is hardly fair, Lidynne.' cried King Nahvib, but he smiled gently at Sy nevertheless.

'Yes, I suppose I am Lykrosian really,' said Sy, somewhat dazed.

'And the protection and power of Gax is yours.' Lidynne paused, exchanging a look with her hsuband. 'It may be that the news you have is worth a great deal, for the gift of prophecy was promised to the line of Iryk the

Mighty many hundreds of years ago, for his service to Gax. There is said to be a seer, or prophet, in every generation of the royal family. It has been ten years since I realised none of my children had any such gift, nor any of their cousins that I knew of. I often wished I could ask Amryn, but had accepted it was not to be. Maybe now my questions shall be answered.'

'Then let us hear the lad speak,' said King Yacconi, 'For any information is vital, especially at such a time as this. Come, Sy, I don't care if you are Sytrannian, Lykrosian or what! Only let us hear what the gods have allowed you to see.'

'As it pleases your majesties,' Sy bowed and began his story, 'Jayak and I were speaking, after the battle, it was just chance, really.'

'There is little left to chance in such a battle as this,' muttered King Nahvib.

'Maybe you are right. Well, Jayak was praising Klara's healing efforts, sure that I would know of her role in the prophecy, as I would the others who make up The Three. But I had not heard the official proclamation, only somehow I had names in my head.'

'Names of who The Three are?'

'Why, yes, it seemed obvious to me.'

'It often does, the gifts we possess are so strong we cannot hide from their conviction. But I had been given names who were not, if you have the names who are…'

'Indeed I do, must you hear them now?'

'Here, write them down,' said Yacconi, pushing a piece of paper towards Sy, 'I will not have any overhear our words, it is too important.'

It seemed like an hour it took Sy to write the three names, though probably it was just a few strokes. When the gathered kings and Stec saw the names, their eyes met in wonder.

'This explains much,' said Stec.

'Indeed, we were close enough in our guesses. And the names here fit well, at least, I think so.' Queen Lidynne looked at the others.

'Yes, Lidynne, Sedryk, I admit I was wrong, yet so near really, so near in one way!' King Nahvib laughed, 'Oh L'ra, that I worship a goddess of adventure and still miss the way in all your games! But these answers are very clear, I will not doubt your way now. Lidynne, Stec, I owe you both an apology. Please, I ask your forgiveness for my distrust. The goddess humbles me in this news.'

'Accepted!' cried Lidynne, 'And happilly, for my games room has been a sorry place without your company.'

'Accepted,' smiled Stec, 'And do not be too hard on yourself, the goddess has wanted us to search for these answers. She likes to use unexpected people, we have never quite known what to look for. After all, I did not know I wanted to be a priest until she chose me. I think all The Three have been chosen for the ways it will surprise them, Els included.'

'But what of the others? And how do we tell the public? Do we make a counter-proclamation?' asked King Azabar.

'I don't think we should make this public,' said King Nahvib slowly.

'I think Nahvib is right,' agreed Sedryk, 'The people named will need time to adjust as it is. There is also an element of danger involved.'

'And if the Demon Lords' people know the proclamation, but not our current thinking, we have a great advantage. Let's give out this knowledge carefully, only telling people when they need to know, even those named.'

'But some will need to know quickly, Nahvib.'

'You're right, Sedryk. I think we should ride to our own countries at once,' King Nahvib declared.

At Istalan's main gates, King Nahvib and his company were gladly met by Drayk,

'I have lots of news your majesty, much has happened

352

since you left to fight in the West,' The First Minister told him, his words falling out of him quickly.

'Then I will hear this news at once and you shall hear mine, for what I have seen and heard is also important. Things are happening faster each day, Drayk, I feel the end to this war is nearly in sight.'

'I will take you to the drawing room, for your wife and friends need to greet you.'

'Do I need to explain everything to everyone right now?' King Nahvib frowned.

'Not to everyone, no.' said Drayk with a slight smile, 'But those who await you now have a lot to tell of what they have experienced, what they have learnt. I do not bring you straight from such a hazardous trip to see minor advisors, but friends whose news will strengthen your resolve.'

'You are mysterious Drayk, I must follow you now, for your words awaken the excitement I already barely contain.'

In the drawing room, Drayk opened the door and Nahvib's heart jumped. Karryn looked more beautiful than ever and Nahvib's first thought was what had become of the cloud she had been so afraid of. He was also pleased to see the three magi looking well, confident rather than harassed. Then he saw the figure on the sofa, resting, a little tired, but otherwise well.

'Lady Taheya!' he cried, 'Now I begin to understand Drayk's secrecy, for seeing you is a pleasant surprise indeed. How long have you been recovered?'

'Since Queen Karryn discovered the traitor in our midst and broke the hold the evil has had on the palace.'

'Yes,' said Drayk seriously, 'Jayak was being honest when he said he never cast anything at Queen Karryn. It was Karryn herself who found Cyru in contact with Demon Lords, drawing on their power to confuse people's minds. Once we realised who it was, it was easy to deal with the problem.'

'Indeed, we all felt a great freedom when Karryn gave

us the news. We placed Cyru in the palace dungeon at once, for he is so given over to the Demon Lords that he still tries to contact them and make spells. We have placed him under a powerful holding spell, so great it took the three of us to cast it.' Pocack shook his head, 'I had no idea the cloud Karryn spoke of had even effected me, but as soon as we had contained Cyru, I felt observations and awareness come back to me. He is probably beyond saving, he has drawn so much power and corruption from that evil.'

'At least we have stopped it, we are free, as are his friends, for his evil must have held the others back. Dayx was quite irritable, angry about Klara leaving, resentful of Hwym's success. As soon as we prevented Cyru casting, Dayx was the joker we are all used to,' elaborated Durrew, 'I don't know how Karryn knew to look for Cyru that day, but glad we all are that she did.'

'There is one reason Karryn knew where to look,' Nahvib took his wife's hand, 'My dear, I owe you an apology. I was hasty to disagree with you only because I felt you were threatening my position. I should not have been so selfish. Whatever roles we have in this war, we should use them to compliment each other. We are husband and wife, king and queen, nothing changes that, whatever surprises the gods give us.'

'Of course. Nahvib, I spoke without understanding myself, we were both confused. I'm just so glad to see you back safe.'

'You were meant to be confused, you above all others.' Nahvib looked at those gathered to greet him, 'There are few I trust with this knowledge, but you are amongst those. Karryn was the only one here who could pierce that cloud for one reason only – *she* is The Guardian, not I.'

'Me?' Karryn laughed, 'But what makes you think that?'

'The battle of Long Grasses brought us more than just a physical victory over the Demon Lords,' said King Nahvib. 'The gods rewarded us with a new chosen warrior

354

and a new seer.'

'Who are these?' asked Pocack,' For we must give our hand to them if the gods have raised them to help us.'

'King Yacconi is the Royal-Warrior, young Sy is a seer.'

'Sy?' said Zritz, 'How funny, the newest seer is a Sytrannian, right under our noses.'

'Close to us, maybe, but no Sytrannian. He is Lykrosian, Queen Lidynne's nephew, it appears.'

'Amryn's son? Gods, Skrella and Roro have been looking for him for years now, we must tell them.' said Pocack, 'But carry on, King Nahvib, what is Sy's input here?'

'Sy knew The Three, even though he had never heard the proclamation.'

'His Three are different to ours then?' Durrew realised.

'Yes. I have told you know that Karryn is The Guardian, but there is another you should know about. I can't tell you everything now, for there is too much at stake. Lidynne, Sedryk, Stec and Yacconi all believe we should keep the proclamation public as if that is all we know.'

'Lull the Demon Lords into a false sense of security, you mean?' Pocack said, 'Might work.'

'So how am I to carry on now?' asked Karryn, 'What must I do?'

'Listen, listen to the gods and you will be guided,' said Pocack. 'This is what you have been given to do.'

'And you have already begun to do it,' said Durrew.' You spotted Cyru, you have eliminated one threat already.'

'And you saved Jayak, it was mostly down to you that he stayed here and wasn't killed, or banished forever,' said Zritz.

'We should have known many months ago, a year almost,' realised Pocack, 'At the time of the wedding and coronation there was a strange glow around you, something I couldn't explain. I talked to Skrella and Roro,

355

but though they had seen it too, they couldn't explain it anymore than I could. There hasn't been a coronation and wedding at once in many years, we didn't know if it was just the gods blessing your union. Now we know. Congratulations, Karryn!'

'Thank you. Now that we have no immediate threat and Nahvib is back with us, I can see two things we need to do.' Karryn's voice was stronger now, for all her shock, she had accepted her destiny.

'Go on,' her husband prompted.

'Firstly, we must look to training and arms. Although we have won the last battle well, I do not think we can sit back. The gap between the battles of Volcano's Gorge and Long Grasses is much shorter than that between Green Forest and Volcano's Gorge. Besides, our recent victory probably means we are nearer to the final battle than we might have thought previously. The new information the gods have given us probably means we may need it sooner than expected.'

'Karryn is right.' said Drayk, 'I will talk to the council. Lins and Frani need to talk to our allies, check what troops can support us – and how they will get here. Zachari may need to draw on some of our financial resources quickly, we must check what we have.'

'Don't forget that the temple is armed.' Durrew reminded them. 'There are many young guards who will fight for their goddess. They are highly trained to do so.'

'Yes, I think Rayth will gladly take up arms against those who did such evil to her friends.' said Zritz.

'And thank L'ra we have the benefit of Roro and Skrella's wisdom. They will know when to attack and how. If we consult them, we are likely to lose less lives.' pointed out Karryn. 'My next suggestion,' she smiled as they turned her way with such confidence, 'Is that we pay greater attention to our young people. They need to be well trained, but also well advised. These people have known great turmoil in their young lives, we must give them the opportunity to talk. Otherwise they become resentful, lacklustre in their ways. Anyway, many parents entrust us to look after their young people, I will not ignore such responsibility.'

'Spoken like a true guardian,' said Pocack, 'You are right, there are many dangers in forgetting all our fighters are people and some of them are still inexperienced in many ways. Yet we can do this, as you showed when you brought them to attention in the gardens that day.'

'Good. Let us begin, for now I know who I am, nothing will stop me fulfilling the role the gods have given me!'

Chapter 28

That first day back home after the Battle of Long Grasses was a hectic one for all. Although only a few Sytrannians knew the truth, the effects were felt upon everyone. The magi decided to hold an emergency lecture to reunite their students, hoping that this time there would be no more traitors. The lecture hall was packed, for all were glad to welcome back the returning heroes and to tell the news of their own excitements. Cyru's absence was obvious to all, but so was Dayx' returned good cheer and all looked at Sy with wonder, for his news had spread fastest of all.

'Did Cranff really lose an arm and a leg in the battle?' asked Dayx. Sorab, winding himself between their legs, widened his eyes.

'Only an arm, silly!' Klara told him, 'Goodness, I'd have thought that was bad enough without people adding to it!'

'He'll be all right, though, the wound was healing well enough,' Hwym said, reaching down to scratch Sorab's head.

'I'm sure you're right, Hwym,' said Dayx, 'I've doubted you too much in the past, but that's all over, along with all Cyru's evil. It's good to have you back.'

'Thanks,' the Northerner was grateful, 'It feels different here already.'

What would you know? Els thought to herself, managing a smile as she picked up Sorab, you've only been here five minutes.

The talk soon died as the three magi came to the stage.

'Greetings, students, heroes all!' cried Pocack, 'For all of you have fought well, whether at home or on foreign land. All of you have conducted yourselves with honour and we thank you for it.'

'Well done,' said Zritz, 'For this is a time when we need heroes and all will be called to act beyond their previous experience and learning, though we use those

358

things where we can. One, indeed, three battles, are fought and won, yet they will be worth nothing if we lose the final fight.' His voice grew more serious. 'We must prepare ourselves with still greater depth for the things that are yet to test us.'

'To that end,' Durrew stepped in, 'We will be changing our class structure somewhat. You will all have the same opportunities, so that all can reach their greatest potential, not just in their strongest areas, but also in their weakest.'

A few groans replied to this and somebody muttered about 'wasting time in listening when I could be casting'.

'Nobody's time is wasted in this!' Pocack said, sharply, 'If there had been more of us listening at the right time, maybe we would have found out about Cyru earlier.' This silenced the students and Durrew continued,

'Zritz and Pocack will take healing and communicational warfare.' He announced, 'I will lead casting and defence, King Nahvib and Queen Karryn will see to fighting skills, although there will obviously be points of overlap in all groups. Your timetables are on display outside our office, please check them before the end of the day, we will begin tomorrow.'

The assorted talents murmured their approval, but talk soon spread to other things. Many were surprised at King Nahvib and Queen Karryn taking quite such a prominent role in the practicalities of the fighting and Jayak smothered at grin at his knowledge.

Despite some confusion, most students were elated at the changes and the excitement they brought. All were quick to see when they had to attend their different lessons and what they could expect to learn there. The victory of the latest battle had made the promise of the prophecy a reality. Now, all Sytrannians wanted to be a part of the final battle on their homeland, none more than those who had come to train in its capital.

It was a great day for all, but those who had fought at Long Grasses had barely rested properly yet and were exhausted by the time evening came. Els was half asleep by dinnertime and fed more food to Sorab than she ate herself. *'Thanks,'* he said.

'Please, help me out,' Els replied, *'I really can't eat any more.'*

Alleri, next to her, couldn't stop yawning and Jayak laughed at her, though his own eyes were bleary.

'I was going to ask who would stay up for a drink,' said Dayx, 'Celebrate everyone coming back. But it doesn't look like I'd be able to keep anyone talking for long!'

'You're right, I am afraid I must find my bed soon, or I will fall asleep at the table,' Alleri agreed.

'Me too,' Els sent, *'I should go now, I think. See you all in the morning.'*

''Til the morning, Els,' Klara called, gratefully taking Dayx' arm.

Most of all, they were glad that they knew today's tiredness was only the result of hard work and not of dark powers they could not see. It didn't mean, however, that all could sleep uninterrupted.

Els fell asleep easily enough, she was so tired. She had barely given thanks to L'ra and repositioned Sorab on her bed when she fell asleep, without having a chance to even arrange the bed linen. The first hour, she slept in peace, her body and mind finally resting from all that they had been through. Then she began to dream and from that point on, her mind knew no rest.

In her dreams she saw many different scenes, yet one person was in all of them. Through every valley, every forest, down every street in Els' dream landscape, Kyrria walked. It seemed, most of the time, as if Els walked with her, watching her friend point things out that she could not see for herself – the dark shapes hiding in trees, small birds whose colours vanished as they took to the trees, lights in houses that Els had thought uninhabited. Then she saw crowds of people, all those that she knew well, laughing and talking. She saw Sy chatting with Jayak, Alleri watching nearby. She saw Klara and Dayx welcome Hwym, Queen Karryn arrive and add her own greeting.

Then the trees grew lighter, shrank smaller and the floor become wet beneath her feet. Now she could see her family sitting in their house, Mavri and Gron trying to get Cam to explain more, Gron shaking his head. Els heard every word, saw every gesture, but could add none of her own. In her mind, she turned to ask Kyrria what was happening, for the priestess had not spoken yet, but when she asked why she was being shown such people like this, Kyrria wouldn't tell her. She simply held her hands out, seeming to implore Els, though to do what, the sorceress could only guess.

Els spent the whole night replaying such scenes, over and over. Sometimes she saw different people, but the same faces of people she knew well were in many scenes. Each time she hoped to tell them something, but neither exerting her powers, nor searching for her notepad and pencil, brought any luck. Every now and then she would turn back to Kyrria, see her old friend smile and indicate that she wanted her to do something, but what, Els could not discover that night.

Els was not the only one who spent that night trying to make an impact on a hostile dream landscape. In Lykrina, Queen Lidynne also muttered and groaned in her sleep, keeping the unfortunate King Sedryk awake as well.

In her dream, she kept trying to reach a group of young men caught by a pack of Demon Lords, already tiring from their wounds. Many times she set out across the desert between them, but the further she walked, the further away her allies were. She called on Gax, asking the hunter god for help and a horse galloped up to her. But Lidynne found she could not mount the horse, no matter how hard she tried to. A voice called out to her, 'Tend to your wounds, tend to your wounds before you aid the others.' The queen looked everywhere about herself and her horse, but could see nothing wrong.

'Where?' she cried, desperately, 'Where are we wounded, how?' The voice didn't answer her though, and Lidynne realised with horror that the young men were being killed in front of her and there was nothing that she could do to prevent it.

Stec had the clearest dream in many ways. Perhaps this was because he was expecting it, for he had asked for guidance many times in recent days. At first, he was the least startled when he dreamt of friends in trouble, for he saw L'ra and strove to hear her words.

'It will seem as if all is darkness, as if a great night sky descends upon your friends. But remember, it is only a trick of your enemy, you will not heed it Stec, not if you obey my orders.'

'Always, I will obey you, dear goddess,' Stec assured her, 'Since you named me High Priest, I have not run from my duty, but embraced it.'

'Then embrace your faith closer yet, for times more terrible than you can imagine will befall Rima, both in the lands of your friends and in the city of your birth.'

'I won't fear, not when you protect me,' Stec replied, but his eyes widened as he saw the images about him.

Alkar struggled alongside Abrim to hold off ranks of Demon Lords, with no way to defeat the fire the evil ones threw at them. Sky City's buildings, after holding in battle once already, now fell in ruins, crushing to death people that Stec knew well, people he had entrusted to the goddess.

Then he was on the border between Akrin and Sytrannia, miles from Istalan. Yet he could see the smoke from his great distance, hear the terrible cries of people he loved. And the cries were not battle cries, not many. For the most part, they were cries of a people lost and confused, mistrusting their rulers, desperate to survive. Stec glanced around for Els or Jayak, surely they would know whom to help, surely the young sorceress and her friends could make an attack, even where others could not. But as he reached the capital, he found the same confusion attack his mind. He knew it was the same trickery that had been attempted on him at Sky City, but still he could not shake it off. Suddenly he found he could not remember if

362

Els knew who the Healer and the Guardian were. Alarmed, he couldn't recall them himself. Jayak would know, wouldn't he? Wouldn't he? But Stec was lost now, how would he even find the allies in this jumble?

'L'ra? L'ra, you must help me, I know you will!' he called.

'Indeed, but you must make a choice.' L'ra showed him again the picture of Sky City's collapse. 'You want to aid your own people, to prevent the terror that lies hidden no longer, but rather fights your people in their hearts and their very souls. How may you do that you ask?'

'Yes, only tell me how I can help Alkar, tell me!' cried Stec.

'You must do no such thing!' shouted L'ra, her might more powerful than ever. Her hair flowed out behind her, thrown back by the wind that howled around her with the force of her divine magic. Her jade eyes glittered and her golden robes swirled. Her beauty was as full of terror as of love and her gaze never moved from Stec's face.

'You make the last choice you need to in this final call to arms.' The goddess warned him, 'Your adventures have taken you from one side of the land to the other, from homeland to foreign shores, from a struggling politician, to a powerful Priest-Warrior. But such gifts can have no impact unless used most wisely and so I give you this choice. I know this is difficult, but in the final battle you can only save either Sky City or Istalan, I make this solemn promise that the one you leave will fall.'

"How can I decide that?' Stec cried, 'Why do you test me like this?'

'Test you? I want to free you, Stec. My anointing is not such that you must be pulled to my will like a dog on a chain. The choice is hard but the choice is yours, Stec, I only show how much I trust you.' Tears glittered in her eyes but then the goddess was a mherl and the animal looked briefly at Stec before turning and walking away. Then Stec's vision showed him both devastated landscapes and it was as if he were on a bridge between the two.

On the one side, Istalan was all confusion and now Stec saw Els trying to find Jayak, while Queen Karryn sought The Sorceress with equal desperation. Stec looked around for The Healer, but the one he searched for was nowhere to be seen. Were we right, have we lost The Healer? Questions buzzed through Stec's head, but it was of no use unless he joined with his friends, fought alongside them one final time.

But how could he do that when his home city, the place he had fought to sustain in the wake of Queen Wertle's betrayal, was crashing into ruins on his right-hand side? He looked at the buildings crumbling, saw children trapped, soon to be crushed, children he knew, whose parents had trusted that he would look after their children. Then there was Alkar, he had left his fellow priest in charge as a temporary measure, he had returned to save Alkar from this burden. And Abrim, though a worthy leader, was new to such fighting, how could he be expected to gather troops against this evil. He couldn't even see Saluna, where could she be? Stec knew if he didn't help them, his countrymen could die.

Whoever I leave, their city will be ruined, they will be lucky to escape death. And L'ra has promised me no escapes, no secrets are left to aid us, she has promised me only the ruin of a city – and I must choose which one!

* * *

In the Dark Lands, where Hrai had been the only human to dare to walk, now Xanesh and Quivviam, highest of all Demon Lords, prepared to call others to join them. Their robes were as dark as L'ra's were dazzling and the light in their eyes was hard with the hate behind it. As they walked to the large table that held so many of their evil tools, they made no noise, for the very form of their bodies had been transformed when they were born into evil.

Quivviam paused at the table, her sleeve dangled lightly on the map of Rima, where dark patches showed where Demon Lords held sway over many people. She chuckled, a dangerous sound, yet even she could not deny the bursts of light that now covered equal amounts of the map.

'This cannot be, Xanesh, everywhere the allies gaineth on us!' she cried.

'Hss! The discovery of Cyru at Istalan ist the worst of it, if we have someone left there at the end, we can still undermine their plans. Still, oft I told thee I wasn't sure about Cyru, we should have chosen someone stronger.'

'Oh quiet, Xanesh! Thou hadst no better ideas, we were desperate then. Things are not so good now. They have triumphed in the third battle and we have lost many men who worked for us, not to mention the High Lords who were taken.'

'They were not so many,' Xanesh argued.

'Enough! We can hardly afford to lose mighty Demon Lords at this stage, we will need all our magic to triumph in the end. If only we had taken more of theirs,' she said, 'If Els hadst but been lost to them at Green Forest, that would have made the other battles easier.'

'She hath L'ra's protection, I am sure of it. There is not much we can do about her. When we alloweth her to reach Istalan's port in the first place, she was halfway to safety.'

'But Cranff, or Stec, it would have smitten the gods' people hard if either of them had gone. We should have had Cranff, I thought we had. I could feel how close he was to death, the life was draining from him and still he fought his way back. I don't know why, why did we not foresee any problems?'

'Quivviam, there is no point worrying over our losses now. We have to decide who to target next, where we can weaken them.'

'Thou ist right. If we continueth leading our brothers and sisters in the dark magic, then we must decide quickly – but correctly.'

She looked intently at the map, Xanesh following her gaze. Though Quivviam proudly noted the large, dark, almost black, patches in some areas, time and time again her eyes returned to those areas that were a mid-grey and close to the areas of light.

'These are the places we needst target!' she cried, 'Where our influence hasn't yet been tested, where it could be stronger, but is at the moment small enough not to attracteth suspicion.'

'And near enough to affect their light,' Xanesh agreed.

'Yes! Like blotting out their sun with our clouds of darkness. Didn't some of those fools down in Istalan speak of a cloud pressing upon them? Well, they have seen only half our power so far. Now we shall press harder, crushing their foolish faith when they see how even the gods protecteth not against an enemy they invite in.'

'I agree. But who will helpeth us?' Xanesh hissed, excited at the idea of new minds to control. 'Let us choose someone more powerful, someone who will fight it, to start with!' he laughed.

The two looked again at the picture of Rima and Quivviam pointed to areas upon it, 'A politician, a priest, a king and a wizard.' As she said this, her finger touched the map at each person's calling and a blue flame, brighter than any natural flame, struck the map and burned as Quivviam cried the names of her chosen.

'Thou art ambitious, Quivviam, let us hope this is enough to bringeth their downfall,' Xanesh said.

'Dost thou doubt me? My magic is strong, Xanesh, look!' she snarled and Xanesh saw the flames grow brighter and higher before his eyes.

'Thou reacheth these people!' he cried, 'We hath a chance yet!'

'Of course, the dark magic is strong and all hearts have their secrets. Our flames burn most brightly in such places, our power transforms their souls.'

'Forever!' cried Xanesh. The light in his eyes was hard enough to destroy any human, but Quivviam's reaction was quite different.

* * *

It was a bright morning in Istalan and King Nahvib woke up secure that he had everything he needed to achieve the final victory. His allies had all proved their trustworthiness and skill in battle and were close by, ready for their next chance to face the enemy. He now knew who The Three were – here he cast a fond glance at the still sleeping Karryn – and could start to think about how he and his various advisors might use this. That the battle should actually take place on Sytrannian soil! A part of Nahvib was scared by this word of the prophecy, but another side of him was proud. Where would it be? he wondered. Perhaps L'ra's Town, he knew those at the temple considered this a suitable place, for the Gods and Demon Lords had already fought hard for that crucial town. In his heart though, King Nahvib felt it would be here in Istalan. The capital had seen so much power, so much change. Why, Els had come here first, all the way from the Northern kingdom. I must arm those at the ports, set up some kind of signal system in the desert, he thought. And defences! We must have equipment in the desert, we mustn't let them attack us to find ourselves short of arms. We must check all the young people can fight on sand, it won't be like it was at Long Grasses. Thoughts came one on another to the Sytrannian king and he was ready for his morning meeting before either Drayk or the magi.

Els, however, was hardly ready to get up, so it was a shock when Klara knocked on her door.

'You're late!' the wizard called, *'Everyone has started their breakfast already.'*

'What?! All right Klara, coming soon, tell them.'

'Sorab, you should have woken me!' Els smiled at her pet, *'Somebody needs to.'*

'You needed rest,' Sorab replied, turning around and stretching out, *'You are busy.'*

'Well, I can see you're going to rest!' Els laughed, *'I*

367

however, have work to do.'

Kissing him on the head, she swept her hair into a high knot and smoothed out her clothing. Els realised she had not spent many nights in Istalan alone, for her time there since her return from the North had been so fraught and more of it spent in L'ra's Town, Sky City or Lila-Cirith-Ak than Istalan itself. So much has changed since I shared this room with Jayak, she thought. He isn't the same, Els said to herself, for all he may have friends again and people begin to trust him, he will never see himself as he did before. Then again, how well do I know myself? I have walked on every continent, yet where do I really belong? She wished she could speak to her mother, wished her family had the same powers she did, but there was no point in wishing, any more than wondering. The past is done, she thought, mostly glad, but with some sadness for the things that she knew were lost forever.

She was smiling by the time she arrived for breakfast, though, her neat hair and tidy clothes convincing most that she was wide awake. Alleri, however, noted the dark circles beneath Els' eyes and wondered what had caused Els to sleep so poorly.

'Afternoon!' she said, hiding her concern.

'Very funny, Alleri! So, I slept in? Everything's been pretty draining lately, give me that.'

'Ah well, I suppose sorcerers need more sleep than the rest of us, keep you at full power, huh?'

'Alleri! There's no need to be quite so sarcastic!' Jayak nudged her.

'Jayak, learn to laugh again, please!' Alleri said.

'Excuse me?'

'Look, Jayak, we're actually glad to have you back. Yes, you messed things up, but, Gods, that's over, we're on the same side now. You are allowed to enjoy being here. We do like you.'

'Yes?' Jayak's voice was softer than usual.

'Yes!' agreed Dayx. 'If you had a point to prove, sounds like you did more than your bit in the last battle.

Came back with it won and all your friends in one piece, didn't you?'

'Yes, Jayak, Alleri says what we all think. It's good to have you back.' Klara added.

'And you, Els?' Jayak looked at her with hope and fear.

I haven't seen him look so scared since the time with Kyrria, since we saved him. When have I spoken to him properly since then? She realised she had almost lost not just one friend, but two, and knew the Demon Lords would have liked her to. I will not be held back by doubts, she thought, I know he is different, I know we have all grown up since that terrible time.

'Alleri's right, what happened before is over,' she smiled, *'I forgive you, Jayak, so stop frowning and start laughing, like my friend says.'*

'You forgive me!' Jayak cried, happy, but startled. 'Of course, I had forgotten, the battle has been all in my mind except the pro - .' A strange look came over his face, as if he understood something at last. 'Anyway, thank you. And you!' he paused to hug Alleri, 'I have to thank you as well, that you should encourage me this way, when I have been so arrogant and selfish in the past. Alleri, I owe you, I won't forget it.'

'Don't worry, I won't let you,' Alleri said, her eyes serious even as she joined in her friends' laughter.

Chapter 29

King Nahvib frowned, 'I don't like this, not a bit.' He held up the letter that had recently arrived, the ornate seal lying on the table before him.

'Why not?' asked Pocack, 'What is it? We have already fought there, they ought to be safe now.'

'That's not what King Hurburt seems to think.' the Sytrannian monarch said darkly.

The gathered council looked concerned. The last thing anybody needed now were unforeseen problems, it could damage everything. The noblemen thought of how the preparations might be effected, how much money they could afford to give towards helping their allies. The magi thought of the spiritual impact – how much more trouble could the Sytrannians take and still thank their gods? When was the goddess going to show her hand? All knew the emotional impact of more trouble and confusion, after Cyru's betrayal, people needed a chance to regain their previous confidence, they needed to live in the hope of victory, not the despair of loss.

'Tell us.' said Nobleman Zakkari, 'Tell us now and we may be able to help.'

'King Hurburt says,' Nahvib sighed, 'There are increased Demon Lord attacks in his kingdom. Green Forest, after what we did there, is largely protected, but surrounding areas are badly affected, as are towns in the middle and towards the West.'

'I suppose we should have expected it on the Western side, we shouldn't have expected the Demon Lords to throw all their power onto those lands and ignore the North,' Lord Drayk said.

'Yes, and where else have they gone that we don't know about?' said Noblewoman Orlanda, causing the others to exchange worried looks.

'Worse, King Hurburt believes his court to be riddled with traitors and is unsure who he can trust there to rid him of this scourge,' Nahvib continued.

'What does he want us to do? That's really what we must know,' said Zritz, his voice thin, but his elderly eyes still bright, awaiting the next move as eagerly as he might at one of Lars' gaming tables.

The others nodded but did not speak, so much depended on each individual event now that the end was near. Durrew wondered how much longer the kingdom could take such tension, how much longer this war must go on. He was not alone, for all those assembled were praying not just for victory, but for a quick end with it.

'He says that although he understands our needs are also great and would not willingly disrupt our part in this fight, he must do so.'

'Then he wants aid? We can spare none,' cried Orlanda.

'He asks for no Sytrannians, no allied forces, he knows we need them too much.' said King Nahvib, to the relief of his council. 'However, he recalls his warriors, until he can be sure his kingdom is clear.'

'His warriors must go back? But that means...' Drayk's voice trailed off in horror.

'Exactly. We lose Cranff, Hwym and Macie, along with all the Northern forces.'

'King Nahvib, is this right? Now, of all times!' Pocack asked.

'I know what you are all thinking,' said the Sytrannian ruler, 'But in all truth, I can see no way around it. Stop!' he quietened Drayk with one look, 'I know you will talk of the bearing this has on the prophecy, but don't think I haven't considered that. I like it very little, but I think we best help King Hurburt and ourselves by sending warriors to him and praying they can help him quickly enough to come to our aid later.'

'So be it. Let us hope they are quick indeed,' Drayk said, his face grave.

He was not the only one to be feeling very serious at that

371

moment. Alleri's concerns however, were not immediately with the war, but with herself. She had been feeling strange for some days now and had initially put it down to the after-effects of the Battle of Long Grasses. That had convinced her for the first couple of days, but it was nearing a week since their return and she felt no better.

She felt terrible pressure in her head, yet until recently she had hardly ever suffered headaches, Klara had said she was one of the few people not to ask for healing from them. It had begun with a slight pain but gradually built up to such a stage that she could feel it behind her eyes and her casting was completely spoilt.

Alleri had decided not to tell anyone; after all, they all had their own problems, and she had decided just to drink lots of water in an effort to clear it. For a time this had worked, but then she had found it build again and a terrible irritability with it.

She had been talking to Els, Jayak and Hwym, noting to herself how much better Els and Jayak were getting along, when she had come over dizzy, barely able to hide it from her friends. But it's nothing to do with that, she told herself, I'm not bothered about that anymore, let Els have whom she chooses. Nevertheless, the pain had consistently worsened and she now lay on her bed curled up, crying in agony.

She had begun to hope that the others had forgotten about her. Perhaps it was better to embrace the pain and the comfort it offered. A small flame appeared in her mind, faint, yet bright in its green intensity. A part of her knew that it was this flame which caused the terrible pain in her head, knew that the next thing it would tackle would be her soul. But another part of her thought why should I fear it, what have I left to fear? This side to Alleri wondered if anyone would ever miss her, wondered if the flame wouldn't give her more than her friends ever had. Then someone knocked on her door and Alleri sat up with a start.

'Who is it?' she asked, all caution and no welcome in

her voice.

'It's Jayak,' the sorcerer answered. 'Are you feeling all right? You looked pale in class, you weren't as talkative as usual.'

'I'm just feeling a little strange. Leave me alone, I'll be down for dinner later.'

'If you're sure,' Jayak said. He walked off and as his footsteps died away, Alleri thought she had got away with it, had put him off completely. Then she heard Jayak stop in the corridor and his footsteps move back towards her room. She held her breath, willed him to believe she was asleep, tired and ill, nothing more. Then his hand rapped sharply on her door and she winced at his determination.

'Alleri? What do you mean you feel strange?' Jayak hit the door again, harder this time, 'You let me in right now, or I'm going straight to Pocack!'

'Stop making such a fuss, I'll let you in, all right?' Alleri fought to sound normal and opened the door for her friend with as cheerful a smile as she could manage. Maybe she would have convinced Dayx or Klara, but Jayak was a sorcerer and so strong an attack could not be hidden from his powers.

'Alleri? Gods, look at your face! Sit down. What's happened to you?'

'I've got a headache, a bad one. It's not fun but really, I'll be fine, just leave me be.'

'Not likely. When my oldest friend, the girl who normally makes most noise round here, suddenly wants to be left alone, I'm worried. When did this headache start?'

'I don't know, a few days ago. It doesn't matter.'

'It does to me. Why didn't you tell me?'

'What, interrupt your getting to know Els all over again? I'd hate to,' Alleri lowered her eyes, he wouldn't understand.

'It isn't just a headache, though, is it? Alleri? Let me look.'

Alleri stopped, she wanted to order him out of her room, but she was tired and it was Jayak asking.

'It hurts here, it makes me go dizzy, then I start to fell angry...jealous.' She bent her head and Jayak sat next to her. Gently, he placed his hands on her forehead, rubbing at the skin there. Alleri groaned, but Jayak didn't stop his probing, the only change was that he now reached out to touch her with his mind as well. His hands continued their motions; feeling Alleri's soft curls between his fingers, Jayak groaned too, for he could feel the pain, both in her head and in her heart. For now he could see the evil eating into her mind and soul, the green flame that burned with a promise of a world free of cares, a world where Alleri would be strong and her human conflicts forgotten. But it was not really such a happy place. Its dreams may seem attractive, that was how it gripped Alleri tight, in spirit as much as in the body, but Jayak knew that the place where the flame burned strong would consume any who left this world for its cold fire. Jayak knew, for he had walked in that place, nearly given in to that sweet poison before his friends had dragged him back from it. They had risked everything they had to offer him a path out of it and he was not about to desert one of them now, Alleri least of all.

'It holds onto you. It calls to you, doesn't it?' he asked, not accusingly, but with all the sympathy of a fellow victim.

'Uhh. Yes,' Alleri moaned. 'I wanted to tell you, but you were all so busy, you especially. You're so concentrated on patching thing up with Els, I didn't want to get in the way of that. I know you love her. Why should I distract you from trying to tell her that?'

'You know that do you?' Jayak's voice took on an edge, though his hands kept up their motion, his fingers pulling Alleri's hair back as he continued to gently knead her forehead. 'Alleri, this is not about Els or anyone except you. I wish you'd come to me sooner, it's serious.'

'It is?' Alleri pulled away from Jayak's hands, turning to face him with fearful eyes.

'Alleri, I can see this headache is from a terrible source.

374

The Demon Lords obviously seek to destroy us one by one. Don't worry, you won't have to battle this on your own.'

'Thanks Jayak, I don't think I could.'

'Well, if you know that, you know more than I did anyway. Let's walk through the gardens to the office of the magi. It'll probably help to get some air.' He took Alleri's shaking hand and was relieved when she was able to stand. 'Take it slowly,' he warned. 'We're just going outside to look at the gardens if anyone sees us, looking for the others maybe.'

'It'll look funny if anyone notices you holding my hand,' Alleri whispered.

'As if I care about that. Come on.'

Jayak's idea was not as far-fetched as Alleri feared, for many of the young people were outside, sitting in the sunshine that warmed the flowerbeds. Dayx and Klara were admiring them together and Els was beginning to wish she had taken Sorab in the opposite direction.

'Cheer up,' the mherl cried, *'Who's that?'*

'Hey! Els!' a voice called and Els was glad to see Macie, though she brought Hwym with her.

The two warriors looked sad, however, and both were burdened with bags and weapons.

'Is the battle come so soon?' Dayx asked, rising to greet his Northern friends.

'Not here, but in the North, yes. We must return,' Hwym explained.

As ever, you abandon others as soon as something becomes difficult. Els wrote, holding the paper to Hwym, ignoring Sorab's sudden nip to her leg.

'It isn't like that,' sighed Hwym, 'The king has called us back, there is nothing we can do.'

'He's right. We go back with Cranff and the other Northerners now, there is no choice for us. Things are really bad there. We have to stop our enemy there otherwise their numbers will increase again,' Macie told them.

'Makes sense, I suppose,' said Dayx, 'Mind, I'll be sorry to see you go.'

'Me too,' Klara said, 'Especially when we have fought together.'

'We'll come back as soon as we can, hopefully in time to help you in your own battle.' Hwym looked at Els, but she refused to answer him.

'Really?' Sorab asked.

'We have to go, Hwym,' Macie said, 'Bye Els, Klara, Dayx.'

'And you Alleri, Jayak,' Hwym said, acknowledging Jayak and Alleri's arrival in the gardens with a wave.

'Have a safe journey, good luck,' Jayak shook Hwym's hand briefly, moving back to take Alleri by the arm.

Hwym and Macie walked off briskly, they had said their goodbyes and they could delay no longer. Sorab ran towards them, squeaking his own goodbye, before running back to Els. Hwym wanted to look back, to say farewell to Els one last time, but what was the point? She didn't care for him. So he strode off, his bulging bag slung over his shoulder, laden with items gained during his time in the South. He had tied his flute, spearheads and some tools to his belt, for he was overburdened with battle preparations now. Concentrating on tying them tight, he didn't notice Els until she was nearly upon them. Macie turned as she heard Els' footsteps, for she ran hard to catch them, but Els had no business with her. Hwym followed Macie's movements just in time for Els to thrust a scrap of paper into his hand. She looked at him once, then fled back to the others, turning the corner of the gardens so as to be out of Hwym's sight before he could call her back.

'What is it?' Macie said softly.

Hwym opened the paper to find just four words written for him: **Good Luck. Return Soon.** After that was a smudge and the paper had been torn. Perhaps Els had meant to continue, but what was left gave Hwym enough cause for hope. Only the tiniest amount of hope, maybe, but he smiled as he answered Macie,

'Els was just wishing me luck, that's all,' he said.

'That's all? Honestly Hwym, we have to get you back here fast,' Macie laughed.

'Then let's catch the boat out and aid our king quickly!' Hwym said and the two of them made off at once.

In the gardens, Klara greeted Els.

'You're upset. Els, Els dear, it's all right to cry, I know how you miss him.'

'I'm not crying.'

'Then why is your face wet? Els, it's all right to admit you like Hwym, it's not like we don't know.'

'How can you know? I don't even know what I want. Leave me be. I just want to get on with the war now, let's all concentrate on that, shall we?'

'Of course. But I'm here if you want to talk about anything, anything at all.'

What would you know? Els thought, You're so tied up in Dayx, how do you know what it feels like to be alone, to wonder why you feel the way you do? There aren't any questions in your life, Klara, how can you begin to understand mine?

'Els! Wait a minute,' Jayak came after her, Alleri with him.

'Jayak?' She hastily dried her face on her robes, *'What now?'*

'Els, we need you. Alleri's ill, I'm sure it's the Demon Lords.'

Els looked at Alleri, noting her grey face, her hand holding tight to Jayak's.

'When did this happen?' she asked the sorcerer.

'I only found out today, I think she's been like it a few days.'

'Days, days of flames,' Alleri murmured. The skin prickled on Els' neck, Alleri's words reminding her of Jayak's struggle with the Demon Lords.

'This is bad. Her voice speaks of fear, but also an attraction I think,' Els sent.

377

'I know. There is much here I recognise. I want to take her to the magi now, will you come with me? Will you help?' Jayak pleaded.

'You know I will,' Els told him, *'We won't allow it to take hold, not this time.'* She took Alleri's other hand and they walked her past the oblivious Dayx and Klara, as if they were merely out for a stroll in the gardens themselves.

They knocked loudly when they arrived at the magi's common room, scared to risk losing the slightest amount of time in healing their friend.

'Jayak? Why knock so desperately, surely-' But then Zritz saw Alleri and brought the three friends inside.

'Gods. How long?' he asked.

'Days,' Els and Jayak said together.

'Then it's serious. But she doesn't seem to have given in to it, you found out. And I don't believe we have had ill magic cast by this one.'

'No. Maybe if we work quickly we can save her,' sent Jayak.

'Lie her down on the couch there, let me see what I can do. And I'll send for the others, we won't try this alone.'

'Good.'

'We'll start though, there can be no time wasted in ridding your young friend of this evil.' So saying, Zritz placed his hands over Alleri and called softly, his old voice trembling, but the power in his words clear as Alleri moaned and twisted in discomfort at them. Jayak replaced his hands on Alleri's forehead, calling on the gods to turn out the evil that tried to consume her. Els cast spells of weakening upon the enemy and though she could not hope to destroy the Demon Lords in such a way, yet the air filled with moans that did not come from Alleri's mouth.

'What is going on!' cried Pocack, entering the room with Durrew. 'I got your call, Zritz, but I hardly expected such...another victim? I thought we were clean here, I thought we were safe.'

'Nowhere is entirely safe,' said Durrew. 'Wherever there are people, there are all our weaknesses to bring us to danger.'

'*You are right Durrew,*' Els answered, '*But we can halt the danger. I think we have enough power in this room to do that.*'

'*She's right,*' Pocack lifted his hands close to Zritz' and Durrew joined them. Their chants grew stronger and the air crackled.

'Don't take it away!' screamed Alleri, 'Don't take the pretty flame. I need it, I need it!'

'No you don't! Jayak cried, 'You need your friends, you do not need any powers that come from such an unnatural source. Alleri, they will break you.'

'Why? Because I am not a sorceress? Because I cannot fight as she does? Who am I without such power? Who listens to me unless I can fight using such strength?'

As Alleri's words revealed her anguish, so the air above the magi brought the green flame into view.

'Listen not, Alleri!' screamed a dread voice, 'Thou canst win affection here. Whereas in our world, my world…' The voice oozed its false flattery, 'Thou shall be queen among Demon Lords, thou shall reign with thine Xanesh, powerful beyond all measure. Can thou turn away such joys? Mine realm awaits you, Alleri, with all its glories.'

'He lies! He doesn't care for you!' Jayak urged Alleri to hear him. 'This power causes you pain, and will cause others more if you let it. Remember what you told me once, when I lay enthralled by the lies they told me. Remember how you urged me to rejoin my friends, to choose the love this world makes real not that conjured up by evil for its own ends.'

'*Alleri, oh Alleri, come back to us!*' Els sent, '*We cannot leave you. And you are still strong, stronger than Jayak, for you have shared the knowledge of this illness with your friends. You know you want to be rid of it. And as for talk of power, I may be a sorceress, but I am nothing without my friends to aid me. Alleri you know that, as well as I! Do not let the Demon Lords, this Xanesh or whoever,*' *provoke jealousy where there is cause for none.'*

'But there is cause! You know I speak of Jayak,' Alleri sobbed.

'And does that mean there is cause? Because you feel so strongly, must I feel so to?' wept Els as she sent. *'Alleri, we have wasted time in fighting when we could have been loving, there is no need to quarrel. I love Jayak no longer and I know he has no more feelings for me than friendship.'*

'But he has been so close to you, arguing, trying to make amends, always close.'

'Maybe, at first,' Els acknowledged. *'But much of that was guilt on both our sides. Yet once we left that behind, only friendship has been the conclusion, nothing more.'*

Jayak looked at Els, as amazed as if she had broken a long spell, to talk of his friendship without regret, or anger. Though he followed her lead, he often turned back to Alleri and his calming hands never left her head.

'You know that? You know friendship is all either of you wants? That is not what they told me,' Alleri's tears flowed, yet she was listening now and quiet.

'And why should they tell you what you want to hear? That does them no good and you no harm!' Els smiled, *'If you had only asked me, I could have told you I was only glad to be Jayak's friend once more, for I have come to realise that, as he has. I have forgiven his wrongs and we are friends, Alleri, nothing more.'*

'I wish you had spoken earlier!' Jayak sent, *'For I was so intent on repairing friendship with Els, I did not think any of my former friends would forgive me enough to love as you do Alleri.'*

'They poisoned my heart, for all I could see was the two of you. I could see nothing beyond that. Curse them for their evil hold! Forgive me, for I have thought many bad things about both of you,' Alleri sent. As she said the words the Demon Lords had hoped they would never hear, the flame wavered and died. The room's natural light returned. The magi sighed with relief, but their students

scarcely noticed.

'Of course I forgive you, such mistakes are easily made in these troubled times, but it was a mistake to hold such thoughts, Alleri. I do not love Jayak. I think I love another, though I seem doomed never to be able to tell him that. Indeed, I may well never see him again,' Els told her friends. *'You have the chance to tell each other, to make the thought real in word and action. Take your chance, you are fortunate to have it.'*

She left then, only pausing long enough to see Jayak take Alleri's hand. A pain shot through her, but it was not for the sorcerer, only for one whose talents she couldn't name; whose face she did not dare hope to see again.

* * *

'At last you show my children some care,' said Ellari, mother to all.

'I show your children much care, I have invested many talents in them and great are the friends I give to my people. You should know I can be trusted to look after my followers. I only desire that they should make their own steps. That way they are aware of their power,' L'ra smiled. 'And now they know they have the means to break this evil themselves.'

'More important is that you have taken them from the grip of evil. You must admit, the power of my people in foreseeing events has been most valuable,' Gax reminded her.

'I thank you, hunter. Now you must turn to those the Demon Lords threaten next, I fear for the king and politician whom Quivviam and Xanesh wish to ensnare.'

'And you can't forget your priest,' Ellari said.

'Hush! You think a priest of mine shall be corrupted?' L'ra tossed her hair. 'Goddess of children, you do not know what powers I place in my followers. I assure you, no Demon Lord will shake the will of one I have chosen!'

'Even so, we need to enlist the Elementals, for their

power is great,' said Gax. 'The mightiest of hunters is grateful for a good wind to speed the chase and steady ground beneath his feet.'

'Indeed, their efforts make the difference in the end, for time stops not for either side and the evil ones will doubtless deceive our people with delays. Go, Gax, speak to our brothers and sisters of the elements, while I see where this adventure finds all my people.' L'ra made off abruptly, There was much to be revealed yet, before the humans could fight with all their talents.

Chapter 30

Though Alleri's green flame had died, other flames still flickered across Rima, growing or falling according to how they were received. Some were quickly cast aside by those stronger than their lies, but others were as eagerly invited by the weak and desperate.

Having failed to win the allegiance of their chosen wizard, Quivviam and Xanesh moved their attention to their other key victims.

'A flame? In my mind? What evil is this?' demanded Stec, seeking the advice of Alkar at once.

'The same flame, I think, which the Demon Lords use in many,' sighed Alkar.

'What?' cried Stec, 'I did not invite such a thing in. Help me, Alkar, for I know I cannot rid myself of this alone.'

Stec was fortunate that his purpose was clear and his need for help apparent. Alkar, along with the few novice priests in Sky City, spent the night in prayer until a joyous morning brought Stec out of a dreamlike state.

'L'ra be praised!' he groaned. 'I would not have my skills given over to evil. Thank you Alkar, brothers.'

After that, Stec and his fellow priests went about their business with renewed energy. Perhaps, however, they should have given more attention to politics than they did magic, for not every council member was pure of heart and one of them put up no resistance to an orange glow.

Even if Stec had kept closer eye on some of his friends, there was little he could do about troubles on the other continents. Battles raged in the Northern continent, endangering the allies so desperately needed in the South. On the West, men were lost rebuilding homes in the grasslands that had so recently been battlefields. In the South, some may have expected things to be easier, for surely preparation was a gentler task than warfare itself?

But preparation led to debate and argument and many

grew envious of the role others played. Though few would say so aloud, some from other countries wondered at the prominence of Sytrannia in all this. There were some whose hatred of themselves was easily transferred to King Nahvib and the allies. More than a few with little skill looked jealously on Els' talents and Nahvib's army. One such bitter soul ignited the spark inside with great vigour and a sickly flame sent yellow shadows about his kingdom. For this was the soul of a king, one whose power was clung onto with a desperate mistrust.

'I take your power!' he cried, 'For my neighbours give me none, only taking my troops to help themselves. I have tried to show them how much they need us, but still they have not listened. You Demon Lords, your names are strange and your power dark, but it is mighty and might I must have!'

The monarch screamed in triumph, while Quivviam's servants saw her sharp teeth gleam even in the mist beneath her hood.

So it was that even while Nahvib and Karryn planned their defences and trained their subjects, still the kingdoms allied to them fell. Els, Jayak and Alleri were present the morning they heard that Cassal had fallen and the afternoon brought the terrible news that Liance was under siege. Of Cassal's other neighbour, they heard nothing and so they could only assume that Rucilia had also fallen foul of their enemy, despite their best efforts.

A week later, one of Sedryk's generals noticed smoke rising in worrying plumes across Izk's plains. He rode close by with his troops, but they were attacked by men waiting behind rocks – men wearing the king's uniform. Vastly outnumbered, Sedryk's troops were forced to back off after losing two men to highly sharpened swords. It was a shaken group of soldiers that returned to Lykrina and Queen Lidynne was greatly alarmed by their tale. She decided to send word to King Azabar and sent an armed guard with Noblewoman Okka, who oversaw foreign affairs. However, when they did not return after five days, Queen Lidynne wondered if they were coming back. She dared not risk anyone else. Lord Dekkomas volunteered but Queen Lidynne forbade him,

'After what happened to Lady Taheya when she left Izk? After the disappearance of Noblewoman Okka? I may have sent her to her death. I will not risk another!'

Soon, Queen Lidynne and King Sedryk had more to worry about, as their subjects began to fight each other, seemingly over nothing. Soldiers were dispersed to deal with the crowds while the queen watched in sorrow, to see many of her people killed trying to attack her castle.

'At such a time? Don't they understand we need to stand together? What have I done wrong?' she asked.

'Your majesty, many people were delirious and talked of things quite…strange,' said Nobleman Uran, 'This is surely the work of Demon Lords. Our people are normally very supportive of yourself and King Sedryk.'

'He's right,' agreed Dekkomas. 'This is not how us Lykrosians behave at all. It is obvious to me that the Demon Lords have excited any mild feelings of disagreement into hatred and fear. We have to look upon this as an attack from the enemy.'

'You are right,' sighed King Sedryk, 'Well, I will have to try to send word to Akrin, Sytrannia and Izk, let us pray someone is still able to listen to us.'

Against all hopes, King Vistar did receive the message brought by Lord Dekkomas, for though Akrin's situation was serious, it had not yet reached the severity of some of its neighbours.

'Ah, Lord Dekkomas, it saddens me to hear your news, yet I cannot say I am surprised,' said King Vistar.

'Then you have heard what has been happening? Are you in contact with others still?' Lord Dekkomas asked, eagerly.

'Sadly, no,' Vistar told him, 'I knew things were wrong, for nobody has seen an Izkan or a Zarittian in some time. I also have several problems of my own. A large section of my army deserted last week. I've sent others to find them, but they've scattered. Even the ones we have found have been pretty incapable of explaining their actions. Some killed themselves before we could question them.'

'Then I will divide the troops who came with me,' decided Lord Dekkomas. 'One third shall return to Sedryk and alert him to your situation. Another third shall go North to Sytrannia, to tell them of the terrible developments we know of. The other third shall remain to assist you, myself included.'

'Thank you!' King Vistar shook the First Minister's hand vigorously. 'I welcome such help for the hour is desperate, but we will not be defeated, I know it! Gax be praised that you come to us now!'

Lord Dekkomas' heart raced. In all the trouble and confusion, here was the youngest of all the Southern rulers eagerly taking up a chance to fight back. This may be the test that makes him, just as it breaks others, thought Dekkomas.

Zarrit was quiet and many would have rejoiced to see such apparent calm. But this was not a quiet born of peace, rather of preparation. There were no fights to be seen, but neither were there open discussions, people walking in the park, children playing. Everyone was inside, watching, waiting.

Even in Kreab's great castle, the same was true. Though Queen Ashla sat with her husband and her council in more quiet than she had ever shown, the restraint was hard on them all. Having refrained from joining the Battle of Long Grasses, they had spent their time in arming their soldiers and fortifying the capital. Their road system was now complete and the royal children, along with two trusted handmaidens, had been taken to an ordinary house on the other side of Zarrit, disguised as peasant children. The two oldest children, eleven and nine years old, had protested greatly at this but Ashla was unprepared to take chances. Now all she had to do was decide what must be done to force the enemy into view.

'I know the enemy is here, in Zarrit,' she said. 'We must flush them out, find where they hide.'

'This would be easy if we faced a foreign enemy, or if only the high lords came, cloaked and firing magic at us,' said Lord Bik. 'But so many of the Demon Lords' people are just that – people. We cannot easily tell what is inside a man's mind if he does not immediately act on it. While the people under such evil influence are awaiting their instructions, we have nothing to prove ill will.'

'Lord Bik is right,' said Noblewoman Caree. 'I know you feel the need to act, Your Majesty, but we cannot do so without proof.'

'Then you suggest we wait here until they strike?' cried Ashla, 'Sit drinking tea and discussing the more interesting aspects of this war as if it is another game to play? I cannot abandon my people to evil, you know some may not survive the takeover of their mind by these forces. Not unless they receive help quickly.'

'How do you propose we find them?' asked Lord Bik.

'Maybe we could use a person of magical talent, a wizard or the like?' suggested Nobleman Ernst, 'Get someone to scan minds, eliminate the innocent so that we could arm them, find those given to evil so we can heal them, or kill them if need be.'

'Nobleman Ernst, I can tell you are more given to working out finances,' sighed Ashla, 'That is a commendable idea, but not a practical one. We do not have enough wizards able to do this; it would take a wizard of much experience, if not a sorcerer. We are not equipped for this, we haven't the people available for it.'

'Then couldn't we borrow some?' asked Prince Griorg, 'Send for help to our allies? Nahvib has many such people, surely we could send someone over the border to find some to help us?'

'No!' cried Lord Bik. 'Don't you remember what happened to Lady Taheya when she tried to send word there of others' troubles?' Bik's hands shook as he addressed the prince, 'I will not send anyone to Sytrannia, I will not risk a life on such a pointless gamble. If King Azabar had thought more carefully, perhaps poor Taheya would not have been the victim of such an ordeal.'

'Hush!' said Nobleman Anbar, 'I know Taheya's attack was of great distress to you, Lord Bik, but you cannot use that to insult King Azabar. As foreign minister, you cannot expect me to let such comment go unrestrained. Yes, King Azabar made a mistake, but he no doubt made the choice that had seemed the best to him at the time. There are none of us who do any more than this.'

'Forgive me.' said Bik, 'I mean no ill to King Azabar. But this situation is frustrating beyond belief. What can we do?'

'There is one thing that might work,' Queen Ashla spoke slowly, 'What would these people want, these ones maddened by the Demon Lords? What would their aim be focussed on in an attack?'

'Well, hm!' coughed Caree, 'Probably Your Majesties, I should think.'

'Absolutely,' agreed Anbar, 'They need to bring the country into chaos to make it ready for their evil Demon Lords to take control of it. You and Prince Griorg would need to be gone in order for them to do that.'

'Then why don't we draw them out?' Ashla said. 'If I was to appear to take a trip somewhere, say with only my handmaidens to accompany me, wouldn't this prompt action?'

'Ashla, don't be so stupid. It's far too dangerous!' Prince Griorg snapped.

'But it would reveal our enemy, then we could really fight.'

'Your Majesty, it would be very risky,' said Lord Bik.

'Of course it would,' agreed the queen. 'But this whole war is and I cannot allow my people's lives to be risked without making some effort of my own. If I had wanted to escape danger, I would have arranged to hide with the children, but I did not. Griorg, don't look so shocked! It is a risk, but not a run into death. My handmaidens are well trained, they don't just do needlework, you know!'

'I know, but, dearest, I could lose you without even being able to try to protect you,' the prince looked as if he had already defeated.

'Maybe not!' cried Noblewoman Zorne. The youngest of the ministers and the most recently appointed, she had held back from the conversation, listening to the points her colleagues made. But now she saw where her input could be made and she couldn't hesitate, though they turned to her with amazement.

'Your majesty, you appointed me mostly to sort out our troublesome infrastructure – our transport, I mean.'

'Yes, yes. But what affect does this have now? I know we can travel more quickly, but I can only go with my handmaidens, otherwise it will look like an attack, that way we will never find our enemy,' Ashla gently told her.

'Only your handmaidens can go with you, yes.' said Zorne, 'But there are many places where others could hide, if they were to go ahead of you.'

'Is this true? It could work if it is.' said Lord Bik.

'The work was finished in a hurry, you all know that. Not that any of it was overly rushed,' Zorne added quickly. 'But there are still many piles of materials left, rocks and some temporary buildings the workers stayed in during their long shifts. If a trusted group of your soldiers were to arrive there unseen, Queen Ashla's carriage could take the coastal route and then wait to be attacked, knowing that help is already available.'

'It will work, I know it!' Ashla cried, 'Come, my dear, you must see the sense in this, I will scarcely be in danger if support is already in place. I think Noblewoman Zorne's idea is an excellent one.'

'If the soldiers left under cover of darkness, it could well work. It will show us who our enemies are and in a reasonably small fight we may show our power over them. The risk to your subjects is much smaller this way.' Bik said.

'Very well,' said Prince Griorg, 'I will trust my ministers in this, for you have studied warfare longer and more thoroughly than I. But I must insist that I be present in the group to ambush our enemy. I will not see my wife go off into a collision with the enemy without helping her.'

'Of course,' said Bik, 'I suggest you, myself and Noblewoman Zorne head up this group.'

'Me?' asked Zorne.

'It was your idea and you know these hiding places. Yes, you. Come let us choose our soldiers immediately, so we can carry out this scheme as soon as possible,' Bik said.

'Meeting dismissed then!' cried Ashla, her mind already on explaining this task to her handmaidens.

Things were worse still over in the East. There were many people there who had failed to learn the lessons of the Elementals' fury and now proved willing to listen to voices far removed from the gods. Persuaded to follow the Demon Lords, they openly mocked the words brought to them by the priests Stec had sent to them, turning on them with violence.

Once they had dealt so furiously with their own kind, they turned their attention to the gods. Cursing the gods, they laughed at them, choosing instead the destructive passion instilled in them by the Demon Lords. They deliberately sought out ways to spite the gods and ruin their work, often forcing those priests left alive to watch this heresy.

In Myrria, they scorned the goddess Myrrine by throwing waste into her rivers, pouring oil and muck into the lakes and sea until the waters bubbled with dirt and a foul mist hung in the air.

Raz growled in fury to see his country, Razia, extinguish all flame and become a place of darkness. Looking down from the Divine Realms, he raged at not being able to find a fire in a single hearth, for he had offered these people warmth and light and now they rejected it.

Cala wept to see the skies above Calan polluted by the foul-smelling smoke of spells cast from evil books. Not only this, but the people controlled by the Demon Lords scaled the tallest buildings in order to bring down their highest turrets and roofs, in some cases destroying whole floors of houses quite casually. The goddess of the air searched for the priests who might help but more often found dark-cloaked figures amongst the people. 'The Demon Lords come, when can we act!' she asked.

'Soon, I hope, for my land will not take much more ruin before it is left in useless pieces!' agreed Tadir. His distress could well be understood, for though Tadria's few volcanoes lay dormant, Demon Lords and their underlings had found other means to destroy the very earth itself. They chanted horribly at the ground and tiny cracks began to run along it. Then the men dug and kicked, even clawing at the soil and rock beneath to cause greater damage. 'This plunges us all into despair! Let it end now, L'ra your people need your intervention!' the earth god pleaded.

'No.' L'ra's voice was clear and she spoke with the highest authority. 'The hour is not here. We act only when our people will benefit from such help, otherwise we lose our chance and the war will swing to our enemy's advantage.'

The other gods grumbled, but they knew L'ra's care for her people.

She would work whatever miracles were necessary to bring certain people to the right places and so they trusted that her plans would work. Nevertheless, it was a restless time for the gods while they waited for their time to intervene.

Two whole weeks had passed in which the Demon Lords began to show their hand across Rima, without exerting their full power. During this time, only Sytrannia, Akrin

391

and Lykrosia remained in any real contact with each other. Even this was often punctuated by mislaid messages or confused communications where attacks or destruction of equipment caused delays.

'Ah! This is more hopeful,' King Nahvib said.

'Queen Lidynne and King Azabar bring help. Wonderful news. The sooner we fight here in Sytrannia, the sooner the prophecy is fulfilled. When are they due to arrive?' Karryn asked him, scanning the letter.

'Five days hence. So we have that much time to fortify our desert weapons, check our roads are kept clear unless in an emergency, run our troops through their final preparations.'

'That should be easily accomplished, the men are ready for action, this waiting has been the hardest part.' Karryn said.

'You say that my dear, but let us not talk too easily of the warfare, for this final battle will involve all our strengths, that I am sure of,' the king said.

'Well, our young people are better equipped than most, especially now they seem to have sorted out their differences.'

'Thank goodness! If we had only known about Alleri and Jayak,' Nahvib said.

'I know,' said Karryn, taking the king's arm, 'I am very glad that we knew each other's feelings from the beginning.'

'So am I. Though we met in deathly danger, I knew from the start I would not part from you. Gods be praised we were clearer than these youngsters.'

'Ah, that must be what made the difference – you are that much older than them!'

'Karryn, you provoke me!' King Nahvib said, but they were both laughing now and it was a while before they thought of sending for the council.

Four days later, the king and queen were discussing matters with their wizards. Their confidence rose to see

392

Els and Jayak participate so effectively in developments, now that their differences were resolved. Their excitement turned to dismay, however, when Drayk, Orlanda and Horik arrived, looking greatly alarmed.

'Your Majesties,' he bowed, 'There is disturbance, in the streets and it's serious.'

'What of it?' King Nahvib shrugged, 'Name the street and we can send men to deal with it.'

'That's just it, it's several streets, not just the one.' Drayk told them.

'Why?' asked Karryn.

'It must be the work of Demon Lords. The people who cause trouble in the streets are not the usual criminals we have kept an eye out for. In fact, many of those we were concerned about have asked if they can help us. No, it is ordinary men – and women – who have taken up arms against their neighbours. The brawls do not begin in bars this evening, but in shops and gardens, anywhere where people gather.'

'How do we know these are not just private matters getting out of hand? Has anyone spoken to these fighters?' asked Nahvib.

'Yes, do they speak of flames, or of strong emotions? Hate? Fear? Anger?' Els asked.

'Yes, has anyone asked them what they're doing?' Alleri said.

'Soldiers, innkeepers, priests, many are those who try to stop them and all have argued with them, to no avail,' Drayk said.

'Yes, the best we can get out of them is that they hate the king and queen, that they want revenge,' said Orlanda sadly.

'But what have we done to deserve such rage?' asked King Nahvib, shocked.

'It is not what we do, darling, rather what the Demon Lords lead them to. It must be time for the final fight. We will face it together, we will overcome it,' Karryn assured him.

'But it is not time. This is not what we calculated, us or our allies,' said King Nahvib, 'We are not ready.'

'Everything is in place, people, weaponry, defences. These youngsters are well prepared,' Karryn countered.

'Most things are in place, but not all!' cried Jayak, 'I know I cannot fight, for The Three are not together!'

A terrible silence held them for a moment. The walls of the classroom seemed to close in on them, as they all felt the danger, so long awaited yet so suddenly arrived, press at them.

'We have little choice!' decided Karryn, breaking the silence with a strong call to those around her, 'Let it be known that I, Karryn, Queen of Sytrannia, am The Guardian. I lead you into battle this day, trusting that the other two follow. In the name of L'ra and all the gods, choose your weapons and follow me!'

Chapter 31

Queen Karryn led her people out into battle, her heart pounding, her muscles tensed for action. Though dressed much more practically than on her wedding day, the same light shone around her, this time stronger than before. Nahvib came just behind her, the same sword he had used at the Battle of Long Grasses held firm in his hand.

Drayk and the council followed. Their physical training was limited, but part of their duty was to protect their king and queen and they heeded this promise. The First Minister had found his sword as soon as he saw trouble in the city, realising that the desert defences would play no part in Sytrannia's war after all. Noblemen Zakkari, Lins, Frani and Horik had taken axes from the armoury as they had sped after Drayk to King Nahvib and Queen Karryn. Noblewoman Orlanda had taken the jewelled knife she normally only wore as an accessory. The council were ready.

Pocack whispered spells of protection as he stepped out with Zritz and Durrew. He had made mistakes in the past, missed clues that the Demon Lords were at work. This time, he intended to serve his king and queen with all his might; he would overlook nothing that might help them. Energy crackled around him as it did his colleagues, they worked magic beyond any they had used in their lives. This time, the test was more serious than any they had gone through before.

The young people were no less determined. Els walked tall, with even Sorab holding his head high as he scurried alongside her. She knew she was The Sorceress, now she could act on that knowledge. Thanking L'ra for her powers, she mentally ran through the spells she might need as she made her way outside. Jayak and Alleri flanked her, they knew protecting their friend could risk their own safety, but they embraced the challenge together. Dayx and Klara followed them. Though Klara had begun to suspect she was not The Healer, she nevertheless carried what potions she could, for she would help heal where she could, no matter what her title was.

Cyru's absence was particularly painful at this time, only a few months ago he could have been expected to be found alongside the other wizards. Cam and Hwym were also missed, but there was little time to dwell on such feelings. The battle was here now, everything else would have to be dealt with afterwards.

They were all too aware of this urgency as they strode out into Istalan's bright sunshine. The town bustled, but not with trading and chatter, only with violence. Men usually known for buying and selling were using their wares to hit people over the head, some threw money in peoples' faces to blind them to attacks. Women wrapped scarves around their neighbours' necks and strangled them, or tripped them on the ground, where blood already mingled with the yellow sand.

'Back! Back you evil ones!' cried Karryn, 'Sytrannia's Queen and Guardian assures you, give in and seek our help, or die serving the agents of evil. These Demon Lords work only evil, flee from it or perish at our hands!'

'How can we tell which people are bad?' asked Dayx.

'Their eyes.' said Els, *'Look at their eyes and you know they are not themselves, not real men or women any more.'*

It was true. The others looked as Els spoke and found they could quickly distinguish those who fought merely to save themselves, their family or property, from those whose eyes glowed a sickly yellow, with no spark behind it. There was no emotion in such eyes, only blind dedication to the Demon Lords, no thought of anything else. Their blindness gave them away and the gods' people found their enemies easily.

'As you trample on this earth,

As you soil this ground with blood,

So the earth shall turn from you,

So the ground shall hold you back,' Dayx chanted, as

396

he called on the ground itself to avenge the damage done. The earth trembled and many marvelled at the young man's skill in using the elements. Rima's ground, though covered in fine sand, held fast a whole line of people, seeming to stick to them as they struggled.

At the same time, Alleri used her magic to seek the strongest evildoers in the crowd and targeted these with spells of confusion, so that they lost sight of their chosen victims and began to fight amongst themselves. She threw people back across the marketplace and cast a protective wall around the palace, so that no friend of the Demon Lords would be able to pass the gardens. As she cast, Jayak used his sword to hew down her opponents, protecting Alleri from all harm.

Els wielded great magic, beyond even her previous battles, for now she used everything the goddess had given her. The fire she had held back when caught by the bandits flowed now like water. Waves of flame hit the attackers advancing on Queen Karryn, carrying them away in a flood of terrible pain before they could cause any damage to her.

'Thank you!' shouted Karryn, 'I shall cause my own wreckage, let me see where I can help.' She saw group of teenage boys caught in a fight with older men. At first she prepared to help the boys, then she saw that they held the men at bay despite their apparent weakness. When she looked in their eyes there was only that dull yellow. Karryn advanced upon the teenagers, sword in hand she hewed them down. One got as far as raising the broken pipe he held, but Karryn struck him down, while the older men, encouraged by this rescue attempt, turned on the others.

'Where next?' one of them said and Karryn threw him a broken chair leg from a nearby stall.

And so the battle started, with makeshift arms and a fierce energy on both sides.

In Calan, Stec fought more desperately than even the

Sytrannians. The palace was mostly smouldering ruins, now the crazed people turned on the houses. The High Lords walked openly among them, often they would shake a fist at Stec and Alkar, laughing madly. Stec, however, had little time to fear such treatment.

'Stec, what can we do?' Alkar asked him, 'People are dying, we haven't enough houses to shelter them all. Should we hang on to the remains of the palace here? Or should we protect an inn or the Council Building, somewhere big enough to hide several people safely?'

"I'm not sure,' Stec said slowly, 'I'm not sure what to do at all, Alkar. There is no easy solution, not now, not in this violent end to it all.'

'Well, I have my horse nearby, let's ride to the Council Building, see what Abrim, Saluna and the others want to do. They have had the most practical ideas, in Wertle's absence.'

'As you say, Alkar, perhaps they will have some ideas,' Stec sighed.

He was already disturbed by what he saw in Sky City, but nothing prepared him for the horrors that met the two priests as they galloped up to the Council Building. Abrim lay dead in the entrance hall, the pool of blood around him already beginning to dry. Saluna stood waiting for them, long dark hair flailing behind her in the fierce gale that hurled about the hallway. But it was her eyes that L'ra's priests noticed first. Though her stance and her terrible act spoke of great anger, there was no spark even with that, only the dull yellow stare of one who was listening to an inner voice drowning out any reason.

'Saluna? What awful deed is this, why?' asked Alkar, overcome to see an ally killed not even in battle, but rather thrown aside by one he had trusted. 'I fought alongside Abrim at the battle of Volcano's Gorge, he was a brave and noble man, how could you do this?' he cried, aghast.

'I can do anything!' smiled Saluna, 'No more need now to listen to you men try to run everything, no need to walk a step behind those who think themselves so much greater than I. Look at him now! I have great power and I will use it.'

'You cannot. This is an evil thing Saluna, stand back from its hold on you, let go,' Alkar entreated her.

'Quiet, priest!' Saluna cried, and a ball of fire came from the centre of the gale. It hit Alkar and he fell to the floor, face blackened, body still.

'Saluna, you shall pay for this dearly!' shouted Stec and crying an ancient word of power, he flung his axe into the middle of the unnatural storm around his former friend and political ally. The wind froze and blew apart in fragments of ice with a frightening whistling sound. Saluna ran then, for all her new powers were no match for the Priest-Warrior and she knew it. Stec ran headlong after her, he would kill this dangerous woman before he did anything else and so he ran faster than he had in many years.

Chasing Saluna took him past a landscape of chaos and ruin. People scurried around, hiding from their own neighbours in terror. Children wandered about, their parents dead or lost in fighting. More and more people Stec saw bore the terrible mark of the Demon Lords in their eyes and Stec's heart ached. Yet all that he saw only made him more determined to stop this evil, to halt its attack on the land. He had killed several men of the Demon Lords when he met a High Demon Lord coming over a hill.

'This is not your land!' cried Stec. 'This land serves L'ra and Cala. We will not be swayed by your evil.'

'Many have been!' chuckled the High Demon Lord, 'Are you sure of your words?' Advancing down the hill he removed his hood. Stec gasped momentarily, for the face he saw was a mass of mist with only red eyes and sharp white fangs gleaming in its gloom. Part of the priest felt he could snatch the face and it would disappear like fog, but he dashed such futile thoughts away to answer the High Lord properly.

'I am sure of the goddesses!' he cried, 'I need nothing

more for my powers to work!' He swung his axe with the same conviction he had shown before Saluna and as it hit the ground, the earth shifted, bringing the Demon Lord to his knees. Then Stec raised the axe and swung hard. He hit the Demon Lord at the neck and his body shuddered and groaned before falling apart, cracking into two dry halves, while the face disintegrated as if it had only been fog all the time.

'Now for you, traitor!' cried Stec, for he could see Saluna behind the hill and knew he had to be rid of her. Trusting to the weapon in whose use he had found L'ra's blessing, he swung his axe again. At first, nothing appeared to happen. Then small dents appeared in Saluna's face and on her bare arms, almost like stones were being thrown at her, though none were visible. Then cuts appeared in her chest and she staggered, dizzy with the blood loss. At last, a great hole opened in her head and she fell to the floor, finally dead. Stec guessed that she had been punished with the same wounds she had inflicted on others and his own blood ran suddenly cold.

He ran back to Alkar to find the priest unmoving.

'It's all right, Stec, go on without me,' Alkar croaked. 'Save Sky City.'

'I can't.'

'What do you mean?' Alkar groaned, 'You're the Priest-Warrior, you can save the city or no-one can.'

'That's just it, nobody can, nobody will,' Stec said, 'I'm sorry, Alkar, L'ra's given me a choice, here or Istalan.'

'Then you must choose Istalan. I'm…sorry I can't be there. Tell, tell them at… L'ra's Town, won't you?'

Stec wanted to tell Alkar he would be all right, but blood trickled from the Sytrannian's mouth and he made no movement. Stec could not deny what was happening, much as he wished to.

'Alkar, I will tell the whole town you died with honour. If I am still standing at the end of this war, I will inform King Nahvib and the nation of Sytrannia shall mourn you for your efforts.'

'If the goddess is pleased, that is enough. Make sure you tell them at the temples too, of how and why this happened,' he shuddered then, dreadfully cold.

'I will, we won't forget you,' Stec said, 'The destruction of the Demon Lords will be complete, the rebuilding of Rima to the gods' plans will be accomplished. None of our efforts will be needless.'

'I... know. Good...goodbye, Stec.'

'Farewell, Alkar, brother,' Stec said.

He didn't stop to wonder over the way things had turned out. Once he saddled Alkar's horse, he only stopped to let some of the Sky City soldiers know of Alkar's death, then he pushed on towards Istalan. He rode hard, pushing his horse on until he reached Myrria. Once at Ocean's Flow he commandeered a boat from the people there. No-one tried to argue. Stec's face was fierce and the Myrrinards had already heard the dreadful news of Sky City's turmoil from King Norryn and Queen Naida. So they lent him a ship, the captain and sailors trying to encourage Stec with news of their quick progress across the Myrrine Straits. But Stec was not to be drawn in conversation. All the hours they travelled the waves, Stec spent looking across the ocean. He was waiting, waiting to engage in the final battle. He hoped he was ready, he prayed he was. This was the last chance, for Istalan, for all of them.

Stec wasn't the only one to be thinking that. In Istalan itself, things were increasing desperate. Though the allies fought well and had great power amongst them, the Demon Lords had influenced more people than they had expected. The fighting was intense and emotionally draining where the allies often fought old friends or familiar traders.

Els searched the crowd, trying to keep sight of Queen Karryn. Knowing The Guardian, she wanted to keep track of her. I want to fight alongside her, The Sorceress is meant to be with The Guardian, where is she? Els thought to herself. She couldn't find Karryn, but decided to fight a group of the possessed not far from where Alleri and Jayak were, hoping to keep them available if either she or they needed help. Further away, she could just see Zritz and Pocack, but Durrew had last been seen bandaging an arm wound near to the palace. Els guessed he must be trying to sustain the spell on the palace.

'Durrew? Need help?' she sent.

'If you can from where you are, it would be very useful!'

Els joined Durrew in his casting and the protective spell around the palace grew stronger. The magus gave a sigh of relief and threw himself back into the battle, where Els quickly lost sight of him again. Sorab nipped at her ankles and she spun round to see a new enemy attacking.

'Die, servant of the goddess!' cried a High Demon Lord, casting dark red smoke at her that made her feel faint and giddy.

'You won't kill me! Your strength is not enough for the powers L'ra has bestowed on me! You shall die, for this land will not keep your sort here, spreading evil.'

Els cast light from her hands. She had worked this spell before, but now it invoked bright golden globes and she knew the goddess was with her.

'These are from L'ra, see if you can take their might!' Els sent, casting the spheres straight at the High Lord.

He doubled up, the smoke around Els evaporating as he burned where the globes touched him. Els shook, horribly reminded of the bandit camp. But this victim of her magic was no child, no innocent, so she watched him burn before she moved to find her next foe.

'Alleri? Alleri, stay close!' Jayak cried, cutting through the hoards of Demon Lords aiming for King Nahvib and Queen Karryn.

He moved fast, his sword cutting down many of the Demon Lords approaching the royal couple from their left, while Alleri was free to cast on the group trying to reach them from their right. Heavily hooded, the group had clearly been sent to attack the most important of the gods' people. Although some were ordinary men who had been turned bad by the dark magic, nearly all were hooded. They also concentrated hard on their prey; they had no time to kick ordinary people over, to start small fights. Jayak and Alleri knew these High Lords and their men came with a purpose, they just hoped that theirs was greater.

'More behind, near the port!' Els sent.

'How are we meant to get rid of them all? It's an awful lot to handle.' Alleri replied.

'I know, but you and Jayak see if you can draw them away from the palace. If that is their goal, they will be torn between that and the king and queen. It might give us some time to attack some before we turn on the rest.'

'I'll try. Hang on, Klara and Dayx are near,' Alleri said, *'I'll get them to chase from the palace, head them our way. But watch yourself, they'll want you, too.'*

'I'm not too worried, I expect our reinforcements will turn up soon, anyway,' sent Els.

'Yes,' agreed Jayak, *'Isn't King Nahvib expecting the Lykrosians and Izkians to arrive today?'*

'So I heard. Let's hope they don't keep us waiting long,' said Els.

But after a night of fighting, the sun rose on a still mainly Sytrannian fighting force. The devastation of a day and night spent in battle had taken quite some toll. Market stalls had been hastily taken over by healers trying to help those wounded, as well as healing the souls of any who seemed to be resisting the Demon Lords. Many soldiers had taken serious wounds and Klara and her colleagues had left the battle entirely to cope with the wounded.

The battle had moved out from the palace and into the city. The people of magic were holding back the dark forces but were now fighting for their lives. As their desperation grew, the Demon Lords' fighting had intensified. Dayx fought possessed men alongside the magi. He had no thoughts for Klara now, only these

403

yellow-eyed, vacant bringers of death occupied him. For he was determined they would not bring death to his lands.

But there was still a lot to cause concern.

'Where are the Lykrosians and the Izkians?' asked King Nahvib.

'I don't know, but we could do with their help soon!' cried Karryn, 'Demon Lords are approaching and they have already ruined many buildings in the town there, look!' Following her gaze, King Nahvib saw how right she was. The houses beyond the market place were wrecked, stones crumbling, walls falling in. Their subjects held off the attackers with what weapons they had, but magic was clearly needed. High Lords spread from the area and though Els was approaching them, the royal couple knew they needed more help.

'Let's at least catch up with Els, for the magi and Drayk's men hold the central ones,' Nahvib said.

'Yes, if we can hold these off then we can stop them taking over any more ground.'

'They have enough already!' Nahvib shouted over the terrible noise of battle, 'Where are Lidynne and Sedryk? Surely they wouldn't have let us down? Is this because we disagreed over the prophecy? I thought all that was forgotten with the new information Sy gave. Lidynne wouldn't have gone to the other side, would she?'

'Not my aunt!' cried Sy, riding alongside the pair.

'Are you sure? And where did you get that horse?' King Nahvib cried.

'From Vistar, his men are here, with fresh horses and fresh men.'

'It's not enough!'

'But it will help, 'til we have more magic and more help. We should be grateful for Vistar's aid for we need all we can,' Karryn said.

'Yes, for the moment.'

'My uncle will come!' Sy insisted, 'In my mind I see him riding here, as I do the temple people, and more allies besides.'

'Then this is good news! Ride on favoured seer, but leave some Demon Lords for us!' King Nahvib said.

Karryn wondered what he had meant about more allies, but was swept on into the battle by the cries of her people.

At the temple of L'ra, Skrella and Roro prepared not for lecture, nor prayer, nor domestic chores, but for battle. The armoury Els had walked past with only a curious glance before Kyrria's funeral was now open and young priests and priestesses were passing out weapons for distribution. The huge axes used by guards on duty were handed out to half the priests, while the others took thick chains, ready to throw at Demon Lords, to ensnare them forever, for the chains were cast with strong magic and would hold them fast in bitter pain which would prevent them casting or contacting their Chief Lords.

'Now we do battle, at last!' cried Rayth, throwing chains to Timo, who caught them swiftly.

'You're not afraid? It is no dishonour to feel such in the face of terrible fighting,' said Arrok. Though old, he carried chains of his own.

'Fear? I only have to hear poor Plarina's screams and I could fight for many a night,' said Rayth.

'Yes, Kyrria and Plarina's torment goes with us in battle, we will fight for all the goddess' people,' agreed Timo. Gone was the confused boy who had avoided lectures and made hasty decisions. Here instead, was a young man, ready and willing to fight for what he believed, whatever the powers stacked against him.

'We have all grown and changed,' sighed Arrok, 'The temple will never be the same again.'

'Nor should my place remain an unchanging island!' called a thunderous voice, though its sound seemed ready to break at any moment, to crack and crumble into laughter.

All looked towards the statue of their goddess. The mherl at L'ra's feet grew duller in colour until dark fur stood out in place of gold and a live creature stepped from the plinth.

This time, however, the creature didn't change into a woman. Instead it turned to face the statue it had left. Gold melted from it to reveal L'ra, more beautiful than ever. Some of those present had met her before, many in dreams, a few in person, as Mavri and Els had done. Nobody, though, had seen her like this. The loss of the metal from her couldn't take away from her beauty, or her power. She shone with a radiance that would have blinded ordinary people. But these were none, these were L'ra's own soldiers and well she knew it.

'Your strength is great, amongst such trial and torment,' she said, voice ringing throughout the whole temple, as everyone listened in aWestruck silence. 'Now I come amongst my people, so that you shall know my strength, my power is with you; and my heart is glad.' She smiled, dazzling the temple folk. 'To see your hope in me and how you fight such terrible deeds. I know my own people and shall defend them to the very last, however it ends.'

'But L'ra,' Rayth said, 'Surely you know what will happen, surely the Demon Lords cannot win?'

'The answer to that you will soon see. I cannot say the hours to follow will be easy, but you are right, I have talents yet to play. For this time, all the gods play their part, strange as that will seem to many.'

'Then we must move out? You would have us join the fight right away, noble L'ra?' asked Skrella.

'Indeed, faithful Skrella and Roro. Lead out your people and gladly. This is no time for skulking. I ask that you follow your goddess in all, no matter how strange the people, gods, or circumstances around you. For they will be, they will be.'

'Mighty goddess, we follow, gladly!' Roro cried, striding after L'ra. The priests and priestesses came after him, their weapons in hand, and their faces at once excited and grim.

At the same time, to the Northeast of the temple, the king's

406

sailors waved through the strangers who greeted them. None of them had seen these people before, but they didn't hesitate in letting them through the City Gate. The visitors had brought papers, but it was not their production that caused the easy passage to Istalan and Sytrannia.

These things might have persuaded the desperate king's men, but instead it was the forces that gathered with the travellers that lent power to their entrance. Four great powers, unseen to Southern men, gathered, loomed behind them. The powers were mighty, fearsome to their enemies, but to the guests they were none of these things, for they bore the newly arrived along with their might.

'Gods!' cried Nai-kin and none could deny his words.

Chapter 32

The market place was suddenly ablaze with yellow fire.

'Perhaps we're rescued?' cried one merchant to those who fought beside him, but his words died as he saw the creatures that descended in the flames. The two beings were clearly Demon Lords, but unlike any who had been seen so far. Taller than anyone present, they burnt the ground where they walked, smoke curled from their fingers as they touched people. Their hatred was more concentrated than anyone's, worse than the most crazed fighters', worse than the angriest man's or the harshest monarch's. It was so thick, the Sytrannians could smell and taste the evil in the air. Some fainted or were sick, their senses were so attacked by these Demon Lords.

'Turn from me as you like, but I will kill you all the same!' cried Quivviam. 'Thine gods are not here now, can you fight us, dare you?'

'Surely thou canst,' said Xanesh, his voice low, yet Jayak liked this less.

'Alleri, is there no magic you and Dayx can perform against this?'

'Hardly! I'd be sorcerer now if I could!' Alleri groaned. 'But the magi might, maybe these new Demon Lords don't know where they are.'

'Do we not?' laughed Quivviam, 'I spy your feeble magi and I will hunt them down!' she laughed and as she did, her hood slipped back. Uncaring, she didn't return it to her head and Xanesh, joining her in laughter, also brought his hood down to reveal his head. That's if head was what it could be called. The mist seen beneath all the Demon Lords' hoods was revealed as more substantial than that, yet it was far from being skin, or anything that a human might call a face. It was strange material, weaving in and out of itself, something like wool, or tree roots tangled in upon itself. It made room for facial features, but never settled around them. But perhaps it did not want to.

The eyes were yellow like their slaves', burning brighter but still an evil shade. It was no sunny colour, more the colour of a once-joyful flower now rotten. The dreadful tendrils of the face parted for sharp fangs to show through, ready to bite and destroy just as much as the Demon Lords' evil magic was. Even these dangerous fangs, however, looked greyed and unclean. Many felt sicker at this sight, others ran, but Els and her friends stood firm.

This is it, Els thought, this is the end, and now we see the planet change. And I am here! How odd, she thought, almost detached from the battle for a moment. After so many miles, so much learning and fighting, sending and casting, all its worth is shown now. The Gods and evil lords do battle and I, I am one of the people to help decide. Little Els, a long way from uncertainty in Garrtron, I fight great evil – and in such company. Then she knew what she would do. I trust Jayak, I know Alleri and Dayx have rounded up many brave townsfolk and Vistar's men have ridden in, she realised.

'Aashti! Vanya! Hold this evil as long as we need you. It may be a minute, an hour or a day. I do not know, but in the meantime, I will find Queen Karryn, The Three shall meet.'

'Do you know the third?' asked Aashti, ever practical.

'No, but he or she is not here in the marketplace, I feel it. Karryn is known, it is to her I will go, I trust L'ra to the rest.'

'Then go, Sorceress, and let your calling guide you. We'll warn the magi, so they may hold off the second group of Demon Lords, allow you quicker movement to Karryn. Be brave, it's only Jhrik-ansi again, just with more people, that's all,' Vanya didn't know if she believed her own words, but she knew Els could reach the queen, now it was down to those in the marketplace to hold off evil. Just for a little time, just a little, Vanya reminded herself, grimly.

With an equal courage, the priests and priestesses of the

409

temple poured out from its walls, their natural powers stronger under L'ra's guidance. They had had no thought of human help, being so overwhelmed by L'ra's appearance. But the goddess of adventure had not stopped at amazing them with her own power; still she worked to show them the unknown power of the men who were allied to them.

'Surely not?' cried Rayth, looking to the Northeast. A group of men, yes and two women amongst the party, had made it beyond the port, though only a little nearer the palace and marketplace than the temple folk themselves.

'What? More men possessed by evil?' asked Arrok, trembling a little.

'Hardly!' shouted Timo, 'These people have journeyed far to aid us, for they have travelled from the North, across The Great Sea they have sailed to reach us. There are Hwym and Cam, who I know well.'

'How is this?' asked Skrella, frowning, 'For the king and queen are expecting help from the East and the South.'

'Can we trust these foreigners then? L'ra?' Roro asked the goddess.

'Foreigners? These people are no strangers to you,' L'ra smiled.

'But I have never seen them, only Rayth and Timo can really claim to know any of them.' The chief priest was puzzled.

'But your young priests and priestess do well to speak what is in their hearts. Their joy shines rightly, but – ah! I see it is not only I who shall tell the tale, for your friends do not come alone.'

As the Northern group came nearer, the temple folk stopped in their tracks, the more hesitant priests shaken at what they saw. Four powerful shapes loomed behind the strangers, like L'ra, larger than the humans yet no less real. If anything, they seemed more substantial, more a part of the world than the men and women they brought.

'What evil is this!' cried one of the older priests, 'What creatures besides Demon Lords could hold such power?'

410

'Only the gods themselves!' boomed a voice and a man came forward. At least he was shaped like a man, though taller and broader by far and his voice rang on his listeners' minds as much as their ears. 'I am Bronv and these, my brothers – Cridf – whom they call messenger - and Lok – whom they call aged from his wisdom which speaks of many years; silent and watchful, my sister, Fess, she who finds all, be it word or object or deed.'

'The prophecy! The prophecy speaks of great and unforeseen help,' cried Arrok, 'We thought we had this in the West, where King Yacconi came to help us, but no, now you bring us Northern gods. L'ra, this is an adventure to end them all,' he shook his head admiringly.

'So she takes the credit now?' frowned Bronv, though he too, laughed.

'We both have played our parts well, though my people are most loyal.'

'What of Els? Her life began upon my land, didn't it?' Bronv challenged L'ra.

'Yet my talents aided her where your people cast her out!'

'All my people? Take care, for I have chosen these folk wisely whom I bring,' Bronv chuckled.

'All right!' Roro cried, 'We have heard bits of your story it seems, and Els we all know, just tell us how such different and – I thought – unrelated Gods come together in this war and we can carry on with it!'

'Very well,' began L'ra, 'It was, I would say, about three thousand years ago, maybe four – '

'- nearer four, I think,' Bronv interrupted.

'Four, then. The worlds had been made and they were happily formed, our people lived upon our Rima in peace. At least, for the most part. But then an evil we had hoped to hide came and walked among them. No great trouble had been caused as yet, but these two, Quivviam and Xanesh they are called, wandered in and out of fragile minds, hinting at dark thoughts. Worry crept amongst our people, who had never feared before. Eventually we

411

realised we would have to move to another part of Rima, hoping to defy them. As gods, we whispered words encouraging people to move elsewhere. But Bronv and I were troubled by difference on this and became divided,' L'ra looked sadly at the Northern god.

'They lived near the coast, many people here, where you call it Istalan, or on the coastal line of what they named Zaritt,' explained Bronv. 'But we didn't solve our differences. L'ra's people moved South and mine Northwards, over the Great Sea, to lands that would need work, lands that would distract them from evil.'

'Yet I hoped the Southern sun would do the same and for a while we both felt we had succeeded.'

'But all the while, the Northmen forgot L'ra's adventurous spirit, the Southerners forgot how to find things, how to communicate as easily as they had once done,' Old Lok explained.

'Lok showed us the errors of our paths and at about the same time, we found out about Hrai, and his communication with the dark ones. They had had few followers, these Demon Lords as they were already known by then, but Hrai gave them an opening, an invitation,' L'ra continued.

'Then,' said Bronv, *'We found those like Els, people of talent rare and strong, that we decided must be used in war. Though my people's belief had forced my action to take away one power, L'ra was able to bless her with talent, as I have others, some I bring with me today. Where are the rest of the gods?'* he asked L'ra, *'Do they wait?'*

'They are in Istalan, ready to give their wisdom to those they choose.'

'That The Chosen may be united?'

'Exactly so.'

'Then we must go on, I would not miss the final destruction of Xanesh and Quivviam, for they have upset my plans for too long!' And the chief god of the North led the way into Sytrannia, as if he had never left it.

'Els! See if you can take on the smaller group there,' advised Pocack.

'Why? I could as easily help you with the great numbers you have, then turn on these,' The Sorceress answered him.

'Yes, but I think what Pocack suggests is that we don't necessarily want them to know your strength, if possible,' sent Durrew, 'Help us here and then slip off to Nahvib and Karryn.'

'Certainly! Feel L'ra's power!' Els cried into the bitter souls of the Demon Lords, this hurting them as much as her magic. But her powers still cast mighty wounds upon her enemies. This small group suffered, not from flames, but from sickness, as Els' power showed the allies' disgust at these servants of evil. For this group were no recently turned townsfolk, rather they were committed to evil, seeking it as Hrai had done. The bodies blistered, strange wounds seeped foul liquid and their eyes ran thickly, so that they could hardly see.

A little North, Jayak and the others gained hope as they saw Els defeat her immediate enemies and head for the King and Queen. Alleri's magic scattered slivers of glass through the bodies of Demon Lords. At the same time, Dayx' mind, caught up in commanding the earth itself, was struck with the cold fire Quivviam brought. Injured, unable to feel his legs, he thought he had also lost control of his mind to see Western horses in the distance.

Apart from Els, the magi struggled to hold their large group of Demon Lords under their influence.

'They are slipping from us!' cried Durrew.

'Not while I live!' shouted Zritz, 'L'ra, grant us allies that we may hold this foe, let few leave, let us hold them here. Others we need for physical attack, but let us hold their minds.'

'Help to attack? I knew I had spent too long in talk!' called Rayth sprinting towards the magi, Timo and Cam trying their best to catch up.

'I hear all who serve me!' cried L'ra.

'And I lend speed where it is needed,' added Cridf.

The young people set to without delay, for Cam had travelled miles to help his sister and he used his axe readily for the cause.

'A good time to return, young Cam! And an interesting introduction to young Reesa,' called Pocack, but the rest of his encouragement was unheard over the noise of battle. The cries of the wounded and dying were desperate, as were many of the shouts for help, both to the Gods and to the Demon Lords. At the same time, Timo's chains rattled repeatedly, striking Demon Lords and their men to bind them, or trip them and drag them to the floor.

'The war is ours!' cried Rayth, her axe hewing several enemies down.

The remaining Northerners could have done with some of her confidence, for they fought more desperately than most.

'Where is the girl?!' shrieked Quivviam, her mind searching all other minds, while Xanesh tried to torture answers from people.

'Hold them!' instructed King Vistar. 'Friends come and Els still runs. We must hold these if we can!'

'To the end, then!' agreed Hwym, thrusting his spear right into the middle of the crowd. Demon Lords and possessed alike fell, taken in by the speed and power of so slight a weapon. They were better prepared for Gron's sword, but this didn't stop him, for his anger was as great as his fear.

'She'll be well, fear not!' he called to his wife, but Mavri was already busy helping Klara and did not hear her husband. Perhaps it was as well, for Gron's strong words were not well supported by his white face.

Not an hour had passed since the Northerners' landed, but it felt like days. Blood of all races had been spilt and only their purpose kept them going.

'I don't know how much longer we can manage,' said Klara.

'Can we afford to stop?' Mavri asked, both inwardly noting the strange accents of the other.

Had they really been managing on their own, then they would have been lost. But they were not alone. Each of the gods had their own people and their own message.

'You used the earth of Rucilia wisely, use this earth as well, Royal-Warrior, and it will serve you,' Tadir told King Yacconi, as he arrived with his army.

The other Elementals were equally determined to assist their followers,

'Hold the port, let only my allies come!' Myrrine told Nai-kin.

'The winds will speed your horses!' Cala reminded Queen Ashla.

'Their fire is dead, but mine lives and I lend its power to your fingertips this day!' Raz told Dayx, who was startled to see huge flame leave his fingers, directed purely at Demon Lords.

'Cam, use your speed, be quick to help your friends and you will serve me well,' called Cridf

'Find those you must help, no matter who they are, how strange to your eyes. Only let me, and I will guide thee,' Fess told Gron.

'Know my wisdom and take it into battle with you,' said Old Lok, suddenly appearing close to Pocack, much to the chief magus' amazement. The old man staggered a minute at the god next to him, but he quickly realised that might had been invested in him and sprang at his opponents with renewed energy.

'Don't think on the things you lack, only upon those you were given, some that you barely know. I command you to know them and see where you should use them.' The man Bronv spoke to would never have expected himself to have been picked on as of any importance. He turned, confused, from where he fought alongside those he

415

had once distrusted, now known as friends.

'Me?' he frowned.

'I have given you gifts so you must use them. Look at your recent work, here and in your own lands. Know who you are. Look at your power and do not run from it any longer. Run with it, run to those whom only you can help.'

'Mavri, your care of your children has been tested and you have shown your strength. Aid these people here like your children, for the future of all Rima's children depends on this!' warned Ellari.

'Trust your horses, for I have blessed them with speed and judgement in their strides,' Arram told King Vistar, 'Treat them well despite your fears and urgency and they will know where they should run, they will hear when their kin from other lands call them.' Vistar nodded in gratitude, he had already seen King Yacconi's Western group arriving, the smoke churned up by their horses travelling across the desert showed their approach and he rode on to meet them, hoping to fight the Demon Lords with two great armies.

'Both seer and prophet must join the hunt!' roared Gax, 'Lidynne, break from your foe and join us! Sy, take people to the South of the fighting, for The Three will be threatened, each before they meet. It may be mental or it may be physical, an attempt to kill or maim them to prevent their meeting. L'ra's adventurers are nothing without the power of the hunter and I bring that to her side now. Let those Gax gives strength and knowledge to show it now. Lidynne, Sy, I call upon and arm you!'

Then L'ra called, not to one, but to all those she had positioned so carefully. Even she tingled with anticipation, for it was one thing to talk of adventure but another to see it, as she did now. So she called to her chief priest first, for he had served her well, but must continue to do so.

'Stec! Chief Priest Stec, hear my cry and obey!'

'I hear you,' cried Stec, intent on L'ra's words, though he did not stop riding. He had made it over the straits to Akrin now and was near, painfully near, to where the vital

416

action lay.

'Then hear me well!' the goddess cried, 'You can unite The Three. Cut a path through the masses here, reach Jayak, and tell him to pass on his knowledge, to bring close those who he knows must be found together. Then you must find Yacconi. You will not kill Quivviam and Xanesh, but you can hold them 'til The Three come together in readiness. Do you understand, Stec?'

'As much as I can. So much has passed, Alkar and Saluna, my home in flames and my friends in danger. But I understand what you ask of me, L'ra, and I will not fail you in it.'

'I know, brave priest. Today, there is nothing left to fear.' L'ra stretched out her right hand and the tears that fell from Stec's eyes ran freely down his cheeks, though he felt peaceful, in a way he had not done in many days.

Then she turned her attention to the others she must contact and her voice searched the minds she knew well, knowing their thoughts better than they did themselves,

'Royal Warrior! You fought hard in your own land, fight with no less power and heart here!' she cried. 'Assemble horses and meet your brother from the East. You can hold your enemies between you. Neither need be afraid, for though Quivviam and Xanesh make a terrible sight, they will not touch you if you draw from me. For I will save them for The Three to challenge, then great evil is met with great good and the battle ends the war!'

'Karryn!' she called the young queen. 'Since your coronation you have been invested with great power, you have two roles in this battle. You know this, deep within yourself, you know that you have your role as The Guardian and a greater role, a role that must join with this. Know these things you must be and do and take them, take them for me!'

Then she turned her attention to the youngest of her chosen people, she reached far for Els' mind. The sorceress felt a prickling on her mind, the surrounding battle disappearing for her as L'ra's word for her became the only clear thing.

'Yes?' she asked, listening intently for the word of her goddess, *'What do you want of me?'*

'Only what I have always asked. Know me, know your power, and use these things with wisdom.'

'As you ask. Can you tell me the one I seek? This is the only thing I need to know, the only thing that would complete your people as a fighting team, those who can deal with beings of great evil, those who can win your war.'

'You ask many questions but I will supply answers when it is the right time.' L'ra smiled then, 'Fear not, only fight on and I will bring you to the other two. The Guardian, the Healer and The Sorceress will meet and soon, but do not search for it.'

Els nodded and moved on, casting the globes L'ra had placed under her power, showing she gave honour to what L'ra had invested in her.

Then L'ra cast further to a mind she had not spent as much time in, only nudged when a decision had had to be reached. A mind which did not know her well, either, and would be surprised at such high level of inclusion in her plans. She touched the mind, stirring its owner. Greatly she wanted to enter it with power, yet she knew to do so would cause terrible fright and turn the person from battle, making them useless to her or any of the allies. No, she would only prod this mind, cause it to move beyond where it stood, firm in battle yet not crucial to events. The Healer must move closer, take up the position, yet would only do so through the power of her people, so she led The Healer this way. After all, thought L'ra, there was not long to wait now.

Caught in ferocious fighting, Alleri and Dayx were glad of Hwym's help. Yet this did not prevent them being drawn ever closer to the eagerly waiting Quivviam and Xanesh. The two highest Demon Lords waited with calm. Casually, they killed Istalan's minor citizens while they waited for their larger foes to collapse from tiredness and give in, hoping that a real cause for celebration would come soon.

'Alleri, we are losing Jayak!' cried Dayx, 'Look where he is.' He illustrated his fears by pointing at Jayak, his gift with the Elements used to cause sun to shine upon the area he indicated.

As Alleri followed Dayx' light, she could not deny the terrible truth. Although they had kept sight of each other, Jayak had gradually slipped further South. The young sorcerer was now almost as close to King Nahvib and Queen Karryn as to Alleri and Dayx.

We shouldn't allow him to get separated like this,' cried Dayx, 'he cannot use magic, we must protect him!'

'Yes, though we may die trying,' answered Alleri.

'Alleri! Don't be so defeatist!'

'I'm being realistic,' she replied, 'I'm weary, Dayx, I cannot remember how many hours or days I have fought. We have both used more energy – physical and magical – than we ever have in one fight. And look at you, your mind is unclear where that thing touched you, you need Klara. I don't even know how well I could help Jayak, I only know I cannot let him die trying to reach Els or the king and queen unprotected.'

'Maybe there's no need?' said a third voice. Alleri and Dayx turned to see Hwym standing beside them. They had seen his arrival, yet they hadn't realised he had moved so close. He had left his fellow countrymen behind and had clearly sought his Southern friends out.

'I could go,' he insisted.

'But you're, you haven't...I mean, well...' Alleri struggled to explain herself but she didn't need to.

'I know I have no magic,' said Hwym, 'But I have something neither of you have – energy. I have only just arrived, carried by mighty Gods and ready for battle. I may not wield magic, but I know what to do with my spear and nothing will stop me finding Jayak to protect him and Els. I know you have seen me jealous, but not any more. If Els is to be with Jayak, I cannot change it, but I will help them

419

both for I like Jayak and I love Els, no matter how it ends - '

'- you don't have to worry about that any more,' Alleri began to explain but couldn't continue, for Hwym was ready to depart again.

'I know, I'm not worried about that. Let's end the battle. I shall see you at the finish, Els and Jayak with me!' he cried and ran Southwards, his lean frame covering ground very quickly and never losing grip on his weapons or equipment all the while. They shook their heads amazed, but hopeful.

It was strange that, when the odds seemed so stacked against them, still the allies hoped, and their hope grew, rather than died, with each passing hour. Nahvib was fighting a desperate battle amongst a crowd of Demon Lords and Karryn was now nearer to Els. It seemed that it was impossible for the queen to try to reach Els without brutal attack, but suddenly Karryn stopped and stood proud, hair tumbling about her cloak, eyes blazing.

'I fear no Demon Lord!' she cried, 'I am The Guardian-Warrior and I will protect those you seek to destroy!' the same glow that had surrounded her on her coronation spread out and the Demon Lords near her shrank back, while the allies rallied at Karryn's cry.

Els heard, and decided to make a dash to join her fellow warrior and partner in the prophecy. She ran hard, but had not noticed the Demon Lords to her east. They were nearer Els than Karryn and the words of the queen had enraged them, not hurt them like those closer to the queen. Stopping their killing, they used all their powers to cloak Els' mind to their presence. Sidetracked by the direction she now raced in, their spell worked. Though all the others around the area could see them, Els was quite oblivious to the menace which gained on her with every minute.

A little to the Northeast, Jayak strained his eyes to see Els. With all the fighters, though, it was useless. He could make out the gold glints in her robes, but that was all. Determined to follow Els, he hacked at the possessed in his way and had killed several when he saw he was not alone. Hwym speared Demon Lords and they groaned at the agony caused by so simple a weapon. At last, they were all dead, only Hwym and Jayak stood, panting heavily as a result of their efforts.

'I wondered when you'd turn up.' Jayak smiled, 'I can't argue with your timing.'

'I had to help, the spear doesn't look like much but, well, it seems to kill just as well as anything else.'

'You'd better move quickly if you want to catch Els,' Jayak told Hwym.

'You don't mind, then, that I've come back for her?'

'Mind? You haven't heard then?' Jayak laughed, 'I've made my peace with Els. Alleri and I are together now, all that has gone before doesn't matter any more. Which reminds me, Hwym, I have also had cross words with you in the past and stood obstacles in your way.'

'It doesn't matter, like you say, it's over now.'

'Then you would be friends?' asked Jayak.

'Of course, why shouldn't I?' Hwym held out his hand to Jayak, 'I've said enough mean things about you, anyway. I forgive you, Jayak and I hope you can me.'

'Nothing would make me happier!' grinned Jayak, shaking the Northerner's hand vigorously.

The two young men felt as if a fog had lifted from their spirits. As they realised their fears had dispersed, they looked at the battle with a new energy. But Els had no such newfound clarity and the Demon Lords were closer than ever. Suddenly, the surrounding Sytrannians had vanished and the Demon Lords were in full view of Jayak and Hwym when they leapt upon Els. Though her voice was as silent as ever, she screamed with all her mind and her friends grimaced to hear such cries.

'Where am I? What am I seeing?' she sent, as the Demon Lords attacked her mind.

'We must get to her, we must save her!' cried Hwym.

'I agree, but how?" Jayak replied, 'The distance is still too great and there are too many Demon Lords to be taken

421

on without magic.'

'Then use magic!' cried a third voice and Stec rode up to them.

'Stec! What happened, you look awful!' Jayak cried.

'Thank you!' the Priest-Warrior smiled, 'I could do with more support, but never mind. Many of my people are dead, Sky City falls, but Istalan will not. Seize these fresh horses Norryn lent me and we attack.'

'Three men against ten Demon Lords? High Lords, with those highest two on their way here? Are you mad?' Jayak said.

'Am I? Use your magic Jayak, for you can!' The priest said.

'What?' Jayak was afraid Stec would be wrong, but they needed something now, so he stretched out his hand towards the Demon Lords. At once, rain poured upon them, missing Els, but piercing the clothes of the Demon Lords, for it rained not water, but liquid metal.

'I can! I am able to cast again!' Jayak cried, looking at his hand in joy and confusion, ' Then what Sy thought was right, it is - '

'- Just as you thought.' Stec halted his words, 'But none of that matters, simply take us to Els and all will be complete. I believe we will see all warriors and The Three soon and then we end it. Come Jayak, Hwym, I shall lead the way, but use your skills when we fight, for mine are nearly spent.'

The three allies praised Arram for the provision of such fine horses, for though the Demon Lords had backed away from Els, there was a long way to ride and without such means of travel, they would never have reached her in time. But in minutes they were close enough to cause the Demon Lords to turn their way, angry yellow eyes glowing and hands raised to cast.

'Stop!' cried a powerful voice. 'Leave these in our hands!' It was Xanesh and his anger was very clear.

'Yes, let us destroy these useless people the Gods call mighty.' agreed Quivviam, 'They think they have power, but what can they do now? No Gods are near and we easily escaped your magi. I say we kill the Sorceress first!' She stretched her hand out towards Els, even her face stretched tendrils of her strange form in Els' direction, but the warriors were quicker.

'You shall not touch The Three, while I yet stand! cried Stec, jumping from his horse to stand and face Quivviam.

'But how long shall you stand?' called Xanesh, striding to join Quivviam. 'What is one man against the highest of Demon Lords?'

'But there is more than one man, more than one warrior,' answered King Yacconi, walking forward to stand with Stec, sounding calm enough, though his muscles were tense and his men murmured behind him. 'I am the Royal-Warrior, when myself and the Priest-Warrior stand together, you fight not just two, but all the power that the priesthood and royal lines of Rima bring.'

'Good words, mortal king, but I do not see The Three and as Quivviam says, I think we shall kill the sorceress without much trouble.'

'Not with my protection!' Karryn stood in front of Els.

'Protection?' Quivviam laughed scornfully. 'You may guard her, but you are no sorceress yourself, neither can you heal her. I shall take you on, while Xanesh fights these feeble men.'

She leapt at Karryn, grey claws grasping, while, as she promised, Xanesh threw himself at Yacconi and Stec. But Quivviam found Karryn could not be easily defeated. Though the Demon Lord raised her hand and brought savage winds down towards her enemy, none touched Karryn. Quivviam tried hailstones, though they were not natural, but globes of lead she hurled at her enemy. Still nothing happened, they fell away from Karryn, as if reluctant to touch her. Xanesh was in equal trouble with the warriors he fought. Stec's priestly power meant anything Xanesh hurled at him rebounded to attack the Demon Lord. As Xanesh poured his efforts into stopping Stec's power, Yacconi attacked him. The fearless Rucilian swiped at Xanesh and was himself surprised, though delighted, to see his blows caused cuts to the Demon Lord's body.

'This mortal wounds me with his faith!' shrieked Xanesh.

'He shall not hurt me, I seek victory with more power!' cried Quivviam.

As the Demon Lord moved to defend her fellow hater of men, Karryn seized the opportunity to move Els to safety. She took hold of the sorceress and carried her to the shelter of nearby ruins, hoping to rejoin the fight as soon as she saw Els could be left alone. But Stec and Yacconi held the Demon Lords to the fight and Els did not stir except to moan gently. 'You live, young Els, but you must move and defend yourself to stay that way!' Karryn groaned, 'Els, wake up, for I cannot protect you forever without letting the other warriors weaken.'

This is no good!' cried Jayak, 'Come Hwym, we must help Queen Karryn.'

'Us, how?' Hwym asked,

'If we look after Els, at least Karryn can join the others,' Jayak explained, 'And we would know Els is safe.'

'Well, that's a good enough reason.' Hwym looked in Els' direction. 'Come on, let's go to her while the fight is too strong for them to notice us.'

So the pair crept past the warring demons and men to where Karryn still held Els in her arms. The queen looked up in fear at their footsteps, but smiled to see friends and allies instead of enemies.

'You come to look after Els?' she asked.

'Yes,' said Hwym, suddenly more determined than ever.

'Then I am free to join the other warriors until Els is ready. The Gods thank you, Hwym!'

'And Jayak,' said the Northerner, but looking to his friend, he found Jayak had already left and joined King Yacconi's men in waiting. 'Els?' Hwym called gently,

'Are you all right? I know you must be weary of this fight, but it is yours, ours I mean.' He pushed back her robes to place his hand on her side. 'Is it this?' he asked, 'Does your old wound trouble you?' he thought he felt her move then and so he carried on, softly talking, carefully stroking her scarred side with his gentle hands. Els' eyes opened and she managed a smile. *'Hwym?'* He heard her say and was so happy at seeing her awake that he didn't notice she had discarded her notebook and spoken into his mind.

'If you want me, I am here,' he told her. Seeking to distract her from her pain, Hwym pulled out his flute and delicately played it.

'The music, it's from the Festival.'

'I, I've been wanting to play the whole piece…for some time,' Hwym said.

'You should have, I'm glad to hear it.'

'Good. Your wound, does it feel better?' Hwym touched Els' side again without thinking, 'You seem more yourself now. I was so scared when I saw you lying there like that.'

'You had no need to fear, your strength has healed mine.' Els looked at him, hazel eyes searching his blue ones.

'What?'

Els stood and took Hwym's arm, *'Look at all you have done, in each battle, in every group of friends.'* She paused and then she placed a hand on his other arm, joining the two of them. *'Look at what you have always done, with your words, your touch, your music. You have healed me, Hwym, where no other could have.'*

'But you're saying…' His eyes widened.

'Yes, I am!' Els' laughter burst through Hwym's mind, casting out all doubts, leaving only joy and the truth it spoke.

'I am The Healer!' he cried, and his words echoed across the ruins of Sytrannia, proud and strong.

'I am The Sorceress!' cried Els and her words rang through many minds.

425

'And I am The Guardian-Warrior!' cried Karryn, 'We are The Three and we shall defeat evil!' To the NorthWest, Nahvib wiped tears from his eyes and the magi rejoiced with him. It was Drayk who ran to explain their emotion to the Lykrosians. They had no idea of what had happened, having arrived in secret. Sadly, they had had to move along the coastline, for they had had no Izkian allies to support them.

The Three stepped towards Xanesh and Quivviam, while Stec and Yacconi melted back. They were ready to lend aid, but the Three were ready to fight with all the gifts of the gods, this was their time now.

'Three? Three question our power!' screamed Quivviam and she conjured poisonous snakes and hurled them at her enemies. But Hwym raised his hand and the snakes calmed, turned into harmless desert snakes and fell to the ground. Xanesh tried to cause the ground to shake, but Queen Karryn's power was rooted in her love for her land and Rima's soil would not move for her enemies. Then Quivviam and Xanesh joined together, standing next to each other. Their hands melted together, the strange tendrils of their faces merged and a terrible yellow light shone from their beings. The light was cast outwards, so overpowering with its sickly glow that Jayak, Stec and Yacconi stood to protect the ordinary soldiers from its glare. Karryn moved her hand and a sheet of mist stood between the allies and the Demon Lords. They increased their power and the mist shimmered and dissolved, but Hwym sang. His magic was not that of destruction, so the Demon Lords were not killed, but the tune he sang was a melody of such gladness that the soldiers nearby were healed and the Demon Lords were distracted. Not for long, but long enough for Els to use her magic. She cried out in her mind with a terrible might, *'For the glory of all the gods, L'ra, I ask your blessing!'* The Sorceress' body shuddered and waves of sheer power came from her to hit the Demon Lords.

'This...power of the gods does...not...defy us!' shrieked

426

Quivviam, still trying to cast fire at the allies, though her body groaned at these new blows.

'You...cannot...we are...many,' cried Xanesh, 'We have...people...' but even as he said the words and tried to help Quivviam, his voice grew weak. For all his words, his people were silent and he was no match for sheer good. Hwym and Karryn continued to hold off the Demon Lords, while Els' casting reached a level she had not dreamt of.

'You!' cried Xanesh.

'I will...defeat...,' Quivviam tried to threaten, but her powers were exhausted and, with her fellow Demon Lord, she fell to the floor. As The Three concentrated their powers on them, the Demon Lords twisted and shrank. Their final cries were awful and even Stec and Yacconi covered their ears. Eventually they were gone, just shrunken twisted bundles of roots and robes left of what had been Rima's greatest threat.

'Thanks be to L'ra, and The Three!' cried Stec.

Amazed, overjoyed, Els, Hwym and Karryn looked at each other. The day had come, the war was ended. Now, at last, they could live in peace.

Epilogue

I should be worried, King Nahvib thought to himself. Stec is yet to arrive, Lidynne and Sy are more interested in testing the wine than in being ready for the ceremony and there is no Izkian monarch to come. I'm not anxious, though, he realised, Stec is on his way, Lidynne and Sy know when they are needed, Taheya will represent Izk. He sat back at one of the decorated chairs and smiled, completely relaxed.

In the six months since the Battle of Istalan, many had learned not to worry. They had come through so much and survived to tell the tale, they were determined to enjoy the life they had fought so hard for.

'It's a good day for it,' said Lady Taheya. She walked slowly towards King Nahvib and leaned heavily upon Lord Bik, but her progress was steady.

'Yes,' agreed King Nahvib, 'It will make Stec's travels easier.'

'And Roro and Skrella will be happy to have such fine weather for so glad an occasion,' Bik said.

'Yes, where are all the young people?' asked Taheya, 'I haven't seen anyone yet.'

'Don't even ask!' laughed Queen Karryn, 'I have spent all morning admiring outfits and giving advice, I trust they will all be ready when the time comes.'

'You should not be so busy at all,' Nahvib pretended to frown.

'Don't be silly, Nahvib, the baby is not expected for months yet and I am no invalid. Besides, Klara has tested that many potions on me, I don't think anyone in the Kingdom is healthier than me.'

'The youngsters are all ready then?' asked Taheya.

'Yes,' Karryn smiled, 'Alleri looks wonderful, it is good to see her so confident. As for Jayak, Hwym and Dayx, I think they compete as to who has the most interesting coloured outfit! I have not seen Els yet, but I am sure she is almost ready.'

'And I hear her parents have arrived?' asked Lord Bik.

'Everyone who fought alongside The Three, everyone who came to do battle will be here, it is only fitting,' said Nahvib.

Silence fell then as the leaders remembered those who had fallen in battle, those who had survived, but remained scarred. Still, above all of this, they knew today was a chance to celebrate survival and reconciliation. The guests at today's ceremony represented every race on Rima, not to mention every power. Grey-haired military hero King Yacconi would sit beside Stec, Calan's High Priest; Gron and Mavri would be placed in the same row as King Nahvib and Queen Karryn.

'Els? Are you ready?' Alleri asked, *'Come on! I won't go down there without you.'*

'All right. I haven't been part of anything like this before, you know that.'

'Look, Jayak and Hwym will be there already, come on.'

'Very well,' Els came out of her room and Alleri gasped. The sorceress still wore her long robes, but the dress underneath was of a lighter green and covered in delicate embroidery. Twists of Northern silks carried Southern jewels and Alleri laughed at this mixture of the cultures.

'Is it true your king has come?' Klara asked, joining her friends.

'Apparently so. It's been a while since I saw him or Lord Cranff.'

'We'll be late. I can't arrive in the new temple late!' Alleri hustled her friends along.

They crossed the sands from the Town House to reach the new temple where the others waited inside. The new building towered over L'ra's Town, but was unguarded, for the townspeople trusted the gods' own protection, after all, they had survived the Battle of Istalan and the goddess had not left them without a priest.

429

Inside the temple, the noise was incredible. Alliances so recently formed were generously built on, many languages and accents blending together. Old friends were welcomed back and Stec's throat was soon sore as he explained the building of Calan's new city as, Ak-e-Teffaar, 'Victory of the Many' in the old language. Many turned to admire Els as she took her place beside Hwym and he was not without his own admirers, for all knew his new status now. Jayak and Alleri smiled to see their friends as happy as they were. 'I hope they stay here after they marry,' Alleri said.

'I'm sure they will,' Jayak replied, 'Gron and Mavri seem to get on well enough with King Nahvib and Queen Karryn.'

'Visiting will be easier if Nai-kin gets the money for the fleet he plans.' said Dayx, 'Imagine that, taking a boat to the North as quickly as taking a horse to Lykrosia.'

'Leave the politics for one day, won't you?' smiled King Vistar, leaning over from his seat behind the young people, 'you will have to wait until Nahvib and I reach agreement, give us a few months yet.'

'Quiet!' hissed Queen Elaina, 'You are as bad as Sedryk, and look, here come Skrella and Roro.'

The priest and priestess stood before the very mixed crowd and turned to welcome another good friend.

'Come, Rayth, this is your day, let us bless your endeavours,' Skrella said.

'Thank you,' the priestess said and shyly stood between the two.

'L'ra be praised,' began Roro, 'That you give L'ra's Town a new High Priestess, one who has learnt much and given generously of her talents.'

'Thank you, goddess,' said Skrella, 'That you give the town a priestess who will carry on Alkar's work, one who has seen terrible things in battle, but attacked the enemy with the goddess in mind, seeking her will only.'

Tears rolled down Els' face and Hwym put his arm around her.

'I'm not sad,' she told him, *'Just happy for Rayth after all that has happened, she's all grown up and, I'm just happy, that's all.'*

'I know. So am I,' he said.

There were many tears throughout the ceremony and Stec himself trembled to see Rayth so powerful. Another new beginning, he thought, I wonder what the future holds for that young woman? He smiled to see Alkar's work taken on by another. Looking around, they all wondered about the future, for many new relationships, friendships, marriages, and alliances, beckoned. One thing united them, they had stood by the Gods and the Gods had stood by them. The future will not be dull, thought Stec suddenly, that I know for certain.

Acknowledgements

I'm very grateful to everyone involved in Pen to Print, especially Anna Robinson for her input, expertise and support. A big thanks to Kirstie Smith for reading drafts and providing plenty of technichal support and tea. Thank you to my other beta readers, Lisa Webb and Pippa Leach, and everyone at the East London Association of Christian Writers group for their constructive criticism at various stages. Not least, thanks to my family for their encouragement throughout the process.

Lightning Source UK Ltd.
Milton Keynes UK
UKHW04f0841260918
329500UK00001B/14/P